The House at Sandalwood

The House at Sandalwood

Virginia Coffman

G.K. Hall & Co. • **Chivers Press**
Waterville, Maine USA   Waterville, Maine

This Large Print edition is published by G.K. Hall & Co., USA and by Chivers Press, England.

Published in 2001 in the U.S. by arrangement with Pinder Lane & Garon-Brooke Associates Ltd.

Published in 2001 in the U.K. by arrangement with the author.

U.S.   Hardcover 0-7838-9422-8   (Romance Series Edition)
U.K.   Hardcover 0-7540-1658-7   (Windsor Large Print)

The text of this Large Print edition is unabridged.
Other aspects of the book may vary from the original edition.

Set in 16 pt. Plantin by Al Chase.

Printed in the United States on permanent paper.

British Library Cataloguing in Publication Data available

Library of Congress Cataloging-in-Publication Data

Coffman, Virginia.
    The house at Sandalwood / Virginia Coffman.
        p.   cm.
    ISBN 0-7838-9422-8 (lg. print : hc : alk. paper)
    1. Hawaii — Fiction. 2. Ex-prisoners — Fiction. I. Title.
PS3553.O415 H68 2001
813´.54—dc21
                                                            2001016746

*For Donnie and Johnny and those
few remaining Kamaainas who remember
the Hawaii of 1935 and all the territorial years*

One

"Judith! What a sight you are!" Dr. Ito Nagata remarked as we shook hands and he kissed my cheek lightly. "When I saw you across the lounge just now, you might have been a statue, you were so still. A lovely statue, of course," he added gallantly, taking the chair opposite me in the little glass alcove of the rooftop cocktail lounge. "You are looking wonderful, considering the — that is, you are looking wonderful."

I smiled at the brave effort of his flattery, but whether it was flattery or not, it warmed me to the heart. This was my first real welcome in Hawaii. He apologized for the absence of Stephen Giles, the man who had sent for me. "He meant to meet you at the airport, but he's in the midst of the most touchy negotiations on the new dock strike. It's what happens the next day or two that will make or break negotiations."

I said I didn't mind. After all, Ito had paged me by phone at the airport and explained. And in my turn, I explained the immobility he had noticed in me. "I was thinking over what I've just seen since my plane came in. Everything. Everyone's clothes. Or lack of them. And that glass elevator in which I whizzed up here, for instance. To tell the truth, I found it a little scary. Even the furniture in here. Everything in this too-modern world. And of course, I was enjoying the view. It is fabulous."

Dr. Nagata snorted. "It is hideous! Michiko and I get out to Waikiki as seldom as possible these days. Honolulu — all of Hawaii, in fact, has become a stone jungle. Hideous."

I admitted he probably was right. "But anything with a rooftop vista is glorious to me these days. And I never saw water so blue."

He was immediately apologetic. "Of course, I should have realized how it would look to you after. . . . Ah, our waitress. What are you having, Judy? Good Lord! Who gave you that mess?"

I was amused at his expression. "It looks like a fruit salad, doesn't it? The waitress suggested it. A Mai-tai. It ought to be very healthy."

"For *malahini* tourists maybe. Bring the young lady a martini. Gin. Olive. Very old hat. For myself, I will have rye and water."

I congratulated him. "You have a remarkable memory," I said. When the waitress had left us, I leaned across the little table toward Dr. Nagata.

"I suppose Deirdre's husband, this Stephen Giles, told you how he offered to employ me. It made my parole possible. Have you any idea what Deirdre's trouble is and why they want me?"

He was evasive, and that wasn't like the man who had been a friend of my family since my childhood, twenty-five years before.

My niece Deirdre's infrequent notes had told me nothing during the year since her marriage. She simply dropped inconsequential and odd, troubling little hints in her atrocious spelling.

> *Stephen says I can wear the gorgeous fuchsia-colored bikini I chose, though he says it looks vulgar on me because of the color. . . . Everyone is darling to me on Stephen's island. . . .*

But apparently, the small village of pure-blooded Hawaiians on Stephen's family island wouldn't come to a dinner party Deirdre gave. She complained later, "I have no friends. . . . Stephen hates me. . . ."
And then, on a new tack:

> *My Stephen is so good to me. He brought me a present. . . .*
> *Stephen doesn't take me to Honolulu one-half often enough. Please, dear Aunt Judy, get out of that place and come and make him do it. . . . They must let you out sometime. I heard Stephen's friends whispering at my birthday party. They said it had been an awful miscarriage of justice and you hadn't really done that thing to Mother. . . .*

So they were still debating the death of Deirdre's mother, my sister-in-law, almost ten years after a jury had rendered its judgment! Now I asked Ito Nagata, "What kind of man is Stephen Giles?"
"He's impulsive. Does things on hunches and so forth. I think I know him pretty well. And

9

frankly, I like him. Also, Michiko's Korean Uncle Yee is Stephen's cook — a real worldbeater. So I hear quite a lot about Stephen and Deirdre. Then too, I'm often called over to Ili-Ahi professionally — since I'm handy, and they know me."

"Heavens! Hi-what? Sounds like a fish."

He laughed. "Ili-Ahi is one of the smaller Hawaiian islands. You know of it through Deirdre's letters as Sandalwood. That's the English translation. It is more or less owned by the Giles family, and some of the pureblooded Hawaiians. They keep it as private as possible. Until recently, they didn't want tourists unless they were invited by Giles or one of the Hawaiian families. Now, all that is to be changed. Stephen has big plans."

"Sandalwood certainly sounds more romantic than Ili-Ahi."

"Same thing, though. Incidentally," he reminded me, "it was the gold from the sandalwood trade in the early days that piled up the Giles fortune, which had pretty well gone down the drain until Stephen took over at his father's death."

I looked out at the enormous expanse of changing Pacific waters, vivid green near the foam that marked the uneven shoreline, then turquoise and sapphire and finally deep, endless blue.

Deep and endless. Just as my life had looked to me some nine years ago. But those incredible

10

depths were crossed at last. I was free. I asked Ito anxiously, "Is Mr. Giles sincere? He must have known Deirdre was too young for him. That is to say, not so much too young as too immature. Of course, she had all that money."

Dr. Nagata was honest, but I could see he tried to be fair.

"The money may have weighed with him, but only subconsciously. Deirdre was on her best behavior every time she and her school friend, Ingrid Berringer, met Stephen. And as to his age, Steve is only thirty-four — your own age."

"I am thirty-three."

He said seriously, "Of course. I'd forgotten. Anyway, this Miss Berringer had a crush on him too. That would make him more irresistible to Deirdre. She was always a little spoiled, you know."

"I don't know. After all these years she may be a total stranger in spite of our letters. But when I was twelve and my brother Wayne went off to Korea, I promised him I would take care of her. I felt very grown-up about that promise I made. He adored his baby, and there was no one else to look after her. He assumed Mother would be her guardian, but Mother was never very well after Wayne died, so — well, I'd promised. And Deirdre was always an enchanting little minx."

"Was Deirdre's own mother ever sober enough to look after her?"

"We thought she might be in time, when we first heard about Wayne's death, but Claire

11

Cameron just went on downhill."

"Uphill, you might say," he put in reflectively. "Seems to me she lived a high time there before. . . ."

He broke off.

"It was probably those men who latched onto her. That and the drink. Anyway, she used to forget Deirdre for months at a time. There was one year I remember, she sent us a Christmas card and ten dollars to get a doll for Deirdre. Then, the next time we heard from her was on New Year's almost thirteen months later. She sent a box of balloons and New Year's party noisemakers." But I didn't want to think about Claire Cameron. I said, "Let's talk about something more interesting."

Ito troubled me by his intense concentration on pleating a cocktail napkin. "Are you sure you haven't done enough for the girl already?" Before I could interrupt indignantly, he added, "People expect Deirdre to be grown-up and capable of managing a household, playing hostess, all the rest. But it just isn't working out that way, so Stephen talked to Michiko and me. We . . ." he shrugged. "We told him everything we knew — and suspected — about your . . . your rotten break."

"No!"

"Now, Judy, Ili-Ahi certainly needs a housekeeper, or a manager, and since you're Deirdre's aunt and she trusts you, it seemed so natural. But I may as well warn you, there are a few other

12

problems besides this business of Deirdre's being too young to run the estate."

"Ito! Is she pregnant?"

He shook his head. "No, it's something quite different. Months ago when Deirdre arrived here, you recall, she was with a friend from that exclusive girls' college the courts sent her to."

"Yes. She was with the Berringer girl. You mentioned her."

"Ingrid Berringer. After a few months in Hawaii the Berringer girl was going on to Tokyo and Hong Kong, and then was to return home. New York State, I think." He took a breath. The paper napkin was a handful of pleats. I laced my cold fingers together, wondering what was to come.

"What about her?"

"Her father and her fiancé, boyfriend, whatever — are here looking for her."

"After almost a year!"

He avoided my eyes. "They've done what they could in Japan and Hong Kong, but now they are backtracking. It seems there's no record she ever left Hawaii. She was to pick up her visas here in Honolulu, and never did."

"But she must have written letters to her family. She could have . . . there are a hundred things she could have done. This has nothing to do with Deirdre and Sandalwood, surely!"

He straightened and smiled as the waitress brought our drinks. "Michiko predicted I would say the wrong thing. Didn't take me long. Now,

13

look. The Berringer thing probably has nothing whatever to do with us. You are going to drink that martini, and powder your nose, and we are going to go down to the suite Stephen keeps on the fifteenth floor, and I am going to present you to your new boss. Or your nephew-in-law. This is one nephew who's older than his aunt. Drink up, Judy."

I looked into my glass, swished the ice cubes around and said thoughtfully, "It's a good thing I am here. This Stephen Giles doesn't seem to be interested in protecting his wife, if he does nothing about gossip like the Berringer business."

He ignored my bitter remark. "How is the martini?"

"I'm going to sip it slowly. I found out how necessary that is when I drank my first martini in more than eight years."

"Pretty wonderful, that first taste, I'll bet."

"Vile. Absolutely vile. For a little while I couldn't imagine why people drink so many of them."

He laughed but agreed that I had a point there. He lifted his glass, saluted me.

"Here's to beautiful Judith Cameron. May it be all *pau pilikia* from here on in. Troubles all over," he explained. "Those are the first Hawaiian words for you to learn: troubles over. *Pau, pau pilikia,* now that you are here."

I appreciated his attempts to bolster me up for the all-important interview with Stephen Giles, but I was quite shaken by the problems that seemed to surround my niece.

"I'll take care of her. Ito, she is all I have left in the world."

He studied me. "You haven't changed about caring for people. But you have changed in appearance. In the old days you were pretty. But actually, you are lovelier now, in a different way."

"Prejudice. Prejudice," I murmured, but I was touched.

I finished my cocktail, even ate the tough-skinned olive, but there was no postponing it. Sooner or later I had to face the interview with a man I instinctively mistrusted. He might own half of Hawaii but he hadn't been able to protect his wife from fantastic gossip.

As we left the cocktail lounge and went to the glass cage that crawled up and down the outside of this high-rise hotel, Ito said, "By the way, my Michiko introduced Deirdre and her friend Ingrid to Stephen, you know."

"How did that happen?"

"They were all on the plane from San Francisco — Michiko and the girls. Stephen was at the airport on business when their plane came in. So Michiko made introductions all around. Well, the girls kept after Stephen . . . I don't think he was too keen on either of them at first. But they persisted. Deirdre can be very winning, as we all know."

The elevator arrived. I said, "Here we are. I don't think I'll ever get used to these glass bugs

15

clutching the outside of a building. It doesn't seem natural, somehow." Then I gasped as I pressed against the glass wall and got my first real view of the surrounding scene. "Fantastic! I never saw so many swimming pools. And coco-palms everywhere. They seem to punctuate the whole landscape. And those high-rise build-ings!"

The beach itself was scarcely visible, but the Waikiki surf was there, unforgettably green, turning aquamarine farther out, and on the ho-rizon finally becoming a deep, penetrating blue.

"Don't look down," Ito advised me, pointing off to the right, toward the greenest mountain range I had ever seen. It was the kind of green that one sees under the first, light, spring rains, pure and rich, wreathed in clouds. "Off *mauka*-way. That's the Koolau Range," Ito went on. "The city is piled up against it. And one of the residential districts beyond, that's Nuuanu. The highway to the Pali runs along that narrow valley and climbs up beyond the range. The surf to your left. *Makai,* we call it, toward the sea. And straight ahead. That's *ewa*-way, toward town. Ewa is a sugar plantation. Now. You know as much as most *malahinis* know."

"I never saw anything so green!"

He shrugged off my admission of this, my first view of Hawaii, but I could tell that he was pleased. Like many people, he allowed himself to condemn his own home, but he would have resented it if I had agreed.

16

"Everything smells like flowers," I said. "From the minute the plane put down, I felt it, as if the air were perfumed."

"Hawaii," he said simply but felt it necessary to add, "smells more smoggy every day, though."

The elevator came to an abrupt halt at the fifteenth floor and we stepped off into a hallway so modern, so antiseptically sterile I felt chilled by the memories of public institutions that it evoked. I was so disturbed at this unexpected sight and feeling — which I had to accustom myself to at any time and without notice — that I clutched Ito Nagata's arm. He looked at me with concern and with that sympathetic understanding my brother Wayne and I had discovered in him long ago when the three of us were schoolmates in Los Angeles.

"You don't have to spell it all out with Nagata," Wayne used to say, and Ito still knew without being told.

"The suite isn't this bad. Quite pleasant, in fact. You may be helping Stephen entertain part of the time. He has a number of business meetings here every month."

"Isn't it funny? I'm not afraid I can't handle the job or Deirdre, but I am afraid to meet the man. Chills are running up and down my spine."

"Why?"

"Fear of failure to be what he expects of me — some kind of superwoman. I tried to explain in my letters, but he seemed to think I was more

17

competent that I am."

"You must think positively. You will find you have given yourself a whole new life. And about time, too."

There was no use in my repeating that a new career as a housekeeper was not my motive in hurrying over to Hawaii the moment I was free. He knew that. My only living relation, my niece Deirdre, and her problems had brought me to this place.

"Here we are." He knocked, then opened the door. We went through a formal foyer, with oyster-white walls accentuated by a low tabaret of teakwood and a stark black-and-white matted drawing in thick Japanese brush strokes on each wall. The only color — and what a startling contrast! — was provided by the vase of three bird of paradise stalks on the tabaret. Each great birdlike head had all the colors of the sunset, with the added detail of a tongue of blue flame in the center.

The foyer opened on either side. To the left was the comfortable living room, with cushioned cubes, couches, small end tables and cocktail tables, an old-fashioned console television set that looked seldom used, and at the end of the room a balcony overlooking the narrow beach, the palms, the incredible proliferation of high-rises, and finally Diamond Head. Even I could not fail to recognize that landmark, I still couldn't identify a dark mass reaching out into the sea.

Ito Nagata pointed to the balcony. "The *lanai.* With that view you can almost forget the high-rises when it's dark enough. Stephen has a bedroom beyond the living room far to your left. On the right, the formal dining room is used for conferences. The kitchen is beyond." Both the living room and the dining room opened onto the *lanai,* with the surf far below in all its endless shades.

I looked into both large rooms. I was much too nervous to admire or even notice the furnishings of which Ito was justifiably proud. Michiko Yee Nagata, his talented wife, was responsible for the interior decorating. She had done a great job. But all I could think of now was the series of mysterious problems involving my niece and her husband, who had sent for me with the obvious expectation that, by some magic, I would solve everything.

"We seem to be early," I remarked as my companion ushered me into the living room.

"Make yourself at home," he said. "I'll get you a drink, and — ah — mustn't forget these."

Looking up in surprise, I saw him taking several long leis of flowers, fresh, moist, smelling of gardens in the early morning, from behind the little bamboo bar across the room against the bedroom wall. He brought them to me and dropped each over my head separately as he kissed me on the cheek. I recognized the white carnations, but the pale lei made up of what appeared to be small bells was exquisite. *"Pikake,"*

19

he explained, and then, "pink plumeria . . . the cheap ones. But the most popular."

I loved each of them, but I agreed that I loved the "cheap ones" of pink plumeria best. The scents rose around me, delightfully romantic, and somehow softening my fears as well. I had felt cold for so long, my emotions frozen within me, that these flowers seemed to offer the first key to the freeing of those emotions.

I was still thanking Ito Nagata when he went over to the bamboo bar again and waved away my thanks. "You deserve it. Besides, Michiko knows about it. No hanky-panky." I laughed. I felt genuinely happy for a few minutes.

"But no more drinks, Ito. I have to get used to it gradually."

"How about coffee?"

"Fine. I'd like that."

"Kona coffee. Nothing like it in the world."

I smiled. Ito Nagata had certainly become a loyal booster of Michiko's native state. Nor could I blame him. From my brief observation it was not for nothing that these islands were called the Paradise of the Pacific.

There seemed to be coffee brewing constantly in a glass Silex. At any rate, he had a cup of steaming coffee ready for me within a minute or two. I accepted it with gratitude. I had raised the cup to my lips when I heard the hall door open. I was glad I could continue drinking the coffee without revealing my sudden new inner disquiet. I was certain that the stride and the slammed door and the human cyclone entering the room all represented my niece's husband and my prospective employer, Stephen Giles.

A little overwhelming at first glance, he was a trim man with a bronze look about him — his complexion, his hair, his throat, even his shirt and bare arms. At least he wasn't wearing one of the loud aloha shirts sported by everyone who returned from the islands. But he was even more informal that I had been led to believe. His attraction for Deirdre and her friend Ingrid was obvious. He looked vividly alive. He had deep-set hazel eyes, a splendid high-bridged nose that dominated his face, and a mouth that I suspected might be both sensuous and tender. He came directly across the room and stood over me, studying everything about me. Now that I saw him close up, I wondered if he didn't also look stubborn, but perhaps I was simply perceiving a man who was used to getting his own way.

Ito and I sat nervously, and Giles began the conversation. "So this is Deirdre's aunt!" He added with a smile, "Her young aunt."

Before Dr. Nagata could say anything, I told Mr. Giles coolly, "I am Judith Cameron," and put my hand in his when he offered it. He had a strong grip.

He said with unexpected frankness, "The newspaper pictures didn't do you justice. And red hair. Have you a temper?"

21

"Auburn. I have learned to control my temper, I hope."

"I'm always trying to control mine, although I sometimes wonder if I will ever conquer it."

Then he went over to the bar and made himself a drink. It appeared to be Scotch on the rocks. Immediately, Ito Nagata took his own glass and wandered away toward the dining room. I wondered if his departure had been prearranged. Mr. Giles brought his drink to the couch and sat down beside me, stretching his long legs out before him. The late-afternoon light cut across the room, highlighting all his features and giving them a harsh look I hadn't noticed at first. "Miss Cameron — Judith, that is — I don't know where I could have turned if you had failed me. I am in your debt. You came over here to help me. . . ."

"To help your wife, as I am sure you understand, Mr. Giles."

"Stephen. Yes, and I thank you for it. Deirdre will be immensely better with you to guide her."

A little thread of a frown told me he was hesitating about something he wanted to say. But I think he felt that he didn't know me well enough to venture into those dark problems — Deirdre's real difficulties that had brought me here. *Were there dark problems?*

"Well," he said after a silence between us, "I'm afraid I can't take you to Ili-Ahi as I hoped to. I am in the middle of negotiations on the threat of a dock strike. I needn't tell you what

22

dock strikes do to our economy. Dr. Nagata has been good enough to say he will take you to my home immediately, where Deirdre is expecting you. The property in your charge will be on Ili-Ahi, as the island is called. To avoid confusion, our house is referred to as Sandalwood. Same thing, actually. But I hope you will occasionally help me to entertain at business receptions here in Honolulu." As I looked at him, he put up one hand as though to ward off my objections. "All perfectly respectable, Judith. What I need is a woman to manage these things at home and here on Oahu. That's it."

"I will be glad to help in any way."

He smiled and I understood quite well why Deirdre and her friend had pursued him, as Ito Nagata suggested. Giles said, "You are rather too attractive to be called Deirdre's aunt. There will probably be gossip. Especially as my wife is too . . . too young to manage her household."

"I couldn't bear any gossip that would hurt Deirdre. But as for myself, I am not afraid of gossip."

"No. I don't believe you are. And Deirdre will depend on you a great deal."

"All the better. Deirdre will bear up — I know she will," I assured him and added with a flicker of amusement, "I promise to do my best and not to give anyone grounds for gossip."

He laughed at that. "You sound Victorian." As I opened my mouth to deny this, he asked the curious question: "You aren't superstitious, I hope?"

What a very odd question to put to a house-keeper! I assumed it had something to do with Deirdre's problems. But I couldn't recall that my niece had ever been afraid of black cats and stepping on cracks in the sidewalk. "I'm not superstitious," I said, "though I think you should know that I won't walk under ladders."

He found this also amusing. "Very wise. Now, if you will excuse me, Judith, my charming young 'aunt,' I'll leave you in Dr. Nagata's capable hands and get back to those damned negotiations. I hope I can get home to Ili-Ahi tonight. But if not . . ." He shrugged.

He got up quickly, downed his drink and called to Ito. A minute later he was gone.

I stared after him. "Is that all, Ito? Just like that?"

Ito Nagata said with a sudden, unexpected reserve, "He's accepted you; you're in. But be careful. Don't go rushing around making an enemy of him just to protect Deirdre. I like Stephen Giles, but he is a stubborn man. I wouldn't want him to turn against me. Or you, for that matter."

"But why would he? I hope whatever I do will be for Deirdre's sake."

"Deirdre may not be perfect either, you know. Try and weigh things. Don't go out on a limb in supporting her against Steve. As I say, he's a fair man, but he might be very difficult if he thought he was being crossed."

I understood, and I agreed with him. But at the moment I saw no reason why we should be enemies, Stephen and I, so long as he remained a good husband to my niece. And I must remember also, when Ito Nagata was giving me his undoubtedly excellent advice, that Ito had always felt I sheltered Deirdre too much. It was the only subject the Nagatas and I disagreed on.

Two

I had some vague notion that we would cross Oahu, Honolulu's home island, and perhaps take a motorboat across the bay that Deirdre had mentioned in some of her letters, in order to reach Stephen Giles's island of Ili-Ahi and his home, the fabled Sandalwood. I was surprised, though not yet uneasy over the complications and the length of time it took to reach Deirdre's new home. We took an interisland plane northwest from Oahu, half an hour later touching down at the airfield on what Dr. Nagata called Ili-Ahi's "parent island" of Kaiana, one of the major Hawaiian group, since Ili-Ahi did not have a landing field of its own. A young man from the little airport office came out and informed Dr. Nagata, "Your jeep is under the willows over there, this side of the Keawe thicket. Leave it in the breezeway near the beach and Sam and I will overhaul it soon as we get a break."

"Thanks, Tiji. See you at the *luau* Sunday."

I looked around this part of the island of Kaiana as Ito Nagata dropped my suitcase and make-up box into the jeep. Even at this hour, with sunset gaudily reflected on the tangled woods at the far end of the airfield and on the patch of what appeared to be giant ferns nearby, the island presented a hundred sources of mystery of concealment to a stranger like me. How lost Deirdre must have felt! The difficulties of reaching Ili-Ahi were like a Chinese puzzle box containing endless smaller boxes within. Deirdre was virtually a prisoner at Sandalwood House once she had reached there.

Ito offered his hand to help me up into the jeep, and then we bounced and rattled over a small, unpaved road while the other three plane passengers, intending to remain on Kaiana, took a hotel limousine along the paved highway in the opposite direction.

Ito glanced at me several times while I studied the rapidly darkening foliage that overhung our little road.

"Troubles?"

"Oh, no. I was only thinking. I hadn't quite realized before how much jungle there is in Hawaii." He smiled but I suspected he was still worried about something, either Deirdre's problems or my ability to cope. "You aren't against greenery and vegetation, I hope. You'll find a good deal of it here, and more so on Ili-Ahi."

"But I like greenery and flowers. And believe me, I can get along without so much of the pushing and shoving and intimacy with strangers that I knew too well for eight years." I raised the divinely scented leis from around my neck and sniffed at them. "It's only that I had a slightly closed-in feeling there for a few minutes. It's no place for anyone with claustrophobia." I was afraid he might think I had changed my mind about what I had come to do, and I added with what sounded to my own ears like an overdone enthusiasm, "But I adore my flowers — the lovely flowers you gave me. They are perfect."

"Not quite, I'm afraid." Ito was looking at me, or rather, at my neck which, as a matter of fact, had begun to burn a little. I put my hand to my throat under the cool, moist leis, laughing uneasily.

"Sunset and the Dracula hour. Why are you looking at me like that?"

He smiled. "I am afraid one of those leis was strung with wire. Not a very common trick these days. Anyway, it has scratched you." He took out a linen handkerchief, and I put it to my neck. When I glanced at the much creased linen there was a thread of a bloodstain. A little troubled, I laughed again and lied.

"Don't look so serious, Ito. It's not some bad omen. I don't believe in omens. I wouldn't dare. My new employer was very explicit about that. He even asked if I were superstitious. I suppose if I'd said I told fortunes with tarot cards I'd have been thrown out on my ear."

Dr. Nagata slowed to let a group of giggling brown young children of all races cross the road and plunge into what I could only think of as a sinister-looking jungle of monstrous, twisted growths, half of which appeared to be uprooted. They looked as if they had gigantic spiders on their backs, with their roots growing in all directions. Dr. Nagata asked me in a puzzled way,

"Stephen talked to you about superstitions? Good Lord! I wonder if he takes them seriously now."

"Takes what seriously?"

"Old wives' tales," he said in a sharp, annoyed voice. "Some time ago there was trouble at the site of the Sandalwood Heiau, that series of cottages for tourists with a layout for parties or *luaus* — that type of thing. Matter of fact, I invested in the *heiau* myself. Anyway, it had all gone to seed, you might say, until recently. They couldn't make a go of it. Stephen's father lost his shirt and killed himself, so Stephen had to start again from scratch. And all, they say, because the cottages were built on the site of an ancient *heiau*. A sacred place in the islands."

Slightly apprehensive after looking around this desolate spot, I asked, "Is Ili-Ahi anything like this island?"

"Not nearly as big, and not as civilized." That shook me. Could anything be even less civilized than this place? "No towns on Ili-Ahi. Sandalwood is the plantation house. Not much by Big Island standards. Then there are cottages in the Hawaiian sector. They grow taro and some experimental crops. The object is to bring back something of the old pre-*haole* life. No, I don't just mean Caucasians." He corrected himself. "*Haoles* are foreigners. These Hawaiians aren't happy with the civilization brought by the Asians, either. Anyway, what isn't under cultivation of sorts is jungle. And an area of fields on the west, where some cattle are run."

It didn't sound promising. I thought this island was remote enough. I wouldn't mind it so much for myself. I would almost prefer my own company after the crowded conditions I had known for the past eight years. But I wondered how a young girl like Deirdre had reacted.

The jeep bounced along and quite suddenly jostled us out over the sand on a series of planks that ran into a shed at one end of a long, narrow strand of beach. The breezeway Dr. Nagata's friend, Tiji, had mentioned.

Now what would we do?

The answer was obvious, but not quite what I had pictured as the way visitors arrived at Ili-Ahi. A simple motorboat with a good working engine. It seemed very unpretentious and to me, at least, pleasant. But Deirdre must have been surprised. Surely, this wasn't the way an impressionable young girl would expect to arrive at the home island of her fabulous husband. Or had she and her friend Ingrid visited the island before Deirdre married Stephen Giles? Although he was certainly attractive, I had not been in a position to admire the charm and masculinity of males for a long time. I told myself that in view of Deirdre's apparent problems, her husband should have better defended her — against the elements as well as other people. But I knew I was assuming too much. Stephen Giles could hardly be aware of all the possible dangers concerning my poor niece. I had hoped my conviction in her mother's death had closed the past for Deirdre. Stephen might not know all about that time of misery and suffering we had shared. Or did he?

We stepped into this boat that looked like an overgrown dory, and Dr. Nagata started the motor after a couple of sputtering attempts. It was past sunset, but violent and startling rays on the western horizon still made the immediate world look as if it were on fire. I could see now that there really was a small land mass — an island? — northwest, beyond the wide entrance to Kaiana Bay, but in this little boat, and among these exceedingly choppy waters, I felt less than secure. I dropped one hand into the water, which was crimson in the light.

Dr. Nagata called to me proudly, "Gorgeous sunset, isn't it?"

We were getting a terrific feedback from the foam and waves cutting all around us and I could only agree, "Gorgeous!" as I wiped my face. I put on my sunglasses again, trying to see where we were going to land along that dark, forbidding coast. There was Stephen Giles's celebrated island of Ili-Ahi, with its more-romantic English translation of Sandalwood. But I need not have been concerned. Dr. Nagata knew perfectly well what he was doing. He headed in toward a tiny dot of light that proved to be a kind of stake coming out of the water about six feet high and topped by a flickering electric light that burned continually. (At least, they had electricity here.) It was covered by a bright copper hood. This hood, upon which the sunset rays gleamed, was the actual light I had seen at a distance. The electric light itself was far too dim.

Ito Nagata explained. "This little channel is one exit point of a genuine river."

"I had no idea an island as small as this might have a river."

"Indeed, yes. Not anything to match Kauai's river, but it's bigger than a brook. It cuts across the island, more or less from the northwest peak, the highest on the island, down through swampy areas, between the Sandalwood Heiau's abandoned cabins that Stephen has taken over, and onto this spot on the southeast of Ili-Ahi."

With stunning suddenness, the sun disappeared and we found ourselves landing at a small, rather unsteady plank dock, in the deep gray dusk. I put away my sunglasses. I had to blink several times to see anything behind and around that copper beacon light on the spit of land that reached out into the channel between Ili-Ahi and the Kaiana Bay. For a minute Dr. Nagata stopped moving. There were curious hushed little sounds around us, like sibilant whispers. Thickets very like those I had seen on Ili-Ahi's parent island of Kaiana grew close along the shore. There was only this hundred yards or so of sand and coral outcrops where the stream emptied into the sea. Not such a good swimming area here — the coral would cut up anyone's feet.

As Dr. Nagata joined me, I noticed that he now carried a big flashlight. I laughed, pretending to be more amused than uneasy. "This really is a primitive place. Are there no lights on the road?"

"Yes and no. There are no roads as such on Ili-Ahi, though Stephen has a jeep and so do the Hawaiian villagers on the other side of the island. But there are lights on this path to the house. Just a little walk through those trees there. We'll probably be met." He reached for the copper cover of the lamp at the wharf and pressed a button inside the lamp stand. "Buzzer. It rings in the main house."

I took up my make-up case. He lifted the heavier suitcase out of the boat and we started along the dark path toward the big house, which was still unseen. There were more light standards lining the dark, twisting way at infrequent intervals, and I found myself hurrying from one pool of light to the next with Dr. Nagata almost striding to keep up with me. A pungent, not unattractive odor of moist earth and bitter roots pervaded the lush, green growth. Now and then there were softer, flowery scents. One could almost sort them out individually, haunting little reminders of the plant life all around.

"Frightened?"

"A little. It's this jungle, or whatever it is. The trees are so tightly laced together. And beyond the path . . ." I pointed out with my make-up case, ". . . it's soggy and wet. All that

33

moss and decayed wood. And, I suppose, thousands of insects and snakes."

Ito dismissed this with a grin. "Nothing poisonous. There is so much rain at the higher altitudes that the stream spreads out all through this area. It's mostly swamp, but by day you will see some of the most incredible blossoms and flowering trees through there. Don't go dashing into the area, though. There are ways, trails — like this lava path. Ah! I told you it wasn't far. Look ahead and to the right. Higher. The path rises steeply here for a minute or two, but at the top and on the right you can see the two screened *lanais* at the rear of Stephen Giles's house, one on each floor. We'd have called them balconies back in L.A."

I gaped at the sight. The view from those *lanais* plunged straight down into the wild, swampy growth far below. We were silent for a few seconds and again I heard the little rustling sounds all around us. Everywhere serpent branches and roots — one as bad as the other — twisted and writhed, even overhead. The still-bright sky above was concealed from us by the intertwined branches and leaves. Everything rustled; nothing was still.

"The place seems so alive," I commented, as Ito Nagata obviously expected me to say something.

I was saved from further comment, which doubtless would have insulted his beloved Hawaii, by the approach of a huge, almost black

Hawaiian man coming down the steeply sloping path to us.

"Kalanimoku!" Ito called. "I am back with the lady, as you see. Has Mr. Giles called? This is Kalanimoku, Judith. Butler and majordomo of the island. He likes to be called 'Moku,' for short."

"Stephen called," said the Hawaiian, a man of imposing girth and what appeared to be solemn dignity until he smiled, which was frequently. He had a wonderful smile. "He said he would try to return sometime tonight. He also told us to expect the lovely young lady. His very words, miss."

I was embarrassed but certainly not displeased and thanked Kalanimoku, "Moku, for short." It did my ego a great deal of good, after years of thinking how very old I was growing. To have everyone refer to me as a young lady. The Hawaiian took my baggage and looked as though he could have carried a few steamer trunks besides. In that semidarkness he was easily seen, for he wore an aloha shirt of astounding, variegated flowers, a pair of white slacks that must have been specially ordered to fit him, and gold-colored sandals. In spite of his outfit, he still managed to look very like a photograph I had seen of the statue of King Kamehameha I in front of the Iolani Palace.

We passed the side of Sandalwood, Stephen Giles's grand old wooden family home, as we reached the top of the little trail that wound onward past cabins I could faintly see, half concealed in thick foliage beyond the house. What was it that Ito Nagata had told me about a tourist village, left unfinished due to bad luck? Superstition again. These cabins were all dark. Clearly, no one occupied them. As we went around to the broad front of the Giles house, I could hear the rushing waters of a stream somewhere, probably on the far side. I wondered if the stream plunged down into that swampy morass below the two *lanais* at the back of the house. I hoped it would look more inviting by daylight.

There were Japanese lanterns strung along the front of the house, giving a festive air to the little clearing. Beyond was the darkness of the forest and those unfinished cottages. No, not a forest. Probably what Ito would call a thicket. I was beginning to understand very well why a girl Deirdre's age should need a housekeeper to care for her husband's estate. But she had also lived for years in exclusive schools with no parental guidance and no authority beyond that of the busy and indifferent courts. She had no way of knowing how to handle this kind of situation.

I forced my thoughts to a more cheerful direction.

"Here we are, Miss Cameron," Moku announced with a magnificent gesture of welcome.

From the long, shallow veranda I stepped through a small entry into a living room that occupied the west front of the old wooden house. Sandalwood must have been a splendid house at the turn of the century when such Victorian structures were still much admired. The high walls were beautifully papered in a green-and-gold motif of pagodas and exquisite Oriental figures. Curiously enough, both mandarins and willowy Japanese females in kimonos and huge obis appeared along the walls. I wondered whose idea that was. Although well cared for, the wallpaper appeared very old and probably could never be duplicated. The room was so long and elaborately furnished, I suspected it was only used for parties, perhaps in conjunction with *luaus* out in the area in front of the house. Nor was it well lighted at this moment — there was just one hanging lamp in the shape of a Japanese lantern on a chain at the far end of the room to give us any light.

Dr. Nagata took my arm, and I followed Kalanimoku through the dark, narrow central hall. Suddenly, a door near the far end of the hall opened from a lighted room. An extraordinary silhouette appeared in that light, which cast a deep bar of brightness across the mat carpeting the hall floor. What appeared to be a gigantic red hibiscus bush stood there staring at us, expressionless. This woman in the hibiscus-flowered *holoku* was nearly six feet tall and must have weighed well over two hundred pounds — she looked solid and regal. Her heavy black hair was worn severely back from a forbidding and intelligent wide forehead. The chocolate-colored eyes, darkly outlined, reminded me of a magnificent cobra who had once out-stared me in a San Francisco aquarium.

I whispered to Ito, "Someone out of Captain Cook's journals?"

"She's mighty important among the purebloods across the island. Stephen borrowed her to run things until you could get here. She did it as a favor, but she is no servant." Then, he called loudly, "Good evening, Ilima. This is Miss Cameron, Mrs. Giles's aunt, who is going to take some of that load off your shoulders. Judith, Ilima is Moku's wife, the queen of Ili-Ahi, and one of the last descendants of Queen Liliuokalani's family."

I can't say I was reassured by this information. My knees had a strong inclination to sink in a curtsy, which I would have been expected to perform, had I been in Hawaii in 1893 when the last queen was deposed for American political expediency. I worked up a wide smile and was grateful when I saw the flash of her large, even teeth when she greeted me.

"I am glad to meet you, Miss Cameron. You have arrived in very good time to help us. It is fortunate that you are a mature woman. You will perhaps know what to do."

I looked to Ito Nagata for an explanation, but I could see that this was a mystery to him as well. Mrs. Moku offered her hand which I took quickly.

"You will want your baggage taken to your quarters first, Miss Cameron, and will perhaps wish to change your shoes."

This last puzzled me considerably, but she led me away from Ito and the huge butler, her husband.

I caught a glimpse of tree tops and enormous leaves beyond the lower floor *lanai* before she ushered me up the stairs to the room assigned to me. Throughout the house I noticed the odd odor of dampness, wet leaves, decomposition, mud, and then, unexpectedly again, the strong scent of tropic flowers. Fortunately, I had also the delicious and comforting odor of the flower leis Ito had given me. I started to address my companion by her full name and for the first time since I had met her, I think she was amused.

"I am called Ilima. It is easier. Here is your bed-sitting room. You are only one door away from the upper *lanai* at the back of the house. This window across the room looks out upon the trail by which you came here. If you look to your right you will see the *emu* in the ground in front of the house. That is for roasting the pig for the *luau*. Stephen thought you might not like the direct view of the gulch on the other side of the house opposite your room. From that side by daylight you can see the waters of the Ili-Ahi River, several tributaries running on down into the swampy area below the *lanais*. I hope your room is satisfactory."

I looked around. A comfortable bed with a headboard; an old-fashioned and so-handy three-mirrored French dresser; a small round table of inexpensive but beautiful rosewood; a comfortable, slightly shabby couch with wicker sides that looked as though they might tear one's stockings, except that no one wore stockings here in Hawaii. There was also a charming table lamp with a brass teapot base.

I felt a small stab of pain as I recognized the lamp. It had belonged to my mother. Deirdre must have kept it with her at the exclusive girls' school to which the courts had consigned her after my trial.

But why was it in my room now? Was it Deirdre's idea? I hoped that it was. I cleared my throat to conceal any signs of emotion.

"What a very unusual little lamp!"

Ilima stared at it. "A *haole* design." I knew that *haole* referred to foreigners and assumed this was meant as a derogatory comment. She added, "Such things are of the missionary sort."

"Yes, very." I began to unbutton my coat, a well-fitted, coachman style popular a couple of years back. One of the matrons had chosen it for me when I became housekeeper in the office of the female warden we referred to as the "Super," a very understanding woman. I tried to sound noncommittal. "So the family is descended from missionaries."

"No. But the little lamp —" I felt rather than heard her pause. It was almost nonexistent. "— it has been in Mr. Giles's family for some years. I thought it suitable in here."

Not so, I thought. You take possessions and pass them around as if Deirdre had nothing to say in her own household, but there were still those who cared about her.

"You will be tired, but we need you badly, Miss Cameron. May we see you as soon as possible?"

"Certainly. At once, if you like." All this haste suggested a crisis of some kind. "I had better see my niece first. I rather expected her to meet me." This must have been perfectly obvious to her. Was Deirdre ill?

"Would ten minutes be agreeable to you?" she asked. "Everything will be explained." Her remark did not reassure me. She left, passing her husband, Moku, in the hall. He brought up my bags, which seemed odd. If there was a lordly "butler" here, there certainly must be boys to carry my suitcases. I asked him as he was leaving, "What other rooms are on this floor?"

"The family bedrooms, ma'am. Not that there is much of the family left. Steve — Mr. Stephen — has the small front bedroom and bath on the other side. Mrs. Giles has the front suite across from him, two doors beyond this one. But she prefers to spend a great deal of her time in the room opposite." He pointed across the hall.

"But why does she have two — ?" My question was so abrupt I hardly recognized my voice, and it was not my business. But apparently Deirdre and her husband did not share a bedroom or even a suite, and still she had another room

41

where she spent much of her time.

Moku shrugged his great shoulders.

"She seems a very young lady. She likes to disappear. These are called pranks. Excuse me, but 'pranks' — that is the word that people use. It is an old word that my mother used, not suitable to a modern young lady at all. Anyway, my daughter Kekua is her friend, and she tells me that Mrs. Stephen plays jokes. Several times she has tried to go off to Honolulu alone. That could be dangerous. Mr. Stephen does not always know. He used to visit Honolulu once a week until the strike deadlock on the docks. Now, he must visit there several times in the week. But it would be dangerous for Mrs. Stephen to try to go alone. She cannot seem to understand how to run the motor in any of the boats. My daughter is a real veteran at running the motorboats across the bay but she cannot teach Mrs. Steve. Mr. Stephen also tries to teach her, and to see that she swims well, in case — but . . ."

"No," I agreed weakly, remembering times that seemed to me very long ago. "Deirdre liked the pools but never learned to swim very well. She wasn't fond of learning. But then, she was always so . . . dear, and we never wanted to force her."

Moku looked away, avoiding my eye. "Yes. I think everyone must love the little lady, even my Kekua, who once had a childish crush upon Mr. Steve. But that was before . . . Well, can we expect you in a few minutes?"

I told him I would be down immediately and then, when he left, I found myself locking the door. Recalling where I was, I turned the simple skeleton key to unlock it and put away my suitcases, still packed, in the closet. There was an adjoining bathroom, a barn-sized room obviously used as a bedroom or perhaps a sitting room in the old days. It had a modern porcelain toilet, but the bathtub was large enough to drown in, and stood high above the floor on gaudily carved legs. I loved it. I only wished I might plunge into a tub-full of hot water at once, to rest and relax. I was exceedingly tense. And I was worried.

Three

I took a couple of minutes to recover that calm Ito Nagata had imagined he saw in me at our afternoon meeting. Then I went down to meet Ilima Moku. I chose the front staircase, however, still hoping that I would see Deirdre somewhere, that some door would be open in this empty house and she would come dashing out in her impetuous way. The place seemed deserted. The wide front stairs had one landing at the turn and creaked madly. I announced my presence by footsteps that seemed even noisier because there were no others to echo them.

I met Ilima in a remarkably pleasant kind of all-purpose family room at the back of the house opposite the big kitchen, the serving pantry, and the dining room across the hall. Because of the intense growth of foliage everywhere around the house, the light from two table lamps brought two pools of golden light to this "family sitting room." I guessed that elsewhere on this or other islands in the state it would still be dusk, with the orange and vermillion post-sunset light still giving a semblance of day to the world. Ilima and her husband were both there, obviously waiting only for my arrival, and I was startled to find a young woman, who was also present. She was still breathless and Moku explained that she, Kekua, had been running to "report" to them.

Kekua was a lush, gorgeous girl with her mother's great earth-brown eyes, which were unreadable, and a figure whose rich, dark curves would have delighted readers of *Playboy* magazine. She was clearly more modern than her mother and father, but the royal blood of Hawaii was evidently still present, even though she wore a miniskirt and what appeared to be a bikini top that was far from adequate to fill its purpose.

"Kekua grew up with Stephen," Ilima explained and I remembered the girl's father saying that his daughter had a "crush" on Stephen Giles. But Kekua, flashing her father's magnificent smile, corrected them now as we were introduced.

"I didn't exactly grow up with him. I happen to be ten years younger, but we all played together, Steve and the rest of us in the village. Matter of fact, once or twice Steve earned money babysitting for me. He wasn't too crazy about it, and I must have been a brat, but Mrs. Giles didn't believe in allowances. It was work or no money," she laughed. "And now we work for him! How's that for the world turned upside-down?"

Moku cut in gently, "Kekua, we can talk about this later, after we find Mrs. Steve."

It seemed odd to hear them talk of my niece as "Mrs. Steve." She had always seemed so child-like, but of course, I hadn't really known her after she was twelve.

"I suppose we'd better get with it," Kekua

45

agreed. "But we've been combing the island. Poor Yee — that's the Korean cook —" she explained to me, "he and two of our men from the village are wandering through the Ili-Ahi gulch behind the house here."

So we had finally reached the crucial matter after all this awkward rambling. But possibly they didn't know how deeply I was involved with anything that concerned Deirdre.

"Is she lost? Was she out walking?" I asked them all. "Please tell me! I am her aunt, you know. There are no other close relatives. Where should I start?" I looked from one to the other. Ridiculously, I felt as if I were ready for a quick sprint out the door, as if the woman they had been searching for was still a child of five or six.

Her husband and daughter looked to Ilima as their spokesman. The massive and queenly woman straightened a little.

"Yes, Miss Cameron. We didn't like to tell Stephen. He is so busy with this waterfront deadlock."

"It may go either way tonight," her husband put in. "So we thought, since you knew young Mrs. Steve well and all . . ."

"Yes, yes! Please!"

Maddeningly, they all looked at me again. Ilima said, "Everyone from Sandalwood is out scouring the island. The servants here, and my own people from the village. We thought you might know how the young lady behaved — the kinds of places she hid — when she was in your care."

I walked up and down the room, trying to pull my thoughts together, to remember.

"She ran away as a child when there were problems, but I did begin to understand something of her thinking. I always found her. But you see, I don't know any of the hiding places . . ." Remembering the old days, I rephrased this. "I mean — any of the safe places on the island. Where did she go when this happened before?"

"We've covered that," Kekua put in brusquely. "A little glade across the island on the trail to our village. It's below Mt. Liholiho. There's a series of falls, and the falls run into the river. But she wasn't there this afternoon."

Finally I understood the "problem" Ilima had mentioned to me when I arrived. But the idea of trying to find a Deirdre determined not to be found, on an island full of jungles, falls, mountains, and unknown if nonpoisonous insects was appalling.

"Can you tell me why she went off by herself today? It might help if I knew what triggered this."

Kekua shrugged. "I'd been to Honolulu looking for a job. Steve was busy; so I talked to his office manager and then caught the noon plane to Kaiana. I operated the motor across the bay for two passengers. Paying passengers." She told me confidentially, "I pick up a little mad money like that now and then. One of the men was a fascinating *haole* and . . ." She stopped as if she found it hard to picture the other man. "The other was younger. I took them to see Deirdre, but she wasn't in the house. It's funny, because Mother had seen her only half an hour before."

Ilima nodded. "She saw them. I am sure of it. Two Caucasians."

Were we getting closer to the real reason for Deirdre's flight?

"Who were these men who came to see my niece? And why couldn't they stay?"

Ilima reminded me, "They were strangers and there is no possible place for them to stay, unless they are guests of Sandalwood or with friends in the village. One of the men from our village, Andrew Christian, was making a trip back across the bay and agreed to take the two gentlemen to Kaiana. They said they would spend the night at the new Kaiana Hilton."

"What did they want with Deirdre? Why not see her husband? Who are they?"

Ilima said, "The name given, I believe, was Berringer. I don't recall the younger man's name."

Kekua hesitated. Then she smiled broadly. "He wasn't the kind you would remember. But Victor Berringer . . . 'Vic,' the other man called him. Ah! Cold as ice and smelled of money. Not friendly at all. But a man with lots of power. You can tell. I think it was something unpleasant he came to —"

"Be quiet."

Moku and his daughter looked at Ilima. It was easy to see that the queen of Ili-Ahi still held her sceptre.

"You do not talk like that about a *haole,* and a *malahini* too! A man older than your father. I did not like his eyes. But you are right in one thing, my daughter. His eyes were like cold waters far out from shore."

The name was familiar but at the moment I was too upset to care about the cold-eyed strangers who had intrigued Kekua.

"Perhaps if Deirdre could see me," I suggested and started to the front of the house. "I could walk about. Do something. Be seen by her if she is hiding somewhere around here."

Moku hurried after me, his impressive bulk shaking the hall floor.

"Maybe with a light. Here. I left one on the veranda." He added, "She will return soon. She has done so before. Let me show you the places where she goes sometimes to read or to draw the flowers here and to press the flowers. She makes little patterns. Very pretty."

I looked back as we crossed the dimly lighted huge living room. The woman and her daughter were talking. The older woman gave her a little push as if to send her after us, but Kekua said abruptly, "I know Mrs. Steve better than you do. She isn't going to thank me for interfering."

Outside the house as we crossed the grassy

clearing, Moku took my arm.

"Careful. The *emu* is just to your right." I avoided this pit, at the same time seeing the movements of the island's population for the first time. Two men with Oriental features, Japanese or Korean, I thought, came around the veranda from the jungle-covered gulch below. They had found nothing, but looked drenched although they wore shiny slickers and boots. It was odd to see such cold-weather clothes in this climate, but even across the clearing my companion's flashlight recalled the mud-encrusted boots, and the water dripping off their rain slickers.

Then Moku inadvertently reminded me of the real identity of the man who had come all the way to Ili-Ahi to meet Deirdre. He remarked, "The younger man who came over to meet Mrs. Steve had not so much force. He seemed afraid."

"Afraid!"

"I mean to say, embarrassed. Not wanting to come. He said while I myself heard, 'She is pretty and gentle. She marries the man. It is always the way. It is not a crime to marry the man another woman wants.' "

So the men were concerned with Ingrid Berringer who had been with Deirdre when they met Stephen Giles. Recalling Ito's hints about Ingrid, the girl who seemed to have vanished, I realized her father would not be visiting the island on a social call! Deirdre had always preferred peace to quarrels, and it was undoubtedly this timidity or gentleness that caused her to run away instead of meeting these unwelcome visitors.

"Miss Berringer's father, was he really angry?" I asked.

He did not want to say so, but it was apparent that Ingrid Berringer's father intended to make trouble.

We passed two women, one Japanese and the other, a younger, Filipino girl who, Moku explained, worked at Sandalwood House to earn her tuition at the university. He introduced us. The pretty Filipino girl said, "We've looked everywhere, Moku. Except —" She glanced at him with what was an obvious attempt to keep her suspicions from me. "You know. Those places."

"What places are they?" I asked when the two women had gone on to the house.

"They have been following the river's course, except near the cottages. Our river runs past them and empties into the gulch behind the Giles house. It was the cottages they did not enter."

These must be the cabins built by Stephen Giles's father: Sandalwood Heiau, the development that killed him.

"Hadn't we better look through them?" I suggested. Our path crossed a little footbridge at this point, and I got a good look at the side of one of the cabins in a glade and facing the river. It was an imitation of the original Hawaiian grass

51

huts, although there were windows and the grass was painted straw. But I found it charming. And I remembered suddenly that when she was small, Deirdre had a little pup tent on the back lawn and insisted on covering the canvas with acacia branches to imitate South Seas grass huts.

"Let's look in there."

"Ah, Miss Cameron . . ." He was so obviously upset, I realized I had said something either shocking or alarming.

When we had crossed the dark little bridge, I turned along the path that led past several cabins facing the river. The river itself was calm, looking jellylike under the first stars and the occasional flashes of Moku's light. He barely caught my arm before I had gone beyond his reach.

"No, Miss Cameron! The *heiau* is hated. You are on the *heiau* land now. Everyone is afraid of it. You would not find her in those cabins."

"Why, for heaven's sake?" All around me the coco-palms fluttered and rustled, although I felt no breeze. They seemed very busy, like gossipers whispering.

"It is a sacred place," he began. I said I understood that. "There are certain memories connected with the *heiau*," he went on. "The *kahunas*, that is, the priests in the old days placed it *kapu* for what Steve's father intended. *Kapu* — forbidden. It should not be a place for *haoles* to make money and to bring their *malahini* friends and soil it with their *haole* ways."

I thought I understood his objections, but they weren't helping me to find my niece.

"We might just look past the cabins," I suggested tentatively. "I wouldn't do anything to . . . soil them with my *haole* ways, but I feel we could then eliminate this area and go on, for a little while."

He did not stop me, but I found myself alone as I went on, feeling my way between new, moist growths, bushes, young trees, and what seemed to me a surprising richness of great multicolored blooms: hibiscus, plumeria, orchids, and red blossoms that glowed in the distant glitter of Moku's flashlight like fireworks sprays. As I moved beyond the area of his flashlight and became accustomed to the blue-dark, I discovered that the starlight overhead seeped through, offering at least a minimum of light to see my way past the cabins. I glanced in at the first of these and saw how the entire project had not been completed. There were three steps — mere plank steps — up to the doorway. Several cabins nearby had no doors. The interior of the first cabin, left unfinished, showed me that the general family room was to be an imitation of the ancient grass huts, but probably with luxurious, Waikiki kinds of touches. There were no windows, and the flooring was carpeted with blown palm fronds, dust, dead flowers, endless greenery. And no doubt a great many insects. I slipped on something that appeared to mash like a beetle, and felt another creature scamper across my instep as I rushed out and down the steps.

Little streams had been cut away from the river to run between each cabin, their banks lined with flowers, often blooms I had never seen before. It was all picturesque, but sad and deserted. The scene made me think of so much of the art practiced and exhibited by the inmates of the minimum security sector of the women's prison. Their work was so often cheerful and bright and happy. But unfortunately, when I was an inmate there, the twittering buyers had always wanted gloomy, downbeat art, "the way it really is," as more than one of the ladies remarked, her diamond-studded hands momentarily blinding me. The deserted cabins before me spoke all too clearly of "the way it was."

It was darker further inside the grove and after glancing in at two more cabins, I looked back through the trees. Seeing that Moku must have given me up, I decided to take a shortcut back toward Sandalwood, across the next little footbridge. Surely, Deirdre would have returned to her home by now.

The cabin across the bridge was one of those Stephen Giles must have worked on recently. It looked quite charming surrounded by hibiscus, tiny pastel-colored orchids growing wild and a lovely golden-blossoming tree. The scent of the plumeria was almost overpowering. I made my way under the window, through underbrush that, however exotic, could have used some pruning, and noticed that recent work had been done on this and the next cabin. The windows were in and the rooftops with their simulated grass-hut look were very realistic without being impractical. I turned, went back a little way up the steps to see if I could discern any of Stephen Giles's touches in the interior. The moon was out by this time, but it was not high enough to be of much help. I stepped inside, but realized I would be unable to see anything except especially dark bundles of rags and canvas left by workmen in the far corners of the living room. I was just turning back to the steps when one of those shadowy bundles moved. The floor creaked.

I must have cried out. I remember I had visions of ancient *kahunas* cursing this ground and of ghastly dead warriors rising up, angered at my intrusion. In my panic I backed against the door frame, staring. The bundle in the far corner unfolded, was thrown off. I heard Deirdre's voice, still so oddly young and innocent, before I could make out her face. She rushed toward me, one sandaled foot still caught in the canvas that dragged behind her.

"Judy! I can't believe it . . . I was never so glad to see anybody! It *is* you, Aunt Judith?"

I had been so dumbfounded by her resurrection from what looked like an old gunny sack that she threw herself into my arms and I found myself hugging her before I could see her. She was crying. I felt my cheeks wet with her tears, and my own.

"Of course, it is! I came as soon as I could, dear. You knew I would, didn't you?"

"It was awful. I was so scared!"

She came out of the cabin with me, holding tight to my hand as she had done when I found her in her childhood, after she had run off. The repetition of this action of many years ago was disturbing to me. She shouldn't be doing this sort of thing any more.

"Deirdre! For heaven's sake! You didn't have to see those Berringers. You are a grown-up, a married woman. You needn't see anyone you don't want to see. Your husband will handle it if you can't. Although, it's better now to begin to handle problems yourself, rather than leave them for others. You really should have begun long ago. Dear, do you want people to think you are a coward?"

Deirdre looked around anxiously as we hurried through the Hawaiians' sacred grove toward the welcome open space in front of Sandalwood, where the rising moon cast the *emu,* the gently bending stalks of orchids, and even the unkempt grass in long shadow.

"It was awful in that cabin. I kept very still so nothing would find me. I don't care what people think. I *am* a coward!"

I laughed and after a momentary hesitation, Deirdre giggled.

"Yes. Stephen wouldn't let them hurt me. He's so wonderful. Have you met him?"

"He was very kind."

"But he has to be away all the time. Whenever I need him, he's always got some stupid meeting or other."

I had no way of knowing how true her complaints might be and felt that I wouldn't help anyone if I took sides in a matter between husband and wife. The best tactic, I thought, would be to play down complaints of both Deirdre and her husband unless I felt Deirdre was being seriously harmed by Stephen Giles's deep devotion to his business. We saw Moku coming back from beyond the unfinished cabins in the little grove. He must have circled the *heiau* while I wandered among the cabins. I was looking in that direction and Deirdre startled me by clutching my arm tightly.

"She's going to be angry."

I saw Ilima's imposing figure on the veranda. She seemed absolutely without expression, but her presence itself was forbidding, even to me.

"You must remember that is your house, Deirdre," I told the girl. "Yours and, of course, Mr. Giles's. It isn't necessary to be rude for you to stand straight, like Ilima. Just hold your head up, smile, be polite, and give your orders to your servants."

"But she isn't a servant."

"Then," I reminded her, "she shouldn't frighten you, because she's just a person standing on your veranda, after all."

This seemed to be an entirely new notion to her. I took advantage of her temporary confidence to ask her, "Why did you hide in the *heiau* if it frightened you so? Wouldn't it have been better to stay in your room until Mr. Berringer left? Not," I added, "that I approve of your running away like a child."

She sighed. "It was nice when I was a child, except for mother being the way she was, of course. But I hid in the cabin because I knew Ilima and Moku wouldn't go in after me. They see ghosts and ancient gods there. They're more afraid than I am."

Her persistence in pretending to be that child I had loved and cared for during the periods when we couldn't locate her mother puzzled me more than anything else that had happened since my arrival in Honolulu.

Because Deirdre was so obviously afraid of the massive and queenly Ilima, it pleased me that she went up to the veranda and stood her ground, saying to the older woman, "I'm awfully sorry I kept you here so long, only I was looking over my husband's work in the *heiau*. My aunt will be my housekeeper now."

I whispered, "Thank her."

But it was too late. Ilima stepped down to the grass, nodded slightly to both of us and strode off along the path across the island to her village on the far shore. The queen had retired with all of her honor and dignity.

Almost at once Deirdre seemed to forget the hours she had spent like a cowering animal in the unfinished cabin. She rushed into the house complaining that she was starved.

"Michiko Nagata's Korean Uncle Yee is the cook, you know," she said. "And a wonder. He terrifies us all, even my husband. Yee! Where are you?" she yelled and then tried to duck behind me.

The serious, severe face of Mr. Yee appeared in the dining room doorway as I was trying, unobtrusively, to get Deirdre on her way upstairs to bathe and change before dinner. We were both covered with dust, leaves, dirt, and possibly insects as well.

Yee asked, "Mrs. Stephen will take a tray in her room?" He was speaking to me as if Deirdre had mysteriously vanished. He added, "It is usual, on nights after there is this long delay."

I agreed and we went on. Nelia Perez, a pretty Filipino college girl, met us on the upper floor.

"Good evening, Mrs. Steve. Your bath water is ready. Nice and hot. You want to jump in?" She glanced at Deirdre's long, disheveled chestnut hair, and nodded to me. I released my arm as gently as possible from Deirdre's tight grasp, and said cheerfully, "I'll see you later, dear," and went into my room.

I felt mentally exhausted as well as physically tired. Every bone and muscle was weak as water. I fell into the big, comfortable chair by the little round rosewood table, and closed my eyes momentarily. I still didn't know, or wouldn't admit to myself that my body was actually less tired than my spirit. I had known something was very wrong here, but I had thought and still told myself it was a physical problem of some kind that could be rectified by a little common sense.

Deirdre was simply new to her position as the wife of an important landowner. She was young. She would grow into her position — I thought it would only take patience. I decided I must explain that to her husband. Fortunately, he was a man one could talk to, directly and to the point. He didn't seem unreasonable.

Sitting here taking it easy wasn't going to help matters. I took the clothes out of my suitcase and hung them in the small but adequate closet, reflecting that there wasn't much I owned that would be useful in the humid sultry weather of the Islands. At least I wasn't penniless. I had a small income that would take care of most of my wants, and then too, Stephen Giles had insisted that I must have a reasonable salary, as he called it.

I ran warm water and bathed in the huge bathroom, loving the old and wonderfully big tub. Then I slipped on a violet chiffon caftan of several layers that I had bought in Los Angeles before my flight. This restored to me something of the femininity that I felt I had lost during the long years past, and when my dinner tray was brought to me by the small Japanese house woman, I felt luxurious and contented, assuring myself that everything would be straightened out in no time. I would soon be able to think about the rest of my life, where I would go, what I would do. . . .

I had no idea what I would do. Lately, I had not thought beyond my release and the settlement of my niece's problems.

"*Mahimahi*. You will like, please," the Japanese house woman explained. "Very good fish. And Island spinach. A little poi. So health. Very good health. Coconut pudding. Tea."

I thanked her and she shuffled away. She wore a *haole* dress but her small feet were cushioned in Japanese *getas*. She was right about the dinner. It was delicious and the *mahimahi,* as prepared by Mrs. Nagata's uncle, was superb. When someone knocked an hour later, I assumed it was the Japanese woman, come to take my tray. I called out casually.

"Come in," I said and then scrambled up in disarray when Stephen Giles walked in, impetuous and positive, apparently never having asked himself if my equally spontaneous "come in" would be for him. In spite of my annoyance I was also amused. He and Deirdre were a great pair — there was at this moment something of the confident boy about this very masculine male.

He saw me reach out toward the open closet for a robe that would look a little less obvious than this sexy business I was wearing. But as he watched me, I gave up the attempt. He was smiling a mischievous, warm smile. It was not difficult to see why Deirdre adored him.

"I'm sorry," he said. "I'm afraid I have the bad habit of walking in anywhere and at any time.

They tell me my manners are no better when I'm working out labor problems. Do you suppose that's why I have so much trouble persuading the ILU to see things my way?"

He seemed remarkably persuasive to me, but then, this persuasive power probably would be more effective on females.

Watch it, I thought . . . and watch yourself, Judith Cameron. You aren't going to help Deirdre by falling in love with her husband. . . .

Four

I regained my calm and launched into the most important problem we had in common.

"Deirdre went for a long walk this afternoon and I decided to join her. I'm afraid it made us late for dinner. That was why she ate in her room. She must have been terribly disappointed to miss having dinner with you, but I am sure she didn't know you would be home."

"It was a last-minute thing. We had a breakthrough on a couple of points and about that time I received a call from here . . . I thought Deirdre might be in trouble."

"No. She's fine. Or was an hour ago." I wondered who had called him. Probably Ilima Moku. I was sorry about it — I had hoped he wouldn't find out.

He stood there a minute looking at me with his arms crossed in a formidable way, and I couldn't imagine what on earth he was thinking, or if he really saw me. I didn't move a muscle. He said finally, "Have you gotten settled yet?"

I said I had. "And I really should be downstairs getting acquainted with the staff. I'm afraid I was so comfortable here, I . . ."

"Don't be so damned humble!" He ordered me so sharply and so unexpectedly, I was roused to a fury that surprised even me.

"I didn't know it was in my contract that I

should not be humble! What else is there in my unwritten contract that I am forbidden to do? Like losing my temper?"

He crossed his arms, looked far less formidable and then laughed. "A red-headed Scot! I know them well. May I sit down?"

"I beg your pardon. Did you want to speak with me about the work here?"

He pulled up the small chair from the French dresser and straddled the delicate back of the chair, facing me as I returned to my own comfortable armchair.

"Miss Cameron . . . that is to say — Judith."

"Yes?"

"You knew my wife quite well as a child. Probably much better than her parents knew her."

"Her father, my older brother, died in a prison camp outside Pyongyang in North Korea."

He nodded. "You must have been very young then."

Twenty-one years ago. And yet, as a twelve-year-old bobby-soxer then, I took my promise to my brother very seriously. My father had died on Guadalcanal when I was three, and after my brother died almost ten years later, mother seemed to lose her frail grasp on life. She couldn't believe that life could ever be good again, and when I was eighteen, she was gone, dead in less than ten days after a simple cold turned into pneumonia. But I had learned to manage the house, the cleaning, the cooking, even the hiring of mother's nurses and the occasional cooks who came and went when we could afford them. Nearly half the time during those years, Wayne's widow, a stunning blonde, had left Deirdre with mother and me. This was especially true after Deirdre's bad attack of rheumatic fever when she was five, which left her with a damaged heart that had never quite grown strong again. After mother's death came the terrible times when Deirdre's own mother, now an alcoholic with little control over her actions, made life miserable and terrifying for Deirdre and, eventually, for me.

"I was young." I smiled. "Once."

He waved aside my little joke, which was only half a joke. "Yes, yes, *Aunt Judy*." He emphasized the title. "I hope we may accomplish one thing, at least, before you are done with Ili-Ahi. We must persuade you that you are not some ancient crone come to slave away for your keep." And then came that tiresome question: "Why have you never married?"

"I have been engaged." He looked far more interested than the question warranted. I felt that he would sit there looking at me until I gave more details, though I couldn't see what this had to do with my qualifications as a housekeeper. I saw him glance at my hand. I raised it, turned it over. "It was a long time ago."

"You stopped loving him?"

"I went on trial for murder."

He didn't even blink. "In that case, you didn't lose much. He must have been singularly stupid."

"As a matter of fact," I began hotly, "for all you know, I may have had my heart broken over him." Something about his expression, his clear gaze, made me backtrack. "But of course, I didn't. Hearts are very flexible. Mine mended and, as I say, it was a long time ago."

"I'm not sorry." He held out his hand, took mine briefly. "Deirdre is delighted to have her problems loaded onto your shoulders. They look pretty slim to me. Can you handle the load?"

"Deirdre will do very well, Mr. Giles. Just give her a little time."

He worried me by making no reply to this. He got up, set the chair back, and started to leave. I was relieved. I had felt uncomfortably conscious of him ever since he came into the room. In the doorway he said, "He really was a fool, you know."

I didn't immediately understand him. After an embarrassing few seconds, I finally realized he meant the man I'd been engaged to almost nine years ago. By that time I could think of no way to answer Stephen Giles, but apparently he didn't expect an answer. He added, "Thank you, Judith. For my wife, and for me. Good night."

"Good night, Mr. Giles."

He didn't like that formality and pretended to scowl but closed the door. I sat for a very long time, not thinking of anything in particular, sometimes getting little blurred visions of the man I had once expected to marry, pictures of the courtroom and the jury. They had looked so sympathetic, almost all of them. It just went to show. You couldn't tell by people's looks. Gradually, as if I had been trying vainly to shut it out, I came back to the real problem: the childish behavior of Deirdre who was now a grown-up, married woman of twenty-one.

Was it possible her behavior had something to do with the rheumatic fever that had left her with the slight heart problem? I supposed because she was endearing and often generous and sweet, she must have used these qualities to lean upon and cling to her schoolmates and her teachers. In this way she had discovered she could save herself from every problem. Perhaps, too, the bad heart assisted her in this calculated dependence upon others. But the result was that she had grown to her present age without ever facing anything more threatening than a frown. And now this Berringer and his friend with their awful suspicions came trooping ashore to stir up trouble, so she had run away.

What, precisely, were Berringer's suspicions? Did he imagine a delicate girl like Deirdre had somehow murdered his daughter? Physically, it was preposterous. Ingrid Berringer, from the little I knew of her, was far more athletic than Deirdre, so the suspicion was extremely far-fetched. Unless, of course, they were concerned about the way Deirdre's mother died.

Feeling as cowardly as Deirdre, I closed my eyes and my thoughts to that subject and got ready for bed. Just before I got into that comfortable bed and sighed at the exact "rightness" of the mattress (not too hard, not too soft), I went to the window which faced west, and opened it to get the fresh, flower- and earth-scented air. The steep path up through the jungle vegetation from the copper-covered light on the channel dock was directly below the house. It was geometrically shadowed by the vegetation on both sides of the path. For a moment or two I imagined I saw long prehensile fingers, weird figures, endless fantasies, but actually, all these visions were formed by the curious, rich growth of the jungle beyond the path.

The moon was high overhead now. A tropic moon, exactly like the one in movies and the travel folders. I stood there dreaming a little, wondering how my life would have been by this time, over eight years later, if I had married John Eastman. Curiously enough, although I tried very hard, I couldn't remember very much about the face of the man who had jilted me "for my own good," as he put it at the time. Even the color of his eyes had faded from my mind. Maybe I tried too hard to remember. Or maybe he no longer mattered.

I shook myself and banished the thought of my unpleasant past. I looked out the open window, this time toward the front of the house, toward the green open space, the hole in the center that was the *emu*, and beyond, the grove with its half-finished cabins — Deirdre's hiding place. I could see why the Hawaiians felt that the lush little grove was sacred. Bougainvillea and hibiscus, orchids and many less-famous bushes of perfume and beauty could be seen as far away as my window. They were guarded and heavily shadowed by hardwood trees, not the thickets I had seen on Kaiana, Ili-Ahi's "parent" island, but straight, dignified trees intermingled with clinging plants and countless kinds of tropical vines.

I could hear the waters of the stream splashing down into the gulch behind the Giles house but could not see them, of course. I was on the wrong side of the house. The sound reminded me, however, that Deirdre had a private room on the other side, across the hall. Why would a nervous, frightened young woman like Deirdre prefer the view of the noisy, unhealthy gulch with its swampy areas at the foot of the plunging stream?

What was there to see from this side of the house that she feared more than the almost impenetrable swamp? And why did a young bride, scarcely a year married, have her own sets of rooms? Two of them? But there was no immediate answer to this, and speculation certainly was not the way to get a good night's sleep. I gave up and went to bed.

In view of the many things that had happened since I had left Los Angeles that morning, it was surprising that my dreams were so commonplace. All night I kept missing the plane, a repetition so boring it acted as a soporific and when I did wake up once or twice, hearing the distant roar of the stream pouring down into the gulch, I went back to sleep instantly.

I was awakened by an assortment of sounds. Unidentifiable bird sounds, palm fronds rustling against the open window frame, the distant rush of waters. Although the room had a westerly view, it was filled with light, a slightly filtered and changing light. When I got up and went barefoot to look out the window, I noticed fleecy clouds floating overhead. There must have been showers earlier. All the incredible greenery beyond the steep path sparkled and gave off the acrid, earthy odor of recent rain.

I saw several men — Caucasian and Oriental, but none of them Hawaiian — coming up the path from the channel dock. They appeared to be headed toward the grove of unfinished cabins, that uncompleted Sandalwood *heiau* which had driven Stephen Giles's father to suicide. This might be one strong reason for Stephen Giles's own strength and determination. Whether he succeeded or not, I admired his effort. I watched the men move past the front of the house across the green open space. Moku, probably coming to work by way of the trail west of the *heiau,* passed the workers and stood a minute watching as they went into the grove. Then he strode on toward the house.

For many years I had seen California desert views exclusively when I saw outside views at all, and I spent far too long that first morning at Sandalwood sniffing the lush tropic splendor, admiring the multitude of different human types I saw here. It was only when I saw Moku enter the house that I remembered I was an employee, not a guest here, in spite of Stephen Giles's beguiling attempt to make me believe I was "one of the family."

I turned away from the window, showered, and dressed in a pale green cotton sheath. Today I went bare-legged like everyone else in the islands. Fortunately, I had a pair of sandals, somewhat worn, but quite adequate. I was just finishing my hair when Deirdre burst in without knocking, and sneaked up behind me, although I saw her reflection in the three mirrors. Before I could turn, she was hugging me as she had done in her girlhood when she was especially pleased.

"Judy! You really are here. I need you so much. Of course, not when Stephen's here. Wasn't that sweet and dear of him to hurry home from Honolulu last night just because I needed him? How on earth could he know? He's psychic — *that's* what he is. Oh, I love that man! Isn't he divine? Judy, are you struck deaf and dumb? Say something!"

I laughed at this remark so typical of Deirdre. "No, dear. Only waiting for a chance to agree with you."

"About what? Be specific."

"About everything you've said."

"Oh, Judy, you are the first one who's thought I was right about anything since — well, since

71

that awful thing happened and you went away."

Anxiously, I watched her face hovering above mine as I sat before the mirror.

"But you mustn't say that. Or even think it. You have just as much right to your opinion as others have to theirs. You are happy here, aren't you?"

"Divinely!" She hugged me around the neck and almost strangled me in her enthusiasm. We both laughed. "That is," she added as her mobile, young face shadowed suddenly, "I'm happy when I can be myself and not somebody else. The thing is, I was behaving exactly the way I always have. I've never changed. I swear it, Judy! Yet, after I've known people for a while, *they* want to change *me*. They say, 'grow up, Deirdre. Be grown-up, Deirdre. Use your head, Deirdre.' And yet, I'm only behaving just as I've always behaved when they — when they *liked* me."

Her voice cracked just a little on that word and brought the sharp pinprick of tears to my eyes. I avoided her gaze and patted her hands that kept their tight grasp upon my shoulders.

"Everyone likes you, dear. But people are often very busy, or they have headaches, or they're feeling angry over their own lives, and so they snap at other people. But they don't mean it. One of the differences between being a little girl and being a grown-up woman married to Mr. Giles, is that when you are grown-up you understand other people have problems too, and you're tolerant when they forget how much they really like you."

"Wise old Judy!"

I wrinkled my nose at our reflections and she giggled. I said, "Remember one more thing. You talk of their liking you. Don't you suppose they have their needs too? Why don't you start thinking about liking other people yourself?"

She took her hands off my shoulders and murmured petulantly, "Not unless they like me first."

The most obvious explanation of her thinking and her behavior was ready in my mind — the only possible answer: "I'm afraid you have been spoiled, Deirdre. By mother and me, and then by others. There really are other people in the world, you know."

"Do I!" She rolled her eyes which were large and green and innocent as a . . . I was about to say "innocent as a child's," an ironic cliché, but her eyes *were* childlike, mischievous, easily hurt, quick to laugh and cry. Though they looked like mirrors of what was within her still-childish mind, I felt they were more like the green leaves I had seen on the edge of the path below my window. They were fresh, dewy, and young, but behind them was the jungle, the unknown.

"You don't want breakfast in your room, do you, wise old Auntie? Let's eat in the dining room. Very regal and splendid. It's a creaky old place, but fun. Like the haunted house we used to play in when I was a child, before I got sick. Remember?"

"I certainly don't want to be served in my room, but strictly speaking, I shouldn't eat with you and Mr. Giles. I have a job to do here."

"How stuffy! No, you must come, because Stephen sent me to ask you to come."

It was a slight letdown to be told that she had come in here so happily to see me only because her husband told her to invite me to breakfast, but when I realized that I was hurt, I was amused that I was behaving like Deirdre by allowing myself to take offense over nothing. I had evidently made too much out of Deirdre's simplicity and honesty. She was a perfectly normal, slightly unsure young wife in her first year of marriage.

We went together to the big, high-ceilinged dining room with its comfortable but exceedingly old-fashioned look. The furniture was too heavy: the long mahogany table and chair were more suited to a cluttered room in a mid-Victorian mansion. Certainly, it was not suited to the humid, sun-and-showers climate of Hawaii. I suspected it was part of Sandalwood's nineteenth-century heritage. I could imagine how thrilled the Mrs. Giles of that period must have been when her fine, heavy, impressive furniture arrived at Lahaina or Honolulu in an old windjammer that had gone around the Horn to deliver it.

Deirdre hesitated at the long, narrow, paneled

door. I heard Stephen Giles's voice inside the room as he came toward his wife. His voice held the indulgent note everyone who loved Deirdre used with her. Sometimes a note of impatience could be detected as well. As I stood there, I prayed never to hear impatience or exasperation in *his* voice. It would mean that he had turned from her as Deirdre claimed others had turned away after the inevitable flattering first impression.

"There you are, sweetheart. You were such a long time I nearly starved to death. You must be quicker tomorrow if you don't want me to fade away entirely."

She giggled and I saw then that he held his arms out and she went into them. Over her head he smiled at me. "Good morning, Judy. Did you sleep well? I hope the early shower didn't wake you."

Deirdre was murmuring against his shoulder, "You're so silly. Fade away! I can feel your muscles — you aren't fading away."

After a minute or two, Stephen reminded her, "We've got to show Judy to her chair. That's the polite thing to do. Remember, I told you when Dr. and Mrs. Nagata were here? We must look after our guests."

"Of course I remember! I'm not a baby!" Taking his hand as he released her, she brought it around her waist and grinned at me. "Your place is where the place setting is. Anybody knows that. Now, darling —" she said to her husband, "let's eat so you won't fade away."

I went quickly to my place between the settings for Stephen and Deirdre at the head and foot of the long table. Stephen seated his wife and then me, and we held an absurd, long-distance conversation about my flight the previous day, the possible agreement to prevent a dock strike, whether there would be more showers today. . . .

Over the fresh, golden papaya, the excellent coffee, bacon, eggs, and hot cross buns, I tried to bring up the subject of my purpose here. I had not been able to eat half the breakfast offered, but such bountiful meals seemed to be the custom, and there was a graciousness about it. The Gileses could apparently afford all the endless dishes no one touched, and that reminded me of my job as housekeeper. Each time I tried to mention it, one of them switched things around, made a little joke, or went on to mention something else so that I had to think up new opportunities to get the matter settled. But it never was settled. When we all got up from the table, I still knew no more about my real position at Sandalwood. I even wondered if I was invited to breakfast to provide added subjects of conversation in case Deirdre and her husband ran out of things to talk about. I snuffed out this idea but apparently buried it in my subconscious mind, for it recurred several times.

As Deirdre said good-bye to her husband, I started toward the kitchen. I had just gone in through the pantry when the cook, Mr. Yee, pointed behind me.

"Someone is looking for you, Miss Cameron."

I turned and almost ran into Stephen Giles. Momentarily, he had lost the slightly amused, almost parental manner he used so successfully with Deirdre. Now he was businesslike. I remembered my first impression of him: that I felt his bronzed face might be admirable but that it also suggested an impetuous, impatient man.

"Judith, I don't want any rubbish about your being a servant. Do you understand me?" I nodded, but even so he repeated, "Do you? Your real job is to look out for my wife. The housekeeper title was merely to satisfy the red tape, to get you free."

"I'll look out for her — you know that. But I don't like to interfere, and I won't interfere in any way."

I had not been entirely correct about him. His eyes were not hard, though they were serious. "I have discovered Deirdre needs someone — a companion. Someone she can trust. And frankly, you are the only one who seems to have been — loyal."

"Loyal?"

"That's the right word. Through almost nine years that I know of."

In a deeper sense, I thought, it really was the right word. And I realized that we understood each other without having spelled out the problem. Another part of that loyalty.

"You may count on me, I promise you."

"Good." He held out his hand and clasped mine. He turned away, then thought of something. "Did we mention the Berringers yesterday in Honolulu?"

I wasn't sure. I had talked to someone about them yesterday afternoon, but wasn't it Ito Nagata who had mentioned them?

"I know a little about them. Ingrid Berringer was Deirdre's school friend. They came to Hawaii after graduation. Then . . ."

"I met and married Deirdre. It all happened fast." I looked at him and he smiled. "I know. I make up my mind in a hurry. At any rate, the Berringer girl stayed around Waikiki for a few days. She tried for a secretarial job with us but hadn't enough experience. So it is rather odd and annoying that these Berringers should be hounding my offices about the girl. We haven't seen her in almost a year. She was over here on Ili-Ahi a few times before our marriage. And that does it!"

"But then why should anyone be concerned over here on Ili-Ahi?"

"Because there seems to be a story going the rounds that the Berringer girl visited Ili-Ahi two days or so after our marriage."

"While you were on your honeymoon?"

"There was no honeymoon."

That left me briefly nonplussed. Before I could think of any comment at all that would not be embarrassing, he saluted me with a jaunty flip

78

of three fingers to his forehead and went out by a back door that I hadn't noticed before. It was probably near the downstairs *lanai*. By the time I reached the front stairs, intending to go up and see if Deirdre was in her room, I heard her call to me from the veranda.

"Here I am, Judy. Hurry! Hurry!"

Not knowing what to expect, I rushed out and found she simply wanted a companion for nothing more important than a walk across the island to the village where Ilima's people had lived and sustained the pureblood line for almost two hundred years.

As we crossed the green open space and entered onto the path to the west of the Sandalwood *heiau*, the Hawaiians' *kapu* ground, I thought I heard someone call to us. I stopped, but Deirdre pulled on my arm.

"Come on!"

I looked back. The path had wound around a huge growth of bougainvillea intermingled with stiff, shiny vines, and I couldn't see what was happening at the big house except that someone was out in front, waving to us. "It looks like that pretty daughter of Ilima's," I said.

"Let's pretend we didn't see her. I like Kekua, but she is a bit on the nosy side. Judy, come on. I want to show you the rapids and the falls above the river."

She was much too anxious to get me away from the house. I went back a few steps, saw Kekua motioning to me. She was looking very sexy in a white bikini that contrasted with the deep mahogany of her flesh. Tentatively, I started toward her. She began to run in my direction. We were still several yards apart when she called to me.

"They're here. They insist on talking with Mrs. Steve. I was down swimming when I saw the boat come across. Steve's boat missed them by a hair."

With a sinking feeling, I thought that in spite of all the millions of people in the world, she could only be talking about Ingrid Berringer's father. At the same time, I was sure this explained Deirdre's frantic desire to get away from the house. Either she had known they were coming this early or she had guessed it. It was too bad they had missed Stephen Giles on the way down, but perhaps their boats had passed each other. As the two men suddenly appeared on the steep, rising path, I saw that they were alone. A tall, thin, forty-ish man with salt-and-pepper hair, cold eyes, and a certain elegance walked ahead, very much the leader. He was accompanied by a shorter, stockier man with the ingratiating face of a natural follower. I could see that even at this distance. There was no doubt in my mind that the tall, thin man with the frosty hair and eyes was Victor Berringer, and I didn't like to think of Deirdre, confused at best, in the grip of that frosty man.

Five

Kekua went around me, passed Deirdre with a flippant, "Ahoy!" and dashed back to the strangers. Berringer and his friend had stepped up onto the veranda, but as I approached the house with Deirdre hanging back behind me, the tall, frosty man said something to Kekua. She nodded and went off past the bushes masking the gulch at the back of Sandalwood. The man took long strides down the wooden steps toward us.

Deirdre whispered, "Don't let him talk to me. Please send him away."

"Well, then," I said firmly, "you should tell him yourself that you don't wish to see him."

"No, no. He wouldn't pay any attention."

"Tell him and he will go away." I didn't know whether I had convinced her or not until we reached the veranda, but meanwhile, the formidable gentleman reached us. I had been right about the frosty eyes, which were more gray than blue. I was surprised at Kekua's admiration — they looked as though they could cut one down at twenty paces. For a moment, I feared they would cut *me* down! I was momentarily tongue-tied when he demanded of me, "Mrs. Giles! I do not like to be made a fool of. Furthermore, I don't intend to be."

"Then, in the first place," I began, "you really should know that I am not —"

"However you may be used to being treated, madam, I have been trying to speak with you for three days. And this time I will not be put off. May we go somewhere and discuss this thing? I intend to get the answers to some questions. I'm sure you appreciate my anxiety, Mrs. Giles."

"Now, see here," I tried to bring Deirdre forward but she nudged me so hard I was breathless for a couple of seconds.

We had reached the house where the younger, stockier man stood, with a hesitant smile and a hand outstretched to take mine.

"Please . . . please . . ." Deirdre whispered in my ear, and then she dragged along behind me as Mr. Berringer escorted me into the house. I decided to see just how nasty Victor Berringer was going to be in pursuing his absurd suspicions before I turned Deirdre over to him and acknowledged that she was Mrs. Giles.

I looked around the long, desolate living room, saw nothing that looked like a bar, and went into the hall. Then I remembered the comfortable room at the back of the house. The two men followed me, and Deirdre scuffed along behind us. I asked the men to mix their own drinks at the tiny portable bar across one corner of the room. The Japanese house-woman brought ice, and Mr. Berringer's companion went to the bar. Both men took Scotch and water. The male "companion" watched Berringer take up his glass before pouring his identical drink. I was too keyed up to have a drink, and Deirdre didn't even want to go near the bar. Anyway, I wished to keep my wits sharp, as sharp, I hoped, as this stranger. He introduced his companion with a brief movement of his glass punctuated by the tinkle of ice.

"This is William Pelhitt. Willie and my daughter had a — an arrangement. They intended to marry, eventually."

"Intend, Vic. Excuse me. Intend," William Pelhitt put in with a kind of nervous, fluttering smile. "Glad to know you, Mrs. Giles, I've been in love with Ingrid since — well — since she was about fourteen, I guess. We sort of had it settled we'd be married later on, after she got out of that fancy college." He glanced at Deirdre, obviously curious about her identity. I glanced at her and opened my mouth, but Deirdre shook her head faintly.

I thought, well, why inflict this angry Victor Berringer on the poor girl until he has simmered down?

Berringer had apparently stored up endless suspicious little details he could use against Deirdre. Although he was not unattractive physically, I found him quite implacable, a man who saw nothing but his own view.

"Mr. Berringer," I began as quietly as possible, hoping to calm the atmosphere, "I appreciate your anxiety, but your daughter is a grown woman. She told you she was thinking of going on to the Orient, so it seems to me that . . ."

"What theories you may expound, madam,

are of no interest whatever to me. William here received a card from my daughter which suggested that she was on her way to Tokyo, but this seems not to have been true."

"But why? What would make her change her mind? And why should it have taken you so long to discover that she hadn't left?"

William Pelhitt spoke up in an uneasy way, with frequent glances at Berringer, which suggested he took all his cues from the older man.

"You see, she sent the card by surface mail and it came weeks after her last letter, so we figured the card told us where she was going, what she was up to. We didn't hear anything from her after that, for months. Not that this is unusual with Ingrid, but finally, he — we sent cables to Tokyo, and they hadn't heard of her, so we flew there, but couldn't discover a thing. Then we got to checking the last letter she sent Vic, and found . . ."

"But Tokyo is huge. I read that somewhere," Deirdre put in, startling us all. I am sure the men had forgotten her presence. Whether or not she intended it, she sounded younger than ever. I was by now so ruffled at Mr. Berringer's manner I decided to delay Deirdre's introduction.

William Pelhitt looked to me for an explanation of the girl's identity, but in the second or two that he looked at me, puzzled and questioning, I saw another man, one not entirely cowed by his long relationship with his companion. I had a sudden notion that he suspected

Deirdre was the real Mrs. Giles. The pleasant fullness of his likeable face would probably become substantial and plump in his forties or fifties. He seemed far more human than Victor Berringer who was so chillingly arrogant.

At Deirdre's observation about Tokyo, Berringer gave her a scathing look. Quickly and contemptuously, he returned to the matter at hand.

"Is it too much to ask if we might be alone and uninterrupted for a few minutes, madam? I would like to learn what I — what we can before discussing the matter with the local authorities."

Deirdre caught her breath. That gasp troubled me, but I did not pursue the reason for it. I said with false calm, "If you will kindly ask your questions, you will relieve all of us, including yourself." I was at least honest in that. "I would appreciate your telling me just what Miss Berringer's last letter had to do with this persecution of us at Sandalwood."

"Yes," Pelhitt put in, obviously trying to please both me and Berringer. "We owe you an explanation. You see, the letter, as it happened, was written three weeks after the card."

"Don't rattle so! Get on with it!"

"Just let me finish, Vic. The letter said she was coming over here to — whatever it's called — this island, to have it out with that . . . with her friend Deirdre."

" 'With that silly moron Deirdre' was how she described you. A bit offensive, and hardly accu-

85

rate," Berringer added without a smile to soften the remark. "But my daughter often had bad manners. She claimed that if your new husband had faced the truth about you — whatever that was — after two days of marriage, she would have no difficulty in winning him away from you. She was drunk when she wrote the letter. Obviously."

"Obviously," I echoed just as sharply.

He moved nearer, as though to exclude Deirdre and William Pelhitt from our conversation.

As I stared at him, hoping to intimidate him into at least a semblance of good manners, Victor Berringer set his glass on the side table behind me where the sunlight caught it and glistened on the melting ice within.

"I certainly didn't take such a rambling and ill-mannered letter seriously. Not until we had returned to Hawaii from Tokyo and discovered what I consider proof that Ingrid never left Hawaii. Mrs. Giles, when did you see my daughter last?"

I felt like a player who had memorized her lines badly. When was the last time Deirdre had seen Ingrid Berringer? I decided to stick to the brief remarks Stephen Giles had made less than an hour before.

"The last time was after the wedding. I don't know what day, but almost immediately after."

"When did she leave?"

"Very soon."

"Alone?"

I said with perfect truth, "I didn't see anyone with her."

"But did she operate a motorboat, a launch, or was she taken back to Honolulu in a yacht? Ingrid is hardly the sort of girl to operate her own boat. She is a very popular young woman and besides, she would not depend upon her own skill."

"I gathered that."

"Then perhaps you will be good enough to tell me why no one knows how she returned to Kaiana from here . . . *if she did return.* And there is no record of Ingrid's having come in by inter-island plane from Kaiana to the Honolulu airport on Oahu."

"Hardly conclusive. There are other ways of reaching Honolulu. She might have gone by ship, you know."

William Pelhitt interrupted us with unexpected gallantry.

"Now, look here, Vic. She's right. In fact, it's even possible Ingrid went on to Hong Kong with friends, on a freighter or something. And she mentioned Tahiti once or twice. Remember?"

"Without her passport?"

"What!" I was startled and glanced over at Deirdre. She was interested but certainly was not shocked or alarmed. She had been looking from one to the other of us as if we were talking about some intriguing mystery story whose details were entirely foreign to her. And surely, I hoped, they were!

"Without her passport, and some of her clothes."

"We aren't sure about the clothes, Vic. I mean, she might have just — not wanted them."

"Well, we are sure she left her Honolulu apartment without a word to the owners. And don't tell me she always does these impulsive things, William. She doesn't strew passports over the globe."

A door closed somewhere and there were steps in the hall. The servants were probably talking about this odd conference. I heard voices faintly outside the room. Mr. Berringer saw me glance at the door and turned just as it opened and Stephen Giles walked in. He didn't notice his wife at once but saw Mr. Berringer and me. We were standing in the sunlit sector of the room, obviously arguing.

"What is all this?" Stephen demanded. "Berringer, what the devil are you doing here? I thought it was you when we passed in the channel. I told you my wife was ill and knew nothing about Miss Berringer's activities. I also told you I didn't want you hounding the members of my household."

"Your wife seems perfectly fit. In every respect," Victor Berringer added, clipping off each word. "She has answers for everything. She is, in fact, almost too well prepared. I expect her to take the Fifth Amendment any minute."

Stephen was just as authoritative, and had the facts at his disposal. "Then why, may I ask, are you browbeating a total stranger who was two thousand miles from these islands when your daughter visited Honolulu?"

The icy veneer of Victor Berringer cracked a little. In his arrogant, slightly sinister self-confidence, the man had been unshakable. Now he backed away from me, staring. I felt that something had to be said in order to smooth over this awkward moment, yet my real impulse, perhaps resulting from the tension of the last half hour, was to laugh at his absurd mistake. I didn't though. Instead, I said, "Mr. Berringer, you haven't given me a chance to introduce myself. I am Mrs. Giles's aunt and her companion."

"Am I to understand —" Berringer cleared his throat. "This young woman is *not* Deirdre Cameron Giles?"

Before either Stephen or I could say anything, William Pelhitt yelled in what probably was one of his few chances to top his prospective father-in-law, "Don't you get it? *That's* the little lady behind the door."

With all this attention upon her, Deirdre looked as though she wanted to disappear into some other space, preferably to another island. Berringer gazed around the room, clearly expecting to find one more woman who had slipped in while we were talking. He came back at last to Deirdre.

"That child!"

It was a comment even more embarrassing to her husband than to the rest of us. When I knew her as a girl, Deirdre often wore her lustrous chestnut hair in this Alice-in-Wonderland style with a pink ribbon run through it above her forehead and the wispy bangs. Her minilength dress with the Empire waistline didn't make her look any more mature either. Since I hadn't seen her in nearly nine years, I hadn't noticed the almost frightening discrepancy between Deirdre's actual age and the age she appeared to be. There was the child's seeming innocence about her smooth, unlined face, her mouth that was soft and emotional with a child's changeable emotions — she was quickly hurt, quickly healed.

As Berringer took a step toward her, she screamed and Stephen pushed her behind him.

"My wife is a bit shy. I'll ask her anything you want to know. Leave it to me and to Miss Cameron."

I think Victor Berringer was shocked at Deirdre's reaction to him as much as by her looks. Whatever his manner, he was a civilized man, and this may have been the first time a young woman had ever screamed in fear of him. I found myself almost sorry for him. It was an awkward moment for all of us.

Berringer stopped, glanced at me and at William Pelhitt, then answered Stephen after he had clearly revised what he intended to say.

"You will appreciate my impatience, sir. I have been trying to trace my daughter's actions since we received our last word from her. That was almost a year ago. You will admit this is a very long time to have no news of a loved one."

Stephen was obviously moved by this very natural concern. He motioned his guests to chairs and admitted, "I am sorry. I've been in the middle of some tough labor negotiations lately, and I am afraid I haven't —"

Deirdre interrupted in her soft, girlish voice, "But she was like that. She never sent letters. She bragged about it. She never wrote to her father, except when she needed money. She used to laugh when she said it. That's Ingrid. Sometimes she laughed at me too."

I may have been the only one who shuddered. But the men shared my feelings, I am certain. I saw the little exchange of looks between William Pelhitt and Mr. Berringer. They understood now that Deirdre and Ingrid hadn't really gotten along very well. Deirdre gazed at us all now in complete ignorance of any crisis. She had never looked prettier or more charming. Stephen had caught his breath when she spoke out like a thoughtless child. When he responded, he seemed to talk more rapidly than usual, but I didn't suppose the other two men knew that.

"Deirdre, where did Miss Berringer say she was going when she left here the last time you talked to her?"

"But I didn't see her then."

Victor Berringer started to speak to her, then addressed Stephen. It was as if he felt Deirdre were deaf and dumb or an animal, incapable of understanding him.

"If that is the case, how does Mrs. Giles know *when* my daughter last visited the island?"

Deirdre didn't seem to know what he was insinuating. Both Stephen and I attempted to satisfy Berringer. I said, "Sir, as I understand it, your daughter came over briefly and left when Deirdre sent word that she couldn't see her."

Stephen said, "We had been married only a few days before, and we wanted a little privacy."

Deirdre had at least won over William Pelhitt.

"Very natural, Vic," he said. "Hadn't we better pursue this in Honolulu? After all, that's where she left her things, isn't it?"

Three of us snatched at this reprieve. Reprieve from what disclosures, I wondered. I was fairly sure Stephen didn't know either, and we were joined by these little doubts, this uneasiness concerning Deirdre, although none of us had any tangible evidence as yet that would connect her with Ingrid Berringer's disappearance.

Stephen pursued Pelhitt's argument. "Suppose we discuss the matter over another drink. Darling, Mr. Yee is waiting to take your orders for dinner. Judith will help you." He kissed her lightly on the forehead as she stood obediently before him. The two men witnessing this domestic scene avoided my eyes. I led Deirdre out gently with an arm around her waist, and Stephen closed the door.

I was so shaken by the confirmation of my vague fears about Deirdre's condition that I hardly knew which way to turn. Deirdre pointed ahead of us, thinking about her husband's instructions.

"The kitchen is through that pantry. Mr. Yee gets so mad when I tell him what to serve — the menus, you know."

"Just the same, dear, you want to make Stephen a good wife, don't you?"

"Oh, yes! Yes! Above anything in the whole world, Judy. Didn't you feel that way about John Eastman?"

It was a long time since I had thought or felt any way about John Eastman, but the subject aroused surprisingly few bitter memories in me. So few, in fact, that I could say now with a high degree of indifference, "I suppose I did once. I was pretty young."

"Just the same, poor dear, you can't really know how I feel, because Mr. Eastman might have been good-looking, but he wasn't sweet and kind and telling you what to do so you didn't go wrong, like my Stephen. Remember how you used to tell me about my father? He was strong and quick-tempered and red-haired and sort of told a person what to do, and that made life much easier — you know? Unless they tell you what you don't really want to do."

I said yes, I knew what she meant. But how could I point out to Deirdre that a husband was not a father and shouldn't have all the qualities of one? She was asking for trouble in her marriage. I couldn't believe that Stephen Giles, a virile and attractive man, could settle for this kind of a marriage. The only consolation was that this was still their first year together, and first years were notoriously rough. While I was in the Islands, the most important service I could do for my niece and for Stephen Giles, would be to wake Deirdre up and make her want to be Stephen's wife, in every sense of the word. She would have to discover in Stephen the man she physically loved, not just a father image.

I reminded myself now that their private life was not my affair, that it was disastrous to interfere in someone else's marriage. Years ago, I had been exceedingly careful, and had tried to keep mother from preventing my brother's marriage to Deirdre's mother. But this was a different situation. Surely, just a hint here and there, a word or two, some slight suggestions couldn't hurt. Surely, I could help a little! I would just have to be careful so as not to make the mistakes everyone else always makes when trying to "patch up" their friends' marriages. *I would be different. . . .*

Six

Deirdre behaved beautifully with Mr. Yee. She began speaking with a slight stammer and a hesitant use of the word "we" which Mr. Yee misunderstood. She was ready, however, when he showed us what appeared to me an implacable countenance but may have been merely an uncomprehending look. She added, "I mean, Stephen . . . Mr. Stephen, I mean, he likes teriyaki steak and you do it so well. Mr. Yee does everything perfectly, Judy — better than anyone in Hawaii."

Mr. Yee's eyebrows remained uncompromisingly straight, like his trim, black moustache, but I felt, without quite knowing why, that he had softened.

"A *haole* dish," he complained. "They think it is *kepani,* but it is *haole.* However, if it is wanted, I make no objections. I will thaw the meat. Mrs. Mitsushima has made a fruit salad for luncheon. With the chilled chicken to be served also. She arranges these things with a certain artistry, so I permit her to work in my kitchen."

Pleased at her success in at least bearding if not slaying the dragon, Deirdre said, "That is very good of you, Mr. Yee, to allow Mrs. Mitsushima to putter around if she . . . doesn't get in your way. Thank you."

When we were in the hall again, she flashed a

triumphant grin and hugged me.

"How'd I do, wise old Auntie? I gave him plenty of *hoomali-mali*."

"You were wonderful. Absolutely perfect." And she had been. She had handled the temperamental chef with thoroughly grown-up finesse. And plenty of *hoomali-mali*. I didn't need a translation to know that must mean a form of flattery.

"Good! Now I'm going up and do some sketching. I just feel in the mood. I haven't sketched too much since I met Stephen, but I'm so proud of myself — Mr. Yee scares me to death, you know — that I think I can draw something again."

I thought this was a great idea and said so. "And I'll look around," I told her, "get my bearings."

We parted at the front staircase. She had gone up several stairs before she swung around, called to me. She laughed, a very light, wispy laugh.

"Wasn't that ridiculous? That awful man thought Stephen was married to you. He actually did!"

"Utterly ridiculous, dear. Don't think about it."

I went on toward the *lanai*, with what I hoped was a cheerful expression. But I couldn't help feeling slightly crushed at her implication that no doddering, creaking old aunt like Judith Cameron would ever be married to a man her husband's age.

96

The man is just my own age! Ito said he is.

After some effort I managed to work up my sense of humor and was able to laugh at my vanity by the time I walked out on the lower-floor *lanai*. Strictly speaking, the so-called *lanai* appeared to be a balcony that looked as if it might collapse at any minute into the jungle-covered gulch far below. It actually creaked when I stepped onto it.

The gulch itself fascinated me. I was so impressed at the sight by daylight that I lost all interest in the ancient *lanai*. For the first few minutes the thunderous drop of the falls drowned all the other sounds. I leaned over the wooden railing, caught the rainbow spray of the falls, and then traced their descent. There was so much foliage below I barely made out any pool or even the continuation of the river that crossed the island from the northwest mountain where it began. I remembered reading, after Deirdre's marriage, that a mountain on the island of Kaiana was called "the rainiest spot on earth." And the mountain on this island was north of Kaiana. Small wonder this Ili-Ahi gulch was the wettest and most thickly overgrown spot I had ever seen.

I couldn't begin to identify the plant and forest life in front of me and below me. The intertwined plants, flowers, trees, the vegetation both living and dead seemed endless. The fallen leaves, windblown blossoms, endless palm fronds, not to mention the debris washed down the river, had collected here for months or even years. There was more vegetation further along toward the last barriers before Kaiana Channel, which I supposed was a series of ancient lava outcrops or coral reefs. I couldn't tell which they were from this point, although I could see the channel glittering in pools of sunlight, and then, hardly a hundred yards away, the pools turned midnight blue, rolling and angry under the rain clouds.

Either I had grown used to the smell of rotting vegetation, or it was masked by the perfume of the plumeria growing thickly around the house on bushes or young trees. There was a golden shower tree almost on the edge of the chasm, and within the gulch itself, bright vermilion flashes proved to be ohia flowers, scattered among hibiscus and other less familiar blooms.

Even as I watched all this tropic profusion and tried to trace the river after it gathered itself up from the bottom of that violent drop, huge rain-drops splashed on my hair and my nose. I ducked into the hall and shook myself.

A minute later I heard the door to that pleasant sitting room open and Stephen Giles, who apparently had his hand on the old-fashioned glass doorknob, said, "I suggest then that you get any other information you want from the Honolulu police. You should have dealt with them in the first place."

He was answered by Victor Berringer's clipped, precise enunciation. "I fail to see why the police on Oahu would have more pertinent information than your own natives here on Ili-Ahi. Why do you object to our questioning them?"

"In the first place, they are not *our natives*. You may as well say we here at Sandalwood are part of the Hawaiians who own this island in a kind of joint tenancy with us. Anyway, they know absolutely nothing about Miss Berringer. I told you that in our exchange of correspondence. And now, gentlemen, I have a great deal to do. I have meetings in Honolulu and I have some workmen here on a project started by my father, and which I intend to complete successfully. You understand therefore, I can't waste more time. Once again, I suggest you see the police and let them handle the matter. From all I have learned of Miss Berringer, she might have gone on to Tahiti or Australia, or even to Taiwan. She mentioned them all."

"She would need a passport!" Berringer insisted, obviously on the verge of losing his temper.

William Pelhitt, sounding anxious, put in, "Say, Vic, why couldn't she have thought she lost her passport and just have gotten a new one? You know Ingrid. Always mislaying things."

"Because — as I keep telling you — the Passport Bureau says that is not the case. Don't you think they would know? There are such things as records, Will."

Stephen stepped out into the hall, and I hurried up the back staircase to avoid being caught

99

listening. "Gentlemen, I am sorry. I wish you luck, but I'm afraid you are searching in the wrong place. Miss Berringer is undoubtedly thousands of miles from here at this very minute. She was a very self-sufficient young woman and doubtless found some transportation where she didn't need a passport. You must know that a yacht, a ship of some kind, could put in at any island in the Pacific and its owner could bring Miss Berringer ashore during the night without the local officials being the wiser. During the occasions I met your daughter, before my marriage, she used to joke about such things — 'being swallowed up in the immensity of the Pacific,' is how she put it. She joked about these things one day at lunch. Asked Deirdre if it wouldn't be fun to go to sleep as herself and wake up as someone else. But you know all this. If I'm not mistaken, I wrote these details to you. Good-bye, gentlemen. Can you make your way to the dock? I'll take you in my boat if you like."

"Quite unnecessary. We have the boat we rented from the Kaiana Hilton. Come along, William."

Their footsteps and receding voices told me they had decided to obey Stephen's obvious command. A few minutes later, from my room, I saw all three men headed down the steep path to the little landing on our side of the channel. I didn't like to hound Deirdre, but her husband had made it clear that my real job was to look after her. As a companion, or as a warden? I wondered.

I started toward her suite farther along the hall and knocked. There was no answer, and then I remembered that she liked to use the room across from mine, overlooking the heavy jungle vegetation that masked the Ili-Ahi stream before it plunged over into the gulch. Why she should prefer this to the pleasanter, sunnier side of the building I couldn't imagine. Although hibiscus hedges and a golden shower tree grew along this side of Sandalwood, the path from the boat landing and the beginnings of the wide green open space in front of the building gave the sunlight a much better chance.

I returned to the door opposite my room and knocked. Nothing happened and I knocked again, thinking that if her windows were open the roar of all that plunging water might drown out any other sounds. This time I could hear little scuffling noises which baffled me.

"Who is it?" Deirdre asked in a high, fluting, breathless voice.

"It's Judith. Do you need anything?"

I was sure she considered carefully. Then she told me, "No, but the door is unlocked."

I took this as an invitation, though perhaps not the most happily phrased, and went in. The room seemed to have a curious blue-green hue and for a minute I stood there blinking. I could see my way, but I had the distinct feeling that I was at the bottom of an aquarium tank. Deirdre's infectious giggle brought me out of this dizzy sense that I was drowning.

"You're perfectly all right, you know. People say they feel like choking in here. The room wasn't used very much until Stephen married me. But I feel quite safe here."

"Safe?" I had been looking around at the wallpaper with its fish and great thrown nets, and torches for the night-fishing, but her odd choice of that word surprised me. "Safe from what?"

She shrugged. "Oh, from . . . busybodies and people trying to make me do things or go places when I don't want to . . . or when they won't let me go to Honolulu. They're awfully mean about that. I've gone down to the landing and tried and tried. I've offered them money. But nobody will take me across the channel."

"But I'm sure Mr. Giles will if you ask him."

"He can't, he's so busy. And that's why I'd come in here and curl up in the windowseat and draw with charcoals."

There was an old studio couch in the room, with a beautifully made afghan thrown over it, but as she had said, Deirdre was sitting on cushions in a deep windowseat with the view of palm fronds and hau trees and what appeared to be a keawe thicket, all crowding in at her against the window. Fortunately, she seemed to have no fear of them. Her imagination did not run in that direction.

I, on the other hand, felt exactly like a creature in a fish bowl, watched on all sides. I sensed the same horrible lack of privacy that I had experienced in prison during the first months. Everyone had tried to prepare me for what they called my low and squalid and even dangerous company, but except for two women at different times who were not so much criminal as mental cases, I had found that company far less repugnant than the loss of privacy. I tried not to appear too cowardly, but the truth is, I hated this room of Deirdre's on first sight.

"How is the sketch coming along?" I asked her, hoping to take my mind off this goldfish-bowl feeling of mine.

She looked up and across the room at me. "I haven't started yet." She had what appeared to be a perfectly untouched pad under her hand, but her fingers were heavily stained with charcoals, so the sketch was hidden. I recognized in her my own deep necessity for a private life, and turned off the subject as casually as possible.

"You'll think of something. There is a beautiful golden tree below the downstairs *lanai,* beside the path. And I saw a young tree, or a large bush, toward the clearing. All those delicate white flowers with yellow hearts. If you look up through them at the blue sky, they would make an exquisite pastel. I think they are plumeria."

She wrinkled her small, slightly turned-up nose.

"Flowers! Everywhere you look. There's nothing special about them. Orchids common as — as grass."

"Well, I'll leave you to your art and go and write a letter or two until the weather clears. I would like to get a good look at the island, sort of see it in perspective when it stops raining."

"But Judy darling, it's stopped raining already. Don't mind the overcast. We're practically the rain headquarters of the universe. You'll always see clouds. You run along."

There was no doubt she wanted to be rid of me. Not that I could blame her. I understood her feelings perfectly. Or thought I did. I wished her luck with her drawing and left quickly.

In the hall, I didn't know quite what to do. I couldn't hound her if she didn't want company. The best thing I could do was to give her a feeling of freedom without leaving her entirely unwatched. It was a horrid thought, that she should be watched. A harmless, sweet, endearing young woman who had the rare ability to remain eternally twelve or thirteen years old. What was so terrible about this that we should all join in a conspiracy to spy on her?

Had Stephen Giles any secret doubts or suspicions, any knowledge of something in her life that no one else knew? Would this cause him to conceal her as much as possible from people like Victor Berringer and William Pelhitt? And worse, from others who had no animosity whatever toward her? Perhaps he had a half-knowledge of the kind I possessed, which would always make him afraid for her. But not of her. Surely, not that!

I went down to the lower floor and came across the pretty Filipino college girl who was dusting the furniture on the side of the house paralleled by the river and the Ili-Ahi gulch. She shook her head as I came into another old-fashioned, high-ceilinged room that was obviously Stephen Giles's study. All the well-used props were there, even a pipe rack that was just ornamental, the girl explained.

"Mr. Stephen stopped smoking the day his father died. Not that smoking had anything to do with Mr. Giles's killing himself. Did it with an old hand gun he'd 'liberated' back in forty-five. Poor man. He gambled a lot in the Fan-Tan clubs around the Islands."

"But I thought it was because he lost his money on those bungalows in the Sacred Grove beyond the *emu*," I said.

"That, yes. But he'd have lost on that anyway. They'll never make anything work in that grove. Not even Mr. Stephen can do it, though Lord knows he's worked like a coolie to build up the family holdings since his father died. Mr. Stephen made it back mostly through shipping. He's got cargo ships all over the Pacific."

I thought I better understood the motivation of Stephen Giles, his determination to make good after seeing and probably suffering with his father in the disaster the older man had made of his own life.

I helped Nelia Perez move the books and folders carelessly piled on a typewriter table whose small portable Smith-Corona looked as though it might fall off at any minute. I shoved the typewriter over into a safer position, and then we did what we could to tidy up the big desk beside it.

"If he is like anyone else with a desk full of papers," I suggested, "he probably doesn't want anything moved, but it won't hurt to clean up a little of this dust, I imagine." With the enormous amount of humidity around the house it was surprising that everything hadn't rotted away.

She agreed cheerfully to my helping, and I dusted off the enormous desk top, replacing the stacks of papers exactly as I found them. She had taken another cloth and was polishing some framed pictures set carelessly in front of the books on an openfront bookcase of a very dark wood. Surely, those books needed a closed case, but no one seemed to care, or maybe the books were used often enough so that glass doors would have been in the way. I suspected, though, the main reason was that this bookcase was part of the family heritage. I had not heard about any other members of the Giles family and would have liked to have known who the people in those portraits were. Nelia saw me look over at the frames in her hands and obligingly identified them.

"Mrs. Steve has two sisters and an aunt in Denver, Colorado. And some cousins in Florida. The sisters and his mother all left here after his father's funeral, they say. His mother died several years ago." She lowered her voice and informed me in a heavy whisper, "Mr. Steve's secretary said he helps to support them all. She makes out the checks every month."

"They probably have a financial interest in Sandalwood."

"Maybe."

"Have any of them met Deirdre — I mean, Mrs. Stephen?"

"No, but they all sent nice letters and wedding presents."

So much for that! No wonder Deirdre had been lonesome occasionally. It was only surprising that she still seemed to enjoy being alone now. She must have found her own amusements — at least, I hoped so. I wanted her to be a resourceful person, not entirely dependent upon her husband or me or anyone else. Life would not be so hard on her if she could rely on herself now and then.

I asked, "Do the women at Sandalwood talk to Mrs. Steve frequently?"

"Talk? We all talk to her. I mean, well — if she talks to us, we talk to her. She's a very nice person. A bit shy, maybe, sometimes, but not highballing it along or anything. Very — I guess you'd call it democratic. Of course, she almost has to be, with her —" Nelia's voice trailed off. She was excessively busy polishing a desk lamp on the stand beside a big leather chair that looked old and used but comfortable.

"With her little-girl ways, you mean?" I threw

the remark out casually, and added for insurance, "Rather clever of Deirdre. You see, she always gets her way."

"So she does! I never thought of that. You know, Dave Shigemitsu, my boyfriend, might . . . it's really clever. Everybody always gives Mrs. Steve her way, so she won't cry or get sick or make a fuss. I must try that."

Poor David Shigemitsu! I could see that in building up a protective cover for Deirdre, I had given Nelia's boyfriend a lot of future trouble.

"I wonder if you are going to be working upstairs very soon."

"I could take a coffee break upstairs," she suggested.

"Good. And just keep an eye on Mrs. Steve's sitting room in case she needs anything."

She nodded. "I know. Follow her if she leaves the house, and get her out of a jam if she falls into something."

"Falls into something!"

"Just putting you on, ma'am. Mrs. Steve knows this island better than I do. But there are a lot of tricky places. Nothing dangerous. I don't mean that. Only if she should run away and hide out again, there are a million places for that."

That wasn't a happy prospect. I thanked her, and when we had set back all the framed family portraits she collected the dust cloths and we left the room.

As I went away from the house, taking the path which crossed the island diagonally, I glanced at the cabins in the grove on my right and remembered the last picture I had dusted in Stephen Giles's study. A black-and-white, eight- by ten-inch portrait of his father, which bore the strange inscription: "Stevie, be generous. Be tolerant. This is everything." It had been signed in a dashing hand, "Dad." A good-looking light-haired man with warm eyes; his features, though, made me suspect he was easily influenced and not very strong on principles. The picture had been in a position so that Stephen could see it from that comfortable leather chair. Deirdre's color portrait had been on the desk, between portraits of his mother and his sisters — all good-looking, forceful faces, clearly of Celtic descent. I wondered if that portrait of his father had special significance. Something about the inscription suggested to me that Stephen had found himself very early in life rebelling against his father's weaknesses. This grove, where I could see a half dozen men working now among the trees was a symbol of those weaknesses. Several of the men there were carpenters. Others were working on the many branches of the stream. It seemed to be Stephen's idea that each cabin of the Sandalwood *heiau* should have its own miniature river. I liked it. The water ran over stones, carrying leaves and bits of palm fronds, even blossoms, crushed but doubtless still perfumed. Ferns grew thickly everywhere, but there was also a great deal of mud swept down from the mountain that was the source of

Ili-Ahi's own river. Until I heard the people of this island speak of their river and the river on Kaiana, I hadn't realized how very special such a path of fresh water might be on an island.

I looked up at the sky, understanding what I had never known before, the real meaning of a tropic blue sky. It was an incredibly pure blue directly overhead, but behind me, at so short a distance they shadowed the Giles house, were clouds gray as charcoal. And off to the west, there were more charcoal clouds in the midst of all that blue purity. I went on along the path which followed the river for some distance. Then both path and river were swallowed up in lush, tropic growth and went their own ways. I could still hear the sounds of running water in the distance. And although the river itself helped to produce more humidity, it acted upon my imagination as a cooling agent.

I felt my spirits raised by all this wild beauty surrounding me and even stopped to pick several flowers: a particularly large hibiscus, several small, delicate blossoms from bushes bordering the path, and a strong red flower that looked like a pillar on fire. There were ferns of all kinds. Some fronds not yet in full flower, looking like clumps of coiled tentacles. I found myself hurrying. A thousand sounds blended overhead and around me. Nature's sounds, of course, but I could not identify them, and the odd, distant calls of unknown birds sounded like the voices of loved ones, long dead, calling one's name.

The path wound upward, climbing over the saddle of Mt. Liholiho. Here another, narrower trail split off toward the north and east. As my own rising path gave me a better view of the island, I could see toward the east, a terraced series of taro fields beyond the forest vegetation that had bordered the main path. Ahead of me the trail rose, split off again, the right-hand trail winding upward higher on the mountain. The way before me was a mass of green — so many shades they made me think of Impressionist art — masses of green dots and strokes, all of different shades, yet all blended into the perfect whole. I might have been looking at a Renoir or an early Monet.

Just as I had been told, the mountain peak really did seem to collect all the rain in the universe. I turned and took the lower path which led, surprisingly fast, down onto an open field. Then I saw that there were several fields separated by bright bougainvillea hedges and small trees with twisted gray trunks. Beyond the fields, which sparkled silver from the recent shower I had escaped on Mt. Liholiho, I saw the village of the Hawaiians. I had expected something like the typical grass huts I had heard so much about, but these houses for the most part were perfectly sensible frame bungalows. A number of people were working in the fields, and the ocean beyond the rugged coastline was dotted with small boats. Along the narrow beach I saw great dark objects spread out. These must be the fishermen's nets. How beautiful it would be to see one of those night torch-fishing expeditions, I thought.

Closest to me was a neat, precise and mathematical series of short trees in a grid form. Papaya, I decided, and then had the unsettling experience of seeing a quick movement out of the corner of my eye, and I realized a man had suddenly ducked behind a flame tree this side of the papaya grove. My first thought was that one of the Hawaiians, seeing a stranger coming toward him, had hidden from me. Then I saw the man's feet and trousers. Slacks, perhaps, but certainly the outfit of a mainlander and a *haole*. And that hot-plaid jacket.

I could not picture Victor Berringer hiding from me behind a tree. Whether he wanted to be seen or not, if he were caught, he would bluff it out, as arrogant as ever. This man was William Pelhitt. What on earth was he up to?

If he was hiding from me, he was going to a great deal of trouble. I had no interest in Berringer's stooge. If I knew him better, I might actually feel sorry for the poor man, but in the present circumstances, his chief curiosity value was in his relationship to a man who did worry me. I went on down the slightly descending road to the outskirts of the village. It didn't remind me in any way of postcards I had seen representing Polynesian culture. These were bungalows exactly like those of plantation workers on many of the pineapple and sugar plantations in the Islands. Some were apparently on stilts and rock above soggy ground — the runoff from the mountain whose green slopes formed the eastern border of the village. Others, with their narrow wooden porches — were they *lanais?* — were more like pleasant little summer cottages on some southern California beach. There were numerous people around, especially the men sitting on the porch of the local store — the only store on the island, as far as I could tell. It struck me as funny to see the men sitting in very modern fold-up canvas chairs and wearing singlets or swimming trunks of brightly decorated cloth.

I wondered again what William Pelhitt was doing in this area. Certainly, the wide, dark Polynesian eyes of the men on the porch of the village store looked me over without enthusiasm. I tried not to hurry past but I could feel their dislike and I wasn't sure whether it was because I was a newcomer, a *malahini,* or because I was a *haole,* or even because I seemed to be a female without an occupation. There were no females lazily sprawled out on the porch. As I recalled from occasional visits to country stores on the mainland, there weren't any women lazing there either.

I reached the narrow strand of beach beyond the village, where children were digging in the sand and teen-age youths in loin cloths of Hawaiian craft design were tossing a very modern-looking rubber blackball. Several Hawaiian girls in bikinis stood by, giggling and encouraging their boyfriends. I didn't want to get in their way and had just turned around, realizing I had spent longer than I intended on this exploratory walk when great excitement suddenly swept through the main, unpaved street of the village. Even the workers in the fields moved out to the street, buzzing among themselves in low voices. Several of the men from the store rushed out and started up the little slope on the path I had taken from Sandalwood.

When a youngster from the store whispered something to the ball players, I asked one of the girls near me, "What is it? What has happened?"

Her big eyes studied me — not unfriendly, but very somber.

"You are from Sandalwood House."

"I am Mrs. Giles's aunt. It is something serious, isn't it?"

"They were warned. They all knew. The place is cursed. First, there was the father of Mr. Steve. Now there is more blood on that sacred ground."

This was even worse than I feared.

"Something happened at the *heiau* grove?"

She nodded. She was watching her boyfriend rush past us.

"They called from Sandalwood. Sammy Tiji fell off the roof of one of the houses."

"Badly hurt?"

"He fell onto the teeth of a rake. Bad luck. Just like they said if anybody worked in the *heiau*. It is evil, that ground. The blood will be upon them."

I fought the contagion of that fear. "Upon *them?*"

"Those who live at Sandalwood. They cannot escape. You will see, *haole.*"

Seven

I forced myself to show no fear or apprehension at this clear warning, but when I had left the girl, I hurried up past the village store, heard a man call me and whirled around, confused. I really should have expected Victor Berringer. After all, I'd seen his stooge nearby. He came striding out of the store with his superior air, his total contempt for all who surrounded him. It was fortunate for his conceit that he possessed that air because both the Hawaiians on the porch and those running up the road glanced at him and looked away, almost all of them with overt or concealed amusement. Possibly because he still wore his eastern Establishment wardrobe without a single bow to the customs and clothing of the Pacific islands.

"Miss — ah — Cameron! If you like I will drive you around to Sandalwood."

I thanked him and accepted his offer before I had time to think. But when we found his jeep behind the store, parked on a grassy little patch of ground rapidly going to sand, I finally remembered to ask, "How do we get there? I haven't seen any roads."

"There's a dirt road around the coast north of the mountain and then along the east coast. Not much of a road, but it serves the purpose, I expect. There are taro patches and a few other fields along there, and about all that can get

116

through are jeeps and Japanese trucks of various kinds." His granite face seemed to have flesh and blood behind that immobile façade. He seemed to be trying to make small talk as well. Why was he being so nice to me? "Are you comfortable?"

"Yes, thank you." I looked at him, surprised by this consideration. He was smiling as though we had parted the best of friends, and I thought it exceedingly generous of him under the circumstances. His pale eyes with their unblinking gaze fixed on me for several seconds, troubled and not really flattering, and I looked away, not quite sure why I wanted to avoid him.

We rattled over the ground to the road that wound along eastward below the papaya grove. No other cars were on the road. Everyone else was on the path I had taken, which cut diagonally across the island. I began to get more and more nervous about the condition of the accident victim.

"Do you think the man was very badly hurt?"

"Probably."

I looked at him. He shrugged.

"They say the fellow was impaled through the breast. Not a very happy way to go. Your friend Giles will have some explaining to do."

"My friend Giles," I said icily, "is in Honolulu at this minute attending to the serious business of seeing that the Islands continue to receive food from the mainland. It is very easy to starve out an island state, and we are facing a strike that may do just that."

He wasn't moved in the least. "According to my new friends in the village back there, Giles has been repeatedly warned not to build in that sacred grove, or whatever they call the place."

I was sorry for the workman and for Stephen Giles if he got into difficulties over it, but my first concern had to be for my niece. I had no idea how she would react, or if she would have the faintest notion of what to do.

"Now, I wonder what you are thinking, Miss Cameron. May I hope you have at last come around to my view?"

I looked at him, letting him see my indignation.

"Just what *is* your purpose?"

"My purpose?"

"I can hardly think of anything less likely than your being found in that village. It prides itself on having as little as possible to do with the *haoles* — the whites with their high-rises and their fast cars and their freeways. Yet here you are — you and a jeep. I can picture you in a Cadillac or a Mercedes-Benz, but a jeep!"

"It is merely for my use while I remain on the island."

I could hardly believe it. "You mean, those people are permitting you to remain in their village? The whole object of their private society here is to keep out *haoles* and modern inventions; to keep the bloodline pure."

"They need have no concern. I will not foul

their bloodline." He said it with the faintest edge of contempt, although it was with more indifference than anything else.

"But why did they accept you? Why are you permitted here at all?"

"They have their reasons."

"They must know you are Stephen Giles's enemy."

Suddenly, as he remained silent, I understood. "Of course! You played on that. You know they are against Mr. Giles's building of the Sandalwood *heiau*. If you were sincere about your weird suspicions, you would have gone to the police in Honolulu."

"I have."

That shook me. "You told the police this cock-and-bull story?" Good God! Would they come trooping over to Ili-Ahi putting all of us — and Deirdre — through some kind of interrogation that would not cease until somebody said . . . something?

I grew more uneasy when we rattled over fallen debris from the lush mountainside and he agreed, "I have told them. Made myself something of a nuisance, with Will trying to back me, though he's a feeble reed to lean on." He reached into his coat pocket, and took out an envelope. "They couldn't see the point of this."

I didn't want to take it, which was ridiculous, because I knew what it was, and if the police had found it unimportant, why should I read anything more into the letter and the postcard sent by his daughter Ingrid?

"Read them."

I looked at the address on the envelope with its flourishes and large circles for dots, then I studied the postmark, which was blurred. There was an airmail stamp and the word AIR was printed half across the envelope and underlined with a thick, black ballpoint. Inside the envelope, with a single page apparently taken from Ingrid's earlier stay at the Surfrider Hotel in Honolulu, was the postcard — a brightly colored photograph of an outrigger canoe full of gorgeous bronzed males bounding over mountainous waves off Waikiki.

"The postmarks. Consider them first."

I did so. I could see how anyone receiving a postcard three or four weeks after a letter had arrived would assume that the postcard carried the later information. Few people examine the postmark closely, especially on a casual postcard. Actually, it would take a very close scrutiny to read the postcard's date. There were wavy black cancel marks over it, but after squinting a bit and studying it, I believed Berringer was right in saying the postcard had been sent earlier than the letter. In a slap-dash way, neither the postcard nor the letter had a written date on it. Both started out unceremoniously with Ingrid Berringer's message.

"Read the postcard first," he told me.

I took in the card's breezy message:

Like your rivals, Willie? Deirdre the Klutz is divinely happy. I don't know how she does it with her bird brain. But if it continues, I'm off for Tokyo.

Sayonara, Ingrid

I read the whole thing again. It certainly didn't say much, but I could understand how he and William Pelhitt might think this card was her farewell to Hawaii, especially since they had received it after the letter. I took up the single-page letter next:

Daddy Doll —

Thanks for the check. Yes, I was able to cash it. Ah! Those magic credit cards! I had a murderous fight with that idiot Deirdre. I've decided that when morons grab something, they hold on harder than us super-brains, but I give her about three days before the truth creeps out. Today's the third day. And I'm going to be there at Sandalwood to pick up the pieces in a sweet, understanding way. So help me, the moron will probably massacre me if I lay hands on her property. I've discovered she can be Dangerous When Roused, but just call me . . .

Foolhardy Ingrid

I looked up, furious because the last line was so obviously a joke, and this man had taken it at face value. His absurd suspicion was based on Ingrid Berringer's insulting and nasty remarks

121

about a girl who had been her friend.

"You actually believe that your daughter was murdered, and by my niece? Surely, you have read other letters from your daughter. Hasn't she made remarks like this before? Do you always jump to the conclusion that someone is going to murder her?"

The thin, inflexible mouth creased to a slit for a moment before he said, "On the contrary. Neither Will nor I suspected anything of the sort. We waited. We sent cables. We wrote. Finally, we decided she might have had some — misadventure in Tokyo, so we flew there. We are satisfied now that my girl never reached Japan. In fact, she could not have left Hawaii."

"What about boats? Schooners, fishing boats — anything of that sort. Mr. Giles says ships could possibly land people on Pacific islands without passports, and no one would be the wiser."

"Mr. Giles, if I may say so, is in a better position than anyone to know about ships that indulge in illicit traffic."

Now what was he implying? "Do you think Mrs. Giles murdered your daughter, and Mr. Giles took her body and threw it off one of his ships?"

"No, although I am not sure of anything at this point. But I think there is a great deal of explaining that your niece might be responsible for, if she weren't so infernally protected. I'd like to get her alone for a little while. I'd have the truth out of her soon enough."

"By physical violence?" I asked ironically, trying not to act as thoroughly angry as I was. This was a matter that required careful handling. I could not antagonize him too much. I dared not.

"Not physical violence, no. I am not a physical man. But Ingrid was my only child and blood relation. She is a Berringer. And I mean to find out what really happened here."

"Shall I tell you?"

The narrow cliff road running southward along the east flank of Mt. Liholiho was strewn with muddy ruts and palm and fern fronds blown along this windward coast. We bounced over them. I don't know what his feelings were, but I found my knuckles white, and I was careful not to look over at the sparkling Pacific, which I knew must lie deep and dark under the rainclouds overhead. Berringer did not look at me, for which I was grateful. The road had no wall, no fence — nothing. This was just a way to reach the fields on the easterly sector of the island.

"Since you are one of those know-it-all young women, you may as well."

"You will find that your daughter — if she didn't leave the island — is somewhere in Honolulu enjoying herself with new friends, new interests. One thing did seem clear in this letter and this postcard. Your daughter's interest in marrying Mr. Pelhitt is certainly not very strong."

"There we agree. But he has his uses."

Beyond Mt. Liholiho we finally saw some men in the flooded taro fields. A battered old truck and an ancient wood-frame station wagon were parked in fern clumps. I was relieved when the road turned inward, away from the sea, although we were walled in by enormously tall vegetation. Ever since my first prison experiences with no privacy, I had yearned for the claustrophobic protection of walls between myself and others. But this scene, like Deirdre's favorite room, proved too much even for my love of privacy. Suddenly, the skies opened and we finally got the downpour I had been barely missing all morning. It was over as quickly as it started, but in the meantime we were soaked.

Berringer parked the jeep by running it into a tiny spot, fairly dry, under a huge banyan tree, the only one I had identified on this island. Its roots sprawled out in all directions and reminded me of an ancient but friendly animal in an animated cartoon. I supposed Berringer would investigate the scene of the accident, then leave. I would see if I could do anything in the grove and if not, would go to Sandalwood House and see how Deirdre had handled the situation. She certainly would know about it, since the call to the Hawaiian village and undoubtedly to Kaiana's tiny town had been made from Sandalwood. Kaiana, so close across the channel, would have at least one doctor in the town beyond the Kaiana Hilton Hotel. But Victor Berringer followed me, asking if he might borrow a dry shirt or jacket from Stephen Giles's wardrobe. Since he was soaking wet, I couldn't refuse.

We found practically the entire population of the Hawaiian village strung out along the main island trail, watching the proceedings inside the Sandalwood *heiau,* but not one of the men I had seen in the village would enter the grove. Several of the grove's workmen were discussing the accident, pointing out where the unfortunate man had fallen. He slipped on the palm fronds carelessly lashed to the roof of a cottage. I noted that some of Stephen's employees were of Hawaiian blood, but they were also Japanese or Chinese, Filipino, or Caucasian. Hawaii is famous, of course, for being a multinational state. Apparently the *haoles* did not share the strong feeling of the local Hawaiians that this grove was *kapu* — forbidden — sacred to the old gods.

The injured man had been removed from the scene of the accident. I hurried on to Sandalwood House. Moku came out on the veranda and walked into the house with me, remarking on my soaked condition. I must have looked like a drowned, red-haired rat.

"Never mind about me. Could you tell me what happened? Where is the man who was hurt? How serious is it? Can we get a doctor here soon?"

He shook his head.

"Too late, ma'am. He was dying by the time I got to the *heiau.*"

125

"He shouldn't have been moved. Where did you have him taken?"

"I did not enter the *heiau*, ma'am. Some of his friends who were working with him. They are Japanese, you know. They took him to a boat and —"

I was sickened by this hasty action. It might have brought about the man's death.

"No! No. It would kill him."

"He is dead. He was dead before he was placed in the boat. His brother who works at the airport on Kaiana has been notified. He will meet the boat."

It was an appalling thing, even more so because I suddenly remembered the dead man's brother. I had met Ito Nagata's young Japanese friend when we landed from the interisland plane at Kaiana after our short flight from Honolulu. It made the death seem more immediate, even more terrible than if the victim had been unknown.

"Is there anything I can do?" I asked Moku. "What about the other men who work in the grove? I had better see about something — coffee for them?"

He looked into the dining room. It was empty but I could hear the august Mr. Yee laying down the law to Kekua Moku. The girl kept insisting, "I can't go near it. Pops wouldn't let me."

"Into the grove," the girl's father explained to me. "That is the difficulty about your suggestion, Miss Cameron. You will not get anyone to take coffee to them. But it is a good idea. Coffee and a little of Mister Steve's Okolehau." He must have guessed from my expression that I was mystified and added, "Something Mr. Steve's father kept. Slightly illegal these days. When they can get it, some prefer it to gin or whiskey."

"Yes. Well, you may be right." From the way his expression lightened suddenly, I assumed he was one of those who preferred it. "But I don't feel I can give it to them without Mr. Stephen's permission. Maybe a little whiskey — I don't know. I'll take the coffee myself after I see Deirdre."

He thought this an excellent idea, so I went to the kitchen and found that Mr. Yee had two percolators ready and an old enamel coffee pot.

"Some prefer it stronger," he said. "Although this person — Moku's daughter — refuses to take the coffee to the grove, madam."

"My father wouldn't possibly let me," Kekua announced, with the air of someone who has received the royal command. And in a sense, she had, but she giggled as she said this, which I found odd.

"Never mind. I'll go. I'll get Mrs. Giles and we will both go."

I hurried out past Kekua's father who looked a little uncertain for the first time since I had met him. His ancient beliefs and superstitions had clashed head-on with his natural desire to supervise any large domestic concern. Upstairs I found Deirdre had left her fish-bowl room and for a minute or two I didn't know what to do or where to look. I was sure she had run away again in that cowardly, childish manner of hers. I was about to leave the room when I saw her sketching pad on the floor in the middle of the room. She must have dropped it when she left the room in a hurry. I picked up the pad and turned it over.

I found myself staring into the face of the well-known fictional devil complete with horns. It was frighteningly well done in charcoals and I was amazed at Deirdre's talent. The thing looked at me fixedly in an uncanny way. It must have been several seconds before I realized this was not a fictional devil at all but the face of a man I knew — Victor Berringer.

Here were the coldly intellectual planes of the face and forehead, the pale eyes. Deirdre had used her lightest gray for the pupils. Here were the thin lips with their contemptuous, light curve. In my excitement when I reached Sandalwood I had forgotten entirely about Berringer who was rain-soaked as I and wanted to borrow a jacket or shirt from Stephen Giles's wardrobe. Had he gone upstairs while I was talking to Sandalwood's majordomo? If Deirdre were surprised by him suddenly when she was alone I had no idea what she would do, considering the implication of her feelings shown in this drawing. It would leave Berringer also in no doubt. She had even caught the high, pale eyebrows that gave his eyes their chilling look.

I slipped the drawing pad face down under a cushion on the window seat and went out into the hall again. This time I could hear the murmur of voices downstairs. I hurried down the stairs recognizing a chill, clipped voice I was beginning to know and to dislike heartily. Was Victor Berringer pestering Deirdre again? It was Berringer, as I had suspected, talking to a young woman in the hall. I started to interrupt them but discovered that the girl was Kekua Moku. Caught by Berringer's words, I said nothing and listened.

"You are quite certain then that you have never seen the woman before? Say — a year ago?"

"Miss Cameron has never been to Hawaii before. Then, of course, she's been in prison for just ages. Murdered her sister-in-law. That was the charge. Murdered Mrs. Steve's mother."

"I have some vague recollection of the business. You are young Mrs. Steve's friend, aren't you?"

"Maybe the only one she's got on Ili-Ahi. She is — simple. You know."

I could imagine the girl touching her forefinger to her head. I was enraged by Berringer's reply:

"I suspected as much. But have you ever seen her really angry? Has she ever shown signs of violence?"

I think this startled Kekua, but then she hesitated. The seed planted, I feared it would grow. "No! Not at all," she said. "That is — she was terrified of you. But it's understandable that she would be, because she hated your daughter so much. Even after her marriage she was afraid Miss Berringer would try and get Mr. Steve away."

Suddenly, something stopped these two insidious gossipers. Berringer said sharply, "That will do. She is coming in from the *lanai*."

Kekua murmured something and sounded anxious. In spite of her gossip and suspicions, it was clear she didn't want an open break with her friend Deirdre.

Berringer said, "Thank you, Miss Moku. You have been a great help."

The girl responded breathlessly. "Thank *you!*" and they went toward the front door. From her tone I suspected she was being well rewarded for her lies. Or was she merely twisting the truth?

I saw Deirdre a minute later. She was watching Kekua usher the unwanted visitor out across the veranda. Deirdre's eyes looked enormous as she turned and glanced at me.

"Ingrid wasn't nasty enough. Now she's trying to get at me through her father."

Eight

With an effort I said casually, "Pay no attention. They were trying to involve me a minute ago. Now, as Stephen's wife, you must go out and help the men in the *heiau*. They've had a bad accident. The men will need coffee and maybe liquor." She looked helpless, obviously wanting to avoid any more people she couldn't cope with.

I added, "You want Stephen to be proud of you, don't you?"

She seemed stupefied or else deep in thought for a few seconds, then shook off this mood and agreed, "I do want him proud of me. More than anything."

I hurried Deirdre into the pantry between kitchen and dining room and although a considerable amount of time had passed, no one had taken out the percolators or the enamel coffee pot. Mr. Yee also armed us with plastic cups. This was not very fancy, and I was reflecting that we wouldn't be especially welcome, even if the workers were still there, when Mr. Yee topped my tray with a bottle of saki.

I smiled at the sight. "Coffee Tokyo? You are sure they prefer this to Jim Beam?"

He was not amused. "Madam, I know these men."

I took this as good advice and we went out to the grove. Somewhat to my surprise the workers were still there. They were gathering up tools and discussing the tragedy. Mr. Yee had known what he was talking about. The men did not mix the drinks, but certainly welcomed them.

Deirdre and I poured coffee, but the men, taking two cups, drank the hot coffee first, with a saki chaser. Presumably, the coffee steaming in their mouths heated the saki. I had been pouring for several minutes before Deirdre whispered, "Do you think that awful man will go and lie to the police about me?"

"You've done nothing wrong. Just remember that."

"Ingrid really was horrible. Honest! We'd known each other all through that boarding school, but when we traveled, she was different. Especially after we met Stephen. She was cutting and sarcastic and said the meanest things."

I moved away from the men momentarily. I had set the tray on a huge tree stump in front of what was intended to be the *lanai* of a larger bungalow, and I reminded Deirdre, "You mustn't speak of your friend in the past tense. She has undoubtedly gone off somewhere on her own. The South Pacific, perhaps."

"Don't call her my friend. She was anything but that. I thought she was my friend and she wasn't. So it serves her right — whatever happened to her."

"Deirdre! Stop talking like that. Stop thinking of her as — as —"

"Dead?" she completed the frightening

thought. "Well, I've suspected that for a long time. I don't see why people can't be honest about things and say what they think."

One of the men came over to us. I wondered if he had overheard our conversation. It was hard to tell. "Pardon, Miss. Some of the Hawaiians would like coffee and the saki. Can I bring it to them?"

"Why not ask them to come into the grove and we will serve them here?"

But they were not about to be bribed. We ended by going out into the trail and did what my grandfather would have called "a land-office business." In no time the little saki remaining in the jug was gone and the coffee pots were empty. Deirdre and I returned to the house.

Minutes later, I heard voices on the way down to the boat landing. I looked out of one of the rooms facing onto the steep descending trail and saw the entire work force from the grove, leaving with all their tools and equipment. Obviously, this was the end of work on Stephen's attempt to fulfill his father's dream.

Nelia Perez came in while I watched the men leaving. She was a little nervous and apologetic, which puzzled me until she explained, "I know I was to keep an eye on Mrs. Steve, ma'am. I tried, really. But the gentleman came to see Kekua and I couldn't keep him out."

I pretended a casualness I certainly didn't feel.

"That was clever of him. I suppose you mean Mr. Berringer. Did he speak to you?"

Now she avoided my eyes and made a great play of dusting off the nearest objects of furniture with the palm of her hand.

"A little. Just — you know — nothing questions."

"About me."

She nodded, still avoiding me. "I'll go now, if it's all right, ma'am."

"Were they questions about my past?"

"About . . . how Mrs. Steve's mother died." The girl looked up at me suddenly. "I said you didn't do it, because it was suicide. I heard Mr. Stephen and Dr. Nagata one night. They said no one else was there. Only you and Mrs. Steve's mother, so it had to be suicide." She hadn't finished speaking before she sidled out into the hall. I let her go. Nine years ago I had prayed desperately to be believed. These testaments of belief now had no particular effect, except to rouse a great many bitter memories in me.

I was shaken out of this wasteful, useless depression by the ringing of a little china hand bell. Before I could figure out what this nineteenth-century sound indicated, Mrs. Mitsushima, the Japanese housewoman, stuck her delicate, carefully coiffed head in through the open door.

"Luncheon, miss."

I thanked her and went across to the dining room, but after all that had happened during the morning, I was not hungry. And the time itself seemed wrong. It should be four in the afternoon, at least. I found no one in the long dining

134

room and felt ridiculous. Surely, all this elegance, bright, glittering crystal, the old-fashioned, clean beauty of Wedgewood china, and the soft, worn napery, was not necessary for Deirdre and me. She came rushing in, breathless, and slid into her chair at the foot of the table. My table setting was on her right and she gave me a mischievous grin.

"I'm not late. I'm not! It isn't five minutes since the bell rang."

"You are Mrs. Stephen Giles. And this is your house, and the luncheon bell is yours, too. Remember that. It is you and Stephen who make the rules here."

"So I can be as late as I like."

"Well, not exactly." I heard myself lecturing her and broke off. I was embarrassed, so I laughed. "I sound exactly like a school teacher, and I don't intend to. Please don't think I want to tell you what to do."

"Oh, I don't mind that. You see, I don't pay any attention to what you say, any more than I paid to my creaky old teachers." At my expression, she grinned. "Now, let's eat. I'm starved."

In her usual winning way she managed to get the subject changed and rushed breathlessly into a plan to visit Honolulu.

"I swear, Judy, it's easier for mainlanders — mere *malahinis* — to get to that town than it is for me, an old *kamaaina*. Stephen just won't take me. Ito Nagata's wife, Michiko, and I had a great plan to go shopping together and then meet Ito and Stephen and go to lunch in Stephen's business suite on Waikiki. They have *luaus* here at home every time I turn around, but really, I can't eat roast pig forever. They're not our kind of *haole luaus* either. You have to eat lots of squid — well, octopus, and spinach — that stuff that's like spinach, and poi, one-finger poi sometimes. I haven't gotten beyond three-finger . . . Anyway, they called it all off, after all. I was never so disappointed. I —" She smiled abruptly and lifted out a chunk of papaya on her fork. She ate with gusto, following this with a piece of pineapple.

I didn't want her to think I was watching her and pretended to enjoy my own fruit salad. Her sudden changes of mood, her conversational switches, all troubled me. However, I was so surprised at the many subtle and delicious new tastes in this tropical salad that my spirits were raised and I very soon began to forget all my depressing fears. I had never dreamed that bananas, the fruit I had found commonplace in southern California, the bland papaya, the sharp, ubiquitous canned pineapple, could taste so different when eaten fresh on their native ground.

"Maybe you can make that trip yet, dear. I haven't seen Michiko since she and Ito last visited — in two years. Suppose we see if your Stephen thinks it's all right."

"He'd better! And why shouldn't he?"

"Maybe he thinks Honolulu — especially Waikiki — is too noisy and crowded nowadays. Dr. Nagata told me he can scarcely get Michiko into town."

Deirdre clapped her hands, one of which still held a fork. "Then she'll want to go, to do some shopping."

"Between us, maybe we can get her to go. That might persuade your husband."

She looked uncertain. "He does let me have my way when I tease, usually. When he is pleased with me, he says I'm his little girl. When we were first married, he didn't talk like that. He said — well, it wasn't that way then. I didn't like being married then. Having to behave like you keep telling me. Giving tiresome orders and seeing about whether things are done or not. But he changed after a while and he became different. That's when he called me his little girl. He's been my whole life, ever since." The essential sweetness of her disposition emerged, and her face seemed to shine. "Sometimes, it's heavenly."

I was moved by the absolute and childish frankness with which she described her one year of married life. I was appalled, too. After an awkward silence, I asked her, "Isn't it always heavenly? I mean," I stumbled on as she stopped eating again and looked at me, "does he mistreat you in any way? I hope he is never cruel to you."

Disconcertingly, she did not answer me. We went on with our lunch, she with the gusto that argued an easy conscience and no problems, I trying to make it look as though I shared her innocence and her easy way of dismissing all matters she preferred not to think about. We were ending the meal when I heard the muffled ringing of a telephone. The sound persisted. I glanced at Deirdre. I could have sworn she was waiting tensely to be called, but she did not look up. The ringing continued. When I was getting ready to ask where the nearest telephone extension might be, the nervewracking jangle stopped. Deirdre set her cup down, bunched up her napkin, and threw it on the table. I was glad for her. There might be troubles swirling around her all too uncomprehending head, but it must be wonderful to live in that childish world of hers, I told myself.

The dining room opened. Mrs. Mitsushima entered gracefully, almost cloyingly bashful.

"Excuse me, please, Mrs. Stephen. The telephone from the Kaiana Airport."

Deirdre got up so fast she knocked her chair over. "It's Stephen on his way back home because of what happened to that poor man." She started for the door while I finished my coffee. We were both shaken when Mrs. Mitsushima protested anxiously, "No, Mrs. Stephen. Mr. Steve asks to speak with Miss — with this lady."

My first thought was that the woman had mistaken his message. Deirdre stiffened so quickly I knew her husband's thoughtless request had hurt and disappointed her.

"Dear, he probably thinks you are in the

grove, helping out. He may not know things are . . . settled."

"Yes!" she brightened, but then, as I thought the atmosphere was going to be more cheerful, she slumped again, dejected. "No, he doesn't want to talk to me. I can't interest him. I don't say interesting things."

"Of course, you do. Go along."

"No. I'm a klutz. I do dumb things. And I'm not — I guess you'd call it intellectual. I'm not, really."

I smiled, but carefully, to let her know I was smiling with and not at her. "Don't you know men are not searching for intellectual wives? That's the last thing they want."

"Maybe." But she seemed to doubt what she must surely have discovered long ago. "At first, I know they like people . . . well, girls like me. I'm not hard to take. Then, something always happens. They think I'm stupid. But I'm the same person I was at first. I thought it would be different with Stephen." She said these things often. She must have understood a great deal more of her acquaintances' contempt than they suspected. Her complaint made me swallow suddenly, with a dull, aching pain in my throat.

In the most cheerful voice I could manage, I suggested, "You weren't supposed to know until tonight. Stephen said he was looking for a little surprise for you. I'll bet he wants to ask my advice."

Her long dark lashes quivered. A second or

two later she smiled. "You go and find out, wise old auntie."

I followed Mrs. Mitsushima into the hall. The little woman was fluttering anxiously.

"Such a long time! Mr. Steve will be cross and make noises."

"Does Mr. Steve often shout and make noises?"

"Not often to Mrs. Steve. To Mrs. Steve he is very, very gentle."

I was relieved at this. He might have a temper, but he seemed extraordinarily understanding with his young wife, which was admirable, under the circumstances.

The nearest telephone extension was in Stephen Giles's study. I went in. Mrs. Mitsushima backed out, closing the door with a solicitude that made me self-conscious. The instant I took up the phone I felt that a hurricane blast of Celtic temper was loosed upon me.

"What the devil is going on there? I've been hanging on this telephone for an hour. Is it you, Judith?"

Remembering my own Scottish family with its sudden irritability which I never took seriously, I calmed him down at once.

"Sorry, Mr. Giles. Deirdre and I were finishing lunch."

Having blown off he behaved in exemplary fashion.

"It is about that time, isn't it? Sorry. Could you get away in about half an hour and meet me at the dock? I want to discuss something before I get home."

I didn't like to agree. It was a bad start to have secrets from Deirdre. If she learned to mistrust both Stephen and me, it would be disastrous.

"I don't think it would be wise. By the way, have you seen Mr. Tiji there at the airport? It was his brother who was hurt."

"I've been with them since they brought Sam over. Ito Nagata and I flew in. But it seems to have been too late. Ito and the Tijis were old friends. It's a rotten business. I hope to God it wasn't my fault. I feel bad enough about it as it is. I had the *heiau* setup inspected before they began to work. It seemed okay. Sammy slipped on the brush that had been lashed to the roof — the others all assured us of that. But the brush has been there for God knows how long. . . . Anyway, this isn't your responsibility. How is Deirdre taking it?"

"Splendidly. She and I took coffee and saki to the men. She cheered them up and was wonderful with them."

"I know she was. She is always warm-hearted and good. I never doubted that. But please meet me. I've got to talk to you. About her."

I thought of how terrible this would be if Deirdre found out about it. But if I could reassure him, briefly, definitely, it might end these murky doubts of his.

"I'll do the best I can."

"Good. Thank you. I am more obliged than I

can say. I was really desperate before you came. I didn't know what I was going to have to do."

As he was speaking, his voice faded slightly and I was sure I heard a click on the line. I rushed to cut off anything more damaging he might say.

"I'm sure you haven chosen something she will love, even if it is small. Don't worry about it. Deirdre will appreciate it because it comes from the person who loves her."

There was a long silence. I could hear all kinds of twittering, buzzing, roaring and snapping noises on the line. But after what was probably little more than sixty seconds, I was immensely relieved to hear Stephen say, "I understand. I hope she will like it. Be sure and give her my love."

The study door opened abruptly. Nelia Perez looked in and pointed overhead. Skillfully, she mimicked someone listening upstairs. I nodded. She made an okay sign with her thumb and forefinger and left. I said to Stephen, "I certainly will, and don't worry. She will like it, whatever it is."

He cut off the connection. I waited a few seconds, heard another click, and set the phone back. By the time I was out in the hall Nelia sidled up to me and whispered, "She was listening in upstairs."

I nodded. "Yes. Thank you." I would have to find some excuse to leave the house in a few minutes. I wasn't sure how long it would take for

Stephen Giles to finish his business on Kaiana and come across the channel, but I didn't want him to spend time looking for me down at the landing when Deirdre would expect to see him within half an hour or so.

I knew I would have to tell Deirdre about the telephone call. Presumably, she would be waiting to find out what had been said. In re-membering the part of the conversation she had heard, I could only thank heaven she had not overheard any more. I was going up to find her when I heard footsteps pass the top of the stairs and when I reached the upper floor I saw that she had gone out onto the *lanai* and was leaning on the wooden rail with her chin resting on her knuckles. She didn't look around but called to me, "I'm out here, Judy. Come on out."

The air outside was damp and curiously ener-vating. The perfume of flowers in warm tropic shade, and the greenery everywhere below sur-rounded us in waves. I found my nervousness and anxiety fading under the double onslaught of air and plants. Then Deirdre looked at me, a sidelong, furtive glance entirely unlike her usual appearance of frankness.

"Did he talk very long?"

"No. But he asked me about you, of course."

"I'm not sick! He doesn't have to hire spies to watch me."

"Deirdre!" I felt particularly awful because, in part, what she'd said was very perceptive.

She twisted her lower lip petulantly for a few

seconds before sneaking a hand out to cover mine on the rail.

"I didn't mean you. What else did Stephen want?"

"He was worried about a little present for you. I suppose he wasn't sure. He didn't say what it was, but it will prove he was thinking about you."

Her doubts seemed to vanish. "Judy, it's true. He does things like that. He sometimes asks Ilima when she is here. Or Mrs. Mitsushima. But can't you give me a hint about my present?"

"I wouldn't if I could. It would spoil his little surprise."

Her fingers tightened convulsively on my hand as she looked away toward the steep path down to the landing. I wondered if her husband could have arrived so rapidly, and if she had perhaps seen him from the house.

"What is it?"

"That creepy man. The one who came this morning with Mr. Berringer."

So William Pelhitt was tired of hiding behind flame trees and had come out in the open! His presence also gave me a handy excuse to leave her. I said, "He has no business hanging around here when Mr. Giles isn't around. I'll go and shoo him off. Meanwhile, you can be ready and looking your prettiest when your husband comes."

She panicked at once.

"I've got to change. I want to look my best. I must, you know."

"Right. He'll be here in less than an hour."

"Half an hour," she corrected me.

"I'm sorry. I forgot — half an hour."

She went into the house on the run. I leaned over the west rail and watched William Pelhitt. He seemed to be exploring the area, looking down at the gulch into the tangled thicket that bordered the path on the west. He didn't like that view at all, and turned and walked up toward the clearing. I called to him. He jumped like a terrified fugitive from justice. He was behaving very mysteriously.

I waved to him and there was nothing for him to do but stop and acknowledge me with no real enthusiasm. I went in to the back staircase and down to catch him. He had reached the *emu* and was examining that hole in the ground when I caught up with him. He may have thought I was crazy, or that I had a mad, unrequited passion for him.

"Do they really cook food in that hole?" he asked with distaste, and a clear attempt to get me onto some safe topic. "Don't you eat grit and dust with it?"

"Not that I've heard. Were you on your way to the house, Mr. Pelhitt?"

He smiled vaguely, asking me to understand.

"I couldn't put up with it any longer, being constantly under the gun."

"The gun. Meaning Victor Berringer."

"Right on! And to be honest, I was hanging around here trying to figure out what might have been done with Ingrid."

I was rigidly on guard at once. "What makes you think anything was *done with* Miss Berringer? And even if there were a remote possibility that she had been murdered, it is far more logical that she was killed in Honolulu. That's a big city, full of foot-loose tourists looking for —" I caught myself, ashamed of the insinuation. "I beg your pardon. I have no knowledge of Miss Berringer whatever. I shouldn't have said that."

"No. You may be right about her. It's the not knowing that's so bad."

I moved back from the pit. I had to be on my way to meet Stephen Giles, but I didn't want to start in that direction until William Pelhitt was gone. I started to stroll along the trail that wound over to the Hawaiians' village. He stared at the grove, then, to my relief, joined me on the trail. His eyes were nervous, unsure. His face with its suggestion of flabbiness was weak. I wondered why I didn't dislike him, as I disliked Victor Berringer. But there was a terribly human vulnerability about him.

"I was going to stop by and see Stephen Giles, but I just didn't have the nerve. That man knows something."

"Impossible," I insisted. "Mr. Giles and I know only that Deirdre couldn't have anything to do with your friend's disappearance. Mr. Berringer became convinced today, I am sure."

He looked at me in his troubled way. "Certainly not. I'd put my money on Giles himself. He's the one."

That shook me. I let him walk on and turned back. He stopped but I said, "Good afternoon," and he went on. I waited until he was out of sight, swallowed up in the shimmering foliage that had caught the afternoon sunlight. I came back and looked for another way to get down to the little dock without passing Sandalwood. At the western border of the clearing I walked close to the first tangled gray roots, mentally kissing my best white thong sandals good-bye as they became encrusted with fresh mud.

But among those tangled roots I made out a bridge over the drainoff area from the west fork of the Ili-Ahi River. It was quite a charming little rustic bridge with rickety-looking rails made of the grayish wood that appeared to have been young when these were the Sandwich Islands. The bridge was barely two planks wide, but it served my purpose to avoid being seen from San-dalwood House. The path to and beyond the bridge was in complete shade, like a tunnel, carved from ancient thickets and jungle vegeta-tion, the sort of rich, water-retaining vegetation rapidly being replaced on the other islands by stone monoliths and freeways for an ever-expanding population.

Small as the island was, I suspected a new-comer like myself could easily get lost by wan-dering off this little footpath into side paths. By the time I had crossed the bridge which shook underfoot, I could see an opening in the thicket ahead and hear the pleasant roll of breakers nearing the narrow strand of beach. This took my mind off the constant expectation of finding spiders and other insects in the thicket. Wherever they were, they certainly did not appear to my eyes, or perhaps it was simply that the atmosphere was so dark and thick with humidity that I didn't see what was all around me. I pushed aside the last fern and the giant leaves, the biggest I had ever seen, and watched a motorboat put in at the copper light with two men. Stephen Giles and my longtime friend Dr. Ito Nagata got out. They looked around, obviously not expecting to see me.

I must have seemed to materialize out of the thicket behind them, because they had their backs to me and were staring along the path by which Ito had first brought me to Sandalwood. Stephen started in surprise and turned around as I called. Ito, with his Oriental self-control, pretended he had not been startled.

"Judith," Stephen began, taking my hand to shake it and then holding it, possibly forgetting he had it, he said, "I've asked Ito to tell me as much as he knows about my wife. I think I should know in order to protect her. But whenever we talk about Deirdre's past, we seem to arrive at you. I don't want to pry into your own affairs, but they concern Deirdre."

Ito and I exchanged glances, and mine was quite furtive. I didn't want Stephen to think we shared some terrible secret about Deirdre. Ito said, "I felt certain things should be discussed. We can't expect Steve to be in the dark, if he is going to protect his wife from fellows like Berringer."

"He has moved onto the island," I told Stephen who didn't like this at all. He tightened his grip on my hand.

"Impossible! To all intents and purposes this is private property. We pay enough taxes, God knows! And no one else owns a foot of Ili-Ahi except the native Hawaiians who have always lived here."

"Yes. And they've taken him in. Rented a house to him, I suppose."

"But why? They would resent him as much as we do. A *malahini*, and a *haole* to boot!"

Ito had looked up quickly as I mentioned Berringer's push to remain on the island. In his quiet voice he managed to make Stephen and me suddenly aware that Berringer was not to be removed so easily.

"I'm afraid Victor Berringer has found a way around their objections. If I read the Hawaiians correctly, they want him as a wedge to cause you trouble."

"I've always gotten along well with the village. Moku and his family are among my best friends. Why do they need a wedge against me?"

Dr. Nagata kept his gaze on his own fingernails as he explained what I was beginning to understand. "To get you to stop working on that

149

resort project in the sacred grove."

"Oh, God! That again! I wouldn't put it past them to have caused poor Sam Tiji's death today." He saw Nagata's expression and after an awkward moment he said, "Sorry. I didn't mean that. Judith, do you agree with Ito?"

"I'm afraid so. They wouldn't go near the grove. Not even today when Deirdre and I offered them coffee and saki."

Stephen grinned suddenly, a single ray of light and charm in that hard face of his. "Saki! Whose idea was that? Yours, I'll bet." Then, before I had time to answer, he said, "Never mind. Nothing is wrong with Deirdre. You see that, don't you? You do see that?"

"Nothing is wrong." A little bewildered by this plea for assurance so soon after our discussion of the accident in the grove, I began to feel more secure. Maybe he *was* talking of Deirdre's physical health, after all. "She is perfectly all right. I just left her a few minutes ago, dressing to look her best for you when you arrive. . . . Stephen, you *did* bring a little present of some kind?"

Whatever inner doubts and fears crowded up to threaten his belief in his wife's normality, he managed to subdue them with an effort. In a much quieter voice he said to Ito, "It's these little things that pile up and raise — questions." Ito said nothing and Stephen turned to me, unaware that his grip on my hand revealed the panic he tried to hide.

"I need you, Judith, as I've never needed anyone. You are the only one who can help me with that poor child. And Ito agrees with me."

Nine

Dr. Nagata said, "Steve, you are hurting Judith."

Stephen looked down, frowning, troubled at his own unconscious gesture. His fingers, one by one, released mine. "I beg your pardon. I didn't realize." He had to clear his throat. It was proof to me that his emotions were not secretive. He cared very much about things and people, and he could not help revealing this.

My hand was hot and numb, but it didn't matter. I understood his terrible concern.

"I'm sure Dr. Nagata has told you the truth about my niece. She is not insane or 'sick' or any other euphemism you may use to describe a maniacal killer." I added with biting emphasis, "As I am sure you must be fearing."

"Judith, I didn't mean that. I never for a second believed Berringer's preposterous suspicions." I could see what he was suffering even in this passionate denial, and I was the more drawn to him because I knew so well this awful little prick of doubt that kept returning relentlessly.

Ito walked away from us, toward the beginnings of that solid, well-defined path up to Sandalwood. He said without turning around, "I think Ilima Moku is interested. I see her starting down the trail. I'll keep her occupied."

I was anxious to leave here. I felt like a conspirator, as indeed I was.

"Please ask me whatever it is you want to know. I don't like to be here long enough to disturb Deirdre. She is very sensitive, and sensitive people are sometimes jealous."

"Come over to the *keawe* thicket." I went with him. This was close to the sea exit of the little tunnel path and the bridge I had crossed to reach this spot. "First of all, Deirdre was nowhere near the grove when Sammy fell?"

Annoyed because the answer to this was obvious, I said quickly, "Of course not. You must have asked the workmen with Mr. Tiji." He nodded. "What you really want to know," I went on, "is whether anything in Deirdre's past would make Victor Berringer suspicious of her. The answer is no. Unequivocally."

He looked at me. I returned that steady gaze without blinking. I was used to it. The judge had looked at me like that several times. And worse, my two attorneys had looked at me with that doubt eating away at them. There was always the notion that I was hiding something. The jury, at least, was not a pitying one. And they had been definitely prejudiced against my own story by the calm I had forced upon myself — an almost total absence of emotion. I said to Stephen Giles, "Deirdre did not poison her mother."

"I know *you* didn't."

"How nice to be so omniscient! I congratulate you."

"No. I knew that ten minutes after I met you. And Ito, who knows you better, backs up my belief. Then how do you account for the death of Deirdre's mother?"

I took a deep breath of the salty air with its pleasant, bitter tang from the woods around us. I didn't want to be angry when I answered him.

"If you had read the details of my trial, you would know that we claimed Claire Cameron committed suicide. She merely chose my bedroom and her daughter's birthday party as the setting."

"Who found her?"

"I did."

"Was she alone?"

"Certainly she was. It would have been rather stupid for someone to poison her and then stay to watch her die." I started back to join Dr. Nagata.

"Judith . . ."

I didn't want to talk about it any more. It was a tragedy I had tried to put behind me for almost nine years. I moved on. He caught up with me in a few strides.

"Judith, *was she alone?*"

"Yes. She was." As he joined me, I told him sharply, "I'm very tired of that question. You are not the first to ask it."

"I beg your pardon. But I do have one more question. I think you owe me the answer."

Was he going to keep at the stereotyped questions, the questions that became clichés nine years ago?

"Well then?"

154

At least, he didn't hesitate or use some mealy-mouthed euphemisms. "Was Deirdre abnormal, was she mentally retarded in any way at the time her mother died?"

I couldn't be angry or resent his desperate anxiety to know. His entire life might be bound up in the health of Deirdre.

"Not that I know of. She behaved exactly the way a girl of thirteen might be expected to behave. She giggled and cried and laughed at nothing. She was sweet and dear and sometimes troublesome. She had a temper and stamped her feet, and then gave in and was her sunny self again. She was a thirteen-year-old!"

Ito Nagata had retraced his steps and approached us.

"Coming, Steve?" He added, motioning toward the path. "Mrs. Moku has gone on her way."

Stephen hesitated. Probably, like me, he felt there was nothing more that needed to be said about Deirdre. He offered a hand to assist me over the coral outcropping but I reminded him, "I'll go back the way I came. It will be better."

I don't know whether he understood my reason, and he was still frowning when I passed him and ducked under the tangled branches of the thicket path. It was sunset by this time, and the bridge was almost dark. Not even the tropical sun seeped into this little area of primeval wilderness, but the bright, burning rays of the sunset on the clearing above gave me an easy goal. My tunnel had a clear entrance up there.

Shaking off what may have been imaginary insects, I reached the clearing just in time to meet Ilima Moku who was staring at the thicket as if she were waiting for me.

I said calmly, without excess warmth, "Good afternoon, Mrs. Moku. Did you want to see me about something?"

But Queen Ilima was not to be put down by the likes of me. "No, indeed, Miss Cameron. I am about to take that path through the *keawe*. You will admit that though you are slim enough, you and I could hardly pass on that bridge."

She certainly had me there. I wondered if I dared to smile, but by that time she was on her way, and presently I heard, deep in the thicket, the ominous crunch of the bridge planks under a weighty load. I followed the edge of the clearing until I was within sight of Sandalwood House. Deirdre came rushing out the back door to meet her husband a few yards from the big, golden shower tree. Stephen lifted her off the ground and swung her around before kissing her on her broad, unlined forehead. Her thick, dark hair flew out around both their heads. When he set her on her feet again, he smoothed her hair in a tender, protective and almost paternal gesture, put his arm around her and motioned to Dr. Nagata who came on, smiling. The three started into the house. Just before they disappeared inside, Stephen, holding the door open for the others, looked back at me. He stared at me for a long minute, expressionless. I could not even imagine his thoughts. Someone called him, and he went inside. I avoided the back door and entered a little later by the front.

I tried not to think at all. Nelia was in the midst of cleaning my room. I sent her off to meet her boyfriend and was glad to finish the job myself. I only wished I could spend the evening occupied with something that kept me from thinking.

Somewhat to my surprise, dinner was lively. Everyone tried hard to contribute his share of wit, or at the very least, good humor. I don't think Deirdre found it necessary to struggle for this as I did. She felt happy and behaved as though she had never been otherwise. There were times when I envied her what appeared to be rapid changes in mood and a complete memory blank on anything that might previously have troubled her.

I remember that night we talked about ghosts. Or more precisely, about mythology, which we ended by confusing with ghost stories. In Hawaii, I learned, the two were not quite the same thing, and mythology was no laughing matter to the Hawaiian or even to the *kamaaiana* white person. I found it strange that, with this ever-present shadow of trouble in the sacred grove, Stephen Giles should have flouted all the old beliefs. A man who got furious when the subject was brought up must certainly take them seriously!

Ito said, "Have you ever considered using an-other sector of the island for the resort you are planning, Steve?"

"It was my father's plan. Not mine. I am only carrying it out. But of course I am considering it and have considered other sites. Do you think I'm a blockhead? We've gone over dozens of places, but it always means doing away with something of value to the island. The latest idea was an area they are using for some pineapple experiments. It may mean irrigation problems. But take the area above the papaya grove on the western spur of Mt. Liholiho. It would have made a nice terraced arrangement like that hotel on Maui — what's-its-name? That's valuable watershed. On Ili-Ahi we've got the last of the real primitive forests in the islands. Ecologically, any other place than the grove would do far more damage. There is nothing wrong with the San-dalwood *heiau* location at all. Nothing but sheer superstition."

"Pelé is there," Deirdre said conversationally. She fingered the shell necklace Stephen had brought her as a surprise.

Ito and I were startled, he more than I because I hadn't been sure I heard the name properly, and for all I knew, "Pelé" might be the name of one of the Hawaiians from the village. But before I could ask a question, Stephen spoke out with an almost rude haste that made Deirdre's remark suddenly important.

"Absolutely no reason in the world why the

grove shouldn't be used. No reason."

Deirdre was smiling. She started to speak but Stephen put his hand over hers, and she subsided contentedly. Dr. Nagata and I tried to change the subject, both speaking at once. He yielded to me and my inane conversation.

"Is it true that this will be the first commercial venture on Ili-Ahi?" Commercial venture. What a pompous, stupid remark, like something written by a no-talent advertising agency. Fortunately, Ito took it up at once.

"I don't think Stephen really intends that the resort complex should open up the island."

Stephen seconded that so emphatically we all jumped.

"God forbid! Have Ili-Ahi mined like Oahu in no time? That's the last thing we want, to make this another Honolulu monster. No. I don't want anything more than just to see the Sandalwood *heiau* completed. I want the growth here on the island strictly controlled."

I ventured with some hesitation, "But won't that bring over the very people, the influences you want to avoid?"

"No!" We all looked at him, wondered if he actually believed what he was saying. He insisted, "Controlled growth is the answer. Anyway, I'm only interested in the Sandalwood *heiau*."

"Pelé won't like it," Deirdre threw in calmly.

This time Ito Nagata and I were speechless. Stephen sighed. He kept his temper better than I had expected.

"Darling, Pelé doesn't exist. Pelé is a myth. Someone the Hawaiians used to worship. Like Lono and — well, the *menehunes*. Now, shall we adjourn to the living room for coffee and brandy?"

He could have offered us plain water and we'd have been relieved. Anything to change the subject. Very much to my surprise, once we were in the living room with the pleasantly cool evening reaching us through the long windows, Dr. Nagata began to discuss the gods and goddesses of old Hawaii.

"You know, Steve, even though we may feel that other and older religions are absurd, antiquated, pagan, I'm in a rather odd position. I see the importance of religion — not pagan, not antiquated — in my own family. Or Michiko's family, I should say. These are quite different from ours. We are Christians, but Michiko's aunt and most of the Yees are Buddhist."

"It isn't the same thing," Stephen protested. "I'm talking about fairy tales. Myths. Not religion. . . . Judith, this really is a good brandy. Won't you try a little?"

Deirdre interrupted gaily, "I'll have Judy's share."

I wasn't anxious to make a fool of myself by getting drunk, and I hadn't had any strong liquor in nine years until I started my trip to Hawaii. I glanced at Ito Nagata who understood.

"Very little, Steve. Judith hasn't been used to it."

I thought Stephen was about to apologize and make a big thing out of something I preferred not to think about; instead, he said quietly, "I know," and poured a little into the extra brandy snifter, offering it to me. Deirdre did not ask again. She watched me and giggled.

"You'll see more than a few Goddess Pelés if you can't handle that."

I agreed that she was right and sipped carefully. While the men started to discuss the safety precautions at the grove, Deirdre remarked to me, confidentially, "They don't like me to talk about it."

"Then maybe it would be better not to."

She raised her chin. "I do know what myths are. I'm not an idiot. The people at the village believe in the old gods, and so do I. I went into the sacred grove yesterday to get away from Victor Berringer, and no one hurt me, because they know I'm not their enemy. But I wish you could persuade Stephen that he'll never finish the Sandalwood *heiau*."

I agreed with her in some ways but I was certainly in no position to advise her husband on his business investments. Suddenly, she and I heard the word "Honolulu" and Deirdre rushed into the conversation between the men.

"You promised me, Stephen. You said when Judy came we could go to Honolulu. And Judy hasn't seen Michiko for ages; have you?"

I agreed that I hadn't and would like to see Ito Nagata's wife again soon, but I was uneasy about

Stephen's reaction. While he hesitated, apparently not so set against it as I had feared, Ito put in his persuasion on behalf of the idea.

"It might be a good thing, Steve. Michiko was saying only last night that she wanted to see Judith and Deirdre. She missed Judith yesterday. Had this appointment about the new layout for the Polynesian Artifacts Arboretum. Sort of an ecological Bishop Museum. But she wanted very much to get together with the girls."

I wanted to smile at "the girls" but didn't. Deirdre pleaded, "I've just got to get some new bikini sets. And this awful coral in the cove wears out a pair of my sandals every week."

Stephen straddled the arm of the couch beside his wife. He looked down at her fondly, took a strand of her long hair and wound it around one finger.

"But don't I try to bring you all the sandals and bikinis you ask for, sweetheart?"

Her gaze fixed upon his face. There was a beautiful, almost terrible love in that gaze.

"You bring me everything I ever wanted."

"But you'd rather do it yourself." He pretended to pull her hair and she squeaked.

"Well, maybe now and then. It would be marvelous, darling. Judy and Michiko would go shopping with me and then afterward we'd meet you and Ito at that apartment where you have the meetings. And then the late flight back to Kaiana. We could spend the night at the new Kaiana Hilton. That would keep us from crossing the channel so late in the night."

I felt like a fifth wheel in this little party of two married couples, and I suggested, "I think it would be a wonderful idea for the four of you. But if you wouldn't mind, I have a dozen things to do, and really would prefer to stay here and — I have some dresses to shorten. Things like that. Styles change so quickly, especially hemlines."

"No!" Stephen stopped me sharply.

I wanted to laugh hysterically at this sharp outburst when I was babbling away about hemlines, but instead, like everyone else, I stared at Stephen. He finished his drink, behaving as if he hadn't contradicted me. Did he mistrust his young wife so much that he wanted her well guarded, like a prisoner on parole?

As usual, Ito Nagata smoothed over the awkwardness.

"I agree, Steve. You heard Michiko complaining the other day when she couldn't be at the airport to meet Judith." He gestured to me. "You are quite essential to the party."

So it was arranged, and we all made plans for the next day. Ito Nagata stayed the night in a guest room next to Stephen's with Deirdre comfortably settled in the bedroom she preferred, across the hall from Stephen's room. No one who is an outsider can or should interfere with another's marriage, but it worried me that this condition prevailed. Small wonder Stephen was so concerned about Deirdre in this marriage that was less than a year old.

Deirdre waved a nonchalant good night to me and went into her room. Ito and Stephen talked for a minute or two about the arrangements for the visit to Honolulu. I started to close my door but Stephen signaled to me. Ito was still there in the hall when Stephen passed him and took a few steps toward me. He said briefly, "We do want you, Judith, very much. You know that."

"Thank you. I'll do whatever I can."

He seemed about to say something, but changed his mind. The silence between us lasted perhaps ten seconds, but during that time I was intensely aware of him, of his physical presence, the overwhelming attraction I felt toward him. Recognizing this, I stepped back into my room, with my hand on the door. I tried to smile but I was too nervous.

"You've made Deirdre very happy with this trip."

He watched my hand upon the door. He wasn't fooled by my inane smile, and he certainly wasn't feeling amused. He said abruptly, "Deirdre is the most enchanting child I have ever known. She deserves all the happiness we can give her." Then he added, in a voice stripped of almost all emotion, "But she *is* a child."

He turned and left me. He did not speak to Ito, who had been an uneasy witness to our brief conversation. Ito and I avoided each other's eyes and closed our doors.

When I was ready for bed I went to open the blinds for a look in the morning at the tree tops and the first daylight appearing in the western sky. I stood there a few minutes enjoying the midnight scents of tropic foliage which were delicious to me. I was surprised to hear Deirdre's voice in the hall. She moved beyond my door, toward the upper *lanai*. Or was it the staircase? I didn't want to spy on her, but her conduct seemed odd and I distinctly heard her say, "Thank you again. I'm ever so grateful. You're not afraid to go home alone? Good night."

I hesitated at the window, and while I postponed the decision to cross the room, I lost my chance to identify the person to whom Deirdre was grateful. Could it be one of the people who worked at Sandalwood? That seemed most likely. I took one more long whiff of the night air and was turning from the window when I heard a door close downstairs. Deirdre's visitor leaving.

I moved closer to the window. A minute later I saw Ilima Moku's huge, regal figure striding up toward the clearing and the path to her village.

So the Queen of Ili-Ahi had been visiting Deirdre! It was too much to hope that she hadn't told Deirdre about my meeting with Stephen and Ito Nagata at the landing that afternoon.

Ten

I slept badly that night. I couldn't see how I might have disobeyed Stephen's request to meet him at the landing, but all the same, my conscience nagged at me. I think, if I had been the mere protective "aunt," the housekeeper and companion I had intended to be, I would have found it easier to accept Deirdre's resentment and jealousy now. During that minute or two with Stephen tonight I had known the difference. I had been attracted to the man and sensed that he felt something for me.

But in his case there were excuses. He had married a stunning and endearing young beauty only to find she was a child. A man of great sexual appeal, and probably normal sexual appetites, he found himself bound to a girl who, I suspected, was emotionally too immature for his needs. I did not dare to dwell on Stephen's problems. My concern must be with Deirdre herself, a child cut off from all understanding and love. With her mother's death she lost even me, the surrogate parent.

Sometimes during that night, as during the previous nine years, I resented this chain that seemed to keep me forever hobbled to another human being. Had Deirdre been anyone but the bubbling, loving girl she was, I might have broken those links in spite of all my promises to her father. But I couldn't abandon Deirdre. I could only try to see that she made Stephen a good wife. From the little Ito Nagata and Michiko had told me when Deirdre married Stephen, I understood he was not a man who played around much. His drive was quite different. I suspected his mastery of business, and his stubborn determination to finish what his weak father had begun, were more urgent drives to him than casual affairs would be. That was Deirdre's greatest protection.

On the other hand, there were those minutes when we were together. . . . I knew we shared a physical desire. And it would be disastrous to give in to that under the circumstances.

By the time I got to sleep I felt that I knew what I must do: banish entirely this ridiculous crush I had on Deirdre's husband and rigorously concentrate on helping Deirdre's growth. That would be painful for both of us, but it seemed obvious now that the most serious aspect of her problem had begun with her mother's death. Having faced that, I thought I might know where to start in helping her. If, of course, a layman could help.

With all these good resolutions I finally slept, and dreamed. Although my days and often the nights before I managed to sleep were haunted by bits and pieces of memories, it was strange that I so seldom relived the nightmare of Claire Cameron's death. But sometimes during those predawn hours of troubled sleep I found myself once more returning to that horrible day, trying to keep out of the way of Deirdre's friends at her thirteenth birthday party, while still making myself available in case of emergency.

I awoke with a start in that humid Hawaiian darkness, but with my mind full of those memories. With one arm behind my head, I went over in my thoughts every detail I could recall — trying for the hundredth, or thousandth time, to fix the pattern, find out what really happened:

It was a very warm, dry day. Unexpectedly warm even for southern California at that time of year. I could see the smog settling in flat layers over the sprawling city that was spread out below my home in the Hollywood Hills. I stood on the terrace at the rear of the house, trying not to listen to the silly, lovable chatter going on around the pool, which was on the next level below the terrace. I was wondering if I shouldn't change from my green linen sheath to a two-piece white silk because John, my fiancé, was coming, and John Eastman had a thing for white. And purity in every sense except, of course, when applied to himself.

I remember that John felt Deirdre was a serious obstacle to our marriage. He used to ask me, "How can you try to mother a teen-age girl with a heart murmur, palpitations, and a dozen other ailments? She should be in a decent girls' school where she could be treated whenever she had a flare-up. You can't be responsible for her. You were a teen-ager yourself not so long ago.

Judith, can't you see your way clear to sending her back to her real mother? Let her worry about the girl's birthday parties and her schooling and all the rest."

To this I could only remind him, "Don't you think I want Deirdre to be raised in her own home, with her own mother? If we could just sober up Claire for a little while, she might . . ." But there I had to leave it, the obvious answer unspoken. I was still romantic enough in those days to believe that all Claire needed was a genuine love in order to sober up and become a family woman.

So I waited out the birthday party, hoping there would be no quarrels among the groups around the pool, no hard feelings between two pretty blonde girls over an equally pretty boy who wore his hair surprisingly long for the style nine years ago. I looked over the group, wondering where Deirdre was, saw her with a boy and a girl, all three stretched out in the sun beyond the far end of the pool. Deirdre wore what she called her first "grown-up" bikini set, in black with a white deer strategically placed over the right hipbone.

Deirdre would have preferred to do some strenuous swimming, or the very least, to join the group tossing the big beach ball in the pool, but she had never quite gotten her childhood strength back after her attack of rheumatic fever long ago.

She saw me glance that way and waved to me.

I waved back. Then she sat up, looking puzzled about something behind me, and pointed. I looked over my shoulder, then up at the windows of my bedroom on the second floor of the rambling stucco house. Someone was up there, wandering around — probably one of Deirdre's young guests curious to see the family rooms. But it had been my experience that such curiosity often meant pilfering as well, so I left the terrace and went in through the breakfast room door and up the stairs. I made enough noise to warn whoever was up there. I didn't want to "catch" someone if I could help it. Better just to warn off the interloper by my presence and a friendly greeting. Have it all look accidental.

There was a group downstairs at the buffet finishing up the luncheon — the foot-long sandwiches and the sundaes they had made themselves. It wasn't so long since I had participated in just such parties myself. As I went up the stairs I heard buzzing and whispers and guessed that those at the buffet were watching me. They must have known which of their friends I was about to encounter.

I crossed the upper hall and went into my bedroom. The room was empty but the lively green spread on my four-poster bed showed signs of having been disturbed. Obviously, someone had been sitting on the bed. The door to the small dressing room between my bedroom and bathroom was almost closed. I had left it wide open. I supposed whoever was snooping around had ducked into the bath-room. Amused at the natural curiosity of my unseen visitor, I followed.

Nearly everything on my dressing table had been overturned. Powder was spilled over the little mirrored tray in which I set my lipsticks. The lipsticks themselves rolled on the floor. One had come open and its coral contents were ground into the gray carpeting. I wasn't in too friendly a mood when I saw that. I picked up the lipstick case and, weighing it in my palm, I pushed open the bathroom door which was ajar.

Claire Cameron stood there interestedly reading labels on the various medicines in the glass cabinet. She did not turn around as I came in behind her. In her gloved left hand was one of my initialed lo-ball glasses in which one ice cube wandered alone in what appeared to be a full glass of Scotch, if I knew Claire. She waved the glass toward the medicine cabinet, took a long swallow and remarked thickly, "Not a decent stock at all, at all. But you always were Little Miss N-Namby-Pamby. Don't you ever get headaches?"

Except for the dainty, though now soiled, white lace gloves, there was little left of the girl I had first seen when she was engaged to Wayne. Her soft, pretty face had swollen alarmingly in the years since. When I remembered the beau-tiful, petulant young bride with topaz-colored hair and the fantastically tiny waistline in her New Look wedding gown, I was sickened with pity. She had become a thirty-year-old woman with flabby features and badly bleached thinning hair. She looked ten years older than her true age. And yet, pity wasn't what she needed. She had been unfaithful to Wayne even before he left for Korea. She had never been disciplined in her free, wealthy childhood, and found marriage an impossible constriction. Still, remembering that young bride of long ago, who had impressed me, a gawky teen-ager, I felt sick now at what remained.

I said, "There is aspirin right under your hand. Claire . . . how about going out to see Deirdre before you finish that drink?"

"Later. Ac-Actually why I came."

I began to brighten. Maybe I'd gotten cynical about her. Maybe she did care about her daughter after all.

"She will be so excited! You haven't seen her yet? Come along and we'll —"

"Hold it! H-hold it! Now, look, Goody-Two-Shoes," she waved the drink. The sticky contents splashed over my head and I stepped back, trying not to let her annoy me.

"I'm looking," I said. "What is it?"

Her eyes had once been rather like Deirdre's, large and bright, with an illusion of innocence. Now, bloodshot and squeezed into that puffy face, they were painful to look at and I shifted my own attention, reaching for the glass door of the cabinet and starting to close it. She reached in front of me abruptly.

172

"Where's your God-damned aspirin or what-ever?"

She had already dropped the plastic bottle of sleeping capsules prescribed for me a year before after a bad cold and cough. I had used only the first two capsules before recovering. I picked up the container as she felt for the aspirin bottle. I tried to replace the capsule container but she was in the way and I set it down on the wash basin.

"Claire, how are you? Is everything all right? What are your plans?"

"Be all right, if things go the way I've got in mind. This time it's love, baby. The real thing. His old man is the Guatemalan consul on one of those corny little islands in the Caribbean. Only thing is, we need a little something to set us up. Pablo is gorgeous. You couldn't imagine! But his old man is one of those bastards who keeps squealing that Pablo's got to start pulling his own weight. And Pablo's not the type. No way! Long and short of it is, we're broke."

I knew her income from a trust set up by Wayne came to several thousand dollars a month and was intended to include Deirdre's support, which it didn't. Otherwise, the balance of Wayne's estate was set aside for Deirdre when she reached her eighteenth birthday. During her last two visits, she had persisted in the complaint: "I'm broke." Before I could ask the obvious question, she cut in sharply, "How long'd you expect me to take it from that precious baron? Who'd have thought a real live baron would take a belt buckle to me? Beat me up once too often. So I had to get rid of him. Paid him off. Loused up my allowance for the next year. Now I'm dead — flat broke."

Claire knew quite well Wayne's money had been his own. He had been a corporation lawyer, and his estate was far different from mine. He had earned every cent of it himself. I inherited our parents' home and a comfortable income from annuities. I had trained as a secretary and worked part-time for Wayne's partners; so I asked Claire somewhat dryly, "How much do you need?"

"Fifty thousand. That'll give us a cushion. Pablo's old man is sure to pop off one of these days. He's past seventy. And with my monthly noble stipend, we can make out."

When talking about money Claire seldom seemed drunk. I stared at her. I never had been able to believe what I heard when I talked with Claire. "For heaven's sake, where would I find fifty thousand dollars?"

I must have raised my voice because she sounded awfully loud when she answered me.

"Who's kidding whom? I know Wayney-boy's family had it stashed away. And it better be coming around, because I need it bad."

"Impossible."

Her eyes narrowed. "Well, you'd better make it possible. Because that's what it'll cost you to keep my daughter here."

The implication was too foul even for Claire. I could only laugh.

"What are you trying to do? Sell Deirdre to me?"

She threw her head back, gulped down a couple of aspirins with the dubious aid of her glass of Scotch. She almost dropped the glass. I reached for it, thought of throwing out the contents, then gave it back to her. She pushed by me, walking uncertainly through the dressing room and into my bedroom.

"Sell my kid?" she asked finally, her pale eyebrows arched. "Don't count on that argument. I can be pretty convincing as the grieved war widow who finally got up enough courage to take her child back. But I do feel the kid would be happier with little old you for the next year or so. Just through the awkward age, you might say. Along about eighteen, she will be at an age when I can handle her better." She grinned. "But meanwhile, if I get my money, she can stay here. Believe me, I need that money. Pablo is an expensive luxury, but worth every penny. Now, what about it?"

"Forget it!"

She bit her drying lower lip. "Okay. Then Deirdre goes with me. Now. Today."

"She won't," I said more calmly than I felt. But there would be no end of blackmail if I gave in now. Besides, I didn't have fifty thousand dollars and doubted if I could raise it. She was bluffing — she had to be. I put down panic firmly.

"Claire, if you could just come back to the States — only for a little while — and not . . ."

"Drink? Not see my Pablo? You've got to be kidding. I'll take Deirdre with me. She'll learn soon enough how to live like her mother. It won't take long."

The more she talked the more sickening the prospect became. Deirdre was young, romantic. She could easily be attracted by the sordid life her mother offered. And such a life might kill a girl with Deirdre's medical history. But I dared not refuse to let Claire make the offer. I had called her bluff. It all depended on Deirdre.

"Suppose I get Deirdre and we'll find out whether you can do this thing," I told Claire, my voice shaking when I wanted it to be chill and confident.

She shrugged. "I'll be waiting."

I had hoped when I called her bluff she might give up, but she was playing it just as cool, and I had to carry on. In the hall doorway I heard her drop her glass on the bedroom carpet and curse volubly. I swung around, unable to hold onto my falsely calm veneer. "You'd better watch those playful little habits of yours or you'll wind up dead."

"Miss Lollypops doesn't approve of alcohol? Miss Lollypops wants the world dry-cleaned. You wait until I get hold of Deirdre . . . my kid. She'll be like me in six months."

"Shut up! Or someone will silence you permanently, and I'm just the girl to do it," I yelled

176

back at her and hurried down the stairs.

There were still three or four youngsters at the buffet, and for a minute I thought of retreating, going down the back stairs to avoid them, but I was too ashamed of my own cowardice in trying such a trick and went on past them deliberately. I did wonder how much they had heard, but unless I was badly mistaken, they would hear an even better show when Claire tried to persuade Deirdre to go off with her and share that jolly life with "Pablo."

I crossed the terrace, looking over the low stucco wall once to see Deirdre. She had moved away from the pool-side. I went down the steps. Several of the party were still in the pool. The big, multicolored balloon sailed over the head of a pretty, dark-haired girl who screamed at missing the shot. I caught the ball, and hurled it back, calling, "Anyone seen Deirdre?"

One of the boys bounded high in the water, waving vaguely toward the walk around the side of the house. I thanked him, turned and started back. The narrow, brick-walled walk was empty and I wondered if Deirdre was out in front of the house in one of the guest cars and cycles parked along the semicircular drive. Two boys were leaving with one of the girls. We all exchanged breezy good-byes. I looked at several cars, failed to find Deirdre, and went back into the house. No one had seen Deirdre around the buffet or among those dancing to the hi-fi in the next room. I went the full length of the house to the back stairs and finally went up.

The bedroom door was closed. As I entered the room I heard sounds of weeping — horrible, heartbreaking noises that sent me in on the run.

"What is it? Deirdre? Claire!"

Deirdre was kneeling on the floor at the far side of the bed. She was crying, openly and childlike, without covering her face. I couldn't see Claire. I found myself moving in slow motion around the foot of the bed, and didn't understand my own reluctance to go further. Deirdre hadn't indicated that she heard me come in, and she kept sobbing, catching her breath, crying again. Claire's body lay in an S position on the floor in front of her.

"What happened? Did she pass out? I knew she'd been drinking too much."

Deirdre did not answer me. I took up Claire's hand, then shook her, doing all the unreasoning things people do when they don't know whether someone is alive or dead. Then I heard Claire's shallow breathing. It did not sound like the heavy snoring of a drunkard.

"Deirdre, call Dr. Lowell, quickly!"

The girl did not move. I looked up. "Deirdre!"

She stared at me with her vision blurred by tears. Her fist was clenched. More and more worried, I reached for her hand. She pulled away. I forced her fingers open. A pharmacist's capsule container rolled to the floor. I watched the little plastic bottle as it kept rolling. It came to a stop against Claire Cameron's bare leg. The

178

container was empty. I stared at it. It was my own prescription, the old one whose pentobarbital contents I had only used twice. They were far too strong for me. Finally, I got up enough courage to ask, "What happened, Deirdre? Tell me. What went on here?"

Deirdre shook her head. She sniffed and blinked and looked at her empty hand. I touched Claire again. Without knowing much about death, I felt sure my sister-in-law was in a very serious state. How long ago I had left her I couldn't say. Not half an hour, but the woman had time enough to take the capsules — possibly by accident, mistaking them for aspirin — and time enough for them to threaten her life since she had swallowed several on top of all the liquor.

Deirdre was still in that terrible stupor. I got up.

"Deirdre, dry your eyes and get out of here. Go down the back stairs and out in front. And say nothing. I'll call the doctor. You weren't here. You didn't see her. You understand?"

She made no sign of agreement but clearly understood me and got to her feet. She startled me then by rushing out of the room, and as I dialed my bedside phone, I heard her clattering down the back stairs. I called and explained to the doctor who had treated Deirdre and me for the past year.

"Please hurry! Please! I can't bring her around. If she took them all on top of the liquor . . ."

He broke off the connection in order to call emergency while I was further shaken by my fiancé, John Eastman calling to me from the doorway.

"Good God, Judy! What have you done to her?"

I was shocked then. The pain at his suspicions came later.

Claire Cameron died in the ambulance without ever recovering consciousness.

My fiancé was only the first to utter his instinctive suspicion. My original argument, with Claire, when I had threatened that someone might do away with her, was remembered by all those witnesses downstairs at the buffet. My motives were obvious. Thwarted mother love, they said.

Deirdre seemed to have blanked out the entire episode with her mother in my room that day. And that was for the best, under the circumstances. During the days before my own arrest, I talked to Deirdre several times and discovered also that she knew nothing. She began to speak again but I learned no more except that she had come in and found her mother lying there "sleeping."

"And the capsule bottle?"

Deirdre remembered nothing of the capsule bottle. After several conversations, I did not pursue the matter, and I dared not put her in the hands of the district attorney's office.

Shortly after my trial began, Deirdre was

found wandering through the parched Hollywood Hills and came down with pneumonia. Day after day I sat in that hot, stuffy courtroom with its high windows, wondering if Deirdre would die and I would be locked up for life. The most telling evidence against me was the quarrel between Claire and me overheard by the children at the buffet, my fingerprints on Claire's whiskey glass when she nearly dropped it, the fact that my own sleeping capsules were used, and of course, my presumed motive.

Afterward, I was terrified to have Deirdre brought to see me for fear she would remember more about that day, and we would have to go through the whole business again and possibly ruin Deirdre's young life. She was made a ward of the courts, sent to an exclusive young ladies' school back East, and I never saw her again, although we corresponded in a desultory way.

I had thought when I was paroled through Stephen Giles's influence that I might banish those years and that terrible day of Deirdre's birthday party, but in the humid, flower-scented Hawaiian night I knew that day had never really gone. It might remain with us as long as Deirdre and I lived. But would it remain *between* us?

Eleven

I banished memories at last and slept, to wake up early, from long habit. Public institutions possess at least one superb quality — they teach the inmate to arise punctually. I knew we would be leaving soon after morning coffee but hadn't expected my coffee to be served to me by my hostess. Deirdre pushed my door open with her knee and then, having closed the door with her hip, came in with a tray bearing the glass Silex, which threatened at any moment to slip off. She had also jammed the tray with cup, saucer, sugar, and cream. I leaped out of bed to grab at and help balance the tray.

Deirdre was in a giggling state of excitement. It is curious, perhaps, that her giggle was not generally annoying. There was a musical quality about it, and I had seen her husband smile fondly while she was in the midst of her fits of giggles. That morning her hair was done again in Alice-in-Wonderland fashion, with a green ribbon that was a perfect complement to her large eyes. She wore a raw-silk dress, sleeveless, with a deep cleavage, and the pleated skirt was a trifle longer than a miniskirt. It was a modified silhouette of a 1920s style made popular this year by a Hollywood movie star. I thought it charming and youthful but a mistake for a girl who should have been trying to impress her husband with her maturity.

Then I had an idea. With Michiko Nagata's help I could persuade Deirdre to buy some clothes that would be a trifle more adult. This might help to persuade Stephen that she was grown-up.

Deirdre settled down in the chair opposite me as I drank my coffee at the little table near the window. I hadn't washed or showered yet, but I could see that I had to give in to her whims or turn off those sunny smiles and the endearing enthusiasm.

"I did it myself," she announced proudly. "Went down and tiptoed around. It would have been ghastly if Mr. Yee had popped in. He'd have murdered me with those eyes. A real spook. Although," she added honestly, "he's wonderful at his job."

"I know what you mean. People like that often are. It's the arrogance of ability."

"The what of what?"

Her brief picture of Michiko Nagata's uncle had brought back memories of former acquaintances. "I knew a woman once who'd been the driver for a gang of criminals. Among other things. And the thing we noticed was her unbelievable arrogance. She used to treat us like inferior beings because her crimes were greater than those of her companions."

"But — she was just a driver!" Deirdre murmured, confused, yet interested.

I wished I hadn't mentioned the memory. The

woman was actually the brains of her criminal gang and having been paroled, she immediately rejoined her gang and was responsible for the murder of three innocent bystanders in a Riverside bank. I did not tell Deirdre, however.

"I guess she liked to boast."

Deirdre scoffed. "What an idiot!" She sat there watching me, making me feel extraordinarily uncomfortable, even self-conscious. I was wearing one of the nylon chiffon nightgowns and matching peignoirs I had splurged on in Los Angeles before leaving for the airport. Deirdre said finally, "Would I look like that in an outfit like yours?"

I laughed. "Much better. A dozen years better, dear. Why don't we get you some in Honolulu?"

She wrinkled her nose. "I'd get cold at night."

"That is one of the great advantages of having a husband who loves you," I reminded her.

She was still thinking this over when I went to shower and dress. By the time I returned to take a dress from the closet, Deirdre was there before me.

"Here's a perfect dress for you, wise old auntie. It's going to be just right with the green I'm wearing."

It went with her green as dull earth goes with a spring-bright leaf, but I was ashamed of my first reaction and agreed. The plain beige sheath was one I had owned for ten years, but it looked surprisingly undated with its new hemline.

Ito Nagata was ready shortly after but Stephen

had gone out to examine the grove and to see what had to be done to assure the safety of the next work crew. He explained this briefly to us when we met him at the boat landing. I am fairly sure Ito and I were both of the opinion he ought to give up the entire Sandalwood *heiau* project, but I did wonder at Deirdre's reason for opposing it. During the boat ride while I was shaking off the channel spray, Deirdre brought up the subject of the ancient goddess Pelé again, and I felt greatly relieved when Stephen kept his temper. He asked calmly, "Have you yourself seen her, darling?"

I was certain she would make a flat assertion, as children often do, either yes or no. To my surprise, she tilted her head and ignored the channel breeze whipping the long strands of hair across the lower half of her face.

"I think I have seen her. Honestly, darling. I really . . . think I have."

With his free hand Stephen reached for her fingers which curled up in his. I wrenched my attention away only to find Ito watching me. I wonder if I changed color or revealed any of my inner conflicts. Ito had always understood me too well. He and my brother Wayne grew up together, while I tagged along, the little sister whose red hair existed only to be pulled. But I knew I had them to protect me and sometimes even to understand me. Perhaps now Ito understood me too well.

I had to raise my voice to make myself heard,

for we were now in midchannel and a warmish, blustery wind lashed hard to support us as we moved with the current in a southeasterly direction.

"Has anyone thought the troubles in the grove could be sabotage?"

Stephen smiled a trifle grimly. "I'm afraid that was our first idea. But it's no use. It would have been easy if we could lay the business on someone connected with the dock negotiations, someone from the mainland who wanted to give us trouble. It would have been less easy if our own people on Ili-Ahi were responsible. But we've even investigated that. No dice. It's just coincidence."

Ito and I looked at each other. I think we shared some sort of notion that there was a "curse" on the area, just as some ground is tainted and there are some places where nothing will grow. Deirdre examined her fingernails with an insouciant, cocksure manner which told us plainer than speech that she could explain the whole thing if she set her mind to it. I wondered.

We barely reached Kaiana Airport in time to catch the interisland plane. Michiko Nagata was waiting for us, but being her usual wise and prompt self, she had already gone on board and was motioning to us from the open doorway. She was stunning and immaculate as ever, with her black hair piled high in a pompadour but the ends curled on the nape of her neck, a style that gave all the wide planes of her face a perfect frame. She was not beautiful, but her friends and the admirers of her professional work regarded her looks as far more interesting than those of any beauty. She knew how to make the very best of every feature — something most of us spend a lifetime trying to achieve and never succeed in doing. She was very modern, which often surprised strangers, and there was none of the old-fashioned, prewar "shyness" that often seemed to be part and parcel of the attractive young Japanese woman.

Ito hurried ahead and was the first to board. Ito was a very clever person in his own field and outside his home, but within the marriage itself, I had always suspected Michiko was the wise one. I was even more glad to see her than I had expected to be and rushed after Ito. Michiko and I hugged each other as the Gileses followed us inside. I wondered if Michiko remembered, as I did, our last meeting in that desert institution not far from Bakersfield, California.

We took off almost immediately after Michiko and I were in our seats.

I said, "You are incredible, Michiko. You never change or get older, not so much as a hair, or a wrinkle. Or one pound."

Michiko laughed. "Three pounds, at least, since we last saw you. But you are marvelous. Let me look at you when we aren't strapped into our little barber chairs. You really look better all the time. Even in that place you had a kind of calm I never inherited from my so-called distinguished ancestors."

Michiko never evaded anything, and she was frank. I felt I always knew how I stood with her.

Feeling much better, I said, "We can't both be liars, so let's assume it's true of both of us. But I do wish I knew how you keep so young."

"Ancestors again. You must choose them carefully. Wrinkles are inherited or they aren't. We are trapped by the rash marriages of our ancestors."

How true that was!

When we stopped talking I sat there thinking over past good times with the Nagatas and from that reverted to our more recent meetings when I was still a prisoner. I shivered. Remembrances seemed to linger behind me, just a breath away from my neck. I started nervously when someone tapped on my shoulder. For a brief time after I got over my fright, I believed it was Stephen behind me, and that furiously annoyed me. I had no business thinking of him at all in any way. And worse, I was disappointed when I looked around and saw William Pelhitt.

He was looking happy for the first time since I had known him, and these good spirits did surprising things for his appearance.

"Got away from my keeper, the lord and master," he confided.

Michiko looked around and smiled. I wondered if she too had met the all-powerful Victor Berringer. I asked if Mr. Pelhitt was going to have his fling in Honolulu.

"Sort of. After I check out a couple of leads. I don't suppose you'd be willing to go with me, Miss Cameron."

I had the feeling that I might discover more than William Pelhitt would about Ingrid Berringer's life in Honolulu, and I hesitated, with a glance at Stephen. He had overheard Pelhitt's tentative offer and frowned. We were both startled when Deirdre cut in with bright, uncomplicated laughter, "Judy! Why don't you go along with nice Mr. Pullet? Michiko and I can do our shopping. Don't worry. And then, we can all meet at the Kaiulani Terrace and go on to the apartment together. Isn't that a clever idea, Stephen? Then we'll be paired up right. Not two pairs and an extra."

Stephen said hurriedly, "Very clever, darling, but I think Michiko and Judith had been counting on lunching together, anyway."

"They can always do that. And I think we shouldn't take up all poor Judy's time while she's here. We're lucky to have her at all."

"Lucky, indeed!" Stephen agreed and looked at me, questioning. "But you do —"

William Pelhitt added eagerly, "I wish you would consider it, Miss Cameron."

"Maybe it would be better," Michiko murmured. "We can get together later." But I knew she was curious. Nor could I blame her.

By the time we reached the Honolulu airport it had been worked out among the group that Bill Pelhitt and I would follow up two of the addresses where Ingrid Berringer had stayed in Honolulu and which, as far as Pelhitt knew, Berringer had not investigated. We would lunch somewhere in our wanderings and then meet the other four at the Kaiulani out in Waikiki and go to Stephen's company apartment for dinner.

As we were about to take separate cabs, Stephen found a moment to exchange a word or two with me.

"I know you are doing this to take the pressure off my wife. But I don't like it. Can you trust him? We know nothing about him whatever."

I smiled. "He knows nothing about *me*. And I'm afraid my record is worse than his."

"Don't!"

I realized suddenly that my flippant remark had hurt him in some way. It was strange that we should react so strongly to each other when we had been acquainted less than a week. Strange and potentially troublesome.

"I'm sorry. That was just a touch of humor thrown in to — to liven the conversation."

"Well, don't! You must not. Not with me."

"Here come the girls," I said. "Good luck with your dock strike or whatever."

Michiko and Deirdre came back from the restroom just as Ito and William Pelhitt joined us. The girls and I embraced and they got into a waiting taxi. Before leaving with Stephen, Ito advised me in his usual discreetly low voice. "Don't play James Bond, Judy."

I was almost relieved to be rid of Ito and Stephen. They made me keenly aware of the fact that a young woman had disappeared, that this was not an ordinary afternoon's date, and that William Pelhitt might still be a mere stooge for the ruthless Victor Berringer.

Pelhitt had hired a car and explained as we drove off toward downtown Honolulu, "The first place is near the museum here."

"The Bishop Museum?"

"Whatever it is. I was told the street is in that quarter. It seems Ingrid lived there for a while. Of course, it was a long time ago, considering. Judith — may I call you Judith?"

I had been calling him Bill for several minutes, and I said, "Certainly," trying not to sound impatient. "But as you say, if that was almost a year ago, why is it important now?"

We were driving through an area of Honolulu that I had never associated with the high-rise apartments and hotels of Waikiki or Fort and King and other downtown streets. The area was crowded with bungalows of the style sprawling over southern California in the 1920s and still there. The big difference was in the palm trees which punctuated these bungalows. Los Angeles and its desert environs had been thick and dusty with huge, shedding date palms. On these streets populated with predominantly Oriental faces, the trees were coco palms, which had their own lean, willowy grace.

Bill Pelhitt said suddenly, "You must think I'm pretty much of a cypher, letting my girl go off around the world when I loved her — I really do, you know! — enough so that I've never looked at anyone. Not since Ingrid was sixteen."

I softened a little. I didn't want to pity him. Pity wouldn't help him in the least. But somehow, William Pelhitt always inspired that emotion. It was unfortunate, because he was unquestionably sincere and decent about his feelings, a man caught in a vise by his affection for a girl who didn't love him and by her father, a man of great force and magnetism.

"I do understand. But I think you must face the fact that Miss Berringer is not in love with you. It seems likely that she has found someone she cares for and they have simply not bothered to let her father know about it."

"Until they need money," he remarked with an old, weary cynicism that surprised me. "You won't believe it, Judith, but I was — I am — the only man she could live with. The others will come and go . . . if she's still alive. But you see, I know Ingrid for what she is. And I — care for her that way. Does that sound crazy?"

"Not at all. I think Ingrid Berringer was a lucky girl, if she had only known it. Now, she may be very sorry." I turned to him, realizing I might be more encouraging. "That's probably your greatest card to play. That she will be tired of this life, tired of — whatever makes her roam around like this, with no roots."

He sighed. "I wish you were — I hope you are right. You've been wonderful for me. From the first minute when Vic thought you were Giles's wife, I thought — lucky Giles."

I didn't know what to say. I felt uncomfortable and would like to have changed the subject, but that seemed unkind.

I tried again to bolster him up. "I just wonder if Miss Berringer might come to appreciate you pretty soon. Don't forget, the action you've taken now is very romantic. The dashing man of the world crossing half the earth to see her. Quite different from some casual love — I beg your pardon — casual relationship here in the Islands. Or wherever she has gone. If you will just be patient, I have a feeling that by the time you find her, she will fall into your arms in relief."

He thought this over. I suspect it was an effort to smile, but he did so. As we drove along the quiet residential street, I was pleasantly surprised again to see the profusion of tropical and semitropical blooms everywhere. I still couldn't get over seeing those lovely little flowers called "Vanda orchids" in the shops, growing almost wild on gracefully bending stalks. My companion ventured hesitantly, spoiling my romantic, flowery dream.

"Do I strike *you* as a dashing man of the world?" Fortunately, he grinned and made a joke of it before I could reply. He looked around for a parking place. I was still not used to so many of the compact little foreign cars. They were everywhere, but Bill Pelhitt managed to squeeze between a Mazda and a Toyota and as I

started to get out by myself, I found my companion rushing around to open the door for me.
His gallantry touched me. He looked much
younger, alive and eager, and I tried to convince
myself that a girl like Ingrid Berringer would
prefer this nice, red-cheeked, blue-eyed fellow to
the sophisticated characters with whom she was
probably involved.

She was involved . . .

Even now, looking back on that time, I remember how firmly I assured myself that Ingrid
Berringer was very much in the present tense,
very much alive. And the truth was, I had no way
of knowing — it was mere wishful thinking. But
still, I never once allowed myself to question this
firm assumption.

Bill rang the little doorbell, which buzzed rau-
cously somewhere in the house. A slight, pretty,
young Oriental woman came to the door. Her
figure was slim as a boy's in jeans and a brightly
printed halter top, and she flashed a welcoming
smile. The gleam of excitement in her dark eyes
made me suspect the welcome was influenced by
strong curiosity.

"I am Teresa Asami. You are the *malahini* gentleman who called. My husband is at his job now
but he told me you had found out from the Surfrider that Miss Berringer stayed here a few
days."

Bill introduced himself and me, explained that
he was another of Ingrid Berringer's "relatives."

We were invited inside and in the warm little

living room I saw sprays of orchids, a vase of beautiful bird of paradise and exquisite watercolors in the Japanese style on the walls, in addition to family portraits. There was one eight-by-ten black-and-white framed portrait of two delightfully grinning young Japanese boys in U.S. Army uniform, though they looked scarcely old enough to be wearing anything but Boy Scout uniforms.

"My uncles," Mrs. Asami explained with pride in her small voice. "They were in the Italian campaigns. That was World War Two. You have heard of their motto: 'Go For Broke!' They took it from us in the Islands. It is an old saying. Tommy was killed. He is the boy on the left. But Georgie came home. He is a Toyota dealer out Kahala way."

"It is a wonderful picture. So very expressive," I remarked, but Bill Pelhitt interrupted her nervously, "Was it here that Ingrid stayed? How did she find out about it?"

Mrs. Asami motioned us to a big red plush couch. "Do you drink tea? Or — saki? *Malahinis* seem to have taken a fancy to it lately." We refused politely and she sat down opposite us, with a graceful tucking away of those good-looking legs underneath her.

"My husband is desk clerk at the hotel and Miss Berringer asked him if there was a small place she could rent. 'Away from things,' she said. My husband suggested the bungalow next door. It isn't ours but we rent it out for the owner who lives in Osaka. Afterward, my husband said he should have guessed what she wanted it for." She clapped her hand over her mouth in sudden embarrassment. "I beg your pardon. I do not mean to say that she — that is, we have no reason to believe she did anything improper, and except for her one visitor, she was absolutely alone."

"Please," Bill put in anxiously. "Don't hesitate to tell us everything. We are trying to find her, and any little bits and pieces of information may help us."

She nodded. "I understand. It was only a few days, and when she left she took a small case — an overnight case, I think. We imagined she would send for her things from the hotel, but during her stay here that was all she had."

I knew Bill was frantically anxious, and curious as I was, and I broke in, "The visitor. You say she had a visitor?"

"Oh, yes. That was in the early morning. The day before she left. My husband and I were sound asleep. He works nights. And we heard this quarrel. The young lady yelling 'Idiot! Idiot! Idiot! Just a complete moron!' And several unpleasant things like that. My husband opened the shade but we couldn't see anything. Our windows were open and so were Miss Berringer's. It — it was quite unpleasant."

Bill Pelhitt's fingers closed on the glass edge of the cocktail table. He leaned forward, wanting to hear more. I had quite an opposite impulse. I knew exactly what was coming. If only I could shut her up, get this Pelhitt out of here without discovering the rest, or what I thought was the rest!

"Mrs. Asami," he said, "when Ingrid's visitor left did you get a good look at her? Could you describe the young lady? Was she — ?"

"Describe Miss Berringer?" Mrs. Asami asked, obviously confused.

"No, no. Her visitor. This young lady she was calling an idiot and a moron."

Still bewildered, Mrs. Asami waved her hands as if to clear the air.

"Her visitor? I don't think you understand, Mr. Pelhitt. Her visitor was a man."

Twelve

I am not especially quick-witted, but it couldn't have been more than a few seconds before I suspected this visitor to whom Ingrid yelled "Idiot!" was the person most nearly concerned with Deirdre. It was her husband. Ingrid had spoken of her one-time friend as a "moron" and had made other cutting remarks, and I thought she would probably speak in this way about Deirdre only to Deirdre herself or to Stephen Giles. It was likely that she would try to hurt Deirdre in any way she could. But this revelation of her quarrel with the visitor was almost as damaging as a public quarrel with Deirdre herself would have been. Only it gave one other person grounds for harming her. And for killing her? But the woman was not dead! She *couldn't* be. I repeated this thought to myself. No one had any evidence that she had been murdered. No one!

Bill Pelhitt was puzzled. "But did you see him, Mrs. Asami?"

"Oh, yes. He was a *kamaaiana haole*. About six feet tall and very handsome, I thought. A fine, bronze fellow in a terrible rage. He shouted at her — something about warning her. He was very angry."

Pelhitt frowned and rubbed his temple. He had almost hit on my own suspicion, I was sure, but something seemed to have stumped him.

"Do you think it was someone she knew well?" He laughed awkwardly. "But she apparently knew so many."

Mrs. Asami murmured conventional sympathy but it was not, after all, any fault of hers, and I could see that she was at a loss to console a melancholy stranger.

"I'm afraid that is all we know here, Mr. Pelhitt. Miss Berringer left late that afternoon. We thought she was going on an interisland trip. But when she didn't return — she paid a month's rent — we decided she had gone on to the South Seas. Tahiti. Samoa. She hinted to my husband that she was in love, and that she would soon 'persuade' the man."

Mrs. Asami made a little gesture of apology. "I really am afraid Miss Berringer sounded quite ruthless when she went after a man. That was the impression we got, anyway. Otherwise, there is nothing we can tell you."

Reluctantly, Bill Pelhitt got to his feet. I joined him. I was anxious for him to get out of here before he realized the identity of the man quarrelling with Ingrid Berringer. At the same time I couldn't understand why the answer hadn't struck him as quickly as it had me.

I discovered when we reached the car that Pelhitt's ignorance of the identity of an angry man was based on an absurd misconception. As we drove off, he said with discouragement, "So she was mixed up with a Hawaiian!"

"A what!"

"You heard those Hawaiian words. The man was a half-blood of some kind. All that talk about golden —"

"Bronze."

"Same thing. So she was mixed up with one of the locals. You know, it might be one of the fellows in that Hawaiian group on Sandalwood Island. Ili-Ahi, or whatever they call it. There were some that I guess you'd call good-looking."

I was noncommittal. I didn't want to be a hypocrite and agree with him. On the other hand I was terrified for fear he would realize who that quarrelling man might be. I was reasonably sure that the unidentified man, if he *was* Stephen, had not harmed Ingrid Berringer. But he might well have bought her off, persuaded her to leave, and that might sound bad to Victor Berringer who would be certain to make something suspicious out of it. Worst of all, I wondered when Bill Pelhitt would find out what a *kamaaiana* really was, that a *kamaiana-haole* was simply a long-time Caucasian resident of Hawaii.

"A native," Bill murmured. He said the word distastefully. "Ingrid and a native!"

"Bill, citizens born in an American state are natives of that state. I'm a native of California. You are a native of —"

"New York. Upper New York state. I'm sorry. I didn't think."

I wished I hadn't brought the matter up. I wasn't anxious to fight the world's battles, and I had a headache. I am not sure just when the headache started, but I knew I was getting awfully tired of Bill Pelhitt's company, especially now that I would have to be careful in discussing the things we had learned at Mrs. Asami's. I made a rather obvious gesture of rubbing my forehead and, very ashamed of myself, I pleaded, "I wonder if you would mind driving me back out Kalakaua to the Princess Kaiulani, where I can wait for the others. I have this splitting headache."

He glanced at me, and the muscles around his jaws tightened. After that one glance he kept looking ahead as we started across downtown Honolulu toward the Ala Wai district and Waikiki.

"I guess I've been boring you. I really didn't mean to. I thought it might be interesting, kind of like detective work."

"And it was. Really, it was!"

He further upset me by saying with deep feeling, "Thank you, Judith. That was kind of you to say so. I can't persuade you to go to lunch with me, I suppose." Before I could answer he went on hurriedly, "But I imagine that wouldn't help your headache; would it?"

To accept his negative invitation seemed the least I could do; so I said of course I would be happy to have lunch with him. He cheered up considerably and we drove out to the beautiful Kahala Hilton and had our lunch. I admired the gardens and enjoyed the food, wishing I hadn't gotten used to eating less in the past nine years.

Institutional cooking had somewhat dulled my taste buds.

My companion talked about his childhood with Ingrid Berringer — how he, being somewhat older, became a kind of guardian to the girl who ran around freely, uninhibited, doing as she pleased, while Victor Berringer was busy adding to his fortune.

It was not until we were finishing our lunch and had turned to a discussion of the decorative pools, paths, lawns, and the endless varieties of green outside in the gardens, that I noticed the little man two tables away. His hooded, Oriental eyes dropped their gaze rather obviously as I looked his way.

"Mr. Moto seems awfully interested in us," I remarked.

Bill Pelhitt was far less casual than I. He turned and stared with deliberation at the little man who gave all his attention to the fruit salad he was toying with.

I saw that my companion was taking far too much interest in the little man, and I tried to turn his attention from what probably was a trivial incident. After Bill's reaction, I was sorry I had ever mentioned the Oriental man, who was minding his own business, after all.

"We have nothing to hide, Bill. Let him look."

"I don't like it. Who could have hired him? He is hired. Anybody can see that. He's a private eye."

"Private eye!" I sighed. Bill Pelhitt really had

an imagination. Because the little man had done nothing else to attract attention to himself, I tried to ignore him. When this proved impossible because of Bill's nervousness, I began to make a more careful study of the little man. He wore an aloha shirt with a raw-silk suit, and the outfit seemed a little too obviously "tourist" to be true. He was an Islander, I thought, and as I watched him I became convinced that he really *was* observing us for some reason, possibly in a professional capacity, as Bill had guessed. But who could have employed him? Bill was right, I was now convinced. The most important thing to discover now was the name of the little man's employer.

I smiled at Bill and whispered with what I hoped was a teasing air, "When we leave, let's walk through the gardens. See if he follows."

Bill Pelhitt hesitated a minute but then agreed. "Right. Let's go." He put on a great performance — I was afraid it might be a bit overdone. "What do you say we take a stroll — dear?"

I tried not to laugh but to keep a suitably easy expression.

"Of course, darling. What an enchanting view!"

We played along, walking out across the path, running our fingers through the water of a miniature pool, while I looked back and saw that our Mr. Moto had not left the dining room. Were we all wrong about him? He had certainly behaved oddly until now.

We couldn't really afford to waste any more time, even in this heavenly spot. I suggested at last that we drive back into the center of Waikiki to wait for the others of our party.

"If we go through the hotel he's bound to see us and follow."

I shrugged. "Go around the building — through the grounds and out some side way." He knew no more about the grounds than I did, but after numerous wrong turns and mistakes, we did get back to the car and started into town. There was a good deal of traffic, and I had decided we should try to forget our spooky little pursuer. We could hardly have picked him out of all those trucks and cars behind us, I thought. But Bill was attempting to do so, all the same. He kept glancing at the rear-view mirror and making guesses. He was so persistent about it, he infected me with curiosity once more.

"I never noticed that truck before. Did you see the driver? Pretty small, isn't he? Could be the one."

I scoffed at this idea. "You surely don't think our neat, precise Mr. Moto is driving a truck. Besides, that truck driver is red-haired." I wasn't going to tell him that the driver of the cream-colored Toyota beyond the truck and behind a Volkswagen did resemble our spy. Busy thinking about the spy and his probable purpose as well as his employer, I said very little after that and made the mistake of not answering Bill Pelhitt's second question in a row.

"Judith, have you got something against me — personally?"

I was startled back into awareness by his plaintive question and denied guiltily, "Certainly not. Where did you get that idea?"

"Well, you did have that headache. And then, I suppose I'm not as fascinating as some men you've known." He grinned a little shyly. "Come on, I can take it."

With a frankness he probably did not understand the real significance of, I promised him, "You are a far nicer person than I have been used to."

Unfortunately, he chose to accept this as a declaration of my interest and his free hand squeezed mine as it lay in my lap. He made no other physical advance but I couldn't help being relieved when we reached the best-known hotel row of Waikiki, with the Princess Kaiulani, on the *mauka* side. Across the street, backing on the narrow strip of beach, were the Surfrider and the aged but popular Moana. The latter was the last testament to the romantic Hawaii of Somerset Maugham.

When Bill had parked and was escorting me to the chosen meeting place on the terrace of the Kaiulani, I began hoping the others would have arrived first. I didn't want to spend more time alone with Bill Pelhitt. I was sorry for him but I felt that he was trying too hard to find a replacement for the missing Ingrid Berringer. He got a table and chairs for us and there seemed to be no way to avoid a long *tête à tête*. *Tête à tête?* Did people have those any more? How much I was still a product of the time before my lost nine years! I wanted to be part of today but I was having problems adjusting. Bill Pelhitt ordered drinks for us. I hesitated as usual. I couldn't seem to make a choice. It had never been a problem years ago. My fiancé, John Eastman, had always chosen for me. Now, when Bill ordered the ubiquitous *Mai-Tai*, I accepted it and tried to keep both hands busy pulling fruit out of my glass and sucking on it. It was sloppy, and it didn't even serve my purpose.

Bill reached for one of my hands. My fingers curled under his slightly damp touch. My own fingers were sticky, but he didn't seem to notice. He rambled on with his new theory that a Hawaiian had somehow caused Ingrid to disappear and interrupted himself to say suddenly, "We've thrown off our private eye! We haven't seen him since the Kahala."

"Maybe he never existed."

He found this appealingly funny.

"You just won't let me have my fantasy, will you? Doesn't matter. I'm beginning to feel a little less lousy. And I did feel lousy when we first arrived here in the Islands, Vic and I."

"I'm sorry. It must have been difficult for you. He is a very overbearing man, and then, for you to be on such a mission."

He said something, but I didn't hear it. As I looked up I saw Stephen Giles crossing the terrace toward us. He was looking angry. I supposed his strike negotiations must have fallen through. But I was so very glad to see him! My smile of greeting must have been bigger than I had meant it to be because his glowering look suddenly thawed into his warm, answering smile. This was only one of the qualities that made it perfectly understandable why Deirdre and Ingrid and now Judith Cameron had fallen in love with him. I pulled myself together, and reminded myself of my position here. I could not even afford to think of Stephen Giles if it was going to affect me this way.

Stephen's glance went back to the table where my fingers tried again, more or less on their own volition, to creep out of William Pelhitt's moist grip. I could hardly believe this sight had caused Stephen's frown but as he came up to us, the welcoming smile was gone again.

"You two seem to be enjoying our tourist delights. Have the others been by yet?"

"Not yet," I said with what I hoped was a very casual friendliness. "I hope you've had better luck than we have."

Bill Pelhitt seemed moderately glad to see him and pulled out a chair for him. I took this opportunity to recover my hand. I felt even more self-conscious when I realized that Stephen had noted this movement as well.

"I'm afraid our news isn't encouraging," Bill said. "We visited a woman who told us about a quarrel between Ingrid and a Hawaiian fellow.

Or — as I understood it, a fellow of mixed blood. Probably Oriental and Hawaiian."

I watched Stephen while appearing to have my attention fixed on a greedy young dove strutting across the terrace. Stephen seemed unaffected by the results of our visit. Perhaps he believed Bill Pelhitt's description was correct.

Offhandedly, he remarked, "I imagine we will find Miss Berringer really did go off on her own, or with company, on some private yacht perhaps. Her father seems to hear from her only when she needs money, so she may be supported at the moment." He saw Bill Pelhitt staring at him and colored suddenly. I had never seen him embarrassed before. "I beg your pardon. I forgot for a minute . . . Actually, I had no right to think or to suggest . . ."

Bill sighed heavily and went back to his drink. "Oh, well, it could be true. But somehow, I don't think so. I've got my eye on that half-breed guy, whatever he was called. Judith, what did Mrs. Asami say the guy was?"

Stephen's eyelids flickered at Mrs. Asami's name. Otherwise, he looked at both of us with simple interest.

I said quickly, "*Hapa-haole?* Wasn't that it?"

"Almost. I guess it was."

I tried not to let him see any relief in my manner at his acceptance of an entirely different description. A *hapa-haole* was usually half-Caucasian. A *kamaaiana* was not necessarily the same thing. I felt that I was doing something misleading in persuading William Pelhitt he had heard other words, but although I was sorry for the necessity to lie, I was not sorry I had lied.

Bill Pelhitt tossed a chunk of pineapple from his drink to one of the doves strutting about the terrace, but the independent birds weren't interested. He looked around guiltily, then got up and went across the terrace to pick up the fruit.

Stephen looked at me. "He seems to be a very kind sort of person."

"Seems to be, and is."

"You like him?"

I said lightly, "I like everything in Hawaii." I avoided his gaze, glanced beyond him, and saw Deirdre and Michiko Nagata loaded down with packages heading toward the table. I felt absurdly uneasy as Deirdre looked from her husband's back to me. She was obviously under the impression that we were alone. The girls reached the table just as William Pelhitt came back. It was perfect if accidental timing. He still carried the piece of pineapple and we all laughed as he held it out with the sad complaint: "Nobody wanted it. Even the birds turned me down."

Stephen drew his wife to him, kissed her on the forehead and then groaned at the number of her parcels. She was delighted by his teasing and grinned at me. I had the chilling notion that her grin for me was one of triumph.

Michiko broke up the awkward moment by telling me about the purchases she had made.

"And the prices! Judith, you wouldn't believe

the fantastic prices these days. I haven't bought any clothes here since last winter and everything has skyrocketed. Look at this swim suit. Ito is going to say I paid for it by the inch."

I thanked heaven for Michiko's calm good sense and for the suggestion she made that we have an early dinner and call it a day.

Stephen looked at his wife. "What do you say, darling? Shall we eat earlier and then go home? Not stop at the Kaiana hotel tonight?"

But Deirdre was in one of those contrary moods I recognized from her childhood.

"I haven't done half the shops. Please, Stephen, you promised."

In the end, because Deirdre had always gotten her way, we spent the rest of the afternoon shopping. I thought William Pelhitt would make an excuse and leave the party. But when we went on to that apartment high above the Waikiki surf where I had met Stephen Giles, Bill was still with us. Stephen had ordered a number of dishes popular at luaus.

"Complete with sand in the taro leaves," he explained and Deirdre added, clapping her hands, "Darling, I was so sick of those luaus where everyone sits on grass and gets beetles in their sandals."

Michiko whispered to me while the great helpings of food piled on our plates, "What I wouldn't give about now for a burger and corn on the cob."

Ito Nagata arrived late but joined us during

the meal and remarked to Michiko and me in a quiet aside that Deirdre was looking very tired, but she seemed happy — nervously, excitedly happy, I said.

"Make her rest tomorrow," Ito said to me. "I'll try and get over in the evening if I can. They are expecting a baby among Queen Ilima's family, so you may see me."

"Deirdre is just tired, as you said. I mean, it isn't anything more serious." I began to feel frightened, the way we all felt when her illness as a child was diagnosed as rheumatic fever and was followed by so many other childhood ailments that might have killed her. Was she never to have a decent, happy, untroubled life?

We managed to persuade Deirdre that we should return to Kaiana by the early evening plane. We would still have the rest of the trip to make by boat. She asked Stephen, "Can we come back again? Soon?"

He drew her to him tenderly. "Whatever you like, darling, but you are looking awfully sleepy; so what do you say we call it quits?"

Bill Pelhitt volunteered to drive us to the airport where he would turn in his rented car. The Nagatas left us in Waikiki and drove across the island to their home in Haleiwa on the north coast. I was more than a little sorry to be separated from them. I felt that my presence in Sandalwood was the last thing that would help Deirdre. I remembered Michiko's final words to me and I might even act on them.

211

As everyone was saying good night, Michiko had said to me in her matter-of-fact, unemotional voice, "I want you to promise me something, Judy. If things get sticky on Ili-Ahi, I want you to come to us. We both want you. I don't like the situation on that island, and neither does Ito. Stephen should never have married her, but since he did, she's his responsibility."

"But why do you say that? Did something happen when you were shopping today?"

"No, no. It's simply that the poor dear is much too changeful, too childish. And rather secretive. I always wonder if that childishness is a put-on. It's not a healthy situation. In fact — I don't think it is safe for anyone close to her."

We separated then, waved good night and I got into Bill Pelhitt's rented car with a great deal to think about, none of it happy except Michiko Nagata's unmistakably sincere invitation. Stephen sat in the front seat with Bill, and after Deirdre's odd behavior during the day I wondered what my reception would be when I joined my niece in the back seat.

Deirdre was sleepy and yawned in my face but made up for that in her endearing way by holding out a hand and welcoming me.

"Come in, come in. Wise old auntie. Honey, have I told you how glad I am to have you here in the Islands? Let's get cozy. There's a breeze tonight. Notice?"

I hadn't noticed, but Deirdre's bare arms showed goose-bumps, and she was wearing very little above the waist. Too bad we couldn't get at some of the clothes she had bought. Then I thought of the fringed sash I wore around my waist and which could also be worn as a thin stole. I was untying the knot when Stephen took off his zippered jacket and sent it back to her. Deirdre was delighted as a child, huddling into the warmth that had touched her husband's flesh. Deirdre was the only one who did much talking on the way to the airport. I was worried about many things: Deirdre's health, her real feelings toward me, the awkwardness of my own situation at Sandalwood, and Stephen Giles's unfortunate — to say the least! — visit to Ingrid Berringer, which the Asamis had observed. I only hoped that Victor Berringer with his sharp mind would not hear the full details of Bill's and my visit.

Stephen said nothing except to ask twice how Deirdre was feeling. "Warm enough, darling?" he repeated as we all filed out at the airport. I noticed when we moved to the interisland plane that Stephen was looking strained and seemed older than he had appeared when we had first met just a few days before. He had his arm around his wife now as we hurried along. We were barely in time to catch the flight.

Bill Pelhitt turned to me and indicated the loving couple in front of us. "It's a beautiful thing, if it's genuine."

Startled, I glanced at him.

"You have reason to think it isn't?"

"I didn't say so. But she seems so young for that fellow."

"She isn't, though," I told him. "And you can see they are very much in love."

We were at the plane now as I caught his last whispered remark, "Lucky devils!" He always managed to make me sorry for him when my real fears made me much sorrier for Deirdre and Stephen.

It was just as we were getting into the plane that I saw a small, neat Oriental man, in a light silk suit. Our Mr. Moto. He was standing apart from the few passengers hurrying to join us. I couldn't ignore the fact now; he was watching us, certainly either William Pelhitt or me, and perhaps all of us. When we were taking off I could still see the little figure, straight as a doll, with that imperturbable face turned in our direction.

Deirdre and William Pelhitt chattered during the entire short flight to Kaiana. Both of them may have been simply nervous and could relieve their tension by talk, but I couldn't do so. Nor could Stephen, apparently. In any case, we four were glad to reach the tiny Kaiana airport and take the jeep to Stephen's speedboat where it rocked gently, pulling at its mooring ropes outside an old boathouse.

As Deirdre and all her parcels were lifted down into the boat I looked off across the bay. I thought I could make out very faintly, the Ili-Ahi light on the little point where the boats docked.

Then it disappeared in thick mist that came and went in little patches shrouding whole areas of the bay and channel beyond for minutes at a time.

"I hope there won't be any difficulty crossing." Bill Pelhitt expressed my fears aloud. Deirdre clutched Stephen's arm anxiously.

"We're all right? We are perfectly safe; aren't we?"

With the gentle patience I admired in a man of his naturally spirited temperament, Stephen promised her, "We'll take it slowly. Don't worry, darling." He squeezed her hand, got her comfortably seated to avoid most of the spray and reached up to help me into the boat. William Pelhitt was behind me and luckily extended his hand at the same time. I pretended not to see Stephen and let Pelhitt help me instead. We took off too fast and went into a thick patch of misty fog, but as Deirdre cringed beside me, Stephen reduced the speed, and we saw behind us the faint clusters of lights on Kaiana twinkling in a friendly way between vast regions of jungle vegetation. Deirdre had begun to think about her purchases and started to describe slacks, bikinis, jackets, and dresses to me in detail.

We must have been nearly at midchannel when we heard another motor approaching from Ili-Ahi. The boat came on at great speed and seemed to be on our course. Stephen called across the black waters: "Who's there? This is Giles. Ahoy! Do you hear us?" He asked Bill

Pelhitt to readjust our lights. The one at the bow suddenly cut a path over the surface of the water as far as the coral reefs off the southeast shore of Ili-Ahi. The boat heading toward us at high speed gleamed in our light and we saw its single occupant, Victor Berringer, a powerful and oddly sinister figure, tall and lean, all in gray, almost becoming part of the mist that curtained the channel.

Stephen swung off course to avoid this gray demon, throwing us all against each other and causing Deirdre to shriek, but it was soon evident that Berringer knew exactly what he was doing. The boats missed each other by several yards. We got the heavy backwash from the other boat, and as we managed to get our equilibrium again I felt Deirdre swaying against me. I cried out, and Stephen cut the motor. Bill Pelhitt and I caught Deirdre as she collapsed. Her face was blue-white in the stark running lights of the two boats. She crushed her cold hands against her breastbone and gasped in pain.

"It hurts! It hurts so. Must have — eaten too fast. . . ."

Her heart! I thought, dreading the knowledge. It was as if she were the small child all over again. Wayne's child in pain and danger.

Victor Berringer had come about and cut his motor. He moved alongside. "Damn lights on this tub! Couldn't see a thing. That mist swallowed you up. Can I help you? Anything I can do?"

216

Stephen and I were too frantic, too anxious over Deirdre to answer him immediately. I had never felt so lost and helpless. We seemed to be floating in eternity, holding Deirdre's fragile life between us.

Thirteen

Stephen's worry about Deirdre that night managed to prevent him from a violent confrontation with Victor Berringer, whose reckless speed had brought on Deirdre's attack. Berringer tried to make up for it by tying his boat to ours and speeding our boat to the Kaiana Hilton's dock on the northwest coast of the island we had just left, while Stephen protected his wife's body from jolts and the rolling of the boat. Shortly after, Deirdre began to shiver uncontrollably. We wrapped her in every warm bit of clothing we could collect from each other, but her condition remained the same.

At the big, new, terraced hotel we were lucky enough to find a Dr. Henry Lum who had just been called in to treat a stout tourist with acute gastritis. Stephen would not leave the hotel bedroom where Dr. Lum examined Deirdre and managed to stop her pain without putting her under heavy sedation. Mr. Berringer and Bill Pelhitt remained with me as I drank coffee and hoped for Deirdre's recovery.

When Stephen came out to us endless minutes later, he explained that they were flying Deirdre to a hospital in Honolulu for further tests and treatment. "It appears to be some sort of nervous attack, Judith. Thank God, this doctor is pretty sure it wasn't her heart."

"In her girlhood Deirdre had something our doctor called palpitations, but he said it wasn't too serious at that time," I put in, hearing my voice high-pitched and tense. It would not help if I broke down. I stiffened my back and cleared my throat.

"Then the young lady is recovering? That's good news," Berringer put in when I found my throat so dry and tight with tension that I couldn't express my own happiness at the relief of our worst fears.

Stephen explained to Berringer with a slight emphasis, "As Miss Cameron says, my wife has had a weakened heart since an illness in her childhood. Judith, you will be coming with us? I've hired a plane."

I shook my head. It wouldn't help Deirdre's recovery if she awoke to see me there with her husband. Meanwhile, I didn't know what to do. I wanted to be within reach in order to hear of any changes in Deirdre's condition. She must recover, I thought. She *must* live and enjoy her life after all the uncertainties and illnesses of her past.

William Pelhitt spoke for the first time since Stephen had joined up. After Victor Berringer had joined our group he had crawled back into his shell and was now looking out furtively to see which way the wind lay.

"We — that is — Vic and I could take you back to Ili-Ahi, and you could be handy there for phone calls or whatever," he told me.

I tried to explain to Stephen, who proved the

biggest obstacle to a calm awareness of the situation. The strain he was under showed not only in his face but was also indicated by his anger, his quick-triggered temper.

"Don't be ridiculous! Deirdre can't get along without you. You know that. And I need you." Berringer, who had been gazing out at the pools of artificial light in the gardens, seemed to be caught by this last remark. His head raised. His pale eyes fixed on Stephen, who was much too angry to care. "You know I need your influence with my wife; so stop being so stubborn about it. Come along. Where is that thing you were wearing around your waist? Is it still in the room with Deirdre? Will you be cold?"

To avoid quarrelling in front of these two interested and no doubt hostile witnesses, I said as quietly as I could, "I'll go with you and kiss Deirdre good night. Maybe I can keep her from worrying about her condition." As we left the room, I looked back. The two men said nothing to each other. They might have been in different rooms, except that Pelhitt had his typical nervous tension about Berringer.

In the hall Stephen walked rapidly, taking my arm. I don't think he knew how fast he was walking. I had to run to keep beside him.

"She will be all right . . . won't she? Deirdre is going to be fine after a rest?"

"God, I don't know! She looked so little there. So helpless. Like a kitten. Hurt and shivering . . ."

In our mutual concern we understood each

other and said nothing more until we reached Deirdre's room, where the doctor had called in his nurse, a cool, efficient Chinese woman who looked as though nothing could sway or upset her. She seemed perfectly suited to her task.

Dr. Henry Lum was in the bathroom giving orders to two ambulance attendants. Deirdre looked drained, her young face still pallid, her eyes glittering and bright, but with a stiff look around her mouth, as if the memory of pain was still there. I assumed that whatever drugs had been given her had not dimmed her nervous energy. I left Stephen and went around to the other side of the bed where the nurse sat in a stiff, ladder-back chair. She glanced at me without expression. Stephen kissed his wife and kept her hand in his while Deirdre, obviously happy, turned her head on the high-piled pillows and looked at me.

"Wasn't that dumb of me? I got scared of Mr. Berringer."

"Why not?" I asked her, trying to ease the fright of that near collision.

I smiled. "You were smart — you reacted first. But you're going to be all right now. Your husband will take you back to Honolulu. If you do everything the doctor tells you, you will have all that nice time together, you and Stephen. Like a second honeymoon."

Her face clouded slightly. I wondered if I had gone too far in trying to reassure her.

"That will be *loverly*." She grinned in her

little-girl way. Then her free hand curled up and her forefinger beckoned me closer.

"Thank you, dear Judy. But you won't go far?" She was whispering now. The grin faded. "Judy? Where are you going now?"

"I'll go back and see about the meals and the cleaning at Sandalwood. I'll keep busy."

"No!" Everyone in the room jumped at the tone of her voice. I think I was more startled than anyone else.

"You are the mistress of that house, Deirdre. If you don't want me there, I won't go."

Her fingers clawed at my arm, pulling me closer. She whispered, "Don't go to the island alone. Not you, Judy. Please."

Bewildered, I backed away, stammering some sort of promise. I was terrified for fear I had somehow brought on another bout of palpitations.

Deirdre's shrill "No!" had brought the doctor into the bedroom. He shooed me out impatiently.

"You are in the way. Only the lady's husband should be present. Please go now."

I looked at Deirdre. She nodded to me. "Thanks, Judy . . . for understanding." Her tired smile flickered at me.

I kissed her forehead and then, passing Stephen, I left the room. Victor Berringer was in the hall, looking indifferent to my arrival, yet he was apparently expecting me.

"I see you have decided to be discreet, Miss

Cameron," he remarked cryptically, taking for granted that I would return to Ili-Ahi with William Pelhitt and himself, my chilly escort. He was implying, of course, that it was best for me not to remain with Stephen.

I was angered by this and felt as though I were being pulled between this man and the equally stubborn Stephen Giles. I suspected the root of Stephen's interest in me. He was drawn to me by our common love for my niece, and perhaps a little because he found he had married a girl with a child's emotions and realized that I was more mature. But he loved Deirdre. I felt certain that he did, and I meant to put no more obstacles in the way of their marriage.

Victor Berringer's interest in me was probably more sinister. I had little doubt that he believed me an accomplice, or at the very least, a witness to some plot against his daughter, since he had no real certainty that I had just arrived at Ili-Ahi. I decided, however, that there was no reason why I should have any difficulty in dealing with him. It also occurred to me that I couldn't stay at the Kaiana Hilton tonight in my badly water-stained dress, which I had torn during our attempt at easing Deirdre's pain in the boat.

I shrugged at Berringer's cryptic remark and went along with him. We picked up William Pelhitt in one of the terrace lobbies and drove around the island to the north coast, where a trio of local youngsters were prowling around the two speedboats moored at the rickety landing.

The state of this pier and the shed seemed to indicate to me one of the reasons why Stephen Giles was working so hard. He had recovered some of the power and the labor which had been lost by his impractical father, but ready cash was still a problem. When Stephen had married Deirdre, my brother's legal firm had kept a close watch on withdrawals from her estate. Except for a reasonable allowance of her own, Deirdre had never called upon any other monies. Since her marriage there were no withdrawals at all except near Stephen's birthday when Deirdre wrote asking for her allowance. From the date of her marriage to the present, her allowance had remained in the banks, drawing interest. I admired Stephen more than ever as I realized how he might have used that money legally, yet he had not done so. His father's failure was undoubtedly the motivating factor for him, giving him the pride that demanded he accomplish everything on his own.

The boats themselves were good-looking and recently painted, but Berringer grumbled. "If I intended to stay on that accursed island, I'd get one of those catamarans with a decent sail, and a couple of really fast boats." He strode ahead of us along the little pier and William pulled me back.

"Why did he come over to Kaiana this late in the evening, do you think?"

I had no idea. I couldn't entirely focus on this conversation. I kept wondering how Deirdre was doing. Would she be all right? How serious had the attack been? I asked Bill finally, "What did Mr. Berringer do while I was in my niece's room?"

"Made a phone call." He shrugged. "That's all."

I jumped nervously when I found Victor Berringer had turned and come back for us. He was almost at my elbow when he asked, "Are you coming?"

I nodded and William Pelhitt hustled along after us. I was rapidly beginning to understand this gray demon's deadly effect on Pelhitt.

Berringer lifted me down and then let me find my own place in the boat. This time the lights were fixed to show us a clear path ahead, but we were also helped by the fact that the moon had risen and the low mist shrouding the bay was now gone.

I waited until Berringer had started the motor and we were zooming out across the bay before I said to him, "Too bad you weren't able to carry out your plans tonight, Mr. Berringer."

Berringer stared at me, and he smiled that peculiar, thin-lipped smile that had no connection whatever with his eyes. The only advantage of traveling with Victor Berringer was that we reached our destination in record time, even though we were soaked through by the spray of the churned-up bay.

William Pelhitt helped me up to the little wharf under the copper-shaded light and then tried to assist our navigator, who waved him aside impatiently. While I waited for the two men, I took a few steps toward the steep path to Sandalwood. The area was intensely dark. The moonlight hadn't risen high enough to cut through the jungle vegetation only a few yards away. Pelhitt pointed over my shoulder at the gigantic *apé-apé* leaves flapping in the night air.

"Like elephant ears, aren't they?"

They were so eerie. They reminded me of all the insect and bird life around us. During the next minute or two when I looked into that foliage in a gingerly way, it seemed that all the little creatures hidden in the midnight dark were softly rustling and moving through plant life that was entirely strange to me.

I was relieved when Victor Berringer joined us and we started up the path together. I felt that although he probably did not constitute a danger himself, he certainly was a formidable obstacle to any other dangers.

He asked me suddenly, "Will you be staying at Sandalwood alone tonight?"

"The servants will be there." I wondered at his question. His manner did not suggest an interest or sympathy with my welfare.

"Then the servants do sleep at the main house?"

"Some do. Others, as you know, Mr. Berringer, go home to Kaiana or to the village across the island."

We had passed beyond the tiny creek that crawled away through the jungle toward the thunderous gulch, and were climbing the last yards of the path with Sandalwood House above us. I was anxious to reach the privacy of my own room. At the same time I couldn't help feeling some gratitude toward William Pelhitt and Berringer. Their presence was preferable to finding myself alone on the path at this hour.

The door beside the ground floor *lanai* was locked when Berringer tried it, but the front door opened easily under his hand. I ducked beneath his outstretched arm, thanked him and waved good night to William Pelhitt who had followed us up on the veranda. He gave me a half-hearted little salute. Berringer glanced from me to Bill Pelhitt, his pale eyebrows raised, then said brusquely to Pelhitt, "Well, come along. It's an Olympic marathon to the local Hawaiian paradise."

I locked the door as they stepped off the veranda and onto the grass before the *emu,* but I watched them until they were actually on the path to the Hawaiian village. I pitied William Pelhitt and disliked Berringer, and I supposed that was the extent of my feelings. But I was suspicious of them too. The only odd thing they did in those minutes after they left me was to start on a short-cut through the Sandalwood *heiau* with its unfinished bungalows. At the last second they swerved, turned and went the long way around the grove. Finally, their figures vanished in the foliage that threaded itself over their heads on the village path.

The hall lights were on downstairs. I was grateful for that, but with the electric situation what it was on Ili-Ahi, these lights were dim enough to conjure up shadows in every corner out of all proportion. I was ashamed of my own cowardice as I hurried past the empty, darkened living room. Hearing nothing that suggested anyone else might be present in the house, I began to wish I had gone back to Oahu with the plane that carried Deirdre and Stephen. Maybe I could then have gone out to stay with the Nagatas.

I started up the stairs, heard soft steps behind me, and nearly screamed as I grabbed at the bannister and swung around. Mr. Yee, Michiko's uncle, stood on the bottom step, wrapped in a flannel bathrobe, yet managing to give an appearance of majestic disapproval.

"When it passed midnight, miss, it was thought you would all remain in Honolulu. May I ask — will Mr. Stephen and Mrs. Stephen be here for breakfast?"

"No," I said. "I'm afraid not." I took a long, uneven breath, wanting to laugh hysterically at the scare he had given me. I explained that Deirdre was ill in Honolulu.

He received the news as I might have expected, with complete equanimity.

"Very well."

I said "good night" but he did not reply. He

simply padded off to some room on the ground floor. Greatly relieved at the presence of another human being in the big house, I went on up past Stephen's and Deirdre's rooms to my own. When I had gone in, snapped on the light and locked my door, I became aware of just how tired I was.

Deirdre had looked so pale, so helpless and young, as Stephen said. And she had looked that way once before, the morning of her mother's death. . . .

I won't think of that, I told myself, angrily pushing away the memory. I'll go to bed, get a good night's sleep, and things will look more cheerful in the morning.

When I got into bed I lay there almost too tired, too drained to sleep for a little while. By lying there absolutely still, with the window open above the steepest sector of the path, which lay below me now bright in the moonlight, I could almost block out the distant roar of the falls into the Ili-Ahi gulch and imagine I heard twitterings and rustling somewhere. The world might be asleep, but the denizens of the thick foliage out there were disturbed. Inside the house a light snapped off somewhere downstairs. Probably Mr. Yee's light, I decided, as one particular glimmer outside had flickered and vanished, leaving another patch of darkness.

I lay there stupidly worrying, first about Deirdre's health and then about her future. I hoped when she recovered, she would have grown up enough emotionally to want to establish a full relationship with her husband. But that was their affair, after all. Another worry was my own future. I would have to leave here as soon as Deirdre recovered from her present attack. There were complications in that, too. A condition of my parole had been my employment with Stephen Giles, and I knew for a certainty when I saw Deirdre's eyes tonight that I must not have any further connection with her husband in any way.

If the red tape about my freedom could be cleared away, I wanted to go to some area where I was totally unknown. I hadn't found myself yet, or found the life to which I wanted to devote my future. All I had thought of during the months they were working on my freedom was the post as "housekeeper" at Sandalwood. I had pictured myself keeping busy, accomplishing something so that my freedom would be worthwhile, but I had never seen myself as interfering in Deirdre's life. Now, all that had changed. I had done considerable secretarial work during my imprisonment and this was a field I might pursue. I had taken most of the "super's" dictation in prison. She had been a hard, wise, toughened woman with a streak of understanding that made me think of the women in pioneer days.

While the surface of my mind planned my future and the rest of it kept praying for Deirdre's recovery, I went to sleep. It was only afterward that I remembered being disturbed once, just at that time of sleepy confusion shortly after I had dozed off in the first hour of my sleep. I heard what appeared to be the shrill cry of a tropical night bird. Startled, I listened and several seconds later there were sharp, crackling noises, as of branches breaking. I wondered whether the sudden flight of the bird had been precipitated by the breaking of the branches, or whether the bird's sudden flight had caused the breakage. It must have been a very large bird, I thought. Unable just to lie there imagining things, I got up and went to the window. Even the breeze had died down. The scene reminded me of some primeval glade, absolutely still in the unearthly golden light of the moon.

I stood there long enough to find myself chilled. Then I got into bed, still listening, still half asleep, but I heard nothing else except the distant roar of the creek pouring down into the gulch. I drifted off again and slept soundly until my doorknob was tried several times and I awoke to find it was ten o'clock on a muggy, sunny morning. Someone, having failed to get into my room because the door was locked, rapped a couple of times. Then Nelia Perez's cheerful voice called out, "Breakfast tray, Miss Cameron."

I hurried to the door, unlocked it, and the girl came in with her tray. She seemed surprised at the locked door.

"You are afraid of burglars, Miss Cameron?

You needn't be, here on Ili-Ahi."

"Sorry. I must have done it automatically."

"Oh, sure. I guess you —" she blinked, looking just a little uncomfortable. "Hope you like your eggs three minutes. Mr. Yee says no civilized human being could possibly want his eggs any other way."

"Just right. But really, I don't expect to be served in bed every day. I'll be leaving as soon as Mrs. Stephen is well."

"Poor little Mrs. Stephen. You know," Nelia Perez leaned toward me confidentially. "It's funny about her."

"How do you mean?"

"Well, she locked her door too." She giggled. "Not much of a marriage when a bride locks her door every night." I must have frowned because she added in a hurry, "Of course, she might not be locking the door against Mr. Stephen. I sure wouldn't. But what other reason could she have?"

I drank my coffee absently while I considered this idea, which I realized now was not new to me.

"Nelia, do you think Deirdre is afraid of someone?"

"Or something. I wouldn't be surprised if that's it."

"But what then?"

"Ghosts, maybe. Imaginary things."

I said after a minute, "I have learned to believe in very few things, and ghosts are certainly not among those few."

She cocked her head on one side and studied me. I turned and almost involuntarily looked toward the unfinished cottages of the Sandal-wood grove. She noted this.

"All I can say, Miss Cameron, is there's been something wrong about that grove ever since Mr. Stephen's father started to build in it. I don't say I believe in ghosts and that stuff, but I'm not about to tangle with Mistress Pelé, or Lono, or the ancient *kahunas* who laid down the curse on anybody who — what's the word?"

"Defiled it?" I asked ironically. It was a very bad thing the way this superstition was spreading. Whether it might be a good or bad idea to bring tourism to Ili-Ahi was not my business. But I felt there was endless harm in this spreading superstition.

I got up and went to the window and tried to make out the grove. I saw the cabin corners, roofs, and through the clumps of trees with their undergrowth daily growing thicker, I saw the roof with the dry rushes torn and littered. A man had died there, falling from that roof only days ago.

"I'd better be going," Nelia reminded me, backing away to the door while she kept an eye on me interestedly. She knew what I was thinking about. "Mr. Yee is pretty burned this morning anyway, what with the household being shorthanded."

Not thinking much about it, I said, "Too bad.

Maybe I can help in some way. Is it Mrs. Mitsushima's day off?"

"No. She's here. It's Kekua Moku who's taken off. She usually helps with the laundry once a week. Sheets and napkins and all that. Little Mitsu does the ironing of anything that isn't permanent press."

"Do you have a washing machine?"

"Oh, sure. But with our power what it is, it'd probably be quicker if we beat our sheets against the rocks in the gulch!"

I laughed and promised as I returned to my breakfast tray, "I'll go down and see what I can do."

As she reached the door she thanked me. "But all the same," she said, "Kekua's going to catch it, even if she does have Queen Ilima for a mother. She only works here part time and keeps demanding a better job, but last week she didn't come to work because she was breezing around in a catamaran. And the way she's been living it up lately, she'll get the —" Nelia Perez pantomimed a slash across her throat. She went out into the hall and closed the door.

I felt guilty at having awakened so late and by having allowed my breakfast to be served here, but when I glanced at my bedside clock again, I had a fresh worry. Surely, Stephen might have called to tell me how Deirdre was this morning. I hadn't even asked for the phone number where I could reach anyone on Oahu. As I showered, I remembered that Ito Nagata was the Giles's physician. They must have called him in, at least for a consultation. Having taken the tray down to the kitchen, I went into the hall, found a list of emergency numbers typed on a leather-framed card and called the Nagatas on Oahu.

Michiko answered after several rings. She sounded either impatient or uneasy until she heard my voice.

"Oh, it's you, Judy. You must be frantic. I've heard about Deirdre. They've called here several times trying to get Ito. He's still not back."

"How is she? Nobody has told me a thing."

With her usual common sense, Michiko assured me at once, "She is doing very well. So you may as well calm down. It was just palpitations. Nothing serious."

"Thank God!" I leaned against the little wicker telephone stand, so relieved my knees felt weak. "But you said Ito isn't at the hospital?"

"No. They called here only minutes after Ito left late last evening. He took the last flight to Kaiana and was to be brought across the bay by two of the Hawaiians from the Ili-Ahi village. There was a woman in labor — Ilima Moku's sister. Very important in their hierarchy."

"I had no idea. That must be why Kekua didn't show up today. Is Ito still here on Ili-Ahi?"

"Probably on his way home soon. He said he'd call me from your place or when he reaches Kaiana. Incidentally, if the child is a boy the poor kid is to be called Kamehameha!"

"Not another *K*. I can't keep them all straight as it is."

She laughed and then asked me if I was staying alone at Sandalwood. I understood her meaning, or perhaps I was just hypersensitive.

"So far. But I won't be staying here after Stephen returns."

"Don't be silly. I can't see you going all out with Deirdre's husband. Although I think a nice, exciting love affair is just what you need."

Too late, I thought. Once again I have fallen in love with the wrong man. But the first time my disastrous choice only affected me. The second would destroy the person I loved best in the world. It was not going further.

"Anyway, remember our invitation. It's genuine. Besides —"

I could almost see her frank smile as she added, "if you've got the guest room, Ito's two aunts from Osaka can't pile in on us, as they show signs of doing."

I was amused at Michiko's honesty and promised I would give her invitation some thought. Then we said good-bye and I went into the laundry to sort out the linens for the washing machine. Little Mrs. Mitsushima was upset at seeing me there and assured me that she intended to do the wash as well as the ironing. I pointed out that we would finish more quickly if I helped, and Kekua Moku would have the advantage of being present at home when her little cousin was born.

But Mrs. Mitsushima said this was not so and begged my pardon profusely for contradicting me.

"Kekua is not with the family, please. They call two times. Not here."

"You mean her family called Sandalwood about Kekua? What did they say? She stayed at home last night, didn't she?"

"No, miss."

She walked away and I hardly knew what to say. There were a dozen reasons why the girl might not have stayed at home, especially at a time like this when relatives and doctors and anxious fathers would be all over the place. Still, I wished we could all be sure about her whereabouts. For all her self-confidence she did not seem old enough to be spending her nights quite so casually.

Meanwhile, I had work to do and was glad to be accomplishing something physical, even if it was only the household washing.

When the first load was through its cycle, I asked Mrs. Mitsushima where these linens were dried, since she insisted politely that the small electric dryer would not do for some of the special linens.

"When no guests come, miss, the sheets dry on the *lanai*. Little things — hooks — the cord hangs on the hooks. There is much room — three lines there, three on the *lanai* above."

She went out with me and we fastened the cords the length of the two *lanais*. A slight breeze rustled over the treetops of the gulch but otherwise the day was still hot and sticky. We took the first sheets to the upper *lanai* and pinned the first doubled sheet along the line. Mrs. Mitsushima was exceedingly careful and I found that I too was soon preoccupied with matching the hems so that they would meet. It was a pity, I thought, that we couldn't study all that fantastic array of tropic beauty so close below us. But I knew that if I stopped to look down I would be captivated and unable to go on working. As we started to hang the second sheet closest to the low rail, Mrs. Mitsushima took a clothespin off the top of the rail and pinned it as I did at my corners of the sheet.

She reached for another wooden pin and her oblique dark eyes looked over the rail. The most horrifying thing happened to her face as I glanced at her. Her face appeared to spread, especially about the mouth, until she seemed to be shrieking madly, yet not a sound came from her throat. The pin fell over the rail. Then the end of the sheet trailed and before I could reach her, she crumpled to the floor of the *lanai* in a faint.

It was not until I had lifted her head and shoulders up and was yelling like an idiot, "What is it? What is the matter?" that I thought to look over the rail into the gulch, where the fall of the Ili-Ahi river collected in flowery, rocky pools. What appeared to be a life-sized doll in a miniskirt and halter lay within one of those pools. The water bubbled and foamed around the golden arms and legs.

Fourteen

I must have stared at the little pool far below for several minutes. I felt stupefied. All I could think of as Mrs. Mitsushima began to moan was that Ingrid Berringer had been found at last. But Mrs. Mitsushima gave me my second shock of those terrible few minutes.

"Kekua down there. She falls, you think?"

I didn't know what to do first. . . . Kekua? Logically, it would have been Ingrid Berringer — *she* was the missing girl. But, of course, Kekua had been missing since yesterday. Young, vital Kekua, so used to this island and Sandalwood's dangers, was much too sure-footed to slip and fall in that way. Yet she had done so. It was an appalling accident. Even from this height it seemed evident that she was dead. No living person could lie in that unnatural, twisted position.

I got Mrs. Mitsushima into a chair at the back of the *lanai* and rushed in to the hall telephone. The Moku family were not on the emergency list but I found a listing that might be helpful: *Village Store — Fred Kalanimoku.* I called this number and after an agonizing wait, heard the proprietor's easy, pleasant voice.

"Can someone call Dr. Ito Nagata to the phone?" I asked, hearing my own voice sounding breathless and panic-stricken.

"Dr. Nagata is on his way to the Sandalwood dock in the jeep. Maybe you will see him on the way. A new Kamehameha is born here. You know about that?"

"No. I didn't. Congratulations. I'm very — happy for everyone." I didn't have the courage to tell him about Kekua.

I set the telephone back and called Mr. Yee and Nelia Perez. Mr. Yee was cross because I had interfered with his careful examination of a problem oven. When I told him about Kekua he caught his breath but did not panic or even get excited in any way.

"I will find some of the men in the fields and we will descend the gulch."

"Thank you very much, Mr. Yee. I didn't know what to do. I was frantic."

Mr. Yee nodded gravely. "That is understandable. You are a female."

I was so grateful to him, I let this pass. Then I asked Nelia Perez to take care of the dried linens in the machine, while I went out to catch Ito Nagata who would probably be driven here along the cliff-side road. As I started, Nelia called to me.

"I forgot to say, Miss Cameron, Mr. Stephen just phoned. He was in a big hurry but he wanted you to know Mrs. Stephen is doing well."

Thank God for that! Then I remembered the girl's body in the flowery pool of the Ili-Ahi gulch. "They had better not come back until Kekua is . . ." I couldn't finish. The accident was

240

too horrible, and coming at this time, when Kekua's family was celebrating one of the happiest occasions, it seemed even more ghastly.

Nelia said, "Mr. Stephen wanted you to know he'd call again this afternoon and talk to you."

"Don't tell him about this yet."

"Okay, if you say so. I can't figure how she could've been so clumsy. Kekua wasn't like that." Nelia looked a bit pale, but she was by no means overcome. She made her observation with a kind of scientific detachment.

Tearing my apron off, I hurried across the grass and into the grove. This would cut off several hundred yards from the village trail.

Through the grove I could see half a dozen men and women striding up from the boat landing toward the village. All of them were obviously part Hawaiian or purebloods. They had the deep, polished mahogany skin and the regal, straight-backed walk that made them wear their weight so well. They were all happy, all obviously on their way to meet the newest "Kamehameha." I noticed that the little individual streams on the way to the village were clogged with debris and one of the foot bridges had been crushed, possibly by the boulder that had fallen and had come to rest against a tree stump.

I passed the bungalow set deepest in the grove, with its back window frames facing out on the clearing at the end of the cliff road. I didn't have long to wait. The jeep belonging to one of the

Hawaiians from the village bounced around the last cliff and into the clearing. Moku himself was at the wheel. I hadn't counted on that. Ito Nagata was with him. I signaled to him and even before the jeep stopped with a terrific jolt, he leaped out and came to me, taking my hands.

"You look awful, Judy. What has happened? It is Deirdre, I suppose."

"Yes. That, too." Moku was grinning down at us. I tried to smile but couldn't. I whispered, "Moku's daughter Kekua is at the bottom of the gulch." It was so bluntly said that Ito started and for a few seconds didn't quite understand me. He looked exhausted. He had probably been up for the past thirty hours.

"Dead?" he asked as he reached up into the jeep for his surgical bag. I nodded. I couldn't get any words out. I was too conscious of Kekua's father sitting there above us with his beautiful smile lighting his dark face. I said abruptly: "I'll go back. Can you tell him . . . please?"

"You are absolutely certain?"

I wasn't. I only knew what the little figure had looked like from the height of Sandalwood's creaking old *lanais*. I started back the way I had come, through the Hawaiians' sacred grove. Dr. Nagata and Moku took the village path, Moku still avoiding the grove, and yet they reached Sandalwood before I did. I saw that Moku knew. The strong face looked darker, set in a new heaviness. Moku and Ito disappeared around the east side of Sandalwood, where there ap-

242

peared to be a trail down the side of the falls where the Ili-Ahi river tumbled into the gulch below.

By the time I got to the edge of the steep path up from the landing and got a clear view of that flower-and-rock strewn pool, I saw that Mr. Yee was down there with two other men.

"Be careful!" Nelia Perez called to me from the lower *lanai*.

I stopped abruptly. I was just below the *lanai* on the gulch side of the steep landing path. There was a spot here about two yards long where the shrubbery had broken away and apparently fallen into the pools and jungle vegetation far below. Before this breakaway in the wall of hibiscus and bougainvillea, the bushes had presented what seemed to be a safety wall. Now that they were gone the place was revealed in all its danger. A few steps more on crumbling soil and anyone might plunge into the gulch, including myself.

As I stood there studying that break in the foliage, I remembered the crackle of branches I had heard in the night. It seemed all the more terrible that I had heard Kekua Moku fall and had turned over and gone back to sleep. But what had she been doing out here last night at — what time was the accident? I hadn't looked at my clock, I could only guess now.

But the greatest mystery still remained: her reason for wandering around out here alone at that hour.

Or had she been alone?

Nelia Perez had dropped a clothespin. I looked up. Clearly, she was nervous and her fingers shook but she had gotten on with the work and I found myself equally anxious to try and keep occupied. I went in the door beside the golden shower bushes and helped little Mrs. Mitsushima finish the laundry. When I went out to change the sheets on the lines, I was more nervous and shaken than ever. I couldn't forget that I must have heard the girl die.

When Ito Nagata and Mr. Yee had finished their examination, Moku quietly insisted on carrying Kekua's broken body up from the pool. He would not leave Kekua at Sandalwood, even briefly. He did not even enter the house. As I went to Moku to try and express something of our feelings, I heard his deep, powerful voice very clearly: "My wife was right and I was wrong. None in my family should have worked at Sandalwood after the grove was profaned. It is ended. No more friends. We do not set foot on this ground again. Dr. Nagata, you will tell this to Mr. Stephen."

I tried to speak to him but Moku turned away from me with Kekua in his arms. He had partially wrapped her body in his own bright aloha shirt and Ito Nagata's jacket, and his massive head was erect. He did not look down at the light burden in his arms. Ito passed me on his way to the telephone in the hall. He gave my shaking hand a quick, understanding squeeze. I wanted to thank him, but I knew I didn't have to say anything. That too he understood.

Apparently, the Hawaiian villagers themselves were going to arrange for Kekua's funeral and burial. Ito called a Honolulu number on Oahu instead of the local Kaiana Island people across the bay. I realized that something besides the accident troubled him. I heard him use the title "lieutenant" and wondered if he were talking to the police. Afterward, I started into the dining room across the hall to give him privacy, but he motioned me back as he called Michiko and explained his delay. He told her briefly of Kekua's death, and I could tell that Michiko was compassionate enough not to ask questions about the tragedy. She asked how I was taking it, and sent a message to me before urging her husband to return home soon. Ito grinned at me faintly before promising.

"I will. I'll get back and catch up on some sleep, I hope." He replaced the telephone and added, "She says if things get too rough, don't forget she wants you to keep my aunts away!"

It was dear of her and I said so. Then I volunteered to get Ito some coffee or whisky, but he opted for tea. He drank the scalding brew as I sat down across from him at the huge dining-room table.

"Ito, you think there's something odd about Kekua's fall."

He looked at me over the rim of the cup. I had a curious sense — very unusual because of the

relationship between my old friend and me —
that he was being deliberately bland and impas-
sive.

"Not in the least. It seems very simple to me. It
was Moku who wondered if it were, in fact, an
accident. I think the girl got too near the edge,
slipped, and fell. Probably she was looking at
something below, and . . ."

"She couldn't have been. The bushes covered
the view of the gulch at that spot. Anyway, why
should she do that at such an hour? It would be
dark down there. Nothing to see, even if she
were farther along, at the corner of the
building."

Ito studied the tea leaves. "We have no idea
what time it happened. We couldn't know for
sure without further study and an autopsy. Real
life doesn't turn up those snap judgments coro-
ners and medical examiners are always making
in detective novels."

I took a breath, hesitated, then blurted out,
"But we do know. Actually, we know the very
minute she slipped and fell."

"What!" I had startled him with that.

"What I mean is," I explained, "I heard it
happen, I'm almost sure. But I didn't look at the
clock."

I had his full attention now. He was taut with
suspense. "Did you see anyone . . . what did you
see exactly?"

I explained then about the sounds and how I
had gone back to sleep afterward. "I'm sure

that's when it happened. The only thing is . . . what was she doing out near the gulch at that hour?"

He considered my question. "Conceivably, she was returning from a visit across the bay. Before she fell through those bushes, there appeared to be a fairly strong barrier along the path. And no one knew better than the Mokus where it was in the gulch."

Since he hadn't brought up a possibility that occurred to me during his questions, I suggested, "Could she have just come from some meeting? With a boyfriend, for instance?"

"Do you have a candidate in mind?"

"Yes," I said slowly. "I am thinking of one. When Mr. Berringer and William Pelhitt arrived here the first time, she made it pretty obvious she admired Victor Berringer."

"But he wasn't even on the island last night. Ilima Moku told me this morning that he had gone over to Kaiana to meet someone."

I realized that Ito Nagata knew very little about Deirdre's attack, about our meeting with Berringer in the bay, and the fact that he had returned with me and with William Pelhitt. He knew very little, yet he should have seen Berringer in the Hawaiian village, for I had watched Berringer and Pelhitt take the trail to the village after they left me last night. But had they turned around and retraced their steps, going back to Kaiana? There was the phone call Berringer made while I was with Deirdre and the doctor in that hotel room. Setting up a later meeting, one that was secret from me, and even, perhaps, from Pelhitt? Actually, we couldn't be sure where anyone was the previous night, except Ito and the expectant mother, of course.

A short time later I walked with Ito Nagata to the boat landing. We were both surprised to see one of the Hawaiian villagers there. He explained to the doctor, "I am to take you across the bay. It was agreed when you came to care for Liliha, Queen Ilima's sister."

"Thank you. I appreciate it. I'll just be able to make the afternoon plane."

The Hawaiian got into a handsome boat that I recognized as the one Berringer had used and criticized the previous night. Ito and I said good-bye.

"We'll be getting together very soon, Judy. And don't worry about Deirdre. I'll drop in at the hospital on my way home."

"Don't be silly. You haven't been to bed since — well — when?"

He smiled. "No. I had two or three hours in the night. They gave me a little place to myself, and I made the most of it. I can sleep anywhere and at any time — always could. Wayne used to say that was why I never made the squad at UCLA. I'd go to sleep in the first huddle."

He stepped into the boat and I heard him ask the Hawaiian something. The young man's voice reached me across the water as I turned away.

"I am told to warn you, Dr. Nagata. Sandal-

248

wood is under *kapu.* You understand what is *kapu?*"

"Perfectly," Ito said in a sharp voice. Then the motor started up, and I walked away rapidly.

I didn't know how things would be if the entire Giles properties were put under a curse. The *kapu* of the old-time Hawaiians was as strong as the more familiar "tabu" that we mainlanders associated with the history of the Polynesians. I thought grimly that Sandalwood had already been bad luck for Stephen's father, for Deirdre, for Kekua Moku, and possibly even for Ingrid Berringer.

But this was carrying superstition too far. There was no evidence that Miss Berringer had been here more than once or twice. One might as well say Honolulu had been placed under *kapu,* since she had certainly spent more time in the city. Why I should be thinking about Ingrid Berringer when young Kekua had just lost her life so tragically, I didn't know. Their only connection was Sandalwood. . . . And Sandalwood, like the grove, was under a curse. Was that the connection then? The bad luck had spread to so many I began to ask myself if Ingrid Berringer actually had been murdered, as Berringer obviously believed.

By the time I reached the house, Mrs. Mitsushima, looking very frightened, informed me that Mr. Stephen had called twice and was on the line again, demanding to speak with Miss Cameron.

I ran inside the house which seemed extraordinarily silent in spite of the roar of the falls beyond the far side of the building. I could hear Stephen's voice through the receiver as I picked up the telephone.

"What the devil is going on there? Answer me, somebody!"

I answered. "Stephen, it's a long story. Young Kekua Moku slipped and fell into the Ili-Ahi gulch last night."

"Oh, God, no! That child?"

"I'm afraid so."

"But how could she slip? The approach is masked in every direction by heavy foliage. That poor kid! I'll have to get back right away. I've got to see Moku — see what we can do to help."

"No. I'm afraid not." I explained about the *kapu.* I think I had a hope that Stephen would find this ridiculous and assure me the superstitions of the villagers meant nothing.

Stephen started to say something angrily, stopped, and revealed the frustration that gripped him in this new problem.

"But I've always been their friend. The family has gone overboard to support their independence in every way. They must know how many times we have used every ounce of influence with the territorial legislature, and later the state, to keep outsiders from meddling with their way of life."

I knew that the Giles family even paid Ito Nagata's fees when he was called over on important cases among the Hawaiians. But I also knew nothing would breed resentment more than the paternalistic efforts of the Giles family. I interrupted him.

"Please, how is Deirdre?"

The question reminded him of my anxiety over her and all the truculence was gone. The warmth and concern that were the other side to his quick-tempered nature made me once more aware of my feelings toward him, those feelings that I would have to hide very carefully.

"Judith, I'm terribly sorry. Actually, I called to tell you she is doing well. Every time I've stepped into her room, she's perked up so much. You would hardly know her. The doctors seem to think she has been under a good deal of stress lately. The responsibility of a new household, and — a life she wasn't used to. But she will be fine. Absolutely fine, given a little time."

I was so thankful I managed to forget our other problems for a few minutes. "Maybe if Deirdre could spend some time with you in your Waikiki apartment before returning here, it might help to ease the problem."

"But that suite is an office. Nobody could actually live there. That's no good, Judith. I hate the Waikiki thing. Not a home at all. My home is at Ili-Ahi. It always has been there."

"*Your* home, Stephen."

In a chastened voice he agreed, adding hopefully, "But she liked it when she first saw it. Ito said — by the way, what happened about Ito Nagata?"

"He presided at the birth of Kamehameha Kalanimoku. Ito thinks mother and future king will be fine."

He laughed. "He will have a lot to live up to with that title, poor kid. Was Michiko there?"

"Michiko? No. You called her in the night, didn't you?"

"Yes, but there was no answer until seven this morning. I thought she and Ito were somewhere together. Then, when she answered the phone this morning she told me where Ito had gone, and I supposed she had returned alone. Not that it matters."

I said, "Just a misunderstanding on my part. Please give my love to Deirdre. Tell her I'll mind the store until she gets back. Then she can take over, because I do have a lot of things to do, a lot of places to see." How very odd about Michiko! However, as Stephen said, it was not our concern.

Stephen was angry again. "You agreed. And I need — we need you! Please, don't talk about leaving."

"I've got to hang up now. Someone is calling me. I'm terribly sorry about Kekua. Perhaps if someone talked to the Hawaiian families at the funeral, they would understand how sorry we are. Meanwhile, Nelia and Mrs. Mitsushima and I can handle things here. And Mr. Yee is an excellent organizer."

"I'll bet he is! I'll get home as soon as possible. We can't leave you with everything in your hands."

"No, no! It isn't necessary. We were getting on perfectly well, until Kekua's accident." I said a hasty good-bye and left him on the line. I was not precisely lying when I said I was needed in the house. I heard loud voices in the kitchen. Obviously, Mr. Yee and Nelia Perez were not going to work as a team without a middleman. I intervened as calmly as I could.

"Mr. Yee, I have just received a call from Mr. Stephen, and I believe he may not be here until late tonight or tomorrow; so we had better clear up the work now and not make too many plans about tomorrow until we find out just what Mr. Stephen has in mind."

"But, Miss," Nelia Perez began, "even if he isn't coming, we'd better see about some more help."

Mr. Yee and I looked at her. "Why, for heaven's sake?" I asked. "None of the family is in Sandalwood. There are no guests."

"Sorry, but Mrs. Mitsushima has taken off. Says she is not going to hang around where they've put a curse on the place. And as for guests, I'm afraid there are guests. Two of them. Mr. Berringer and Mr. — the other one."

What were they doing prowling around here? They knew they were not welcome. From the very first, Berringer had made it clear he suspected Deirdre of doing away with his daughter.

253

And William Pelhitt felt much the same about Stephen.

Feeling like a complete hypocrite, I went out on the veranda and welcomed both men with smiles. William Pelhitt seemed glad to see me but Berringer was obviously here on his own business. I hadn't eaten lunch and it was too late now, so I suggested we have cocktails. I arranged in the kitchen to have some crackers and cheese and macadamia nuts brought out to us.

"Where is Mrs. Mitsushima going?" I asked Nelia as we put together the plate of hors d'oeuvre.

Mr. Yee heard us. He said disdainfully, "The female will be taken across the bay by someone from the Hawaiian group. I believe she leaves us upon the advice of Ilima Moku."

Nelia and I glanced at each other uneasily. "Has Mrs. Moku been by Sandalwood since her daughter was taken away?" As I spoke I remembered painfully how much Ilima Moku cared about her daughter, how she influenced and dominated her that first night when I arrived here.

Mr. Yee said, "She would not come here again, miss. The *kapu* is in effect. I believe the message came from a farmer named Ling in the papaya grove."

When the two guests and I were seated on the veranda over our drinks, Berringer came to the point as bluntly as usual: "I won't mince words. Miss Cameron — Judith —" Bill Pelhitt frowned at his use of my first name but rubbed his head immediately afterward, and I wondered if he was afraid his companion would disapprove of even this small sign of private opinion.

"I imagine you came here with some definite matter in mind," I interrupted. "Or did you come because of the grief in the village? You would not want to intrude, I imagine." I must have said this ironically, though I hadn't intended to do so when I started, but he gave me a complacent little smile.

"Quite true on both counts. You are a rare woman, Judith."

I did not ask what he meant by "rare." I wondered why he was buttering me up. It sounded like something he had pulled out of his collection of soothing sayings for effect. Bill Pelhitt explained hurriedly, "We've been discussing the visit you and I made to the Asami house. Vic would like to know your version of her story about the fellow who visited Ingrid."

I laughed, though I wasn't feeling amused. "How like you, Mr. Berringer! You are just like a bulldog. Is it the description you want? I'm sure I remember it word for word."

"I have every confidence that you do." His icy voice was clipped and distinct. "What was your impression of the words my daughter spoke to her visitor?"

"You remember," Bill prompted me. "She called him an idiot. A moron."

"Idiot and moron. Yes, I think that was what

Mrs. Asami said," I agreed.

Victor Berringer put his glass on the table.

"Really rather odd the way my mind works. You might even call it devious." He took a sip of his drink while I waited with a quickened heartbeat. "What I keep asking myself is why my daughter would call this fellow an idiot, or insane."

Bill opened his mouth. I think he was genuinely astonished. "Look here, Vic, I told you. I mean — Ingrid talks that way."

"What are you getting at, Mr. Berringer?" I asked, trying to sound calm.

"There is one person in Hawaii with whom my daughter was closely involved and whom she referred to in letters — rudely, but that is Ingrid! — as an idiot and a moron. I am speaking of your niece, Mrs. Stephen Giles."

"Are you picturing Deirdre disguised as a six-foot male leaving your daughter's bungalow as she was called 'idiot' and 'moron'?" I asked, smiling sweetly.

"This was a man, Vic!" Bill spelled it out. "A man. Mrs. Asami described him. Some kind of half-Hawaiian or half Oriental. She called *him* the idiot."

"Did she say that . . . precisely?" Berringer asked me, the silver pupils of his eyes focused on mine as if he were trying to read my mind, my suspicions, my thoughts and fears. "Or did she speak of an idiot? Did she say 'you are an idiot'? Or was she speaking to this fellow about someone with whom he was closely acquainted. Someone for whom he cared a great deal. And did she really say '*that* idiot'? Which so angered him that he threatened her and warned her never to approach his wife again?"

Fifteen

From the beginning of his little inquisition, I had been dreading his arrival at this point. If Berringer proceeded to investigate the Asamis' story on his own, he would know that Mrs. Asami had seen a Caucasian, and one remarkably like Stephen, who had left Ingrid while in a fury. If Ingrid Berringer actually was dead, Stephen had his own motive, disposition, and opportunity to kill this woman, especially after that threat to her overheard by Mrs. Asami.

But William Pelhitt — bless him — interrupted the dangerous silence which followed Berringer's accusation by pointing out a trifle drunkenly, "That doesn't quite fit, Vic, because Mrs. Asami said it was a fellow with Hawaiian blood. Half a . . . What was it, Judith? Half a-what?"

"Hapa-haole," I lied, ashamed of the lie, yet still anxious to keep Berringer from pursuing this idea. I didn't believe Stephen murdered Ingrid Berringer. I was almost certain . . . ninety-nine percent certain, at any rate, that he hadn't done such a thing. But the suspicion would bring him more grief and I wanted him to be happy. No! I wanted him and Deirdre to be happy.

Mr. Berringer seemed to understand the meaning of the pidgin-English expression, like so many others used daily by Hawaii's citizens, irrespective of their many races and nationalities. But I thought I had better add, "half Caucasian, I think it means."

While Bill Pelhitt downed his next martini rapidly and took a third from Nelia, Berringer took another cracker. I wondered at Bill's condition so soon after two drinks, but decided he must have been drinking before he came here. I wondered why he felt it necessary to remain in Berringer's difficult company so long when he would be much better off back in his home, thousands of miles from this formidable future father-in-law.

"So I am given to understand," Berringer said. "Meanwhile —" He swung around in his chair. "I seem to be the only human being left on this planet who cares what has become of my daughter."

"We care," I assured him, "only if harm has come to her."

"Vic, of course we care! I loved Ingrid," William tried to cover my chilly answer. But I felt that I had carried hypocrisy as far as my pride would let it go. The more I heard about Ingrid Berringer, the less I liked her. And at the moment my only feeling toward her was a resentment that she had caused so much pain and trouble to Deirdre and Stephen.

I stirred, started to get up, hoping they would take the hint and leave. When Berringer simply crossed his legs and took another long swallow of his Scotch, I challenged him directly.

"I meant to ask you, but somehow I forgot. Mr. Berringer, are you a man who loves the sea?"

That surprised him. "Tolerably. I don't think I understand."

There was a certain bitterness in my voice I couldn't quite subdue.

"I was thinking about your journeys across Kaiana Bay last night."

I know he suspected I was leading up to something unpleasant, but he couldn't quite decide what it was.

"Quite true. No one should know better than you and William here. I nearly ran you down. That damned motor! And the lights — totally inadequate. Practically no power whatever. I hope you've let your niece know how much I regret the affair. How is she doing now? Well, I hope." I nodded. "But you are getting at something else, aren't you?"

"That was not your only trip last night, was it, Mr. Berringer?"

"Certainly not, I returned with you. Escorted you to this door behind me here, as a matter of fact."

"I am talking about the third trip you made across the bay last night. Quite late." I thought he was going to deny that trip. I waited, holding my breath. Bill Pelhitt, drinking nervously, was as anxious as I, especially under the cold eye of Berringer, who shrugged and agreed calmly.

"That's true. I won't ask you where you found out — it's obvious. William, you will do us all a favor, one of these days, if you hustle yourself home. Home to New York, that is."

Bill Pelhitt reddened and started to say something but changed his mind. To our surprise he set his glass down sharply, got up and stalked off the veranda. Once he left the veranda he stumbled but kept on his feet. It was obvious that the drinks had hit him badly. I called to him, but he did not look back. I got up to try and make him understand I hadn't intended to get him in trouble. But Berringer stopped me by a remark that completely confused me.

"I can't imagine why it is important to you, Judith, but I am not hiding the fact that I went back to Kaiana last night. I went to meet someone. An employee. And in doing so, by the way, I saw an acquaintance of yours looking very furtive. She certainly didn't want me to see her."

"She?" I could think only of the servants at Sandalwood. It must have been one of them.

"Yes. The doctor's wife. What's-his-name — the Japanese fellow. It was his wife I saw at Kaiana City." He got up, finished his drink and stretched rather elaborately. "You will admit it is hard to miss anyone in a town with a population of about one hundred. A very pleasant drink. You make an excellent hostess."

I merely stared at him. I was trying to sort out this preposterous story he had told me. I finally thanked him with such indifference he obviously got the hint that I wanted him to leave. Unlike Bill Pelhitt and the entire population of the Hawaiian village, Mr. Berringer cut straight through the forbidden grove and met Bill far down the village path. They appeared to be arguing. Berringer seemed to be trying to get Bill to take the easterly cliff road. Perhaps he had a jeep parked there. But Bill was holding back with anger or drunken stubbornness. I didn't go in until the long, gaunt shadows of late afternoon melted around the two men.

I didn't want to go back into the house so soon. Because of our present problems, the ancient walls of Sandalwood gave me claustrophobia. I knew I wouldn't be able to think in there at the moment, and I had a great deal to figure out. I wanted to avoid both Bill and Mr. Berringer, so I avoided the direction they had followed. I had not yet seen the gulch at close quarters and decided I would try to find out just why Deirdre preferred that part of the house parallel to the river and the falls. It was very damp, very loud and, as I had seen from the window of Deirdre's little "studio," it was always dark, because of the heavy foliage. What did she find so fascinating out there?

I had enough common sense not to do anything dangerous or to venture down to the place where Kekua Moku's body had been found, but as it was not yet dark, I took this hour of dusk to follow the Ili-Ahi river. It divided into a dozen little streams, one bordering each unfinished cottage, and then it joined to pour over the sharp cliff's edge into the gulch below. The so-called sacred grove was extraordinarily still at this hour. I followed one particular stream, found the miniature Japanese bridge that had been broken by a falling boulder, and was forced to retrace my steps to find a way around the bridge.

It wasn't difficult. I simply stepped over this stream with its floating debris from the rains high on the mountain above the Hawaiian village. Some day it would be exciting to follow the river to its mountain source. Some day . . . But of course, I wasn't going to be at Sandalwood in the future. How beautiful it was here in the grove with exquisite, pale green foliage lacing overhead, and the wild grass and ferns soft underfoot!

One of those fern fronds was lumpy. I took another step, then looked back. I had stepped on a gilt leather sandal lace. It seemed an odd lace for one of the men who worked on the Sandalwood *heiau*. I was sure it belonged to a woman. That would eliminate every woman on the island except those employed at Sandalwood. It belonged to Nelia Perez. I couldn't recall that Mrs. Mitsushima wore sandals. No. I distinctly recalled those Japanese *getas* that she wore. And none of the women from the Hawaiian village would dare to enter the grove that was sacred to their people. It must belong to Nelia.

I picked up the gilt leather lace, ran the flat surface through my fingers and was about to throw it away when I saw distinct footprints in the earth around the humped miniature Japanese bridge about a yard long that had crumpled, apparently under the fallen boulder. I set my own foot in that first print. It was smaller than mine. Possibly a boy's print, but considering the lace in my hand, I decided it was more probably a woman who had been here. There were more marks around the boulder. But so many men from other islands had worked in the grove that the blurred prints could belong to any of them. What I had found meant nothing, but I kept the lace anyway, without quite knowing why. I found myself lashing the little lace against my other palm as I walked on.

I then followed one of the little channels to the main course of the river. It was growing dark when I reached the corner of Sandalwood House where the river poured past the east side of the building. It was noisy and foaming here. I glanced up at the window of Deirdre's study. The room looked blind and it depressed me to think of Deirdre, who should be here in my place, managing her husband's household. If it hadn't been for Victor Berringer's asinine and dangerous behavior in Kaiana Bay, Deirdre would not be so seriously ill.

Someone in the house had turned on the lights in the kitchen. They helped to illuminate the narrow path here. The riverbank had been built up with a heavy stone wall and I stayed close to the house. I had no intention of falling into the river and being swept over the falls into the gulch below. These thoughts sparked other fears. I began to imagine I heard sticks and other debris crackling underfoot behind me. This was impossible, as the falls roared only a few yards beyond, but the notion of being pushed over into this foaming torrent was enough to make me change my course. I turned back, carefully making my way to the corner of the veranda, with the grass, the *emu* for roasting pig, and the sacred grove beyond.

The grove was dark now, so I went up onto the veranda and snapped on the ground lights in order to better see the remnants of our cocktail party, which I began to pile up and carry into the kitchen. I had made my first trip, set the dusty sandal lace on the tray beside the dirty glasses, and come back for the dishes, when one of the ground lights went out. It was one of those lights strung among the trees that surrounded the *luau* area. The wedge-shaped area of the grove was now darker than its surroundings and it took on all the sinister aspects of a primeval nightmare. The lights nearby that sifted through the treetops cast everything in a green mist, and just as I put my foot out to hold open the door, I looked back once more. Someone was in that grove, in the area darkened by the failure of that electric light.

One of the Hawaiians, I thought. Someone who might want to cause trouble at Sandalwood in revenge for the tragedy that had struck the Mokus. I made a pretense of glancing around in all directions without focusing on whatever or whoever might be hidden there. Then I closed the door and locked it. The lock was far from satisfactory and I didn't like the idea that the creature out there in the forbidden grove was so near the house. I snapped off the outside lights and hurried to a north window in the darkened living room. Nothing moved out there beyond the open *luau* area. Maybe there had never been anything hidden in among those *kapu* cottages.

All the same, as I left the living room I was relieved to remember that Mr. Yee would be around. He seemed a remarkably efficient man. I thought again of the thing I had seen in the grove, and was no longer surprised at the gullibility of those who imagined they saw the goddess Pelé floating through those glades between the cottages. I went into the kitchen and had my first shock of the night.

Mr. Yee had left a note on the long kitchen table. The note was written in a thick-pointed pen, like a Japanese brush:

Miss Cameron,
This being my free night, I have departed for Maui and the home of my cousin. We are proceeding with a chess game that is in a highly anomalous position which I hope to normalize with tonight's careful thought. You will find your dinner at slow heat in the oven.

Y

Remembering the scare I had just gone

through, triggered by that whatever-it-was out in the grove, I found my stomach was not in the least receptive to the idea of food, even Mr. Yee's. I had not heard any sounds in the house since I entered. I listened, concentrating now upon the house itself. Even the creaking and crackling sounds of the old wood seemed to have stopped. I was enclosed by the eerie silence. At this moment I would have given a good deal to hear the voice of anyone who normally belonged at Sandalwood.

I fumbled with the flat, leather sandal lace and ran it between my thumb and forefinger absently as I walked around the kitchen, past the windows. Nothing was visible outside except the foam of the rushing waters that caught the light. It annoyed me to note that no one had closed any of the blinds as far as I could tell, and it was sprinkling now. A temporary shower, perhaps, but it would manage to wet everything all the same. I pulled the old-fashioned kitchen blinds, tested the lock on the pantry door leading outside, came back, and went out into the hall.

I found myself amused at my own fears. I did not like the silence in this house, but I certainly was not anxious to hear the muffled sounds a prowler might make. I went back into the living room, making my way between the wicker furnishings to the long windows. I looked through the venetian blind of the north window. My mysterious gray lump was still huddled out there and was still in the same place. Could it possibly be a rock I hadn't noticed before?

Ridiculous! There were no rocks that large in the grove. Anyway, whatever it was, it hadn't moved in the last ten minutes. I closed the blind and went to the opposite end of the house, to the back door beside the golden shower tree. It was unlocked. Mr. Yee must have left by this door. Or Nelia Perez. I locked the door. I had forgotten about Nelia. Perhaps — just perhaps — she had not gone yet. I hurried upstairs and looked for her, but it was soon clear that she had gone for the night as well.

I snapped on the hall lights and started in to close the blinds in each room. About this time the sounds started again. The wind had come up, driving a sudden, tropical shower before it. In a few minutes every window in the building began to rattle. The upstairs windows were sure to be open. I went into each room to close windows and blinds, remembering with a smile the permanent idea of most old-time citizens of Hawaii that the rain never got anyone wet, and it was somehow disloyal to suggest that windows should be closed.

By the time I reached Deirdre's bedroom suite on the northwest corner of the house the storm broke in full force. I hurried to close the windows and then the long, pink, taffeta drapes. Everything in here reminded me of Deirdre's taste. The big, four-poster bed was curtained in pink — always her favorite color. How carefully Stephen had decorated this room for his wife!

Actually, I thought, my real and secret reason for agreeing to come to Hawaii had been satisfied. Deirdre's husband loved her, and everything I had noted since my arrival only helped to convince me that this was true. During those early months of the marriage I had often wondered whether Deirdre's large inheritance had played a part in Stephen Giles's proposal. Deirdre was certainly attractive enough, but I knew something of her behavior since my imprisonment, thanks to those women appointed by the court to watch over her, so that I had suspected Deirdre might be too young emotionally for marriage. I looked around the room, remembering that she would not sleep here, so the problem remained. But at least, from all I had observed of Stephen's care for her, I was certain that her money had nothing to do with their marriage.

I started to draw the draperies across the wide north window and discovered, just when I had relaxed and begun to feel safe, that the gray lump of matter out in the glade had vanished. The rain was beating through the foliage and I wondered if the thing could have floated away, always hoping it had not floated in the direction of Sandalwood House.

The doors and windows were locked, but still, I thought, it shouldn't take much effort to get any of the ground floor windows open. I closed the last of the draperies and made my way back to the hall. There I debated whether I should be brave and go down to the kitchen to rescue my dinner from the oven, or yield to a baser but more honest spirit of cowardice and lock myself in my room. The idea of risking an accident by leaving the oven on all night seemed a trifle drastic, but still I hesitated. Across the hall was Stephen's room. He might keep a gun there. However, if I were forced to use it, in view of my past history, I would almost be better off dead.

I considered the worst possibility, that someone from the village was waiting to do damage to the Sandalwood *heiau* in vengeance for the death of Kekua Moku. In which case, if I minded my own business, I should not disturb my gray, lumpish companion. Since I was in no position to be found with a weapon in my hands, I would let sleeping dogs lie and hope they would stay put as well.

I went rapidly down the front stairs, not troubling to be quiet. I had left the kitchen and hall lights on. I found nothing suspicious. My oven dinner proved to be a casserole that smelled deliciously of herbs I did not recognize and of Oriental vegetables I had only seen in the windows of San Francisco's Chinatown. I found myself surprisingly hungry despite my earlier terror of the dark.

I had a curious fear now. I wanted to eat at Mr. Yee's big cutting table without exposing my back to the pantry door or the open hall doorway. I pulled a chair around so that nothing but the wall was at my back and ate my dinner, jumping every time the rain hurled a broken palm frond against one of the windows.

I finished hurriedly, put the dishes and coffee cup in the sink and ran water. The water was muddy. I had taken out the cup and saucer and was drying them when I heard a terrific blow against the west windows of the living room. I dropped the cup and saucer, shoved them aside with my shoe, and went across the hall.

The living room was a terrible mess. One of the long, floor-length windows had broken under the onslaught of an entire tree trunk — a slender, flowering tree complete with all its foliage and its gleaming white flowers. I might have been able to move the tree trunk but the room was showered with petals, glistening green leaves, and broken branches, not to mention sheets of rain that threatened to inundate the room and all its broken furnishings. As I stood in the doorway, shocked by the damage, I supposed the rain would be cold, but when I made my way into the room, carefully stepping over broken glass, china bric-a-brac and toppled furniture, I found that warm rain was rushing in.

At least, I reminded myself, I finally had a definite job here. And my childlike fear of the house and its loneliness had vanished before this very real problem. I wondered if a cloth or blanket could be hung to keep out the torrential rains temporarily, although I doubted it. I had always supposed tropic rains came and went. I remembered a note from Deirdre saying that it rained in

Honolulu on one side of the street while the sun beamed down on the other side. Tonight was more like one of our Los Angeles downpours. A long time in arriving, then turning into floods.

I should telephone someone, I thought. But first, there must be something that I could use to block that open area. I waded through debris, reached the trunk while my shoulder and head were pelted with a warm shower. And then the hall lights flickered, faded, came on again, and as I swore in furious panic, they went out.

I straightened, blinked, and tried to focus on the various objects of the room so that I could feel my way back to the kitchen where there was a box of tallow candles next to the cupboards. The damage to this room appeared enormous, but I didn't know how valuable the furnishings were. They had looked to me like late-Victorian antiques. This would be just one more thing for Stephen Giles to worry about. I took another look at the damage and then saw that the rain had stopped beating across the west end of the room. It beat instead against a barrier.

My gray, lumpish companion was much closer now. I gasped as I saw it peering in at me through the broken window.

Sixteen

There was a certain amount of light remaining in the sky in spite of the rain and the night. I could see that the lump was human and male. I was about to run when the creature began to mumble, to make noises that sounded more pitiful than frightening.

"Judy . . . need a little — little help. . . . I'm soaked. . . . Can't seem to get . . . going. . . ."

Good heavens! It was poor William Pelhitt.

I made my way around the tree, managing to slip on several of those glossy leaves, but I did avoid the glittering and dangerous slivers of glass. I got William under the armpits. He was wet through, absolutely soggy.

"Come on. Right foot. Now the left. Watch it! That's glass."

At least he could move. He must have had a great deal to drink before he came to Sandalwood. He wasn't as heavy as he appeared. It must be his bad posture that gave the illusion, this and his lack of belief in himself. That was not surprising in the circumstances, and in the company of Victor Berringer. He was a fool to remain here as the butt of Berringer's contempt and cruelty.

I got him across the room. As we were about to move into the hall, Pelhitt crashed into the door frame. He groaned. He had bruised his temple and the pain must have been excruciating for a few minutes. But it roused him, and by feeling our way, we managed to get across the hall into the kitchen without further disasters. He fell into the chair I pulled out, and while he huddled there dripping water in pools around him, I fumbled for candles, got matches off the shelf beside the candle box and lighted two candles, melting wax into a dish and a saucer for their bases. I was shocked at Bill Pelhitt's condition. A razor-thin streak of blood trailed below the bruise, and I grabbed up the dish towel where I had left it at the time the tree crashed through the living room window.

Bill Pelhitt raised his head, tried a faint smile, which looked more like a grimace.

"If you — throw — I'll try to catch."

I said lightly, "It's not necessary. I always wanted to play nurse."

I tried to be gentle as I dabbed at the bruise but he took the towel and tried to rub off the blood. I winced at the effort it cost him. I offered to take a candle and get antiseptic from the downstairs bathroom but he said, "Not yet, please. Don't leave me alone. Lord, but I'm cold! Can I get next to the oven? It feels warm."

Together, we shoved the chair over to the oven. The stove was electric, so we couldn't count on any more heat until the power came back. I got him settled and taking a candle, I ran upstairs and brought down several blankets. Poor Pelhitt was shivering too much to get out of his sodden clothes, so I threw a blanket around him and asked him to dry himself off. He shook his head tiredly, groaned.

"A drink of water. Never been so thirsty all my. . . ."

I ran the water, threw it out, and ran a second glass full that was only slightly cleaner. "Here. Try this. If the mud doesn't clear your head, nothing will."

He tried to smile and started to drink, the glass shaking in his unsteady hand. I reached over to help him but he stopped me.

"What was that?"

I glanced out around the blind. "Looks like the rain is letting up."

"No, no. Listen!"

We listened together. No doubt about it — there was a rattling noise at the back of the house. Not another tree about to crash through? I remembered the beautiful golden shower tree at the rear door. Bill Pelhitt made a supreme effort to rise but I motioned him back to his chair before the oven. The rattling came again followed by a sudden quiet.

"He's gone," Bill Pelhitt took a long swallow of water and shivered inside his blanket.

I was sorry I couldn't agree with his opinion. The wind and the rain had slowed to a gentle purr, but I was sure I heard footsteps at the end of the hall, and I thought how easily a man might leap over the rail of the lower *lanai* and enter in spite of the locked outside door.

Bill Pelhitt's teeth were chattering but he muttered bravely, "Give me a knife."

On the cutting board Mr. Yee had left one of his good French knives, shining and polished. I passed it to Bill and we waited breathlessly. The footsteps grew louder and before he appeared in the doorway I knew whom to expect. I was enormously relieved and at the same time I felt far happier than I should have been to see Deirdre's husband. It was more than mere relief — much more. A feeling I had no right to be having.

Stephen stopped at the sight of us, looking so amazed in the sudden, blinding light of the candles that I almost laughed. His thin nylon jacket and slacks were as soaked as Bill Pelhitt, and his hair had fallen across his face. He was just as amused at the first sight of us.

"I see you've been out in our local weather. What they call in Honolulu 'liquid sunshine.' "

"We're so glad to see you," I managed to say and then repeated it as if there were no other greeting in the world.

He came in, touched my cheek gently with cold, wet fingers that, nevertheless, were warm to my heart. "Are you all right? I was so worried when I saw the power had gone, and there was no sign of life. I thought they might have . . . you are all right?"

"Fine. But Bill is sick. Please look at him."

As I spoke he was carefully taking the knife away from Bill.

"You won't need that now. You look pretty

276

done in. Here. Let's get you dry." He reached for the fallen blankets, but Bill seemed to resent the attention. Stephen asked him, "What were you doing out in that cloudburst?"

"Visiting Judy."

That took me unaware, but I nodded as Stephen questioned me with a glance. He didn't like this. He seemed upset over Bill's use of my nickname, but at least he was getting Bill dried off.

"I think he has a temperature," I said, but temperature or not, he certainly was suffering from a bad chill.

Bill tried vainly to wriggle out of Stephen's clutches while making half-hearted protests, "Let me go! . . . can d-do it. I'm fine. . . ."

"Quiet!" Stephen ordered him. "You're on your way to pneumonia if you aren't careful. You'd damn near have to lie down in the rain to get this wet." Bill looked at me furtively. I made no sign of understanding how close to the truth Stephen's casual comment might have been, for I suspected Bill had been lying there in the grove since sometime soon after he had quarrelled with Berringer. Apparently, Berringer had gone on, leaving Bill in his unsteady condition, and this was the result. Stephen glanced around. "Look, darling, would you mind —" His mouth twisted a little. "That is — Judith . . . could you get the couch ready in my study? There are linens —"

"Yes. I know where the linens are." I took one of the candles and started out, then hesitated.

"Is there some way we could get Bill warm?"

"I don't need anything. Will you please leave me alone?"

We ignored Bill because evidently he was not quite himself. He very probably was delirious. Stephen suggested then, "There's a hibachi here. We can warm up some of those stones on the path outside the pantry door, wrap them in towels. Pretty old idea and not much use in Hawaii, but they helped my mother once, and you never know." Bill was complaining with as much vehemence as he could muster. Stephen tried to buck him up. "The sooner we wring you out, old man, the sooner you can go home."

But Bill objected querulously even to this. "Don't call me 'old man.' "

Stephen apologized in a careful voice. "Sorry. Figure of speech."

I took the top linens from the shelf in the closet and ran to the study. I stripped the cover from the studio couch and threw on gaily flowered pink sheets and a blanket. I had forgotten pillowcases, but I rolled up the extra blanket I had brought. It would serve as a pillow. I called to Stephen.

"It's all right. Damp in here, though."

They were already in the hall and Stephen supported Bill Pelhitt who managed a small smile. I took his other side and we got him to the couch. He murmured, "Not drunk now. Honest."

"Of course, you're not, Bill. Now just relax.

That's it." I felt his forehead. He certainly had a fever. Stephen nodded. He himself still looked as if the downpour had Scotch-taped all his clothing to his body. I suggested, "I'll help Bill. Hadn't you better change too? You'll find yourself fighting pneumonia if you don't."

"Don't worry. It isn't the first time I've crossed Kaiana Bay and gotten drenched. First, we've got to get the hibachi going. Can you take over while I get the thing started?"

So I sat down on the edge of the couch, rearranging sheets and blankets around Bill Pelhitt. He drew back with an embarrassment I couldn't understand until I realized Stephen had stripped him of the soggy clothes and under all these blankets he was naked.

For some reason I felt as sorry for him as if he had been a helpless child. In other circumstances I might have been surprised or even amused at his sudden modesty, but he must have been through a great deal since the disappearance of the girl he loved, and I liked him nearly as much as I pitied him. I felt that some friend ought to give him stern advice when he felt better able to take it. He would have to stand up to Victor Berringer.

In a remarkably short time Stephen had the little black hibachi smoking and burning in the kitchen and was able to heat stones in the coals of the briquets he used. I furnished towels in which to wrap the stones. It occurred to me, very belatedly, that we must call for a doctor from

Kaiana, but when I broached the subject as we were carrying the wrapped stones to the study, Stephen shook his head.

"I couldn't get through to you half an hour — no, an hour ago, from the Kaiana airport. However, we'll try if he doesn't show any improvement. All right, Pelhitt. You may not believe it but you're going to feel better pretty soon."

Bill's teeth were still chattering but he managed to get out a polite, "Awfully . . . good of you."

His uneasiness over my presence, as a woman and a comparative stranger, kept me from being of much help, but as I could see, Stephen managed very well alone. In spite of Bill's hot, feverish forehead, it was clear almost at once that the towels with their heated stones were exactly what he needed. He calmed down, stopped shivering and in no time went to sleep.

Satisfied that he would be all right for a few minutes, Stephen and I went back to the kitchen to find something that would seal up the broken living-room window until morning. All his exertions with blankets and hot stones and hibachis had dried out Stephen himself.

He remarked wryly, "I thought when I reached the landing tonight that the amount of Pacific water I carried ashore would sink the island." He looked at me. We smiled, although there was nothing very funny about his remark or our situation. We reached for the remaining candle at the same time. His fingers, firm and warm, closed over mine. It took an enormous effort of will for me to remove my hand. Long minutes after I caught myself staring at my hand and wishing — like a child with a first crush — that I could preserve that sensuous feeling between us.

But instead, I said quickly, "I wish I could perk some coffee. We could use it."

"I don't suppose you'd take a chance on a very small jigger of my father's Oke."

"His what?" At least, the moment between us had passed. We were now comrades, not potential lovers.

"Okolehau. It used to be popular — and legal — before the second World War. Something to do with taro. Everything has, in the Islands."

Somewhere I had heard of it before. I remembered that I had wanted to ask about Deirdre, to be certain there had been no relapse, but the house was damp, the jungle around us closing in from all sides, and a little warmth, I felt, would do us good. I said gaily, "Fine. Then we'll try and cover that window in the living room. Have you eaten?"

"Come to think of it, I haven't."

"A little food, or at any rate, something healthy to drink, would do Mr. Pelhitt good, too," I suggested.

"You are a true pioneer's woman, Judith." He touched my chin jokingly, but I think the fact that I avoided his warm gaze might have brought the situation more firmly into focus. He stepped back, returned to the easy relationship he might have shown in Deirdre's presence.

"Great idea about dinner. I'm afraid we'll have to cook on our guest's hibachi."

"I wonder if there are any steaks in Mr. Yee's precious refrigerator. Never mind. We'll find something."

We attended to the living-room problem first. By the light of a third candle we got the window fairly well covered by a huge piece of plasterboard that had been under his desk in the study to protect the heirloom carpet. Stephen's guest was not disturbed. Stephen had put a big Band-Aid patch on his temple. Apparently, the injury, though painful, was not serious. Bill slept heavily but as his body had warmed and dried, his temperature seemed to go down. I left the glass of water near him. He would have a monumental thirst when he began to recover. Some orange or tomato juice wouldn't hurt either. How unhappy he seemed to be, caught in a vise between Victor Berringer and his highly unstable daughter!

While I rummaged through Mr. Yee's carefully arranged foods in the freezer, Stephen went upstairs and changed. He came back through the dark halls only minutes later looking especially handsome in a white turtleneck pullover and rust-colored slacks. He had combed his hair but it was still tousled. I was glad that such a mundane problem as food could keep my mind occupied.

"There isn't any tomato juice," I told him. "I

think Bill could do with quarts of orange juice. But all we've got is pineapple."

"One of the first dates Deirdre went on with me was to the big pineapple factory here," Stephen reminisced. "It didn't matter that we could have bought a glass of pineapple juice anywhere. Her thrill was to take a paper cup to the faucet and watch the juice pour out in front of her eyes. She likes things like that. Fairy-tale things. A not-quite-real world."

"How about some papaya?"

"For me or our patient?"

"For you. The patient gets the pineapple. There aren't any steaks, by the way. Doesn't Mr. Yee believe in beef?"

He reached over my head into the highest shelf in the freezer, felt around and agreed that Mr. Yee had finally showed his Achilles' heel.

"How about scrambling some eggs and having these sausages? I think they are chorizo. Damn! I wish we could heat some coffee. Well, no matter. What do you think of the Okolehau?" He watched as I tasted the stuff which seemed potent enough to cook food without a hibachi. I held onto the top of my head and he laughed.

"There's not much left in the world, and from the look on your face, it's just as well. You know, that casserole looks interesting."

"Chicken à la king?"

"Not from Mr. Yee. I'll bet it's tomorrow's dinner. Chicken in milk — cocoanut milk. Those greens are the tops of taro. It's one of his specialties. What would happen if we heated it tonight?"

I was horrified. "Not me! You forget, I know Mr. Yee's demanding nature."

"Coward!" he teased as he finished his drink and fed briquets into the hibachi until it was ready for my frying pan. Then he straddled a chair beside the table and propped his arms on the chairback. He then proceeded to make me nervous by watching me work.

"Do the doctors say when Deirdre will be able to get up?" I asked while I beat the eggs.

"She was up for a few minutes this afternoon. She's such an adorable —" He hesitated just a shade before adding, "child." There was a little silence. He went on finally, "Judith?"

"Yes?"

"Do you believe, from your knowledge of her, that my wife will ever grow up?"

I didn't look around. "Do you really think you would love her as much if she were completely grown-up and different?"

He laughed and I heard him drumming the fingers of one hand on the table. "Probably not." He started to say something, then broke off in an odd way. I looked back at him. His fingers curled around a bit of leather and he was staring at it. I recognized it as the gilt sandal strap I had found in the sacred grove.

"Oh, that!" I started to explain but he was asking of no one in particular, "Isn't this from one of Kekua Moku's sandals?"

"But it can't be. I found it in that grove beyond the *luau* setup. The one that's accursed or whatever."

He turned the lace over. "But I remember when she and Deirdre bought sandals, quite different, but I remember the discussions they had. Kekua in the grove. Well, it's not impossible. She has —" He caught himself. "Had — poor little Kekua! — had a mind of her own. I wonder what she was doing there. Or was her sandal found by someone? All this means very little, of course, since she slipped and fell." He looked up at me. I was staring at him, puzzled as he was by the girl's unnatural death.

"Could there be something about her death that is — well — sinister?"

"Probably not. She may even have lost her footing because of the loose sandal. But there had to be a reason. From the minute I heard about the rotten business I haven't been satisfied that Kekua could have simply gotten too close to the edge. She knew where the gulch was. She has played around here since she was two or three years old." He took a deep breath. "Ilima will never forgive me. Moku might understand that it was an accident. A horrible accident, which, frankly, I still can't figure out. But Ilima — she will hate us. I can't say I blame her."

After heating the sausage slices, I tried to concentrate on the scrambled eggs, which were finished very quickly. I set this improvised dinner before him on one of the plates from the kitchen set, blue and white but unadorned, with none of the eggshell delicacy of the china used for the family meals. After thanking me for this snack, he ate in what appeared to be enjoyment. I decided to heat up a can of soup for Bill Pelhitt and went in to see if he could drink the pineapple juice.

I found him awake and in spite of a splitting headache he was insisting that he had to have his clothes. He must get home.

"Where is home?"

He started to give me the obvious reply, that he had to return to the village. But he debated this, even while he assured me he had to leave. "I don't suppose any place is home now. Maybe when we all get over this, maybe then I will know."

Offering him the juice, which he drank obediently, I said briskly, "What you need to do is get out of Berringer's hands, out from under his influence. Go somewhere you've never been to before and find a nice girl and marry her."

He looked startled at the idea. "But — Ingrid. . . ."

He really needed a good shaking up. "Frankly, she doesn't seem to have returned all this devotion you've lavished on her. She must have had you spellbound or something."

He drank the juice in one nervous gulp. "No. But I thought I owed it to her to. . . . It's like paying one's respects to the dead, you know —

in my case, a dead romance. I just felt I owed it to her."

Stephen came in about this time. I hardly recognized his hard voice. "You think she is dead. Why? Have you some special reason for thinking so?"

"No. I mean — I don't have any special reason. But I'm sure."

"Why?" The word was snapped out. Stephen's antagonism baffled me.

"For heaven's sake, leave the poor man alone," I put in while Bill not very helpfully shrugged, started to drop his blanket and grabbed at it. "I'll see about your clothes," I said and went back to the kitchen, where everything was still damp, although the doorway into the pantry looked like a Neapolitan clothesline where Stephen had stretched the slacks, shirt, underpants and gray jacket on the backs of chairs. Stephen followed me.

"Must you be so suspicious of him?" I asked, trying not to touch off his uncertain temper.

I could see that he was already wishing he had behaved better. "Sorry. He just irritates me. So damned helpless, and you huddling over him like some Nightingale with the lamp!"

"In my case, it's a candle." I tried to play down his silly accusation. "Anyway, he'll be gone soon. You might lend him some of your things. He is not as tall, and he weighs more, but you must have something."

"Don't worry. I'm way ahead of you. I've laid

out things for him when he is able to get on his feet. But I would like to find out what he knows. Or suspects. I can't see Berringer killing his own daughter — assuming she is dead — but what *are* they doing on the island?"

I began to clear away his dish and silverware. "Stephen, if I ask you something, you will understand this is strictly between you and me?"

"You know that." He smiled suddenly. "Are you about to admit that fellow is in love with you?"

"No. Don't be ridiculous. To people like that, I am one of those efficient nurse types on whose shoulders he can weep so he can unstarch my uniform."

"Do people often unstarch you?"

I was silent for a minute.

"What were you going to tell me that was so secret, Judith?" His unexpected gentleness when he used my name was hard to disregard. I made a special effort to renew my impersonal manner.

"I think you ought to know that Victor Berringer is asking questions about the man who threatened Mrs. Asami's neighbor that day in Honolulu about the time you and Deirdre were married."

"Mrs. Asami's neighbor. The Berringer girl." He didn't seem as worried or as angry as I expected, but he was thoughtful. "I wonder if you think I murdered the girl. And if so, why? Or was she a discarded mistress of mine? Or a blackmailer?" He laughed shortly, but there was no humor in the sound. "Not that she isn't capable of it. She made life miserable for Deirdre." I couldn't avoid his gaze. He was willing me to look at him. "Is that what you have thought of me since you and Pelhitt visited Mrs. Asami? Judith, I swear to you —"

I said violently, "I know you didn't do it! Don't be a fool! But Berringer would love to believe anything, and so would William Pelhitt. The poor man is jealous. After all, he loves this Ingrid character." He stared at me, unable to say anything for a minute. Then he laughed, this time much more cheerfully.

"Thank you for the vote of confidence. But please, promise me one thing. Never refer to *me* as a 'poor man.' "

"I'm not likely to. You are not the sort to inspire pity."

"Thank God for that, at any rate."

I had just stacked up the dishes when I heard Bill Pelhitt in the hall. "Where is everybody?"

He was at the open doorway into the kitchen only a second later, and I very much hoped he hadn't heard our last remarks. He had found the clothes left by Stephen and looked a trifle odd in Stephen's sporty attire, but he was not unattractive.

"I appreciate the hospitality, but I had better be getting back. They might think I've run away because of the trouble in the village. The young lady was always nice to me, and I feel I owe her my presence at the — ah — you might call it the wake."

I didn't know what to do myself about the grief of the villagers. I was a *haole,* a Caucasian, and I was a *malahini,* a newcomer. They were not likely to accept me, but Stephen was almost one of them, and yet, his family, his house, were hated and feared now. I could see that he was debating his conduct as I debated mine.

Stephen said, "No need to leave until morning, Pelhitt. Maybe I had better go back when you do. I have to talk with Moku and Ilima. Make them understand how we feel over what has happened."

But Bill pleaded with obvious embarrassment, "It might be better if you didn't see them just yet, sir. I'm sorry. It's pretty rough having to say it after you've been so darned helpful, but I'm afraid from what Vic and I heard today, there might be trouble if anyone from Sandalwood showed up now. You do understand, don't you?"

Seeing that Bill, in his excessive politeness, was having his own rough time of an explanation, I added, "He's right, Stephen. Really. There couldn't be any mistake when Moku took his daughter away this afternoon. He was very bitter. I felt the bitterness almost as much as his grief."

"And he's not as bad as his wife, the one they call Queen Ilima. I heard them, Giles. No mistake — it goes deep with them."

"But they accept you and Berringer."

Pelhitt had nothing to say to that. He looked drained and tired after the liquor and the effects of the storm. But the fever and chills seemed to be gone — that was one consolation. He asked if someone would be so good as to give him another glass of pineapple juice. I got him the drink and asked if he wouldn't like something to eat. Then Stephen suddenly took the matter out of my hands.

"You've been on your feet and fighting problems all day, Judith. Be a good child and go to bed."

Bill added his concern. "I've caused you a lot of trouble. Mr. Giles is right. You go on. As for me, I appreciate what you two have done for me, but honestly, I'd rather be on my way."

I was tired and worried. I wasn't quite sure why, but so many odd things were happening at once, and besides, I felt I shouldn't be around Stephen any more than necessary. I enjoyed his company too much. He took one of the candles from the kitchen and started up the stairs with me. On the landing he asked in a low voice, "What do you make of him? How did he get so wet? Was he standing in the downpour?"

"No. Lying in it, I think. He had been drinking heavily and I saw him lying over in the grove. I didn't know what it was, but as soon as I saw his gray slacks and jacket, I recognized him."

"Will you be all right?"

"Of course, now that you have come." I realized instantly that it was the wrong thing to say and I elaborated on the remark as casually as possible, "Now that someone else is in the house, I can feel safer." I reached for the candle.

"I'll take you," he said testily, but he was too late. I already had one hand on the saucer. He grabbed at the candle which broke away from the saucer and rolled across the landing. We both knelt to rescue it before the house burned down. I found myself giggling — I really must have been tired!

He rescued the candle and set it back in the saucer of melted wax as I was scrambling to get up. He put his hand under one of my elbows and got me to my feet.

"I love your smile . . . I love your mouth, Judith."

He kissed me. I struggled. I had always regarded a woman who struggled against a kiss from the man she loved as a ridiculous phony. A second later I would have surrendered to the exquisite pleasure of that kiss. But I recovered first. My conscience, the despicable thing I was doing to Deirdre, gave me the courage to break away.

"I'm sorry. I never should have —" I couldn't go on. I wanted him so much. I made my way up the stairs, through the dark toward my room. I heard his rapid footsteps immediately afterward and as I fumbled to open my door, he said quietly, "At least take the light. I won't bother you. But don't expect me to say I am sorry for what happened. That would be pretty hypocritical.

Good night, Judith."

I glanced at him briefly as I took the candle. Whatever he said, or whatever his feelings, I knew he was deeply troubled too. The part of him that needed me was not the complete man. Any other reasonably normal woman would serve him as well. He *loved* Deirdre. And in his special way, he needed Deirdre's dependence upon him. I was certain of it.

I locked the door and found myself crying. It was the most incredible thing. There were years when I had never cried. Now I was all adolescent emotion.

A girl loses her father when she is a baby and has an alcoholic mother who prefers her own form of expensive hell. . . . So I am sent to prison because the girl poisons her mother and then ends up with the one man in the world whom I love.

What made me think that? It was all a lie! I'd never really thought Deirdre killed her mother. . . . Another lie — have I always thought that? And now, was I frantic to cover Deirdre's tracks because I feared she had murdered her rival, Ingrid Berringer?

I was sickened with disgust at my own thoughts. I needed a bath, purging and cleansing. I would scrub until there was no skin left — punish myself. I deserved it for such vicious, self-serving thoughts.

As it happened, that punishment had to be administered in a different way. There was no hot water, so I took a cold shower. By the time I had finished I was so invigorated I began to ridicule myself and ended by going to bed in a much healthier frame of mind. All this flagellation and sell-loathing over a simple kiss! I might as well have been fourteen years old.

How small my personal affairs were, in view of the tragedy to the Moku family! I dreamed vaguely that night, in little snatches of scenes that might have come from a badly edited movie, and I didn't recall them the next morning, except — was it part of the dream, or in my thoughts while half awake at some time in the night? There was Kekua Moku's sandal lace in the forbidden grove. But it should not be there. If anything, it ought to be near the edge of the steep path where she had slipped and fallen. Why hadn't I remembered that scuffed earth around the sandal lace? There was the tiny foot bridge broken by a weight that was very possibly the weight of a human being in a struggle of some kind.

Had there been a struggle on that spot? And had Kekua run and run and slipped, falling to her hideous death?

Seventeen

Mr. Yee was back the next morning, his haughty, dictatorial self and very welcome to all of us. Nelia Perez had hectic tales about her voyage across the bay in his company at the beginning of the storm. Today's humidity was terrific, but the sun was out again and Ili-Ahi looked once more like an opulent tropic isle full of romance and intrigue, exactly like the travel folders.

Stephen came in while I was finishing breakfast to tell me that all the invalids were well and accounted for.

"I checked with Deirdre as soon as the power was on again. She is raring to go and wants to return home as soon as possible. It may be just a matter of days. She was button-holing everyone she met, trying to persuade someone to furnish a magic carpet. But the doctors think, if we are very careful with her, I can take her home sometime this week."

"How wonderful! And if the weather is anything like it looks this morning, she can recuperate in no time."

He agreed as he stole a half slice of freshly buttered toast from my plate. Grinning with pleasure, he looked very boyish.

"I think I've got some men coming in from Honolulu to help complete the Sandalwood *heiau*. We'll lick that *kapu* yet."

I felt that his insistence on fighting against the deepest religious feelings of the Hawaiians on the island was disastrous, but it was obvious I couldn't tell him so. He took a big bite of the toast and looked down at me.

"Aren't you going to ask about your not-so-secret admirer?"

"Oh! Is that the other invalid? I'm sorry — I was thinking of something else. How is Bill?"

"Says he's fine. He and Berringer must have gone over to Kaiana at sunrise. He called from there. Wanted to remind me not to go to the village. I wasn't wanted — that sort of thing. But it's my place to visit the family, and I intend to."

Stubborn as a Scot, and I should know! I remembered his accusing me of something very like that the first time we met. He meant well toward the Hawaiians in their village, but I felt that he did not know those people as he thought he knew them.

I said, "I'll get at the living room and see what can be done. I hope the carpet wasn't ruined, but I have my doubts. Is it very old?"

"Too old. Time for a change. Have we nothing in the house but this infernal guava jelly? Isn't there any grape or currant or whatever?"

I was amused at his taking over my breakfast, but at his mention of the jellies I was chilled by an old memory.

"I don't like dark jellies. They make me think of restaurants and institutions. They always serve dark jellies."

He was quick to understand and lightly changed the subject. I soon saw that the return of the normal, perfect weather had an equally cheerful effect on the rest of Stephen's employees. We had lost Mrs. Mitsushima's services, but the first boatload of men to cross the bay that morning appeared willing to help Stephen complete the building of the cottage complex and went to work at once, clearing away the storm damage. A glazier and his assistant were in the group, and while I cleaned up the living room, they put in the new window.

I did notice one difference in Stephen's new employees. They were all Caucasians. The word had gone out — that was obvious. Because I was worried about the tensions on the island, I found the housework a great relief. When I had the living room fairly clean, there was still the serious matter of the dampness, the stench of wet cloth and soaked wood. I went to the linen closet, looking for a room freshener of some kind, but Nelia Perez had a better idea.

"Why don't you hang *mokihana* around the room. Makes it all smell natural."

"What on earth is *mokihana?* It sounds like a native curse, and we have enough of those already."

Nelia explained that berries found on Kaiana Island were strung, along with fragrant *maile* leaves, to make as good a freshener as could be found.

"At least, that's what my family uses. Mrs.

Stephen has some in the dresser drawers and in her own closets. We might use them and then I could make some more before she gets back from the hospital."

We went up to Deirdre's bedroom, the large pink one that she apparently did not use, and there were leis of *maile* leaves and the scented berries hanging in her closet as Nelia predicted. I took them out for immediate use.

"There are some in her dressing-table drawers," Nelia called to me as I was leaving. "Fresh ones that Mrs. Nagata brought over a month ago," she explained. "They'll do the job."

"Fine." I didn't want to remain here too long. With Deirdre away I preferred not to be wandering around among her personal things.

I was out in the hall when Nelia called me back. "Miss Cameron? In the dresser drawer here. A letter. It's sealed."

"Then don't touch it. Coming?"

She came along, shaking her head. "It's addressed to Mrs. Stephen all right, and I know that writing. Why would that girl write to Mrs. Stephen?"

I scarcely heard her. I had just identified the voices of Michiko and Ito Nagata downstairs and went to meet them. Although they obviously had come here on their way to pay a condolence call in the village, they were excited about something else, some secret. As we went around the house examining the damage done by the storm,

Michiko looked at Ito.

"We should keep it a great mystery. She will appreciate it more."

"What mystery? Appreciate what?"

They wandered around the living room with me, obviously not too impressed by the way I had repaired the damage and refurnished the room. Ito was too polite to be honest, but since decorating was Michiko's job, she shuffled things around and managed to change the entire look of the room by the most minute details. Meanwhile, I followed, feeling gauche and untalented, and also dying of curiosity.

"Ito, what is it? Please don't keep me in suspense."

He watched his wife rearrange the hanging of two matted water colors showing Sandalwood in earlier days, and asked me if I knew that I was important enough to be spied upon. I felt a sudden depression.

"Ito, no! Not the police! I'm on parole. I haven't done anything. They must know that."

While Ito was denying any such idea, Michiko said with amused impatience, "Ito, my love, I hope you don't have to convey bad news very often. That was a terrible way to phrase it. No, Judy. It's something you and we and Steve are all in together. We've got a detective watching us."

"But that is ridiculous. What could the police possibly — ?"

Ito put in, "That's just the thing, Judy. It isn't

the police. It's a private detective. We are being honored by the attentions of a genuine private eye."

"Mr. Moto!"

They looked at me. Michiko laughed. "Perfect description. So you've noticed him too."

"He followed William Pelhitt and me when we were at Kahala the other day. How did you find out about this business?"

Ito said proudly, "That was Michiko's trick. The night I came over to attend the birth of Kamehameha Kalanimoku, Michiko followed me."

"But why, for heaven's sake? Don't tell me you thought Ito was up to some shenanigans!"

Michiko gave him one of those sloe-eyed looks, half laughing, half sinister, that I had always admired. "He'd better not try any. The truth is, I saw that creepy little penguin the day we splurged up and down Waikiki. Then, night before last, as Ito drove away from the house, I caught a glimpse of the fellow again in the car lights. He was parked across the street in a little cream-colored Toyota. So I slipped on sandals and took my car and putt-putted off toward the airport. I figured if he followed Ito, he would be there. Sure enough. He missed Ito's plane by a hair, and I watched him. He telephoned. Then he took the last flight to Kaiana."

Ito put in with husbandly pride and some amusement, "She bought a scarf, took off her belt, looked as unlike our *Vogue*ish Michiko as

300

you can imagine, and followed my — I think TV calls it a 'tail'."

"Only he was no longer tailing my sinister husband," Michiko announced, excitement creeping into her calm, self-reliant manner. "He was on his way to meet someone."

I almost scared myself by my shout: "The man who hired him! And I know who it was. Berringer said he saw you night before last. He tried to make it sound sinister." They were properly impressed by my guesswork. I added, "Actually, it was the other way around. You saw Berringer. I should have guessed. The old troublemaker tried to make me believe — God knows what. May I get you some breakfast? Or is it lunch?"

"Neither, I'm afraid, Judy." Ito's suddenly apologetic manner puzzled me until Michiko explained brusquely. "It's the funeral. Ito thinks we are betraying you and the Giles family, but it isn't a matter of choice. The Mokus have been friends of my family since the years of Queen Liliuokalani. As a matter of fact, they were very good to us Japanese and Koreans when we came."

"Michi—" Ito began, but I said I understood. I had never before heard her speak in such a way about her people, or heard her refer to her ancestors this way, as if she were part of them and they part of her today. She was so very modern in appearance and speech, one was inclined to forget her ancient roots elsewhere.

301

"You are sure they would resent me?" I asked as the Nagatas left Sandalwood. But they didn't even stop to answer me. I did understand, but I was sorry. Sorry most of all for Stephen. I was sure he felt deeply the break between the Hawaiian village and Sandalwood.

I went out into the clearing after the Nagatas left the house. The men in the sacred grove had finished cleaning up and were beginning to dig out stumps and unwanted tangles of vines and bushes. I heard them talking about the damage to the papaya orchards from the storm, which meant more problems for the islanders, whatever their race. Stephen saw the Nagatas as they were leaving. He said something to the foreman and crossed the grove to the village trail. I knew what he was going to do and that he would be disappointed. It might even be dangerous for him.

He stopped the Nagatas, and I could see that they were trying to dissuade him. I turned away. It was awful to spy on him. Besides, I was thinking far too much about him. A few minutes later, making the beds with Nelia Perez, I heard Stephen come racing up the stairs two at a time and into his bedroom. Nelia motioned to me.

"My father says he's bull-headed. But I like that in a man."

"Sometimes it can be troublesome. I'm sure he doesn't realize how the Mokus feel. It might have been different if the work on the grove hadn't started again, so soon."

Out in the hall Stephen's voice called my name sharply.

"Judith!"

I dropped a pillow out of its pillowcase and went into the hall, followed by Nelia's eye-rolling pantomime which said, plainer than words, "Now, you're in trouble," or perhaps, more generously, "Now *we* are in trouble."

I approached him and said calmly, "Yes, sir."

He had just grabbed up a dark jacket and was putting it on in the hall. The color gave him a strangely subdued look, but there was no mistaking his scowl.

"Judith, I wish you wouldn't discuss me with the help."

"You must know the help always discusses an employer."

"This is something you don't understand, believe me. The Nagatas may think they are close to the Hawaiians but they haven't lived with them for a hundred years, as we have. We understand each other." His brief burst of temper had already faded, and I probably should have left it there. Long ago I had gotten into endless trouble minding other people's business. But I tried once more.

"Stephen, you have a moral right. Even a responsibility. I don't deny that. Only, all this can't mean much when they don't want anyone from Sandalwood. They blame the invasion of their sanctuary for Kekua's death. And you've gone back to work on that sanctuary."

"My God, Judith! You've been through it. That grove is exactly like any other acreage on the island. There isn't an inch of it that has any sacred importance, except in their superstitions. And when we break for lunch, I intend to go to the village, to make an appearance and show them the Giles family cares about their loss, cares about that poor child who died."

He reached out to touch my hand, a friendly motion to show that all was forgiven. Unfortunately, the whole impact of his argument hit me, and I pointed out, feeling a little sick at the necessity. "Don't you hear yourself — the enormous gulf between *you* and *they?* A minute ago you included the Gileses and the village as *we*. But every move you make is against their interests and their beliefs."

"Their interests! God Almighty! If the Sandalwood *heiau* isn't going to bring them prosperity, a chance to sell their handiwork and their fruits and even their beef cattle . . . Judith, keep out of this. I know what I am doing. Believe me!"

I was sure he hadn't the faintest idea of their real feelings, but I nodded. I felt so shaken I couldn't speak. I knew he was right in one sense. I had been interfering. But I had an excuse, which was no excuse, under the circumstances. I loved him.

He went down the stairs. When he reached the landing he slowed, nearly stopped, then went on. I wondered if he was remembering last night when he dropped the candle there and we both fumbled for it. And afterward, when he kissed me.

No matter. As soon as Deirdre returned, I would find an excuse and leave Sandalwood, eventually leaving the Islands as well. There had to be some legal provision to get me out of here without violating my parole.

"Well, he's gone," Nelia came out into the hall, swinging a pillowcase over one shoulder. "She's lucky, that niece of yours. In a way." I must have stiffened, because she added in a slightly flurried voice, "to have Sandalwood and the estate, you know."

Having worked with me all morning, she had earned herself a break. She suggested we take our lunch down to a cove west of the river's outlet. "We can swim in the clearest waters of the Islands. And you know how clear most of the waters are around here!"

I thought of the burial service that would be taking place at the other end of the island in a few hours. It seemed insensitive for us to be swimming and picnicking at such a time, but the day was hot and muggy. We had been working for some time, and maybe no one at the village would know. I weakened and we sneaked into Mr. Yee's kitchen while the Gileses' chef was taking his noon siesta. I found that picnics in Hawaii were a good deal more healthy and less standardized than the sandwich-and-thermos lunches on the mainland.

We found bananas, brown and huge, but not

overripe, and a pineapple already cut into long, delicious sticks. We took two sticks, wrapped them and added a couple of rolls Mr. Yee had just baked. For at least an hour that day I felt free of the pinching, nagging worries which had made my stay at Sandalwood oppressive. The little cove was inside the long coral reef and there was coral underfoot, but at Nelia's suggestion I borrowed a pair of Deirdre's old, light beach sandals that she wore when she swam here. By the time I had swum out to the reef and then over to the copper light on the boat landing and back, I felt like a new woman in that buoyant water.

Nelia and I were eating our lunch under the shade of a thick, twisted ohia tree that looked a hundred years old, but Nelia laughed when I remarked on its age.

"They look like that when they're pups."

"Nothing in Hawaii is quite what it seems," I said, growing philosophical under the spell of the humid air and the incredible aquamarine clarity of the water before it crawled up the beach in its lacey patterns of foam.

After a little while, Nelia remarked thoughtfully, "I don't know but what *malahinis* are wrong when they think we are different. People turn out to be just about what they seem. It's just that they are trying hard to be something else, maybe. But — take love and hate. My boyfriend says he's had times when he hated me. After a quarrel, you know. He couldn't hate me so much though, if he didn't actually love me just as much. So if you weigh up both sides of people's actions, you find they pretty well balance. Take poor Kekua. If she'd been having a big love affair, which she wasn't — I'd know — then it would be logical that the man might have loved her enough to kill her if he couldn't have her. That's if he loved her enough. But love isn't what made Kekua tick."

I sat up on one sand-covered elbow. "What made you say that? Was there a lover at all in her life?"

She waved away the notion with scorn. "Whatever killed Kekua, it wasn't any love affair. But between you and me, little old Kekky was doing all right in the dollar department."

I watched a big outrigger canoe sailing across the bay, its mainsail a gaudy red and gold, but I was thinking of Nelia's words.

"You think she was blackmailing someone?"

"That's putting it pretty crudely. All I'm saying is that people are true to their character. If they love something, they can hate just as hard, but the love is still there. And the same goes for greed. Greedy people don't change. When I was a lot younger, they sent Kekua to a school in Kaiana City one time. That's where I met her. She found out I'd driven to the pool on the wind-ward coast with my boyfriend instead of going to the movie house. I had to pay her a dollar a week to keep her from telling my pa, until her family decided to take her home. They didn't like our *haole* ways. *Our* ways, mind you."

Beyond the bright outrigger a prop plane was headed out over Kaiana Bay toward Ili-Ahi. It did not surprise me too much, since my mind was on other things, but Nelia pointed out its importance. She got up, shaking white sand off the deep, marine blue suit she wore.

"That's funny. Looks like that plane is going to land on the island."

Startled, I got up as well. "How can it land? There is no field, is there?"

"On the west coast beyond the jungle there's a field where the Hawaiians keep a small herd of cattle. Mostly beef, but I think there's a dairy herd as well. They haven't had any to sell us lately, or so they say. Now, with Kekua's death, they'll tighten everything up until Mr. Stephen stops work on the grove."

Anxiously, I picked up my beach hat and the hamper.

"If that plane is coming in, they must intend to visit Sandalwood. We'd better be going."

"Right!"

We made our way around the tiny cove and took the path up past the copper light to Sandalwood House above the gulch. We did not look toward the noisy falls or the broken clumps of fern and bright ginger and the darker, prickling bushes that had gone into the gulch when Kekua fell. But there was still the sweet, haunting perfume of those ginger flowers on the moist air, and it was difficult not to remember what happened in this place so short a time ago.

Nelia laughed. "I hope the plane doesn't land on some of those cows, or we'll be getting milkshakes for free."

I couldn't see the humor in this, especially as I now realized that the field she referred to was literally a pasture.

"You mean to tell me there is no landing strip at all?"

She shrugged. "If you can call one unpaved jeep road a strip. A couple of years ago Mr. Stephen and his pilot came in on a belly-whop. No wheels. Mr. Stephen got a black eye and a broken leg. The pilot was okay. But Queen Ilima wouldn't give permission for any more landings. Scared the cows and they wouldn't give milk, or something."

"I shouldn't wonder." Her information indicated that the plane we could see circling above the westerly half of the island was not here on a joy ride.

By the time we were inside Sandalwood, Mr. Yee was standing in the hallway, hands on hips.

"Madam —" (He must have meant me.) "I take it I may expect your assistance when you have shed your wet garments."

"Are you having difficulties?" I asked as coolly as I could.

Nelia sensibly chose this moment to duck upstairs and change while Mr. Yee made me acquainted with what he considered a new catastrophe.

"I am informed by the telephone that Mrs.

Stephen arrives in the airplane. Madam Ilima gave the pilot permission to land. This will take place within minutes if all goes well."

Whatever I had expected, it was not this. In view of Nelia's tale about the last plane to land here, I could only hope all would go well.

"But that is dangerous! She knows there isn't a landing strip here. And she should be in the hospital! Surely, her husband doesn't know about this."

Mr. Yee said, "I was not consulted on the matter of Mr. Stephen's views. Mr. Berringer and Mr. Pelhitt, I believe, visited Mrs. Stephen in the hospital and talked with her. She wished to return to Ili-Ahi. Having talked with her about many things, I am told, they agreed to assist her."

I was starting up the stairs in a great hurry, to get into some other clothing, when I was jolted by Mr. Yee's final statement.

"The four will be asking to see Mr. Stephen at once."

"Four? Including the pilot?"

"No, madam. Including the lieutenant from the Honolulu police department. I believe Mr. Berringer acted as pilot."

Eighteen

I had long ago steeled myself against reacting to shocks of any kind and I went on up to my room, showered and changed. I kept glancing out the window every minute until I saw the three men — Berringer, tall, confident, and powerful, William Pelhitt, looking too hot in the sun and still with a patch on his forehead, and the stranger who was probably Filipino and Hawaiian, a good-looking dark man, with the heavy grace of the Hawaiians I had seen. That would be the police lieutenant. Deirdre was with them, walking a trifle sedately, not running as she usually did, but she looked cheerful and surprisingly perky after her ordeal.

Now that I knew Deirdre had landed safely, I could finish dressing with an easier mind and did so in haste. By the time I finished, Deirdre was already on her way to her strange, greenish-hued room above the river and the falls. I called to her in the hall and followed her.

"It's wonderful to see you, dear. It seems like ages. How are you feeling?"

She hesitated, then turned and smiled, holding out her hands, but for an instant I felt sick — as if she had struck me. She had almost failed to turned around when I spoke, and I knew the delay was real, not my imagination. Something had happened during her hospital stay, something to turn her against me. She had

311

made too much of those moments in her sick-room at the Kaiana Hilton when she looked at her husband and at me.

"I'm fine," she told me coolly. "It all turned out to be a false alarm. Palpitations, they call it. An old lady's disease. Stephen was going to come and be with me tonight but he wouldn't bring me back home until the fuddy-duddy doctors said I could go. Then Mr. Berringer came to the hospital. He was scary at first —" She leaned nearer to confide, "He still is. But he talked to me awhile and he didn't seem so bad. And then, when I complained about being kept in the hospital, he said he'd get me home if I would talk about the days with Ingrid."

"And did you?"

She shrugged. "It wasn't as bad as I thought. I just told what I remembered, and he didn't get mad or anything."

"And you feel perfectly all right. No pain? Everything fine?"

"Of course!"

Why did Berringer want Deirdre home on Ili-Ahi? Did he hope she would lead him to something — some clue about his daughter's disappearance?

"But you shouldn't be climbing stairs," I insisted. "You know that. When Stephen talked to the hospital they told him you wouldn't be released for several days."

"That's right." She squeezed my hands with a more friendly gesture, and her warm, full lips spread in her childlike smile, but her eyes were wary and watchful. "As it happened, Berringer turned out to be a friend. Yes, wise old auntie, I really have friends of my very own." She withdrew her hands with a kind of thoughtful deliberation. "Imagine! I was important to them. They came clear to the hospital, he and that Pelhitt man, just to listen to my opinions and what I had to say."

Without being sure what this meant, I was almost afraid to ask. I knew anything Berringer might want of Deirdre would be disastrous.

"Of course they wanted to talk with you, Deirdre. After all, you knew Ingrid. Was the lieutenant with Mr. Berringer and Bill Pelhitt when they saw you in the hospital?"

She had started into her room. She looked over her shoulder, a trifle puzzled but apparently not in the least suspicious of any ulterior motive in all this.

"The policeman? No. Why would he visit me? He's not my friend."

"And Berringer is? Deirdre, when you first met that man, you were terrified. You drew sketches of him as Satan. Why the sudden change?"

With an insouciance that reminded me of her mischievous childhood years she taunted me, "I changed my mind. Mr. Berringer isn't like you or Stephen. Or Dr. Ito Nagata. He listened to me about that awful Pelé goddess who scared me so."

"What! But Deirdre —"

"In the grove. I saw that thing from my window, that goddess — whatever it was — right after Stephen and I were married. Nobody believed me. Why do you think I moved out of my pretty pink room? I was frightened of that thing, and Stephen just wouldn't believe me. He thought it was because of . . . because I was afraid of him." She bit her lip and looked as if she was sorry she had told me so much.

I said quietly, "I understand. I really do."

This time the faint flicker of a smile was genuine.

"In a way, I was afraid. I was so stupid. Ingrid said I was the most ignorant freak she ever knew. I don't mean about sex and things like that. But about handling men. She said she'd get him back. She said I was an idiot and he'd find out and never want me. But he's not going to find out. I'll never let him know me so well he'd be able to hate me as she did. He's always going to see me the way he thinks I am now. Not — that other me. The one that Ingrid says is an idiot."

I could hardly bear this. To think she would believe the foul, treacherous lies of a woman like this Ingrid Berringer! I could kill the woman myself, or very nearly!

"Deirdre, listen to me. Ingrid Berringer is a jealous female. That is all. You mustn't believe anything she tells you. Women like that always try to hurt you if they think you are vulnerable. You must never let anyone see that you can be

314

hurt by them. Certainly not by a jealous creature like that."

She took a deep breath. "And you, darling Aunt Judy? Are you a jealous female?" she asked me unhappily. Then she went into her study.

I hadn't heard the men downstairs, so I went down in a hurry to find out what they were doing. No matter how they may have conned Deirdre into believing them, they were here for some devious reason that would hurt Deirdre and Stephen. And they had risked her life to further their schemes. I bitterly resented them, but I knew this attitude would accomplish nothing. Following their voices, I went into the living room where I found William Pelhitt regaling his two companions with the tale of last night's storm and the way he had fallen, "fallen into the room through the broken window."

"And here is my young savior," he pointed me out as Berringer and the dark-eyed lieutenant looked around at me. The lieutenant was not unfriendly, but he had the business-like stare of a man sizing me up. I knew the look and the suspicion that triggered such a look. On the other hand, Victor Berringer's eyes regarded me with frosty amusement and something else — a certain curiosity — as if he were genuinely interested in my part of this business. Surely, if he were worried about his daughter, he would, understandably, feel rage and fear and all the heated emotions of any other human being in his situation. I sometimes wondered if Victor

Berringer actually was human.

The men were all standing by the new west window from which anyone could get an oblique, northerly view of the sacred grove. Once Berringer and the lieutenant had lost interest in staring at me, they returned to what seemed to be their chief concern, the grove itself. William had tried to concentrate on me, but I could see that his companions' determined, one-track minds had shaken him. He kept trying, in his heavy-footed, rather endearing way, to play down the seriousness of this visit, but I felt they might as well get on with whatever unpleasantness they intended.

Bill boomed out with almost an excess of cheerfulness, "Hi! Come here and tell them all about how you saved me from pneumonia last night."

"I don't want to play down your rescue from pneumonia, but I would like to ask you what these gentlemen are doing here. According to Mrs. Giles, they took a great chance by landing in some sort of pasture."

"Perfectly adequate landing strip, but thank you for your interest, Miss Cameron," Berringer put in politely. "We checked by telephone with the noble lady who is called 'Queen' Ilima. She described the field minutely, and urged us to make the flight over at our first opportunity. This was our first opportunity. By the way, this is Lieutenant José Padilla. Lieutenant, Miss Judith Cameron, Mrs. Giles's aunt."

The lieutenant nodded. I could almost see his brain recalling certain unsavory notes about my past, but he was more interested in the present serious matters. I agreed with him in that — I didn't like this pussyfooting around.

"I suggest you get on with whatever you came to do and save the amenities for afterward. Mrs. Giles tells me you persuaded her to leave the hospital against her doctors' advice. I don't suggest you try any more tricks of that sort. If something happens to Mrs. Giles, you will be responsible. Now, what did you come here for?"

"She's right, you know," Bill Pelhitt put in, nervously trying to make peace. "Can't we postpone this business for a little while, until Mrs. Giles is better?"

Before Berringer could open his mouth with a customary sardonic remark, Lieutenant Padilla turned to me.

"Miss Cameron, I do agree with everything you say. I am here to see that an area of the grove called Sandalwood *heiau* is investigated."

Since Deirdre had mentioned her phantom goddess Pelé, which she claimed to have seen when she was first married, I assumed they were interested in the sacred grove, but Kekua had died less than two nights ago. What had all this to do with Deirdre's imaginary phantom? The disappearance of Ingrid Berringer so long ago had nothing whatever to do with murder, as yet.

Then I remembered the marks I saw in the grove the afternoon before the storm. "But

Kekua's footsteps and the others were washed away last night. And today the workers must have trampled all over the place."

For the first time Berringer lost his cool self-possession. "What has the native girl's death got to do with this? Get on with it."

"Mr. Berringer, I don't want to supervise the digging until Mr. Giles is here. These men are his workers and I want to be quite certain he is witness to everything that is done in that grove."

The whole situation was far worse than I had expected or even feared. I was sure that Deirdre never dreamed of what she had stirred up, but I said coldly, "Mr. Giles will be happy to satisfy you when he gets back from Kekua Moku's funeral. I had supposed you came here to investigate Miss Moku's death. It seems you aren't even interested in it."

They all seemed upset by this charge, as if it had never occurred to them that there might be something strange and sinister about Kekua's "accident."

Bill Pelhitt and Berringer said almost together, "But it *was* an accident, wasn't it?" and Lieutenant Padilla asked me flatly, "Are you trying to tell me Miss Moku's death was not an accident? If you know something that hasn't been reported, I advise you to make a statement to that effect."

Deirdre's voice settled priorities for us at that minute when we heard her calling as she ran through the hall toward the front door: "Stephen! You didn't go to the funeral yet. I'll go with you. I'm going to the grave, too."

The lieutenant glanced toward the doorway but returned his attention to me immediately. "Mr. Giles seems to be here; so unless you have something pertinent to say about the Moku girl's death, we will have to leave that subject for some later time. Perhaps you would prefer to go in to Kaiana City, or better yet, to Honolulu, and make your statement there tomorrow."

"But I have no statement. I simply thought —"

He turned away with Berringer and went after Deirdre. From the window Bill Pelhitt and I saw Deirdre walk as quickly as she could out across the grass to meet Stephen. He was clearly delighted to see her, and swung her up to him in an embrace that tore at me emotionally. I was happy at this clear sign of his love, but I couldn't deny my own anguish. I really did feel jealousy. Bill looked at me.

"Loves them all, doesn't he? He may be pretty gentle now, but he managed to make my Ingrid love him, and then he threatened her life."

"Don't be ridiculous. Are you responsible for filling that policeman with lies?"

A muscle in his cheek tightened. He said breathily, "Those are no lies. You heard Mrs. Asami. Vic took the lieutenant to question her. Then we went to talk with Mrs. Giles, and Mrs. Giles told him the rest."

"How could Mrs. Asami identify Stephen? Or

did you just guess at someone who fitted his description?"

Bill looked around in that embarrassed way he had that was at once annoying and pitiful.

"I took a wedding picture of Giles and his wife."

"How? When?"

"Last night. In his study. I just borrowed it. A five-by-seven color thing. It will be returned afterward." He pointed to the little domestic scene on the lawn.

Stephen was looking Deirdre over from head to foot, and obviously scolding her, but gently. I closed my eyes. When I opened them Deirdre had turned and was staring back at me.

Beside me, Bill Pelhitt grumbled, "He's talking about you. Anybody can see that. But it's only making her hate you. Did you ever think of that?"

I said, "Haven't you done enough damage? What a detestable, sneaking little man you are!"

His face was enraged. "You don't understand!"

I pushed him aside and went out after Berringer and the lieutenant. They were just approaching Stephen and Deirdre but had apparently announced their purpose before they reached him. Stephen still held Deirdre's hand but he was demanding that they furnish their legal proof of rights to dig up the grove and ruin the work of many weeks.

"Do we need to make it legal, Mr. Giles?" the

320

lieutenant asked quietly. "Wouldn't it be better to give us help, since you have nothing to hide?"

"Darling," Deirdre put in anxiously, "They just want to look at the place where I saw Pelé a long time ago. And then again. Lately."

Stephen frowned. "I have nothing to hide, whatever these fellows may think." His expression softened as his glance shifted to me. I could not seem to avoid his gaze. I couldn't keep myself from reading personal and probably imaginary messages in the eyes of this man I loved.

Deirdre, with her husband's arms around her, clutched his hand in both of hers. "Really, Stephen has nothing to hide. You must believe that. It was Pelé I saw. Or a man who —"

"A man?" Lieutenant Padilla asked softly.

"A man or a woman. Just somebody in gray. Maybe it was a raincoat he — or she — was wearing. But of course it wasn't Stephen. Was it darling? Darling, don't keep looking at wise old auntie. She doesn't know the answer. Or does she?"

I was glad I hadn't been looking his way. I kept to my coolly competent act. I said, "I am sure no one needs me out here. I'll get back to the house." In spite of my effort, my voice sounded shaky and uncertain to my own ears.

I turned and walked away rapidly. I tried not to hear Stephen urge Deirdre, "Go along, darling. You should be lying down, taking things easy. Judith will look after you."

It was an innocent suggestion and, I thought, one that showed his very male stupidity, for the last thing in the world that Deirdre wanted was to be dependent upon me for anything. I heard her childlike giggle and her firm denial, "No, no. My husband needs me and I'm going to stand by him."

Surely, she could have no idea what she was doing to the man she loved!

Much worse, though, the lieutenant asked her to stay. "You must help us find the place where you saw Pelé."

Stephen settled the matter with a firmness that made me admire him all the more. "Lieutenant, I will ask my men to give you whatever help you need. The sooner we conclude this business, the better for all of us."

I had reached the veranda by the time the lieutenant accepted Stephen's offer. From the living room's north window I saw the men who were called off the Sandalwood *heiau*. They looked at each other, protested a bit, but ended by taking up rakes and shovels. They began to turn over ground around the little broken foot bridge and then, as Deirdre pointed out various places with sweeping motions, Stephen came back to the house, calling to Mr. Yee. The cook appeared in the hall.

"I cannot be expected to appear in all places at once, Mr. Stephen. Yes. It is possible to feed the crew. But for the liquor, that is not my responsibility. Coffee and hot saki, perhaps. No more. In a very short time Nelia Perez leaves. After that, Miss Cameron must wait upon all the family and the crew if this matter is not ended by nightfall." The sun had already gone down behind the western jungle-clad slopes and I knew that even in the light dusk it would still be difficult to see what they were doing out there in the heavily timbered grove.

"We'll eat picnic fashion in that case," Stephen said. "Judith — Miss Cameron, is not employed as a servant."

Mr. Yee made no reply to that. He returned to the kitchen. Stephen followed him to the kitchen, then started back past the open doors of the living room. I thought that in my place at the north window I would not be seen but he looked in and spoke.

"Judith, you know I didn't mean that this morning. Of course, it is your business. Anything to do with me is your affair."

I had forgotten all about our quarrel. It meant nothing. But I was nervous for fear Deirdre would overhear us, and said quickly, "I have some things to do. Would you please excuse me?"

He tried to be gentle about it, though he wouldn't let me pass him. His strong face looked so tired, so strained, I longed to comfort him. But I kept a tight rein on my desire to make that kind of disastrous gesture.

"Please. Deirdre will be wondering."

"You were right, you know." I was surprised at

this which, like our quarrel, I had forgotten. I must have shown my surprise. He explained, "I didn't think the village would go so far as to put up a barricade. I always believed we understood and respected each other. And now this. I don't even know what Kekua's death had to do with those fellows digging up the grove, putting us weeks behind in our work."

"Something Deirdre saw."

"Yes. I know that." He dismissed this impatiently. "And all because that woman, Mrs. Asami, heard me quarreling with Berringer's impossible daughter. You may depend on it, I probably would have strangled her — well, not quite that — if she kept on persecuting Deirdre. Calling her an idiot and a moron! Calling her on the phone. She threatened to come to the island. Hounding the child. Saying I would learn to hate her when I realized she was — the way she is. As if anyone could hate that child! I'm surprised I *didn't* kill her!"

We heard the lieutenant call for Stephen and he started to the window, I suppose to signal that he was coming.

I touched his arm. "Not in here, Deirdre will think something is wrong." I did not add "again" but he understood. Deirdre would be certain to think we had contrived this meeting and were talking against her. He nodded and went back through the hall to the veranda.

I dreaded and yet looked forward to the first moment when I could suggest that Deirdre did not need me. Certainly my original idea of serving as housekeeper had fallen through. I glanced out the window across the room. There seemed to be sudden excitement in the grove. Stephen had begun to run toward the little crowd gathered around something I couldn't see. Deirdre had been forgotten. She trailed toward the excited men very slowly. It must be that she at last realized her innocent chattering had brought some deep trouble to the man she adored.

Whatever evidence they had located it must have something to do with the death of Kekua Moku. I decided as I watched, my hands shaking so I could hardly hold onto the curtain, that Kekua had quarreled with someone there in the grove — her blackmail victim? — and that she had either been killed there and taken across the grass to the gulch below Sandalwood, or she had run from the grove and been pursued to her death. But what evidence of such a purely hypothetical scene could they expect to find?

Although I was frantic with suspense, I did not go out there until Mr. Yee and Nelia Perez left the house. It was Nelia who came back and motioned to me. I went out to the veranda then and met her.

"Is it something about Kekua's death?" I asked her, still persisting in my delusion.

"Who knows? Maybe there is a connection."

We started across the lawn on a run. There was still the golden afterglow of sunset across the island, except in the grove where shadows were so deep that one of the workers raised a lantern and the light flared across the area in front of one of the cottages. The steps had been removed and a trench dug from the earth uncovered the cottage foundation. Within that trench was a long, aging, water-soaked bundle. It must once have been a woman's cape. It was natural wool trimmed with white leather, but though the leather was hopelessly stained and the wool rotting, enough of the material remained so that it was identifiable.

"Well?" Lieutenant Padilla asked, more or less generally. "Is anyone prepared to identify that object? You, sir?" This was to Berringer, who looked stony-faced, his thin lips very tight.

"If it is — if it was purchased by my daughter, I was not aware of it."

I was shivering with cold, or with the tight clasp of Deirdre's hand on my right wrist. My right hand was numb. We were all startled out of a dreamlike state of horror by Stephen's voice, wonderfully quiet and steady, although he too looked pale, unlike himself.

"I recognize it. When Miss Berringer arrived at the airport in Honolulu with my wife she was wearing a deep gold wool cape with some kind of leather trim. Around the collar and armholes, I think."

Deirdre's clasp on my wrist tightened and I winced, but when I looked at her, I knew she was on the verge of fainting.

326

"Can we get Mrs. Giles out of here?" I asked the lieutenant. "She is ill."

Stephen turned, caught Deirdre and lifted her light form. "Clear the way, please. You! Lieutenant! I'll be on hand if you want me." Deirdre was frightened, crying and breathing too rapidly, but she had not lost consciousness, and as he carried her to Sandalwood House she hugged him closely, her wet cheek against his bronzed one.

At the same time someone had lifted the rotting fabric from the body and a part of it, the head, probably, was revealed in the trench below us. Feeling sick, I avoided looking at it, wondering if I was going to be able to get away from here under my own power. I heard Bill Pelhitt as he fell to his knees in the dirt.

"Ingrid! God, it *is* Ingrid!"

Nineteen

Lieutenant Padilla might have appeared calm and steady, but he moved fast once the identification of Ingrid Berringer had been made. Nelia and I got coffee ready, with various whiskies handy to lace the coffee for the men who had worked to uncover the ghastly business of Ingrid Berringer's body. Lieutenant Padilla walked across the clearing to speak with Stephen, who came down from the upstairs quarters. They were discussing the possibility of getting the plane off before sunset. They lowered their voices when they saw Bill Pelhitt, who stood on the grass below the veranda steps in a kind of stupor, staring at the grove with its lantern light and phantom figures.

Most frightening, I think, was Victor Berringer. He had started to touch something in the wet, rotting confines of the trench where his daughter's body lay, but even his iron nerve was not up to that horror. He strode back to the veranda, poured himself a cup of coffee, and stood looking into the cup after each swallow. His face still had the granite look with its inhuman chill, but once, only once, he choked as he drank, and cleared his throat in a furtive way.

"I can get the plane off if you can't," he said finally, interrupting the lieutenant's discussion with Stephen. "I demand that you bring this man and his wife in for questioning."

The lieutenant was not impressed. "Mr. Giles has volunteered to return with me and make a statement concerning his knowledge of Miss Berringer's movements in Hawaii."

"And his wife."

Lieutenant Padilla waved this away impatiently.

"Mrs. Giles is unwell. We can talk with her at another time."

"But she could run away!"

The lieutenant looked at him with grim dislike. "Queen Ilima will be here shortly. Mrs. Moku has agreed to remain in the house tonight if our business in Honolulu keeps Giles too long for him to make a comfortable return until morning."

I breathed more easily now. Berringer was still for a minute, shuddered slightly for no reason, and then nodded.

"I don't suppose we can remove my daughter to a decent place . . ."

"I'm sorry. Not yet. I've asked for the cooperation of the county's office in Kaiana City and two men will be here at any time to watch over the grove until all the —" he hesitated "— evidence has been studied. Will that satisfy you?"

Berringer shrugged. "It must, I suppose. William! What the devil do you think you are staring at? Come along."

Bill Pelhitt looked around with a nervous start. "I don't think you will need me, Vic. It doesn't seem to matter any more."

"Are you crazy? What doesn't matter? My daughter has been murdered and you say it doesn't matter? We can't even be sure what the weapon was. A blow. It tells us nothing. I mean to find out who struck that blow. Someone too cowardly to face her."

"We don't know," put in Lieutenant Padilla. "It may have been a blow from a fall. Anything. An accidental death."

"And her burial? That can hardly have been 'accidental'!" He added with cold deliberation, "The man — or woman — who did this is going to pay! And if it was two of them, they are both going to suffer for it. Ingrid Berringer was not some barefoot native girl killed by a jealous *kanaka*. She was Victor Berringer's daughter!"

Unconsciously, Stephen and I looked at each other. I knew he felt as I did, that no girl, whatever she may have done, deserved that epitaph: to be of importance after death solely because she was Victor Berringer's daughter!

Ten minutes later, when three men from Kaiana, including Dr. Lum of the Kaiana Hilton, arrived by boat, Lieutenant Padilla went off with Stephen and the two who had loved the dead woman to the improvised airstrip.

Stephen's last instructions were for Nelia, who would try to act as Deirdre's companion, since Deirdre was still refusing to see me. The knowledge hurt but did not surprise me. As Nelia and I watched the men go, Nelia remarked, "Funny that a man can care so little about his only child, and so much about himself."

"I suppose so. It's hard to know what men like that are really feeling." I didn't even know what Stephen was thinking at this minute, with all his terrible responsibilities and worries. But I was impressed by Nelia's view, which was both cynical and penetrating.

The four men dissolved into the tight-laced jungle growth to the west of the village path. A short while later Ilima Moku came stalking along that path in a red-and-green flowered *holoku*. Queen Ilima's height and bearing and her vivid, deep color were emphasized by the long gown.

Nelia and I were taking in the dirty glasses and what remained of the ice and bottles when Nelia muttered, "Uh-oh. The queen arrives. Get out the red carpet. I'll go up and see if Mrs. Steve needs anything."

Considering the roadblock laid in the way of Stephen's jeep at the time of the funeral, I dreaded a confrontation with the woman. Deirdre must never suspect the reason why the woman was here. She had gone through enough trouble, including her jealousy of me, and the uncertainties of her past, which she had long ago blotted out of her memory, but which existed, I was sure, in her subconscious mind.

I tried to behave toward Queen Ilima with the utmost naturalness. It was not easy. The lady came to the veranda and set one sandaled foot on the step. I said, "Thank you for coming, Mrs.

Moku. It seems it was important to Lieutenant Padilla."

Ilima Moku's proud, dark head inclined very slightly in my direction. "Is Mrs. Stephen in her study now? Or in one of the bedrooms?"

I trailed along after her anxiously.

"Would you mind being very careful in what you talk about, Mrs. Moku? She has no idea that — that —"

I couldn't finish. It was like a nightmare replay of Claire Cameron's death long ago. Once more the threat hung over Deirdre. If she realized that she was suspected of such a hideous crime, I couldn't imagine what tricks her mind would play.

Mrs. Moku had already started upstairs. She did not look back.

"I am not concerned with Mr. Berringer's daughter, you may be sure, but with my own."

This in no way reassured me. Her daughter had been buried only a few hours ago. Her mood could scarcely be charitable. I let her go on. She must have discovered where Stephen had left Deirdre, because I heard her open a door. Feeling like a sneak-thief, I went up after her as quietly as possible. To my surprise, it was Stephen's own room whose door closed gently. At least these horrors had accomplished the object for which I had come to Hawaii. Deirdre must have finally grown up enough to accept Stephen, not only as a "guardian" but as her husband. I heard whispers. Then Queen Ilima backed out, followed by Nelia Perez, who was trying to quiet her.

"Poor thing. She's only just got to sleep."

"This is no matter of mine. Let me see her. I have given my word that she will not run away."

"All right. Just a peek."

With an impressive grace, Ilima moved silently into the room, satisfied herself, and came back out, closing the door with care.

"Very well. But I must take the room opposite. I will know then if she makes as if to leave."

Nelia Perez said briskly, "That's entirely up to Miss Cameron. She's the housekeeper here. As for me, I wish I was on my way home. I should never have let myself be talked into staying here tonight. But Mr. Steve has his winning ways."

Queen Ilima's deep-voiced reply cut like a rapidly flashing knife. "His winning ways have destroyed my daughter. And now another is dead. And on that sacred ground. The *kahunas* put it under *kapu* long ages ago. Who disturbed that ground? The Giles family!"

I ran downstairs and was entering the little back parlor when Ilima called to me. I didn't think it would accomplish anything if I forbade her to use Deirdre's pink bedroom, so I merely asked what she would like for dinner.

"Nothing, Miss Cameron. I will not touch any food or drink in this house. I will go to that bedroom now and remain there. With the door a little open." Having given her ultimatum, she returned to the upstairs region, doubtless to

333

play detective all night.

By the time my own evening was over, although it involved very little work, I was not only praying to have Ingrid Berringer's murder solved as soon as possible, but was hoping almost as strongly that Stephen would make peace with the Hawaiian villagers. Surely, no one could bear this house for more than a few nights without the usual friendly household staff coming and going. The place was a tomb. The roar of the Ili-Ahi falls deafened me at times. Then there were moments when the noise seemed to fade into distant obscurity, and that was worse.

Nelia and I saw each other when she came down to the kitchen for Deirdre's supper.

"No," she said in answer to my first question. "She's not ready to see you yet, but I think, between you and me, she's coming around. She really wants to be friends with you. It's just — well, you know . . . Anyway, all she will eat is toast and soup. Any of the *lomi-lomi* salmon left? That will be for me. That and the pork, and some beer."

I asked about Queen Ilima. "Do you think she will ever forgive the Giles family? Surely, the new baby should comfort her a little."

"It's her sister's baby. Still, Ilima may soften too. Some day."

"Will they ever allow any of us *haoles* to visit Kekua's grave?"

With a nervous little shiver, Nelia said, "The Kalanimokus are buried on that mountain above

334

the village at the source of the river. Unless you're a pretty good hiker, it's no picnic. They've always chosen that area because it is hard to get to, through all that swampy patch at the base of the mountain. Of course, Mrs. Steve is devil-bent to go. She and Kekua were friendly, you know. But you can depend on it, Queen Ilima will never let her leave Sandalwood unless — that is, until Mr. Steve gets back."

In the end our brief dinner together was the only bright spot in the long night. Nelia slept in the guest room, and I in mine. As I closed my door I thought, when this murderer is found — and it *has* to have been a stranger, not someone I love — I will leave here. Or was I hedging? I had said I would leave as soon as Deirdre recovered.

Where would I go? Back to California. Or farther east. There was a world there. Mine had been confined too long — it was time I saw that world. If only Deirdre and Stephen could be happy together, I knew that in spite of my own infatuation, I would be relieved. Enormously so.

I heard sounds occasionally in the night. A wind blew up and when I looked out the window toward the north and west, I could see rain clouds hanging over the distant peak below which Kekua had been buried today. I looked out into the hall several times. Always one light was on in Ilima's room, and always the door was open a foot or so. But Deirdre did not leave her husband's room.

I got back to sleep again and awoke a little

after a clouded sunrise. I may have heard a sound without being aware of it, but when I opened my eyes to see someone standing beside the bed, looking down at me, I blinked and I may have cried out. It was only Nelia Perez, still in her nightgown. She was looking tense and reached out one hand. I backed away, but her finger touched my lips and my eyes opened wide.

She whispered, "She made it."

I tried to ask, "Made what?" but I had to push her finger aside. "What is this all about?"

"Sh! Queenie doesn't know. The old dragon's finally fallen asleep. I could hear her snoring."

I sat straight up in bed but kept my voice down. "Deirdre?"

"Read this. I found it on her bed."

It was one of Stephen's letterheads folded twice and sealed with a bit of Scotch tape. My name was scrawled on the back of the paper in the childish writing that reminded me of Deirdre's letters to me in prison. I had the unpleasant sensation that I was back at the institution. Eagerly I broke the tape seal.

Darling Judy:

Forgive me. I've been horrid. A real louse. Hold off Queen Ilima. I'm going to Kekua's grave and plant a little slip from our shower tree. She always liked it. Please, please don't let Ilima or her family know.

Love,
Deirdre

336

"Good heavens! You don't mean you let her go!" I was already out of bed.

"Not me! My room was farther away from her than yours is. I just heard one of those stairs creak and on a hunch I went to her room. Gone. Evaporated!"

Things didn't look quite so bad to me. "Maybe I can call someone from the village to . . . No. They'd only contact Ilima. But you must know the —" Her face clearly told me that was out. She shook her head vigorously.

"And get the whole gang to put a curse on me! Not little Nelia, thank you! I've my own problems without having *kapus* thrown in my direction."

I knew I would have to go after Deirdre. "A trip like that could be very bad for her. She could have an attack and no one about to help her."

"Excuse me, miss, but she isn't that sick. Whatever palpitations are, they can't be as bad as a heart attack. Anyway, she went under her own steam. I had a hunch, just a hunch, mind you, that she intends for you to follow her. It's all so pat. She knew someone would find the note and give it to you. And she must know you'd go after her."

I was grabbing clothes and dressing. As I gave orders I managed to keep my voice down. "I'll have to go anyway. We can't take the chance that this is some trick of hers. You go to Stephen's room and keep the door closed. When you know Mrs. Moku is awake, make a bit of noise to let her think Deirdre is still there, but keep the door locked."

"I don't think it'll do any good. Queen Ilima is no fool. But I'll do the best I can." She hurried off.

While I got into slacks, I looked out the window. I thought I saw Deirdre in something pink, far up the village path. I scrambled into a turtleneck sweater and pulled it down. I opened the hall door as carefully as Nelia. She was right. Ilima Moku had fallen asleep. I could hear the even sound of her breathing.

I slipped down the stairs and on the ground floor I began to run toward the front door, which would be the shortest way to the village path. The grass around the *emu* was wet and glistening. My sandals and my bare feet were soaking wet by the time I reached the trail and of course, Deirdre was now out of sight.

There were patches of blue sky between the great, puffed clouds with their dark lining, and as I went along the trail, slowing now and breathless. I kept going into shade and out of it. The trail was dappled with sunlight, but off to the west and the north it was raining over the peak of the mountain. I tried to remember the name. Liholiho? Lunalilo? It didn't matter, but thinking about it kept my mind off my legs which were definitely beginning to tire, and I realized I had only begun my hike.

But Deirdre would be tired also. She had only just returned from the hospital. It terrified me to think of a girl with a bad heart hurrying along this rough and twisting trail ahead of me. If I could only call to her, I could at least tell her to take it easy, tell her I wasn't trying to chase or catch her. I just wanted to be certain she didn't kill herself. I had passed this way only days ago but since that time we had gone through a storm that was little short of a hurricane, and the trail was littered with debris. I found myself climbing over broken tree limbs thick with greenery, all soggy and dripping.

I began to catch glimpses of the sea on the west, breathtakingly clear and blue, but beginning to darken in wider and wider patches under the rapidly shifting clouds. I came to a sharp turn that had been masked by the hibiscus blossoms blown across the ground and into a bush where they appeared to sprout beside pale yellow, star-shaped flowers. Beyond the turn, however, I caught sight of Deirdre below and to the east of the village trail. She appeared to be waist-deep in ferns. She must have reached the turn-off to the mountain burial ground, but she had not yet started to climb.

I called to her. Nothing happened. I tried again and then a third time, hoarsely, but my voice was swallowed up in that immense and luxuriant jungle. I made my way through a barrier of broken ferns that still seemed alive. They fell across the trail like hundreds of stiff cobra heads. The wind flung a palm frond in my face and I was momentarily blinded. I screamed and threw the thing away from my face. To my relief and surprise I now saw Deirdre again, in her pink shorts and halter and the little candy-striped jockey cap. She seemed to be on rising ground. She must have started up the mountain.

Then she looked back. I could have sworn she saw me. I waved frantically and called, "Deirdre! Stop! Please wait for me! Deirdre!" But she turned her head away and went on. It was odd and disquieting. I followed, running now. She did not look back at me again. So her note to me had been, in one way, a lie. She was not really apologizing — she was very obviously avoiding me. Or, as Nelia suspected, leading me on. That was a curious thought.

Shortly after, I found the turn-off leading to the burial site of the Hawaiian family. On a small, flat, stone marker was carved simply: KALANIMOKU. I could catch glimpses of the sea on the west beyond a strip of coco palms, their fringe in the path of the wind, fluttering exactly as they did on picture postcards. I turned my back to these and headed east and north, where the path began to rise. The wind hit stronger as I climbed. I was sure I had seen Deirdre somewhere along here, but she was nowhere in sight now. I studied the ground, thankful that the rain squalls hadn't hit this area yet.

Then I came to a fork in the steep, climbing path over very black earth. I didn't know what to do here until I had studied the ground. On the higher climb there were several footprints that looked fresh. Small feet, like Deirdre's. But could I be sure? I took a few steps between the prickly, unknown vegetation on the upper trail and saw a tiny pink knitted ball dangling from one of the bushes. The waistband of Deirdre's pink shorts was decorated with these miniature balls of yarn. It was a sign impossible to ignore, so I started to climb. Almost at once the trail closed behind me.

By the time I had walked for ten minutes, tearing away the interlacing growth that also crawled around thick tree trunks, I began to wonder if I would be able to find my way back. I no longer saw any signs of Deirdre. I had gradually entered a swampy area that was heavily forested, with much of its mossy growth rotting. I remembered that this mountain and one on Kaiana received four hundred inches of rain a year. This was said to be the highest rainfall registered in the world.

Hearing the ripple of water, I was about to turn back when I saw another of those pink balls of knitting yarn on a half-log that formed an uncertain bridge over this sector of the Ili-Ahi river. Although the water flow was heavy here, and raindrops had already begun to penetrate the canopy of immense vegetation overhead, the river at this point was still narrow. Within this jungle world the air was hypnotically thick with flower scents. It was not sweet, but, rather, was compounded of a strange, almost bitter perfume of the flowers' aromas plus the wet earth and the smells of millions of crowded, scrambling tropical growths, almost all unknown to me. The river tumbled past me at this point and downward from some collecting pool near the mountain peak. Then it wandered across the island to the falls beside Sandalwood and on into the sea near the landing for the boats that crossed Kaiana Bay.

Seeing the tiny pink ball on the log bridge, I decided I had been right. Absurd or not, Deirdre was either playing a joke on me, leaving tracks for me to follow, or perhaps, subconsciously, she wanted me to follow. Either way, my spirits were considerably raised. She must mean exactly what she said in the note, that she was no longer angry with me. She would surely have stopped somewhere around here. I was worn out, and I considered myself a strong, healthy woman. I crossed the bridge, which wobbled and shifted under my feet. It was not very stable and had been laid over boulders and on top of a huge, fallen tree trunk coated with lichen and green slime. Lianas trailed everywhere from the trees and foliage overhead that enclosed me. Sweaty and wet all over, I felt as if I were in a bathhouse whose walls were rapidly smothering me.

Bird sounds were faint and far away, but there were rustlings close at hand, so close I could hear, or perhaps sense, the little sounds above the noise of the stream rushing down past me, beneath the trembling log that seemed barely to support my body. Across the log, on slippery, moss-covered ground that seemed to sink spongelike underfoot, I could not even find the continuance of the trail. I must have wandered in this strange, uncomfortable Eden for some minutes before giving up and making my way back toward the log, using the sound of the river as my guide.

If Deirdre had tired by now — and I myself was exhausted — she simply could not have gone beyond this area. I called her name several times but the result was an eerie sensation, as though the sounds of my own voice were sucked in by all the Ili-Ahi swamp's unseen denizens. Then I reached the river at a point a little above the improvised bridge, which was masked from me by a huge banyan tree, at whose feet anthuriums grew, looking artificial as they always had to me. Stiff and shiny, a gorgeous red that was softened with pink, but never quite real. Brushing aside the tangled vines, I heard my name called. Thank heaven! It was Deirdre sitting there across the river, her back against a boulder, her sandals beside her, and her feet splashing in the foam that lingered as the waters rushed by. She waved to me while I wondered how I could have missed her when I was on that shore of the river. Where had she hidden?

"Hi! Led you a chase, didn't I?"

"You led me a chase, all right. Honestly, Deirdre!" I raised my voice. "Why? Don't you know you could have killed yourself?"

Deirdre was looking mischievous but even at this distance her young face appeared strained and very white.

"I know, wise old auntie. Why don't you come and stop me?"

"What I ought to do is spank you."

"Try!" It was a curious challenge.

I made my way around endless tentacles belonging to the banyan tree, its roots everywhere, and reached the point opposite where Deirdre sat, the point from which I had crossed on the log bridge to this side.

The bridge was gone.

Twenty

I thought I had miscalculated the place. I moved out as far as I dared on the slippery ground and looked down the path of the river. It descended rapidly about twenty yards beyond this spot. I couldn't be mistaken about the bridge. It had been here. I could identify each boulder, as well as the big, dead tree where the log bridge had rested. Long ago, several cleats seemed to have worn away from a wooden contrivance that fastened the bridge securely at this end.

Deirdre called suddenly, "Be careful. You'll fall in."

Even though I remembered her many moods, I was surprised at the concern in her voice now. Whatever trick she was playing, there was nothing malign in it, since she obviously wished me safe now.

"What happened to the bridge?" I asked calmly.

"There." With her wet, bare toes she pointed to the river's edge just beyond her feet. The long bridge had come to rest against the shoreline and bobbed there, looking as if it might float away and down the stream that bubbled and foamed below us.

I studied it, wondering what on earth I was going to do now. I called to Deirdre, "I hope there's another way to get down off this mountain."

"I don't see how," she shrugged. "It's all a swampy mess behind you. The trail up to the burial ground runs from this side."

"Now, look here, Deirdre, if you saw that the bridge was going to come loose, why didn't you call out and warn me?"

"Can't hear you!"

I raised my voice, then realized she heard me quite well. She paddled her feet vigorously in the water as she informed me that Stephen had called her late last evening and told her he would be home in the morning. "He said he explained to the hospital why I left. He said you would take care of me, and if I behaved I wouldn't have to go back." She added in a sudden, querulous impatience, "He thought of you. Always you! He even said at the end: 'Tell Judith when I will be back.'"

"Of course he did, Deirdre. I am acting as housekeeper. I should know how many people will be at dinner, if nothing else. What has all this got to do with that log falling?"

Sulkily, she kicked at it. "I did that. It hurt, too. It was heavy. I just slid it off the rocks and let it float right here." She looked up. "Judy, I'll let it go against those boulders and you can step on it easy from where you are, if —"

"If!"

"Darling auntie," oddly enough, she seemed to be sincere in calling me that. "Please promise to go home to California. Or China. Or someplace else. As long as you are here, where Stephen can see you doing everything right, everything better than I can do it, I'll lose Stephen. Won't you promise me, Judy? Please?"

It was heartbreaking that she had felt it necessary to go to this much effort just to get rid of me, especially since I was leaving anyway. She must have planned that I should follow her, knowing I would be trapped by this stream.

"I promise, dear. I meant to leave when Stephen came back from Honolulu."

"Oh, Judy, darling! Swear."

"I swear. Now, do be careful. Don't exert yourself too much." But she was already on her feet, scrambling over the slippery ground. She knelt by the center of the log and began to free it from its entangling vines and the debris washed against it.

"Take it easy," I called, watching anxiously.

"I got it off those upper rocks. I can get it back on these rocks a little farther down. I can do things too, you know."

"Yes, dear. Very clever." But she worried me to death. She was trying to boost the log over against a boulder and looked as if she was exerting tremendous energy. I shifted my foot along the river's edge, tried a rock about two yards out in the stream. The torrential force edged my foot off the rock and my leg plunged into the cold, rushing water. While I was recovering my balance on the shore, Deirdre got the log jammed between a boulder and the fallen tree trunk. She cried out and I waved to her to stop.

"Take it easy, Deirdre. Easy! I'll get across. Don't worry."

She was weeping now in her panic. "It's got to go across. It's got to!"

I ignored this, and ordered her to stop and take it easy while I followed the river bank upstream, climbed around the banyan roots, and examined the river at this level. It certainly wasn't deep, but its power was frightening. I could swim, but hardly in rocky water only a few feet deep. The real danger would come from being washed off my feet and getting a few bones broken, or, even worse, being washed downstream, no doubt cracking my head in the process.

My decision was made for me. I heard Deirdre call out sharply and then, in an agonized voice, cry my name:

"Judy — !"

The inevitable seemed to have happened. Her nervous excitement and her exertions had triggered one of her attacks. I stared downstream, frantic at my helplessness. Deirdre had dropped the end of the log and was kneeling beside a big tree trunk, her fists pressed tight against her chest.

"Be very quiet. Don't move!" I called and then stepped out on the rock again, but slipped as before. I tried to confine my thoughts to this one task. Forget Deirdre. Forget that once I reached her, there would still be the problem of getting her out of this claustrophobic Eden. She cried out again. I forced myself not to look her way. There seemed to be more panic than pain in her voice, but I could not be sure. I considered the area downstream where the log bridge had been propped on boulders and on that rotting tree.

I returned to the area I had been afraid to test. With Deirdre across from me, panicky and crying, I found this area more possible now. I had to make it. There was no alternative. It was like a ghastly chess game played with my life and perhaps Deirdre's life. I chose a flat boulder that appeared to be securely anchored in the stream. The heavy run-off from the mountain peak above poured across the rock, but I felt I could better manage the current than one of the dry but highly dangerous rocks that might possibly overturn under my weight.

I stepped out, planting my foot firmly. It was lucky that I had been firm, because Deirdre screamed in terror as she saw me, and the sound cut through my very bones. That and the current nearly swept me off the boulder, but my toes dug into my sandals and somehow those flat soles fastened upon the boulder. One of the reasons for my choice of this boulder was that the next seemed firm and steady as well. Confidently, I set one foot upon that stone. My confidence — and my foot — were misplaced. A heavy tree limb, twisting and turning as it rushed downstream, cracked so hard against my thigh that it numbed my leg for a minute and I went down under the impact. I was soaked hip-deep but at least I hadn't been washed away. I put one foot after the other, clinging to the soggy, moss-covered log which had helped to support the original bridge.

Deirdre reached out, trying to help me, but I ordered her back. The only good thing in this ridiculous mess was Deirdre's surprising recovery at this moment. I told myself the mysterious "palpitations" would never have let her move about like this, trying repeatedly to touch and help me. There were still signs of her panic. Her face was twisted and tears stained her cheeks but she stood her ground, shaky as she was, so close to the water. I was grateful for her outstretched arm after all. I grasped the tree trunk again only to break off a handful of decayed wood and a hideous, crawling white mass. Maggots? Worms? I screamed, louder than Deirdre had ever screamed. I splashed on toward her out-stretched arm and fell against the riverbank. As she bent over me, shaking me and calling my name, I muttered, "I'm all right. Don't worry."

We looked at each other.

"Deirdre?"

Shivering, she whispered, "I'm so sorry. . . ."

I tried a smile. It wasn't much but it reassured her. "I couldn't have made it without your help. You did it. You saved my life." It seemed to me at that minute only a slight exaggeration. Her hand had been exceedingly welcome.

Deirdre smiled back at me. She leaned against the ohia tree, pressing her knuckles into her chest and closing her eyes, but she did not seem to be in the great pain that had struck her earlier. Perhaps the pain — if it was real and not psychosomatic — had subsided with her panic. She repeated proudly, "I really did save you, in a way. Didn't I?"

I straightened my back and pulled myself up against the tree. I was badly shaken but felt very much myself. It was Deirdre who suffered, and she had added to that suffering by her attempt to help me. The old, childish Deirdre might have collapsed in tears, suffered severe palpitations or worse. I remembered that when her mother died, she had gone into a kind of childish stupor, and she had never grown up since. But today something had taken place that might be more important than all the memories between us. She had overcome fear and pain, whether self-induced pain or real, in order to help me. She had grown up.

I touched her hand lightly. "I'm so proud of you! How are you feeling?"

"Pretty good. It hurts. My chest hurts, but —" She took several short, sharp breaths. "Honest! Not as bad as it was." She looked around at this overgrown jungle, and I thought her voice was fainter. "Do you think we can get going without help?"

"Just give me a few minutes." I tried to rub my foot and leg, but the touch sent stabs of pain through my leg. I knew from past experience that this was merely a muscle spasm and would go away in a few minutes, but it was unpleasant enough now.

"Did you tell anyone where you were going?" Deirdre asked. She spoke with an effort and I looked at her sharply.

"What is it? Not the pain . . . Deirdre!"

She shook her head. It was all in slow motion and she was shivering, but the pressure in her chest seemed to have lessened. The pink color of excitement and pride at her effort to help me had drained from her face, and I was deeply troubled to note that her pallor had returned. Seeing me stare at her, she looked down and mentioned distant bird sounds in some tree across the river, but I couldn't hear them. I wondered if they were real at all or if the river gushing and bubbling past us noisily prevented me from hearing. I began to wring out the fabric of my soaked and dirty slacks. My sweater had remained comparatively dry, but that wouldn't be the case for long. The mountain rain had drifted down to our level, beginning with large, intermittent drops. It seemed to be scattering, which was the best we could hope for, and I had learned how quickly showers came and went here in Hawaii. One was dry almost before the shower had moved on.

"We had better start," I suggested, getting to my feet. I moved away from the river. Deirdre took my right arm.

"Let's go. It's easier to breathe now."

The shower caught us as soon as we left the thick jungle growth bordering the course of the river, but the wind was driving it rapidly on toward Sandalwood. Deirdre huddled under a palm tree, laughing while her teeth chattered.

"I'm so cold . . . so cold! Isn't it silly? The sun's just over that ridge." She was still giggling when her finger groped for me and she whispered, "I — I — can't. . . ." I tried to hold her, but I hadn't the strength, and we went down together. It was a grassy patch dotted with tiny white flowers that our bodies trampled down, but it saved us from the muddy ground.

Deirdre's eyes were closed and her face looked old, drawn and sallow. I called to her, took hold of her shoulders and shook her. It was no use. I felt the pulse in her thin wrist, thanking God there was a response, sluggish but unquestionably present.

I got up and went on a few yards. I could see the ocean between stretches of a papaya grove that had been battered by the recent storm. I went back to Deirdre. I had left her huddled with her head upon one hand. She was moving now like a child who had just awakened from a nightmare, very slowly, her eyes open, yet unfocused. Her hands were spread flat on the grass, shifting as if she searched for something.

"Deirdre! What is it? Have you lost something? Deirdre, look at me."

She did not raise her head. Still searching, she moved each finger in that curious slow motion I had noticed earlier. She began to cry.

"Don't . . . oh, please . . . please don't take any

more . . . I'll throw them away. You can't take any more. . . ."

I knelt beside her, touched her wind-blown, rain-wet hair. "Deirdre, what is it?" She terrified me. She seemed to be in another world. Another time. Gradually she saw me but there seemed to be a veil between us. She whispered, "I could have stopped her. It's my fault. She just stood there and swallowed them. And every time she swallowed a capsule she said, 'come with me and I'll stop taking them. Leave your aunt and come with me. I'm lonely.' And then she went to sleep — and died. I should have gone with her, and she'd be alive today." She was shaking again.

"Deirdre . . . are you talking about your mother?"

She raised her hand slowly, let it fall, felt again over the grass. I think she was talking to herself. "If I find them first, she won't be able to take them."

"What, dear?"

"The capsules. . . ."

I felt unnaturally calm, like a victim of shock, and I knelt there silently, staring at the miniature white flowers, remembering nine years gone by. So that was how it had happened long ago! My defense had been correct after all, only no one had believed it. Not even me. Claire Cameron had taken those pentobarbital capsules with some idiotic idea of forcing her daughter to leave my house. Her drunken condition had done the rest. And the shock of it combined with

Deirdre's false sense of guilt had banished the scene from her mind until now.

I tried to get to her.

"Deirdre, I'm going to walk a few yards and see if I can signal someone on the way to the village. We must be almost directly above the trail."

She nodded. I had at least gotten through to her. When I looked back a minute or two later, she was sitting with her head on her crossed arms, ignoring the rain squall that passed overhead.

I went off the path and made my way between waist-high ferns in the direction of the westerly seacoast. This time I did see parts of the village trail and several men, and a woman, walking in a northerly direction toward the village. Did this mean they knew about us? I stood on my toes, wincing at the sudden, painful reminder of the muscles and flesh bruised by the tree limb that had struck my leg on my crossing of the stream.

I must have looked like a semaphore waving my arms over my head — they couldn't hear my voice, as it turned out — but I felt that nothing had ever been so important in our lives as the arrival of those unknown rescuers. While I waited to see if they noticed me and left the village trail, one part of my brain was registering again the all-important fact that Claire Cameron had unintentionally killed herself. How often I had assured myself of this, and yet, I had always retained that horrible little doubt!

But Deirdre was innocent. She had done nothing except plead with her mother. Deirdre was innocent! I could not doubt that awful moment of delirium when she had reverted to the child watching her mother die. It had been worth everything to know that. It was also a dreadful reflection on me that I could have believed at any time in Deirdre's possible guilt, knowing Claire Cameron's irresponsibility as I did. And Stephen. Had he suspected his wife's guilt in that crime? This knowledge might be the preservation of their marriage.

I waved again, called to them until my throat was raw, and kept waving, criss-crossing my arms. Anything to attract their attention. Then they turned somewhere off the trail into a clump of ferns and young trees. They had turned eastward when I returned to Deirdre but not before I recognized Stephen among them. The woman must be Ilima Moku.

I found Deirdre in the same grassy spot where I had left her and in the same position.

"He's coming for you," I told her gently.

She looked up. "Not — ?"

"Your husband is coming, especially for you." Her red, tear-filled eyes gradually brightened. She stared at my face, as if gauging its degree of truth. I went on, "He will be so proud of you! You were very grown-up and brave when I got into that trouble in the river. You didn't faint or lose control. You were quite wonderful."

I expected this to produce one of her quick

and enchantingly childlike moods of enthusiasm. She surprised me, however, by her quiet,
adult pleasure.

"I tried. I didn't know I could do anything
decent. You were always so good at everything.
But I knew I had to be strong. And I was, wasn't
I? The pain in my chest went away. I didn't let it
get me." She clutched her bare arms. In spite of
the heat and humidity she was chilled and
shaking. The halter she wore was totally inadequate and my sweater was still soaking wet, so I
made no attempt to switch with her. I could only
hope the men would get here before the next
mountain shower.

"Do you think you can walk to meet them if I
help?" I asked her hopefully.

She accepted my idea with a soft smile that
still managed to suggest a burgeoning pride in
herself.

"I might even do it alone. Not that I don't
thank you, Judy, but Stephen must see me
alone."

I understood. I watched her get to her feet diz-
zily. As she swayed I reached out, but she did not
need my help. I could see that these movements
cost her considerable effort, and she murmured,
"I had a dream when I fainted. I dreamed of
mother. Wasn't that odd, Judy? I dreamed I saw
her die." She hesitated. I thought she had stumbled but she recovered quickly. "It's all right. I
think I understand. It wasn't a dream, was it?"

"It was an accident. She was trying to persuade you to go away with her, but she had been drinking and with those capsules on top of the alcohol, she had no chance."

She nodded and then her face lighted and I knew before I saw the path ahead that she had seen Stephen. I did not look at him, but I knew he had reached Deirdre and taken her up in his arms.

Wearily, I stepped aside and directly into Ilima Moku's ample form. Victor Berringer was with her. As I disliked them both intensely, I tried to pull away from their strong hands when they attempted to help me. Was this how Deirdre had felt when someone always propped her up so that she could do nothing for herself?

I ignored Mrs. Moku and addressed Berringer. "What are you here for? Not to rescue Stephen's wife, I'm sure. What are you? Some kind of secret service?"

"Nothing secret, I assure you."

Stephen, with Deirdre in his arms, looked me up and down anxiously. "Judith! You are soaking wet. Berringer, for God's sake, make yourself useful!" He started down the mountain path.

Berringer looked as though he was about to pick me up, but I twisted away and went on, my steps matching those of Mrs. Moku, who helped me down to the village trail and into the Hawaiian village itself. Ilima's husband, Moku, came to meet us, walking heavily as if under a great weight. The loss of his only daughter had broken his spirit. He kindly suggested that Deirdre and I might get into dry clothes. He didn't tell us he was offering us Kekua's sun dresses and Ilima did not refuse. Whatever her feelings about the guilt of the Giles family, it was clear that some of her old liking for Deirdre remained. Deirdre and I changed to Kekua's Hawaiian-print, two-piece dresses. Then William Pelhitt came out of the cottage Berringer had rented and tried to help us into Stephen's jeep. His hands shook as he helped Stephen wrap Deirdre up in a blanket that he furnished when she began to shiver again. She was lifted into the jeep. William asked me then, "Are you all right, Judith?"

"Fine."

"Don't let anything happen to you. Vic, I think I'll go along, just in case Judith needs help, or something."

Berringer cut him off. "You find it very easy to replace Ingrid. She hasn't even been decently buried yet!"

"No! I only —"

While they were arguing, Deirdre raised her head and looked at Mrs. Moku.

"I meant to ask you, Ilima, and I forgot. Remember the note you brought me from Kekua that night when you warned me about . . . You know?"

I lost interest in Bill Pelhitt's protests and Berringer's stinging answers. I was suddenly remembering the night I saw Ilima Moku leaving

Sandalwood after talking with Deirdre. I could only guess that having seen Stephen and me at the boat landing in that intimate and secretive conversation, she had warned Deirdre about me.

Mrs. Moku said in her deep, musical voice, "I remember. My daughter sent you a note about a monkeypod bowl you wanted from Kaiana City."

"But that's the thing." Deirdre pulled her head out of the blanket like a small turtle in a big shell. She did not seem to notice the warm, muggy heat all around us. "It may be a note about the monkeypod bowl, but it was sealed inside the envelope you gave me. On the sealed envelope it just told me to open it in case of accident. But I was in the hospital when Kekua had her accident, and I forgot all about it."

Stephen and I looked at each other. He barked suddenly, "Berringer, will you lift up Miss Cameron? She and my wife need to get home and rest."

As Berringer overcame my objections and lifted me into the jeep, Mrs. Moku said, "I will come too," and managed to get her bulk up behind us in the jeep. Stephen started off at such a speed Deirdre and I were thrown against each other, and though Stephen apologized, I knew why he was hurrying.

Twenty-One

The sun was brilliant now, with the clouds driven far out to sea, but the fury of the recent big storm had left evidence everywhere along the cliff road, in the ruts of the road itself and in the debris piled along the face of the cliff that bordered us on the right. The left side was a sheer drop to those deceptively smooth, piercingly blue waters of the Pacific.

In spite of the moist heat Deirdre was buried deep in her blanket and as the jeep bounded over every conceivable obstacle, Stephen shifted one arm and put it around her shoulders, pulling her to him. The knuckles of his hand touched my bare shoulder. I remained motionless, but I felt that touch. I was sure I would never forget the excitement of it, which was out of all proportion to the slightness of our contact.

"Hold on," he warned us a few minutes later. "We've got some rough spots ahead."

We bounced over rocks, mud, brushwood and half-ripened fruits blown by the fresh rains. I was wondering at the accumulation in this spot, then noted the great piles of logs and boulders along the cliff side.

"Was this the place?" I whispered nodding toward the pile.

"The roadblock. Yes. Berringer and I removed it going north. He seemed pretty anxious to rescue you."

I showed my teeth. "He probably thinks I am the murderer he is looking for."

He raised his voice, smiling a little. I realized he was adding for the benefit of the woman behind us, "Mrs. Moku helped us, too."

Ilima said severely, "I am not an inhumane woman!"

After slowing to a crawl, we managed to get around what remained of the barrier and rattled on toward Sandalwood. I knew that Stephen and probably Ilima Moku were even more anxious than I to reach the Giles house. They wanted to read the note Kekua had left for Deirdre. I myself couldn't yet assume quite as much as they did. Unless Kekua had been murdered. I still remembered those footprints that I had thought were running steps, the imprint of the toes decidedly deeper. She had been running in almost a direct line and she had fallen, somehow miscalculating the masked edge of the Ili-Ahi gulch.

But why was she running? Obviously from some danger.

I kept my thoughts on this matter to avoid thinking of what must happen at once, my departure from Sandalwood and Hawaii. I was happy about Deirdre. I felt that she needed psychiatric help, but that would be a decision between Stephen and Deirdre herself. I had spent most of my life living Deirdre's life, or what I thought was her life. It was time I respected her ability to make her own mistakes and to survive them. My further regret I could scarcely admit to myself, and that was made more poignant by the mere effect of Stephen's hand as it touched my shoulder. I loved him, and he was Deirdre's whole life.

Stephen turned sharply inland beyond the cliffside and into the parking place at the rear of the cottages in the sacred grove. He lifted Deirdre down and reached for me but I avoided him, as did Queen Ilima. Deirdre wavered but insisted on walking under her own power, beside Stephen. They cut through the grove but I knew Ilima Moku's strong feeling about this ground, and when she started on the longer path around the grove, I followed the Gileses. They cut straight through the trees between the unfinished cottages, passing directly over the area, now covered by boards, where Ingrid Berringer's body had been found.

They were stopped on the veranda of Sandalwood House. I reached the steps in time to see Nelia Perez talking to Stephen and gesturing volubly.

"Walking in like that and taking over! I didn't believe you'd sent him and I told him so!"

Stephen turned to Deirdre. "Do you remember where you put Kekua's letter?"

She looked blank and I wondered if she would revert to that childish girl who left problems to everyone else, avoiding any complications. But Deirdre considered the problem and then said quietly, "Yes. That's it. I slipped it into the lefthand drawer of my dressing table."

Nelia exclaimed breathlessly, "I know! I saw it in the pink bedroom. We were looking for *mokihana* berries. Miss Cameron and I. I dropped the envelope back into the drawer."

"Unopened?" Stephen asked quickly.

"Of course. Miss Cameron called me and I forgot all about it."

Stephen moved into the house and with quiet but rapid steps went up the front stairs. We followed, instinctively as cautious as he had been, although I doubt if either Deirdre or I knew quite who and what we were afraid of disturbing. Nelia knew, of course, and watched us curiously. I had just passed the landing when I heard footsteps as the door to Stephen's room opened. There was apparently an attempt to cover up the sound because when I appeared in the upper hallway I startled William Pelhitt who looked more than usually awkward, walking on tiptoe and with his mouth open.

I said, "Good afternoon. I thought we left you in the Hawaiian village."

He stammered, "I — we — that is, Vic sent me — I took the short cut by the trail. Being in Vic's company for too long a time can g-get pretty bad; so I d-decided to drop in and maybe g-get invited to lunch."

"Of course," I agreed calmly. I didn't enjoy tormenting him, but I was furious with him for being the poor, luckless fellow he was. "And when you couldn't find your host downstairs, you came up and looked for him in his bedroom."

"No. You see —" He began to wring his hands. His face was white and he was working terribly hard to make his story convincing. The trouble was, he did not lie well. He had to live his role. "I left something here the other night when I was — you know — sick. It was an envelope. I just didn't want Vic to see it."

"So you left it in Stephen's room."

"No! At least, it isn't there. And I tried the greenish room facing the falls, Mrs. Giles's study. I guess I must have left it in the other bedroom." He reached for the handle of the door to Deirdre's pink bedroom. As I watched him, he caught his breath. The door opened slowly under his horrified stare.

Stephen came out. "Is this what you were looking for?" He held up two envelopes, one with Deirdre's name upon it, the other a psychedelic pattern of bright yellow paper adorned by leis of purple flowers. In the middle of it scrawled in purple ink on the second envelope were the words: "In case of accident to me, Mrs. Steve, please read this, but only in case of accident. Kekua Moku."

"M-may I — it's really mine —" Bill Pelhitt made one last effort, but he didn't reach for it. He must have known he was through.

I heard movement behind me. Deirdre and Nelia Perez, and a heavy footstep on the stairs. I didn't look back. I was painfully fascinated by the scene before me. Stephen surprised me by his own gentleness as he took the bright yellow page from the envelope and read aloud:

Mrs. Steve,

I was coming back from my boyfriend's trailer outside Kaiana City one night a couple of days after your wedding. I was just starting the motor of my boat when William Pelhitt came to the landing. I didn't know him, but he asked me to take him to Ili-Ahi. He said he'd just missed somebody he knew. I figured he was a friend of Mr. Steve's and took him over. He paid me twenty dollars. Another boat landed just minutes before we did. I saw him huff and puff up the hill. He met somebody and they went into the sacred grove. If it was a woman, I figured it was a love-in. Then Mrs. Mitsushima and Mr. Yee came out of the rear door at Sandalwood and headed for the landing. I didn't want them to see me and maybe tell mother, so I cut through the brush west of the landing and legged it home on the trail.

He must have gotten back across the bay in my boat or one of the others that's always left by either Mr. Steve's people or ours.

I never dreamed my passenger had done anything. He was too harmless. But last week I saw him come to Ili-Ahi with the silvery man who has the money. I could see friend Pelhitt hated to come. He was scared I'd recognize him. He almost fainted when he saw me. But old Berringer wouldn't take no. When I realized nobody's seen Ingrid Berringer since about the time I took Pelhitt over here, and what with his pre-

tending he'd never been here before and being afraid of me, I decided to test him. I asked if he'd loan me a hundred dollars. Just like that, he did. I figured I had it coming, and I was innocent. After all, I don't really know he did anything!

But today I asked him how he felt about lending me five hundred and he scrambled together three fifty. He got those ham-hands into my shoulders, told me that was it. I made him promise to meet me in the Grove with the rest of what he owes me. Then I got to thinking I need insurance. This letter is my insurance. All I have to do is mention it and there won't be any rough stuff. He wouldn't dare!

Thank you.

Your friend,
Kekua Moku

Bill Pelhitt put in eagerly, "You see? She says herself she doesn't know if I did anything. And I didn't. I mean, not deliberately. Never, I couldn't even believe it when she fell . . . I swear I only . . ." His eyes, bulging and bloodshot with his terror, seemed his own worst enemy. Their gaze focused suddenly on something in the shadowy hall behind me. He clasped his hands until they looked knotted by the tension he was under.

"I wouldn't hurt a living soul deliberately. I wouldn't even hurt a fly . . . a tiny insect. Not on purpose."

I turned and staring behind me, understood

his terror, the desperate plea in his voice. It had been wasted on two people who appeared to be images in stone: Ingrid Berringer's father, and Kekua's mother.

Stephen took his arm. "Don't say anything else. Not until you have legal counsel. Judith, would you call the Kaiana City sheriff's office?"

Feeling like a coward, I went downstairs to phone, not wanting Bill to hear me if I spoke on the upstairs extension. I had reached the office and was told Lieutenant Padilla of the Honolulu Police was also expected momentarily, when I heard voices as they all came in downstairs. Then I heard Stephen's angry insistence, "You have nothing to say about it. You are going to have to leave him alone. He will be locked in my study with me until the authorities arrive. Is that agreeable to you, Pelhitt?"'

Apparently, Bill agreed, because his broken-voiced reply was too low for me to hear. It was a strange and terrible hour that followed. Mrs. Moku and Berringer went into the living room to wait. She sat stiff and regal on the couch and he paced the floor. At Mr. Yee's demand, Nelia went to help him in the kitchen, and Deirdre said faintly, "I'm going to lie down. Stephen will tell me all about it later. Would you sit with me until I can get to sleep?"

I said, "Of course, I will. I want to see as much of you as possible, because I will be leaving when the police say I may."

Deirdre frowned. "And I meant you to have a

368

wonderful time here. I didn't know I'd feel so —
inferior when you were around."

"Don't worry. I would have had a splendid time and gone over to visit the Nagatas, done all sorts of things. Except for poor Mr. Pelhitt and Kekua. But I do have to begin my new life back on the mainland, if we can get my parole transferred." I lied briskly, "I'm looking forward to that." And then, as I knew it was not quite a lie: "Really! I am. A whole future — out there —"

"Is it — because of what I said today?"

"No, dear. It's because I am a grown-up lady now and I can't cling to my favorite niece forever."

She squeezed me in as strong a bear hug as she could manage and we went up to Stephen's bedroom together. I forced myself not to overdo the assistance. She lay down, pulled the thin thermal blanket up to her chin, and stared at the ceiling.

"I thought I had a heart attack today. But it went away too quickly."

"No. We can be thankful for that."

She sighed. "I suppose he did really kill them, poor man."

"I'm afraid that's the curse of William Pelhitt's life. He was born to be called 'poor man.' "

"I'm sorry about Kekua. But the other one, that's different. She was cruel and cutting and loved to hurt people."

"I never understood, Deirdre. Why did you travel with her?"

Deirdre was thoughtful. "I guess because she treated me like an equal. She didn't have too many girlfriends, but she was glamorous and exciting. It was only after we met Stephen and he wouldn't pay any attention to her, that she began to call me names. Idiot! Moron! All that. You see, until that time, I'd always let her have her way. Let her have any boys that liked both of us. I gave in. But not about Stephen. So she said I'd be a perfect match for her old boyfriend, that she'd trade me her boyfriend for Stephen and then everybody'd be balanced. . . . I suppose she meant Mr. Pelhitt." We were silent, possibly thinking that our own problems had never been worse than Bill Pelhitt's were and always had been. He was a born loser.

I thought Deirdre had gone to sleep but she turned suddenly and gazed at me, holding out her hand. "Judy, I used to dream about mother's death. Horrible nightmares that she was taking those capsules and I could stop her but I didn't. And then I'd wake up and try to remember, and it was gone. A blackness rolling up around me. And this time, when I woke up, I remembered."

"But there was nothing you could do. If she hadn't been drinking, it is very probable she wouldn't have died, so it was an accident. You see that, don't you?"

"Oh, Judy, I see that you suffered all those years because of me."

"What a ridiculous thing to say! If anything, I suffered because no one in court would believe the truth, that your mother killed herself."

We held each other's hand briefly. She closed her eyes. Nelia Perez came in as silently as possible, motioning to me.

"Mr. Pelhitt would like to talk to you. Mr. Steve says it's all right. And the police will be here any minute."

I looked at Deirdre. "I don't know." Deirdre opened her eyes, grinned, and winked.

"I trust you with my husband. I'm a big girl now."

"Can I stay here in your chair and hide out?" Nelia wanted to know. "Mr. Yee's been running me ragged."

I left the two girls exchanging horror tales of Mr. Yee's domestic tyranny and went downstairs past the living room. Berringer stopped pacing to demand of me, "When is there going to be some action?"

Before I could answer, Queen Ilima said sternly, "Be calm, man! You are as weak as your murderous friend."

This upset Berringer so much he stared at her, speechless, and then sat down in the nearest chair. He looked shaken. I wondered if anyone in his life had ever referred to him as weak. It was apparently the worst insult in his lexicon. I went to the study and Stephen let me in. I could see that, in a strange way, he and Pelhitt seemed to have developed a rapport. Possibly he understood why Pelhitt had killed Ingrid Berringer. If, of course, he really had killed her. I still hoped he

371

could somehow prove both deaths had been "accidents." I despised him, but I pitied him profoundly.

Stephen said. "He wants you to understand how it happened, and I think he deserves that."

Bill Pelhitt got up from the couch. He looked extraordinarily well, considering his situation. There was a pride about him that I had never seen before. The slightly fleshy color had returned to his face. I was amazed.

"You don't mind sitting here beside me, just for a few minutes, Judith?"

I almost looked at Stephen to get his opinion or permission, but I made my own decision and sat down before William Pelhitt. In spite of his invitation to me, he remained standing. There was a glow of nobility in his manner and I guessed even before he spoke that he had raised his spirits with some pretense that would help him get through the long and terrible time ahead.

"Judith, I did receive a letter from Ingrid, just before the Gileses were married. She sneered at me. She was crude and vulgar. She said she had met a real man and nothing but her simpleton roommate stood in the way. She said beautiful morons would appeal to me, that I should come over and snap up Miss Deirdre. That hurt. It cut deeply, I can tell you. I brooded about it until I couldn't stand it. I felt my whole world was collapsing. I had to talk to her. Persuade her that I had always been a part of her life and she would come back to me."

Stephen cleared his throat. I said, "You did not tell Mr. Berringer?"

"He would have despised me. And I might have lost my job."

I felt a few grains of my sympathy dissolving in his concern for serving at any cost a man who despised him.

"So you flew over to Hawaii in secret," Stephen prompted him.

"Yes. Vic sent me downstate to New York City to deliver bonds for exchange. It was a very private matter and it had to be done by hand, so to speak. I hurried through that in a couple of hours and flew to L.A. and then to Honolulu. I was dead tired. I couldn't find her at the hotel next day. She'd moved. I was frantic. I figured she must've won over this Giles fellow — sorry, Mr. Giles — so I flew to Kaiana and that's where I met this Kekua and got the ride to Ili-Ahi. And when I came ashore, I saw Ingrid. I rushed up and grabbed her. She was coming from Sandalwood. Seems that Giles wasn't home and Mrs. Giles refused to see her. She cursed me. Said if I'd come a few days earlier I could have taken this Deirdre off her hands — like calling to like, she said. Meaning we were both idiots, I guess.

"I rustled her into the little grove. There was lots of lumber lying about. To be used the next day for steps. Anyway, the ground was torn up and I stumbled and she laughed. Said I couldn't even walk straight. She said even though Giles was already married, she would never want me. Then she showed her teeth. She said I should leave her alone, and when I got mad, she said she was going to tell her father — tell Vic — what an idiot I was and that she'd see I lost my precious job if I didn't stop pestering her. I've worked for Vic since I was fifteen. I've gone right up the ladder. My father was Vic's partner in the old days. He was going to give me the management of the brokerage house in Buffalo if I — when I married Ingrid. I just went crazy. I slapped Ingrid. She fell into that hole. I guess . . . right then she was dead. She never came to. I must've sat on those boards, holding her for an hour. She was cold. She began to — anyway, she was dead. I panicked. There was the trench. I did it by not thinking. I just dug deep and covered her up."

I shuddered. He tried to touch my hand but saw the involuntary retraction of my own fingers and drew back. Stephen said, "Maybe you had better save the rest for later," but Bill Pelhitt shook his head.

"There isn't any more. I hoped and prayed I'd never have to come here again but Vic made me go with him to the Orient. It would have been strange if I refused. And I might've lost my job. And then . . . just as if fate led me, I had to come with him to this very island. This hell hole! All I could do was to make noises like it could have been Mr. Giles here. I mean — I did blame him. I figured he'd led Ingrid on. But now, looking back, I can see how it was. And I walked right into that Hawaiian girl here. But it wasn't only her, that little blackmailer. It was that grave. I got this fixation that it would be uncovered. It just haunted me."

I moistened my lips. "Did you kill Kekua?"

Stephen had raised his head. He was listening. Then he repeated, "You don't have to tell us anything, Pelhitt."

Bill said softly, "I know. But you see, I didn't kill her. She made me meet her a couple of nights ago to pay her another hundred and fifty dollars. I thought I'd scare her. I threatened her and she ran right across the grass to the path. Then she looked back at just the wrong time and fell right through those bushes . . . and fell . . . and fell. . . ." He covered his mouth. His eyes looked haunted. "She . . . kept falling," he mumbled.

Stephen moved to the door. He turned back before opening it.

"I'm afraid they are here."

The room was very still for a minute. Then Bill Pelhitt stiffened, walked slowly toward Stephen. "Better get it over with."

Stephen opened the door and they went out together.

By the time I was permitted to leave Hawaii upon the agreement to furnish my address to the court at all times during the next six months, I was at least satisfied that the friends I left behind me were as reasonably happy as they could be. That was a consolation and a great relief.

With Deirdre back in the Honolulu Hospital, this time for tests and a checkup, she couldn't see me off but she insisted that Stephen drive me to the airport for the morning coast flight. I would have preferred to say good-bye to them both together in Deirdre's room, but I couldn't argue with the new and grown-up Deirdre.

"I owe you more than I can ever repay, Judy," she whispered as she drew me down to the bed with her arm around my neck. "If I hadn't blacked out all those years ago, the jury's verdict would have —"

"Don't think about it. We made our plea and they didn't believe it. They would probably have accused you of lying to protect me. Now, dear, write to me."

"You know I will." She hugged me again, looking over my head to warn Stephen severely, "You take extra-special care of her."

Stephen said he would. Deirdre rang for the nurse, who arrived with a lei of *vanda* orchids.

"Let me do it," Deirdre demanded and I bowed my head again while she dropped the lei, ice cold, over my head, kissed my cheek, and pushed me in a friendly way. "Go on. Take my husband!"

I said, "I never like men who are in love with their wives." At the door I smiled at her once more, we made smile gestures of a parting kiss, and I went out into the hall with the nurse, who looked back with a big sigh.

"It restores one's faith in marriage. They are

such a handsome couple."

"They are, thank God!"

Stephen came out a few minutes later and we left the hospital, making small talk about the weather, which was perfect, and about the prospect that I would have a smooth flight. He asked me once what I planned for the future, and I dismissed the matter lightly.

"I may just enjoy my freedom for a little while." I hesitated. "May I ask you a question?"

"Judith —" He glanced at me, then back at the highway. "You know you can."

"What do you plan to do about the grove after all this has happened?"

I think he was surprised at this subject, which was apparently not what he had in mind. He shrugged. "It no longer seems to matter. I'm confining my interests now to the shipping. We've done well there, and no *kahuna* curses. Nothing stronger than strike threats." He smiled grimly, and explained, though he didn't have to. I had guessed. "It was my father's death, I think, more than the grove itself. I seem to have been the prey of a superstition there that was far worse than the *kapu* Ilima's family believed in. My notion was that if I finished and made a success of the Sandalwood *heiau* I would put my father's spirit to rest. That's a pretty primitive thought for this day and age, isn't it?" I couldn't disagree, though I understood his feelings very well. He shook off these thoughts which even now appeared to trouble him. "Anyway, Deirdre is coming along wonderfully. It was her suggestion, by the way, that she see a psychiatrist, and Ito Nagata recommended someone. Deirdre met the man this morning for the first time. She seems to feel that he is a friend already. Someone to talk to who is paid to listen, as my little girl calls him."

Yes, I thought, Deirdre suited Stephen perfectly. With all his conflicts earlier in our acquaintance, he knew that he wanted his wife to be just such a girl as Deirdre. He added, "When this psychiatrist thinks she can handle it, Deirdre wants to testify, at least get into the record what she saw the day her mother died."

It seemed unimportant now that the years were gone. I tried to dissuade him but he said stubbornly, "She wants to. And I want her to. We've got to clear your name." There seemed no point in arguing about it. I touched the small, delicate orchids around my throat and remembered how much orchids had meant to me when I was a girl. Knowing this was the peace symbol between Deirdre and me, I felt that this wreath of little flowers strung on a bit of twine meant more to me than all the flowers in the past.

At the airport Stephen bought several leis and dropped each one over my head while I protested, feeling ridiculous. We laughed a good deal. He kissed me, a very slight brushing of his warm mouth on my cheek, each time he dropped the lei, but always it was a laughing gesture. As he dropped the last lei and kissed me, his forefinger traced my lips. I saw his eyes, the depths, the expression, and looked away quickly.

Good-byes were yet to come. I had said good-bye to Michiko and Ito Nagata the night before, but there they were, waiting to add fresh leis, cinnamon carnations, *pikake,* white ginger, and my commonplace favorite, pink plumeria, and before I knew it I was crying. It was a wonderful thing to have friends like this, people who had always believed in me, long before Deirdre's memory made the truth official.

Ito hugged me at the last before sending me on my way. "*Me ke aloha,* Judith."

"You brought me my aloha greeting, and now my aloha farewell comes from you, my dear friend," I told him lightly, but he knew the feeling behind my words and understood my gratitude.

We hugged each other again and I rushed to board the big plane. I moved into my window seat, thankful for the dozen leis that doused my own perfume and gave me sufficient excuse for my red eyes. I looked out the window and pretended to make out individual faces. My view was blurred by tears, but I was intensely relieved to be putting two thousand miles between me and Deirdre and Stephen. My relationship with them had cost too much nervewracking tension, too much passion that had to be restrained. And I couldn't help thinking of William Pelhitt. That damnable Berringer family, father and daughter! What pain they had caused!

The plane lifted off the runway, circled, headed out toward California, and I had no more time for tears. Although I occasionally thought of Deirdre's husband, the memories receded further and further into the past. My future was going to be quite different, and it would be free of the strangling ties that had nearly ruined both Deirdre's life and mine. I looked out the window. I had never seen a sky so vividly blue. We were soon far above sea and clouds, but I took the sky for my omen, and my spirits lifted with the soaring plane.